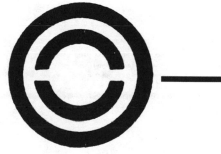

THE CIRCLE REPERTORY

COMPANY THE FIRST FIFTEEN YEARS

THE
CIRCLE
REPERTORY
C◎MPANY

THE FIRST FIFTEEN YEARS

MARY S. RYZUK

IOWA STATE UNIVERSITY PRESS / AMES

It is easy to say this book could not have been possible without the love, support, and understanding of my husband, Ony Ryzuk. In this case, it is too simple but very true.

Mary S. Ryzuk received her Ph.D. in theatre at the City University of New York and now teaches at William Paterson State College in New Jersey.

© 1989 Iowa State University Press, Ames, Iowa 50010

Composed and printed in the United States of America

First edition, 1989

Library of Congress Cataloging-in-Publication Data

Ryzuk, Mary S., Ph.D.
    The Circle Repertory Company : the first fifteen years.

    Bibliography: p.
    Includes index.
    1. Circle Repertory Company—History. I. Title.
PN2277.N52C577   1989   792'.09747'1   88–13704
ISBN 0–8138–0029–3

62,940

Contents

Foreword

WHEN I became Artistic Director for Circle Rep I realized that 1988 was a far cry from 1969 when I founded Circle Rep with Marshall W. Mason, Lanford Wilson, and Rob Thirkield. The resident theatre movement across America had matured, the most important off-Broadway theatres in New York were non-profit artistic institutions like Circle Rep, American dance had had a renaissance, VCRs were in nearly every home, and there was a video rental store on every two blocks in my New York neighborhood. The lives of our audience members had become complicated and busy. They were more selective with their time and came to us for a fresh, enlivening experience.

Marshall had built an extraordinary company, and I was fortunate to be leading a community of artists committed to the truth and humanity in the theatre. They were artists who were are also blessed with a generous and curious spirit that allowed them to be affected by new talents. As we now move into our third decade we are expanding our mission—discovering and nurturing new writers, actors, directors, and designers, creating new worlds on our stage with a vitality that will speak to and challenge our audience. The ability to make theatre accessible to young people today and to enable them to value the unique experience of a shared and living moment is to assure the continued growth not only of our richest legacies but also of the minds that will shape our theatrical future.

In 1969 Marshall, Lanford, Rob, and I shared a common goal: to establish an ensemble of actors, directors, designers, and playwrights who could work together to create living theatre in a collaborative environment. The relationship between our artists was and still is a special one of deep trust and continuing commitment. Our growth as a company has been built on this unique ability to work together to challenge the talents of individual artists: to allow designers to draw on their knowledge of a playwright's sensibilities rather than merely the requirements of a single set; to provide playwrights with a fine body of actors to draw on for their work; and to unite our directors, playwrights, and actors in a process of long-term development. During the fifteen years covered in this book, Marshall developed a truly important artistic institution whose unique vision and process changed the way that American theatre realized its art.

TANYA BEREZIN

Preface

THIS history traces the evolution of the Circle Repertory Company from its beginnings in an uptown loft in 1969 to its fifteenth anniversary as a critically acclaimed theatrical institution in 1984. Culturally, the history attempts to place the Circle Rep within the context of the off-Broadway milieu in which it developed and within the context of contemporary American theatre in general; it also places the Circle Rep within the broader intellectual environment of the nineteen-sixties, seventies, and eighties. Artistically, the history shows that although the company is best known for lyric realism, lyric realism represents only a small portion of the company's output and should not be considered the identifiable style of the Circle Rep. However, since the Circle Rep achieved much of its high visibility through playwright Lanford Wilson, whose plays became closely identified with lyric realism, the term itself became inseparable from the host company.

In its first fifteen years, the Circle Repertory Company evolved from a free-spirited ensemble of actors and playwrights-in-residence to a major developer of new plays and new playwrights, and back to a revolving repertory ensemble trying to recapture its original philosophy of a theatre by artists for artists.

I first became interested in the Circle Repertory Company of New York when I was asked to direct *Slippers in a Cage* for the Barn Theatre Guild in Montville, New Jersey. The play was written by Peter Dee, a Circle Rep Lab playwright, and was produced in 1982 by the Barn Theatre Guild in cooperation with the Circle Repertory Company.

As part of my research for the play, I began inquiring into the history of the Circle Rep, then celebrating its fifteenth anniversary year. The company was a vital contributing force in contemporary American theatre and had received much critical coverage of its work, not only as a developer of new American plays but as a working ensemble unique in American theatre. But I found that there had been little written about the company's historical evolution in the hazardous theatrical milieu of New York City. Thus was born the idea of writing a history of the Circle Rep.

Writing this history has been an adventure of discovery for me, a discovery not only of the company's birth and growth, successes and failures, and joys and sorrows, but also a rediscovery of the varied cultural forces of the nineteen-sixties, seventies, and eighties — the three decades spanned by the company's history. Writing has also been an adventure of discovery of the many people intimately involved in the company's evolution who have given so freely in personal interviews and epistolary contributions to this history, particularly the company's four co-founders: artistic director Marshall W. Mason; actor and director Rob Thirkield; playwright Lanford Wilson; and actress Tanya Berezin.

I also wish to express my sincere appreciation and thanks to all of the company members who directly participated in the creation of this story: Kathy Bates, John Beaufort, John Bishop, Peter Buckley, Jordan Charney, Jeff Daniels, Alan Feinstein, Richard Frankel, Mari Gorman, Bruce Gray, Michael Higgins, Ruby Holbrook, Daniel Irvine, Toni James, Ken Kliban, Bob Le Pone, Christie Peck, Ari Roth, Richard Seff, Michael Skelly, Ted Sod, Milan Stitt, Tom Thompson, and Peter Weller. Particular thanks go to Rob Meiksins, who spent many precious hours in discussion with me during the course of my research; to B. Rodney Marriott, who during his tenure as acting artistic director so generously opened the files of the Circle Repertory Company to me for study and opened the doors of the company's private readings, rehearsals, and labs for direct observation; and to my dear friends, Dr. George Mandelbaum, Mercy College, New York, who would not let me give up, and Dean Jay Ludwig of William Paterson State College, Wayne, New Jersey, who encouraged me to undertake the project.

I must also express my heartfelt gratitude to Professor Stanley Kauffmann of the Graduate School and University Center of the City University of New York, whose stature as a drama critic lends such eminence and dignity to the work he has graciously agreed to support; to Professor Charles Gattnig of the City College of New York, whose friendship and kindness have always been the inspirational foundation of my happy association with him; and most particularly to Professor Vera Mowry Roberts of Hunter College of the City of New York, who so generously agreed to chair my doctoral committee and who has been a constant source of inspiration and encouragement throughout the year it took to write this book.

The adventure has been a fulfilling one. What started out merely as an attempt to fill a void in contemporary American theatre history ended up being a labor of love as well.

MARY S. RYZUK, Ph.D.

New York City, 1986

1969 1970 1971 1972 1973 1974 1975 1976

1977 1978 1979 1980 1981 1982 1983 1984

1

The Climate

A historical note in the Circle Repertory Company's program reads:

> Circle Repertory Company, a not-for-profit institutional theatre, was founded in July, 1969, in a second floor loft at Broadway and 83rd Street by director Marshall W. Mason, playwright Lanford Wilson, director Rob Thirkield, and actress Tanya Berezin. Their goal was to establish an on-going ensemble of artists—actors, directors, playwrights and designers—who would work together to create a living play.

In essence, the four founders accomplished their objective. However, Marshall Mason had predicted from the first that it would take twenty years to build a great theatre company. The brief note in the Circle Rep program does not hint at the eight years it in fact took Mason to realize his vision of a company.

The story of the Circle Repertory Company is one of determination and continuous financial peril. It is the story of four young, talented people who came to New York City in the early sixties with—except for Rob Thirkield—little more than enthusiasm jingling in their pockets. Although it was Lanford Wilson who wanted to keep the actors together after the extraordinary ensemble work of *Balm in Gilead* in 1965, and who then suggested starting a company, it was Mason's and Thirkield's dream, and Mason's unfaltering vision, that finally brought the company together in the inauspicious loft over a Thom McAn shoe store in 1969.

The growth of the company is not merely the story of one small theatre company that "made it" in New York City—it also reflects the emotional climate of the sixties. As Lanford Wilson says:

> Interesting talking about feelings and the times and all that stuff about the sixties. Marshall, a skinny, penniless kid out of Texas—Rob who was a rich kid—Tanya, who had the most plausible upbringing in Philadephia—me with a background so different from that drug scene and all that stealing. We came from such a different scene together here to make theatre and our reaction was a little removed. We didn't really participate. We recorded it. We had to go on field trips to learn how to play *Balm in Gilead*. Not a single actor had ever seen anyone on heroin. They had to go on field trips to restaurants and all-night cafes to study these people because they didn't know them—because we all came from such a different place from the wildness.[1]

The revolution of the young had begun without fanfare, without an open declaration, and had spread almost unnoticed at first, throughout academia, from the college campuses down through the junior levels. Youth was on a rampage far beyond the usual adolescent passions. The uniform of the rebellion would soon be easy to spot: military fatigues, tie dyes, and long hair. There was a definite androgynous overtone— unified, unisexed, and becoming increasingly colorblind.

Mason, Wilson, Thirkield, and Berezin could not possibly know what lay ahead of them when they arrived in New York City in the early sixties. They were in their early twenties, enthusiastic, full of visions for their theatrical futures, and about to grow up in the explosion of the off-off-Broadway movement as theatre began to reflect the major social changes happening all around them.

The Civil Rights Act of 1960 was signed into law by President Eisenhower in May 1960. It set off a myriad of reactions from zealous support to out-and-out murder. The unexpurgated version of Lawrence's *Lady Chatterley's Lover* was ruled "not obscene" by the United States Circuit Court of Appeals in New York in March 1960; the lock was off the door.

It would be a short jump to overt pornography and an even shorter leap to opening up live theatre with ever-increasing challenges to the meaning of obscenity and the very core of morality. With meanings once so clear, now the very words became difficult to define; as never before, they were suddenly open to wide differences in subjective interpretation. In May 1960, Enovid had been approved by the Federal Drug Administration as the first safe method of birth control, and while the scent of a new freedom was palpable, few could foresee the extent of the sexual revolution at hand. Ernest Hemingway's suicide in July 1961 figuratively closed a door on an earlier era, "the lost generation." At almost the same moment in history, a young, vibrant, new president was in the White House giving birth to a new generation of idealists; executive spirit and idealism created the Peace Corps, and inspired young Americans were setting out in great numbers to aid the underprivileged of the world. Soviet cosmonaut Yuri Gagarin orbited the earth, Alan Shepard became the first American astronaut in space, and John Glenn quickly followed with the first American orbit—"Out in space!" "Out of sight!" "Next stop, the moon!" Anything seemed possible. Desegregation was being tested in the south by the Freedom Riders, James Meredith attempted to enroll at the University of Mississippi, Roger Maris hit his sixty-first home run, and although the four hundred American combat troops sent to South Vietnam by JFK in December 1961 had risen sharply to eleven thousand military personnel and technicians by December 1962, the alarm had not yet sounded in the American conscience with any force, and anything indeed did seem possible. Everything was turned on high. Few had "dropped out" yet.

In a sense, the founders' narrative parallels the history of American theatre in the past fifteen years, especially as it progressed through the turbulent seventies. It is difficult to encapsulate a decade, but important to show, even in broad strokes, the vital activities and energies that formed the soil for the Circle Repertory Company's growth.

It was not long before the euphoria of the early Kennedy years disintegrated in ever-increasing violence and with ever-increasing graphic coverage by the media. The colorful canvas suddenly turned black. It became the decade of assassinations and assassination attempts. Beginning with President John F. Kennedy in 1963, the shootings continued and the mighty fell: Martin Luther King, Jr., Malcolm X, Governor George Wallace, Senator Robert F. Kennedy. It was the decade of violent antiwar demonstrations; the murder of Civil Rights workers; the immolation of little black girls in a church bombing in the South; and the drug-induced deaths of such high-profile performers as Lenny Bruce, Jimi Hendrix, Janis Joplin, and Marilyn Monroe. It was the era of long hair, flower children, the pill, hippies, "pigs," communes, and a heavy drug culture that threatened to deepen the abyss between disillusioned youth and the "establishment." The young were "turned on" and "tuned out"—and with alarming frequency they "dropped out," often permanently.

It is little wonder then, in the face of such a staggering chronology of violence to the individual as well as to the national psyche, that when *Time* asked, "Is God Dead?" on its April 18, 1966, cover, many serious people seriously pondered the unthinkable.

In contrast, it would be difficult to even recognize these powerful experiences of the sixties by looking at the establishment theatre. Broadway continued to present the traditional fare of comedies—*Mary, Mary; Never Too Late; Cactus Flower; Entertaining Mr. Sloan; Three Bags Full; The Impossible Years; Slapstick Tragedy; Generation;* big money musicals—*Bye, Bye, Birdie; My Fair Lady; Mame; On a Clear Day You Can See Forever; Sweet Charity; Fiorello!;* and an occasional, difficult to find, serious drama—*Who's Afraid of Virginia Woolf; The Homecoming; A Day in the Life of Joe Egg.*

Off-Broadway, on the other hand, was reflecting the true pulse of the times. Plays like *The Connection* (1959), *The Blacks* (1962), *The Brig* (1963), *In White America* (1963), and *America Hurrah* (1966) were all presented off-Broadway. Off-Broadway was violent, wrenching, angry theatre, the kind of theatre that almost demanded converts rather than audiences. And not only was off-Broadway flourishing—by the midsixties, off-off-Broadway would come into its own as well, with recognition of its activities, its own label, and its own cultural standards.[2]

It is always risky to try to categorize an era or to attempt to trace patterns of artistic development and place them in cause-and-effect relationship. But it seems only natural that the wildly rebellious attitude of the sixties would be reflected on the small experimental stages. Traditionally accustomed to poverty, off-Broadway groups had little to lose and much to gain by deliberately seeking notoriety. And, as in pre–World War I days, off-Broadway was the place to express rejection of the commercialism of "uptown" theatre. Just as groups like the Provincetown Players and the Washington Square Players had questioned the values of their era, so too were contemporary groups in the sixties raising controversial issues and questions. While there are many similarities between the early off-Broadway movement and that of the sixties—notably that off-Broadway represented the best hopes for the American playwright—there are some major differences that should be noted.

The early off-Broadway movement was comprised mostly of literary-minded Greenwich Villagers, few of whom relied upon theatre for their personal incomes. Although they aspired to professionalism and polish in their work, they were mostly amateurs who jealously protected the spirit of amateurism which they felt kept them intimate with the pulse of current writing and free of commercial considerations. The air of literary and theatrical revolt in Greenwich Village before World War I was accompanied by a climate of political and social awareness, including the new Freudian psychology. This new Bohemia, however, was restricted to the geographical location of the Village itself. The lifestyle of radicals and writers such as John Reed, Max Eastman, Theodore Dreiser, Margaret Sanger, Emma Goldman, and Edna St. Vincent Millay did not affect the everyday life of common America to a large degree.

Not so in the sixties. The sixties were flaming with dissidence. New angry voices reached beyond the considerations of the *literati* of the day. With the Vietnam War, political assassinations, a growing drug culture, and the sexual revolution, the stakes were elevated to life-and-death status. The new purveyors of off-Broadway theatre made no attempt to isolate themselves from the public. Fanned by the media, their movement represented a revolution of the masses, not just the Bohemian few.

The off-Broadway revolt against "uptown's" commercialism was still in progress and would continue. But even more important, the revolt in the sixties centered upon presenting the issues of the day with visceral honesty and a hard-nosed rejection of and defiance toward traditional establishment values. Off-Broadway and, even more particularly, off-off-Broadway loudly proclaimed the counterculture of drugs, sex, and hardrock music, and scorned traditional institutions such as marriage, motherhood, and the nuclear family. It proposed in their place an "alternative lifestyle" in its "alternative theatre," which now accepted everything from sado-masochism and homosexuality to wife-swapping, draft-card burning, swinging, and living communally. The true mirror of American theatre was being held up to reflect the times with an almost romantic zeal by off-Broadway. But as the decade progressed and the

Vietnam War took its toll in social conflict as well as casualties, the fervor of what had been hailed as the most idealistic generation in the history of America soon deteriorated.

By the end of 1969, the year Circle Rep opened at the loft on Broadway and West 83rd Street, John Willis in reviewing the previous season wrote:

> The state of the theatre in New York was grim. Attendance was decreasing. Increasing were production and ticket costs, vulgarity without humor, nudity without artistry and obscenity without shock value. Onstage nudity, homosexuality and vulgarity reached the point of absurdity. Broadway's first all nude play was quickly dumped with other rubbish. Except for individual performances, impressive sets and excellent revivals, there was little during 1969–70 in New York's theatres that was not mediocre, depressing and unrewarding.

The Circle Repertory Company would eventually come to represent one of the few "sane" voices that survived from the off-off-Broadway movement of the sixties.

As the off-off-Broadway movement began to soar, many theatre groups were springing up all over New York City. In its early heyday off-off-Broadway groups presented plays wherever space could be found, usually on infinitesimal budgets. Many of these plays were incoherent. The styles that were so right for depicting the ferment of the times eventually faded when the relaxing of war tensions weakened the exigency of confrontational theatre; audiences showed signs of exhaustion at being "yelled at" constantly.

Even during these early days Circle Rep's goals were more oriented to the written word than, for example, were La Mama's productions. Ellen Stewart, founder of La Mama, became one of the most prolific off-off-Broadway producers. In 1961 she opened the La Mama Experimental Theatre Club with a heavy commitment to new plays and new playwrights. Many young playwrights would not have been heard had it not been for Ellen Stewart's enthusiastic and generous support. "By 1967 she had produced 175 plays by 130 writers. During the season of 1969–1970 La Mama alone produced more plays than were seen on Broadway," according to Oscar G. Brockett in his *History of the Theatre*. Notably, it was at La Mama that Lanford Wilson's *Balm in Gilead*, generally considered off-off-Broadway's first full-length play, premiered under the direction of Marshall Mason in 1965. It was the first time they worked together and marked the beginning of an extraordinary twenty-year working relationship.

By 1968–1969, La Mama's main focus shifted from playwrights to directors, since many of the only partially scripted plays seemed to demand intense director involvement. Tom O'Horgan, later director of *Hair, Futz,* and *Tom Paine,* was one of La Mama's most controversial directors. He was highly experimental in his approach to staging, using choral speaking, dance, mime, frantic physicalization, and pulsating electronic light and sound effects, all of which tended to de-emphasize written scripts even further.

Circle Rep's focus was also distinct from the environmental approach of Joseph Chaikin's Open Theatre, founded in 1961, which tried to conjure up transformations through dreams and myths during performance. Much improvisation and free movement in large open spaces was part of the Open Theatre's workshop approach, as playwrights structured the improvised material into plays, occasionally with stunning results, as in Megan Terry's 1966 production of *Viet Rock.* However, it was not common for many plays of an enduring quality to result from this "of the moment" approach.

Much of this theatre did not speak to Marshall Mason who, despite his belief in some essential aspects of experimentation, was a traditionalist at heart. There was much experimentation, exploration, and risk taking, especially in the early days of Circle Rep's operations, but most of it was in terms of theatre styles rather than challenging society to scrutinize its perceptions or of challenging theatre itself to scrutinize its role in society. In this sense it was diametrically opposed to the philosophy of the Living Theatre, a high-profile group of the time. Margaret Croyden's negative assessment of the theatrical fruits of the sixties in her *Lunatics, Lovers and Poets: The Contemporary Experimental Theatre* could almost have been written about the Living Theatre alone:

> As is the case of movements composed of all kinds of personalities, and especially where personality was itself supposed to be an artistic vehicle, some individuals lost sight of their original aim of building an authentic new theatre and got caught up in all sorts of fads and ego trips . . . untried techniques were grafted into undigested philosophies, the gestalt theories mixed with R. D. Laing, confrontation politics with Artaud, consciousness expansion with Yoga, spontaneity with disciplined

exercise, guruism with collective living, freakism with simplic-
ity.

A serious problem . . . was the experimentalists' reliance
on self-expression as a predominant aesthetic—the old romantic tenet. Self-expression became the answer to all arguments
and served to hide a dearth of shallow ideas and unworkable
theatrics . . . it cultivated an intense and limited subjectivism
and bred . . . a new anti-intellectualism.

Deeply influenced by Antonin Artaud's Theatre of Cruelty, the Living
Theatre sharply de-emphasized written scripts in their philosophical
presentations and emphasized mime, ritual, incantation, and stage
movement repeated to the point of entrancement and "exorcism" *à la*
Artaud.

By 1969, the Living Theatre, under the leadership of Julian Beck
and Judith Malina, was a highly political, activist theatre, one of the
most antagonistic of the alternative theatres, demanding intense audience involvement and almost always evoking extremely critical responses. Except for such productions as Brecht's *Man Is Man* and *In the
Jungle of Cities,* critics knew they were not going to see a "play" in the
ordinary sense of the word when they went to see a Living Theatre
performance. In seeing a performance which truly represented the Living Theatre's avowed goal of overturning "classic and experimental dramatic forms to replace them with political protest and moral anarchy,"[3]
critics knew they were in for an evening that at best might resemble a
political rally, at worst an exhausting assault upon their sensibilities.

Upon seeing *The Brig* in 1963, directed by Judith Malina, Robert
Brustein wrote that it was not a play but a punishment, like the sadistic
stomach punches repeatedly suffered by the terrorized prisoners on
stage:

I don't suppose I will ever spend a more disagreeable evening in
the theatre. Instead of organizing a dramatic work, Kenneth H.
Brown, the nominal author, has chosen to function as an absolute mute witness to a typical day in the infernal regions, the
only departure from this terrible realism being the compression
of time. . . . Visually, there is plenty of excitement in the way
Judith Malina has drilled her company into a stolid automatism
vibrating rhythms of pain; but aside from this, there is nothing
to break the monotony of the proceedings, where even brutality
and violence soon grow dull and routinized. One leaves the
theatre with a headache and jangling nerves, having shared all
the agonies of the prisoners except their physical torments.[4]

Other critics were equally appalled, although Brustein reacted with some disdain toward Howard Taubman and Walter Kerr when Taubman called for a "presidential investigation" in noting that *The Brig* is a "far cry from drama," and Kerr sympathized with any audience forced to suffer this "hoosegow."[5]

Whether or not what these critics were reacting to so strongly was "a play" is not important. The production represented a severe point of view, yet set the tone for a good deal of off-off-Broadway theatre. The Living Theatre was the best-known, the most influential, and the most copied group of its kind by the end of the sixties. It had also been around the longest, having started in 1946. Its theatre was startling, astonishing, different, and quintessentially off-off-Broadway, although such a term did not yet exist. The audience was invited to view their communal lifestyle with its nudity, drugs, and free sex, led by more of a guru-type figure in beads than an artistic director. In *The Living Book of the Living Theatre* one is immediately struck by the religiosity of the long list of "I believes," which sounds like prayers. On stage one could not help being aware of the missionary zeal beneath the confrontational explosions; there was the ever-present, unspoken, "Join us."[6]

In Brustein's final assessment of *The Brig,* he is one of the few critics willing to put aside his jangled nerves and acknowledge the bottom-line morality of this approach:

> With this ruthless documentary, the Living Theatre confronts you with the thing itself, trying to break through the crust of indifference which Americans have developed in the face of evil; and the mere staging of the work becomes an act of conscience, decency and moral revolt in the midst of apathy and inertia. Whether the revelation of these conditions will affect that bureaucratic mechanism which creates them, I cannot say. But if you can bring yourself to spend a night in *The Brig,* you may start a jailbreak of your own.[7]

All of this was far removed from Marshall Mason's vision of theatre, which by contrast must be called more gentle; he was not a revolutionary. Although aware of Brecht and Artaud, Circle Rep was much more influenced by the Chekhovian world of realism, mood, profound characterization, and most important, language.

Mason was disappointed with contemporary theatre, especially with the nonverbal and avant-garde styles that were so prevalent:

There was no theatre in America. Nearly all theatre on Broadway was imported from England. Harold Pinter was the reigning great playwright in America at the time. Joe Chaikin was doing very well with his Open Theatre, but again it was all nonscripted. Grotowski was very much in. La Mama was flourishing but flourishing in nonverbal theatre. It was all very experimental, very interesting but not interesting to me. I had always sort of been in the mainstream. I do experimental theatre — *Untitled Play* was an incredible experiment that worked. Others do not. That is the nature of experimentation. It's absolutely essential to have that freedom to fail. I used to think experimental theatre meant a certain kind of theatre. I think all theatre is essentially experimental. The form-play may be traditional but within that you have to create new life. Otherwise it's more of a museum piece.[8]

With the suggestion that most people think of experimental theatre as avant-garde or out of the realm of realism, and thus difficult to comprehend, Mason agreed:

I know, and that gets formalized and regimented in exactly the same way that realism does. I think by the late sixties it really had begun and you knew exactly what they were going to do. . . . Whereas realism, which had been abandoned for a number of years, really held as we subsequently found out when we reintroduced it to the theatre. There was a lot of vitality in it yet and people have responded.[9]

Lanford Wilson held a similar view. Wilson, who had such a responsive ear to the music of language and was intent on becoming a playwright, wanted no part of the nonscripted aggressive approach of the Living Theatre:

I'll tell you my experience with them. I went out to Brooklyn to see one show, *Frankenstein*. It was the only time I'd left Manhattan Island in five years. It was really interesting. It was very good in that it created a monster. It was just amazing. They had the passport scene — or whatever that was — the rubber stamp scene — "State your name and take them to the cell block," the whole rigamarole. This is what I remember — the monster and that section. The repetition, by the fourth one, is very effective. I do that too. And then they went about ten more, and I said, they're not proving anything. It's not really effective anymore by doing that. Then they did about twenty-

> five more and I got very bored. . . . Then I got back into it and broke down completely. Because it had finally elevated beyond any intellectual understanding. It suddenly became about the whole world and about everyone and about me. So I remember that experience very vividly.[10]

It was important basic research for Wilson. He was not sure how he could use it, but it meant something theatrical to him. Although he often used repetition, the kind of repetition that bludgeoned the senses was new to him. It was a theatrical experience that was reflective of the craziness of the times. But Mason and Wilson both wanted to develop different experiences out of the same times. Wilson admits that the visceral experience and the technical idea of *Frankenstein* were valuable, but he consciously rejected the intensely subjective lifestyle that was at the core of the Living Theatre philosophy. It became difficult even to sit around at parties on the floor with a jug of wine with Living Theatre members. Wilson continues:

> And then the word around the Village at the time was they were the most arrogant, impossible, unclean people that anyone had ever been near in their life. They stank and they were so arrogant about, "We're the Living Theatre!" It was like, "We are the only art." So I decided that these people were not for me. They were not the sort of people I enjoyed taking with. I found the play very effective, but it's not the kind of theatre I wanted to do—no.[11]

He was much more in tune with Circle Rep's credo as articulated and pioneered by Mason and Rob Thirkield—an ongoing company of artists dedicated to growing together and dedicated to the development of new American stage literature. As their program states, Circle Rep was looking for an environment in which a group of artists could create independent of outside pressures, and in which an audience could experience a theatre event that was moving, real, and reflective of the human dilemma, rather than politically rallying or cathartic. With this policy, Circle Rep's voice was comparatively quiet for the times. So quiet, in fact, that its work eventually had to be labeled and categorized apart from other off-off-Broadway theatre as "lyric realism." Although there were other off-Broadway and off-off-Broadway groups presenting realistic theatre (mostly revivals or imports), Circle Rep became high profile with its presentations of original, realistic, American plays. In Edwin

Wilson's review of Edward J. Moore's *The Sea Horse,* directed by Marshall Mason at the loft on upper Broadway, he speaks of Circle Rep continuing to present new works that are not experimental in style as had come to be expected of so much off-off-Broadway fare. He felt that this clearly made Circle Rep an exception. In fact, Circle Rep had become one of the few successful voices of realism and poetry in a sea of absurdist, avant-garde, and highly political activist theatre. This voice, which clearly distinguished the Circle Repertory Company, was primarily due to the plays of Lanford Wilson and to the interpretation of these plays by Marshall W. Mason.

2

The Four Founders—
Plus Joe

Marshall W. Mason

Marshall W. Mason was born in 1940 in Amarillo, Texas. West Texas is mainly open-range cattle country. The city was built in great part on the prosperity of the cattle industry and in part on the piled-up hides of slaughtered buffalo. The glamour of the Old West clings with echoes of buffalo hunts and the presence of Texas Rangers still stationed in Amarillo, but Mason holds few fond memories of, and little allegiance to, the city of his birth. His father had been adopted when only a child by the Masons, a poor, childless couple. He too was poor and worked as a salad chef for Texas A&M University when his own son, Marshall, was born.

When Marshall was four years old, his parents divorced. He continued to live in Amarillo for the next two years with his mother and Sam Feutral, the Air Force man she married almost immediately after the divorce. When Mason was in the second grade, and his half brother, Sammy Feutral, had just been born, the Air Force transferred his stepfather to New Orleans.

"My mother had her hands full with two kids and her husband in the Air Force," Mason remembers. "She didn't know where she was going exactly, setting up household in the middle of New Orleans."

Marshall was therefore dropped off with his adopted paternal grandparents in Luling, south Texas, where he finished the second grade. When he went to live with them, his grandmother was seventy-two years old and his grandfather was seventy-six. The plan was that Marshall would join his mother in New Orleans when she was settled, but Mason loved Luling and refused to go. As it turned out, his mother was in New Orleans only temporarily. It was not long before she separated from Feutral and moved to San Antonio, no more than fifty miles from Luling. Mason visited, spent weekends, and babysat for his half brother, but he always went back to Luling where he was being raised as an— admittedly spoiled—only child by his elderly grandparents. Marshall's father lived nearby and would come to visit whenever he could. "He was working in some town in south Texas as a short-order cook," Mason says. "I'm trying to remember. . . . I don't remember. I would see him from time to time and I would see my mother from time to time, but mostly I lived with my grandparents. My father's actual name before he was adopted by the Masons was Thomas. . . . My bloodline is actually Thomas. When either my mother or father came to visit me it was always a special treat. My father always brought me presents. Books, mainly. . . . The only time I remember missing them significantly—that it was a really painful time—was when events like PTA meetings happened. I didn't have any parents to go."

Mason does not remember being lonely as a child. He had a close friend in the second grade, Gene England, who remained a friend to adulthood. Every Saturday morning they went to the serials. His grandfather gave him an allowance of twenty-five cents a week. The movie was nine cents, popcorn was a dime, coke was a nickel, and there was a penny left over for some bubble gum. Afterwards, the two boys played imaginative games based on the exciting adventures they had just seen on the screen. It was not long before Mason knew that he would be in theatre; there was never any doubt in his mind about that. As a child, he sat in the darkened movie house feeling the frustration of passively watching child actors on the screen and instinctively knowing he could do better. There was a tremendous impatience inside the boy to grow up quickly and begin his career as an actor, despite the fact that he was persistently warned by his pragmatic elders that such dreams were unrealistic. Rather than discouraging him, their warnings only increased Mason's impatience. He unabashedly admits that, growing up in an area removed from live theatre, his idols were Marlon Brando, James Dean, and Montgomery Clift. To him, they represented the highest form of art that could be accomplished in films. Behind them he keenly felt the presence of the Actors Studio approach with its Americanized Stanislavski method, and Elia Kazan, the director who became hero and idol to him.

By the sixth grade, his grandparents decided to move to Mullen, a tiny, isolated town of 600 people in the middle of Texas. Mason disliked the quiet town intensely. There simply were not enough opportunities for a boy with his imagination, energy, and drive. Now began a period of transience in the young boy's academic as well as home life that was stimulated by his own vital determination and allowed by his grandparents' permissiveness. Since his father, who had never remarried, had moved back to Amarillo in northwestern Texas, Mason decided to move in with him for the seventh grade. By the end of the seventh grade, his grandparents had moved back to Luling, the town that Mason really considered his hometown. Torn between his love of Luling and the opportunities Amarillo offered, he shifted back and forth between his father and his grandparents, shuttling from one school to another as well—the sixth grade in Mullen, the seventh in Amarillo, the eighth in Luling. It became clear to the young boy with the growing sense of independence that the opportunities of a large city were really advantageous, so he spent the ninth grade back in Amarillo. With so much moving about, however, there was little room to build up any school allegiances; he could barely wait to complete high school, and in fact managed to graduate a year early.

Mason's childhood obviously was marked with a good deal of emotional self-reliance. Although it was never openly stated, there was little room for him in his mother's life; she married a total of six times by the time Mason was in his twenties. There never had been a sense of family between Mason and Sammy Feutral, his half brother, the two never having lived together. In terms of financial security, there had never been much money, living with his grandparents; between the two of them they earned approximately one hundred dollars a month. However, growing up without money, young Marshall's values never became intimately involved with it—money simply was not very important to him. Even much later when critics opened avenues of financial success for him by praising his directorial work, Mason most often did not avail himself of the opportunities. He preferred to remain close to the work he was most interested in—a distinguishing personal characteristic—particularly if it had to do with the Circle Repertory Company, even if the recompense there was comparatively small.

Mason left Amarillo at the age of seventeen and returned only for the deaths of his grandparents and his father. "I was with my grandmother when she died of cancer after my freshman year," he says. "She was at home when it happened and I was with her. My grandfather died about two years later in an old age home. . . . I went back again in May of 1969 to bury my father. He died suddenly, unexpectedly. It wasn't a long illness, a ruptured spleen, something weird. It just happened," he says quietly. "My mother came from California and joined me in Amarillo. I flew his body back to Luling to be buried with my grandparents. I chose for his tombstone a quotation from *Hamlet:* 'He was a man. Take him for all and all. We shall not see his like again.' Which was what Hamlet said about his father. I haven't been back to Luling since."

Mason is not fond of Texas. Since he has been in New York, he has returned twice, both times to Dallas to do a director's colloquium. Mostly he avoids returning. "I find myself artistically, politically, socially, and every way else so in another place," he says. It is hardly surprising that it is a part of the world in which he feels he does not belong. "I'm a real New Yorker. I love New York," he says of his adopted city. "I don't like the criticism I feel inherent in Texas of anything liberal or humanitarian. The real preoccupation with anything economic is distasteful to me. So. . . . "

It is easy to say he left Amarillo at the age of seventeen and never returned. In a sense, philosophically at least, that is true.

He then attended Northwestern University, where he became a protegé of "the great Alvina Krause," whom Mason felt was pure in her artistic beliefs. "To work with her for four years was to absorb some of those ideals," he says.

Rob Thirkield

At Northwestern Mason met Rob Thirkield, the "rich kid," who attended as a graduate student from Wesleyan University and who was so profoundly instrumental in the development of the company. Thirkield was already at Northwestern when Mason arrived. Thirkield had come to the university to continue his studies with Alvina Krause, with whom he had spent two summers at Eagles Mere Playhouse in Pennsylvania, acting and designing sets while still attending Wesleyan. At Northwestern, Mason and Thirkield roomed together. Thirkield remembers him as "a tall, gangly guy with thick glasses, a Texas accent, and a very high, squeaky voice."[1] Mason immediately set about working on the pitch of his voice and getting rid of his accent. "Now," Thirkield says appreciatively, "he almost sounds English." The theatre was a mutual love and became the basis for a strong bond between the two students, although their personalities and backgrounds were extremely different.

Rob Thirkield was born in Glen Cove, Long Island, on July 29, 1936, but grew up in Brooklyn with his parents. His father, whom he remembers as "very businesslike," was a banker who served as vice-president of the Brooklyn Trust Company. His mother was a very beautiful woman. Her father, Thomas Leeming, whose family owned Ben Gay, was head of the Brooklyn Academy of Music and always had four seats reserved at the Metropolitan Opera House. As a child, Thirkield remembers many an evening when great singers from the Metropolitan would come to their house to sing. His grandmother's house in Glen Cove, which he refers to as "rather nice," was palatial, with many rooms, huge white columns, and a brilliant white portico. Thirkield spent a good deal of time at this house as a child. It was a wonderful place for fantasies, with its many balconies, nooks, and crannies. Since his sister was six years older and his brother four years older, Thirkield spent a good deal of time by himself, most of it filled with play-acting.

"We had this old cedar closet full of Japanese costumes," he recalls fondly, "and I'd come running downstairs and start jumping around in a Japanese costume. And my parents said, 'Oh, that's very nice. Now go back to your room.' I always loved the theatre, and I always had puppets for whom I would make scenery. In school, I always acted in the Christmas play and I was told by my teachers that someday I would be an actor. But my family always said, 'Be a lawyer. Be a doctor. Anything but an actor.' But that's what it was for me right from the beginning. My parents went along. No major problem. But not tremendous encouragement either. I never really studied anything else but acting. At Northwestern I took a theatre architecture course, and my parents said, 'Oh! You can be an architect,' and I said, no . . . no I couldn't."

Like Mason, money was never very important to Thirkield, but in his case because it was always there. He never even knew how wealthy the family was until his father died and he helped his mother settle the family accounts. The discovery of the family's worth was a shock to him. Thirkield's money would eventually play an important part in the creation of the Circle Rep. In the beginning he was the only contributor. Even after the Circle Rep received it first grants, Thirkield continued to contribute at least $20,000 a year for the first ten years and often bailed out the company when it ran into financial difficulties.

Mason and Thirkield studied acting together at Northwestern and then directing as a supplement. They remember Alvina Krause as a brilliant woman and an inspiring teacher who concentrated on plays by Chekhov and Ibsen. The traditional thrust of Mason's theatrical views was being nourished plentifully. Thirkield would eventually branch out in different directions. Working closely with Tom O'Horgan at La Mama in his early days in New York and stimulated by Grotowski's "Poor Theatre," Thirkield leaned toward the avant-garde.

At the end of his sophomore year, Mason asked Krause to take him to Eagles Mere for her summer playhouse season, where she took her best students, including Thirkield, every year. She turned Mason down. "I was so depressed," he recalls. "I absolutely believed and trusted Miss Krause. If Miss Krause didn't take me, it meant that I was not one of the best actors at Northwestern. I said, well if I can't be a great actor, I'm not going to stay in theatre. I'm going to do something else. I considered transferring to pre-law."

Krause's associate, Professor Jim Gousseff, realized that Mason was deeply discouraged by what he perceived as total rejection. Gousseff was also aware of what a loss it would be if Mason did leave the theatre department. He took the depressed young man to his home, made him drink a great deal of wine, and tried to convince him that the theatre needed serious people like himself. Even through the blur of too much wine, Mason was adamant; if he could not be a great actor, what was the point? And then Gousseff said, "Have you ever thought of directing?"

Mason thought for a moment. Finally he said, "There is a play I'd like to direct. There's no part in it for me, and I really feel this play, *Cat on a Hot Tin Roof*." Then Gousseff made a deal with him. Northwestern's summer repertory theatre was doing *Oedipus, The Rivals, St. Joan,* and *Midsummer Night's Dream*. He assured Mason that he would get good parts if he remained, took a few classes, and directed *Cat on a Hot Tin Roof* in the fall. "Think it over," he said. "Don't transfer."

Sophocles, Sheridan, Shaw, and Shakespeare, Mason thought. He decided to stay.

When Thirkield heard of Mason's plans to direct Tennessee Williams's play, he clearly remembers saying, "Oh sure, Marshall. Go ahead. Lots of luck!" Although they had studied directing together, Thirkield looked upon Mason basically as an actor. He was not aware that Krause had turned him down for Eagles Mere.

"I found that what I disliked about directors was that they often superimposed an idea on the actors, and as an actor I had resented this a great deal," Mason says. "I felt that the objective was to get the play to really live and breathe and the way to do this was to work with and through the actors and not on the actors. I felt more like the author of the play; I didn't think of it as being the director. Maggie was very real and palpable to me through the actress I was working with. So were Brick and Big Daddy. All of these people were my people. I felt the play was almost Greek in its size. I used the people sort of as chorus. They watched everything. There was never a sense of privacy in the house. They were always being watched. That's an element in the play, 'These walls have ears.' It was very useful. There was a ghost haunting the play and watching. I felt more like a playwright; the play was there, Tennessee wasn't, and I was responsible for it. The play was such an organic part of my sense of the world and what I wanted to say about the world. . . . "

Although Mason's vision of what a director does with a play was totally copied from Alvina Krause, he had a chip on his shoulder because of her rejection of him. Krause came to see a dress rehearsal of *Cat on a Hot Tin Roof* and told him it was very well staged. Mason said, "What do you mean, 'staged'? It's not staged at all. The whole thing is organic. I didn't impose any blocking on it at all." And Krause said, "Well, I just meant that it's very logical and nice work."

At the end of the performances at Northwestern, Krause always gave a critique. There was a full house for *Cat*. She said wonderful things about each of the actors, and then added, "And I assume that everyone is aware of the superlative direction." The audience stood up and applauded. Mason was nineteen years old. He received the 1959 Award for Best Director at Northwestern University that year. "But it wasn't something I chose to do," he insists, "or intended to do or ever do again," even though he suddenly found himself in everybody's eyes as a director.

Now Alvina Krause invited him to Eagles Mere for the next two summers, where he directed *Mary Stuart, Cyrano de Bergerac,* and *The Doctor's Dilemma.*

In 1961, Mason graduated from Northwestern University and headed for New York City, while Thirkield left to serve two years in the army between the Korean and Vietnam wars. The list of their classmates from Northwestern is impressive. Along with Claris Nelson and Dennis Parichy, who would come to New York and work closely with Mason and Thirkield at the Circle Repertory Company, Northwestern also graduated Tony Roberts, Richard Benjamin, Larry Pressman, Penny Fuller, Marcia Rodd, Karen Black, and Paula Prentiss, to whose Cleopatra Thirkield had played Caesar.

Like many young hopefuls who arrive in New York to begin careers in theatre, Mason had his share of frustrations. Not only were there no jobs to be found, either in acting or directing, but just when he thought he could begin to practice his art, serious theatre as he appreciated it disappeared from New York. "Miller and Williams were no longer producing a new play each season," he says. They had almost fallen aside under the negative label of "old fashioned" and an increasingly harsh critical view that their major work was behind them — even though Miller had yet to write the controversial *After the Fall* and *Incident at Vichy* in 1964 for the short-lived Repertory Company of Lincoln Center. At the time, serious theatre in New York seemed to be represented by British playwright Harold Pinter, who was then the critical rage.

One of the earliest plays Mason saw on Broadway was Pinter's *The Caretaker,* which he said infuriated him. As a youth one often makes extravagant statements to express the strength of one's convictions and ideas, which if seriously reflected upon would seem ludicrous. Over the years, Mason has mellowed considerably in his point of view toward Pinter. But at the time, the young man felt all the critics and reviewers were excited because they could not understand what Pinter was talking about. "It might have illustrated nothing so much as their lack of intellectual capacity. . . . They were turned on by 'What is the *meaning* of Pinter?' Pinter is a poet if anything. He had them all fooled. They thought he meant something."

Mason felt Pinter's meaning was very existential and was meant to be sensed rather than understood. Agreeing that the acting by Donald Pleasance, Robert Shaw, and Alan Bates was brilliant and that the production values were exceptional, he nevertheless felt cheated that he could not really get emotionally involved. "I want to get something out of a play when I go to it," he insists. "I do not want to leave the theatre saying, 'What do you suppose that meant?'" He was not ashamed to admit he had not understood the play; in fact, that was his whole point.

For a young man just starting out in a big, unfriendly city that had little room to nourish his ambitions, he had strong, passionate views. But even then he could not be intimidated into changing his opinions by those who had the power to establish criteria. His opinions at the time were based on emotion rather than intellectual assessment, and right or wrong they were the driving force that would establish his artistic direction. All of his feelings about "real" drama were solidifying almost unconsciously. These were the feelings that would translate into the conscious objectives that he would bring to the Circle Repertory Company and that would contribute directly to the attention to realistic detail, and the very style of lyrical realism with which he has become identified. He had an almost missionary zeal to reintroduce realism into the flood of avant-garde absurdism.

Though a bit uncomfortable in rejecting current dramatic fashion, Mason nevertheless hated theatre of the absurd. He was not interested in the absurdity of the human condition presented against an indecipherable cosmos. The metaphysical aspects took the human condition out of the realm of identifiable human experience, thereby losing his interest. With no plot to speak of and no "real" characters in conflict, the situations were simply not dramatic to him. He felt that Edward Albee grew out of a sea of absurdists and inherited much of the grotesqueries. Although Mason could relate to *The Zoo Story* and *Who's Afraid of Virginia Woolf* (more the exception in Albee's repertoire then the rule), *The American Dream,* presented the year Mason arrived in New York (which Albee stated was intended as an American version of Ionesco's *The Bald Soprano*), left Mason cold. To someone with his proclivities, *The American Dream* could only be a stark landscape populated by symbols rather than people.

When he did respond to the absurd play, it had to be packed with emotion—though understated—such as Beckett's *Waiting for Godot*. It is easy to see how Mason might be attracted to one absurdist play and not another. The important ingredient is obviously the humanity and emotional impact, for despite its comic aspects, *Waiting for Godot* is an extremely emotional drama of human despair. The very structure of

Godot's dramatic action, starting with "Nothing to be done," is theatre in which the importance of sequential events is immediately made irrelevant. The oft-repeated words "Nothing to be done" is a painful refutation of man's ability to shape his own destiny. Vladimir and Estragon talk of repenting having been born, of the crucifixion, of waiting for Godot; they contemplate suicide, wonder what they will ask Godot when he comes, eat a carrot, all of which demonstrates that the action is really only one—to wait. This, then, is basically static action. There is no story in the usual sense, but rather a series of images designed specifically to show man's alienation from reality, an alienation that produces the lethargy and anxiety that can result when he feels surrounded by an incomprehensible world.

Mason does not feel that Vladimir and Estragon are symbols. "They are real people," Mason insists. "Very detailed, very rich human beings. Their context is a bit strange. The universe against which they are presented is, perhaps, not a realistic universe, but they are real people. And their despair is monumental."

Ionesco was another matter. Ionesco committed the unpardonable sin of not moving Mason, to whom theatre has never been an intellectual game. It has to "hit you" on all levels. "It has to have something for the mind," Mason continues, "but it also has to move you. It has to be meaningful in human experience terms. Ionesco doesn't write about real people. He writes symbols. When you get so off into the absurd thing, you get into a style that does not interest me!"

But in the early sixties these were the reigning kings—Pinter, Beckett, Ionesco, and Albee. The current mainstream challenged all of Mason's thoughts about theatre. If there had been a balance between realism and absurdism, he might have leaned more to one without consciously rejecting the other. But with realism almost nonexistent, he was forced to sort out his feelings and come to a conscious decision about what he wanted to pursue, and whether or not there was room for the kind of theatre he wanted. To him, the greatest playwrights were Euripides, Shakespeare, Molière, and Chekhov, all of whom wrote about the human experience. The contemporary writers he read and loved as a young man growing up in Texas were Tennessee Williams, Arthur Miller, Robert Anderson, and William Gibson. Plays like *All Summer Long, Tea and Sympathy,* and *The Miracle Worker* were not only accessible but "spoke to him."

He had the Midwesterner's expectations of Broadway as the highest criteria of American theatre. When he found it bereft of the kind of theatre to which he could respond, he gravitated toward the Actors Studio, where he hoped he could work with Kazan, but Kazan had already moved on to the experiment of the Repertory Company of Lincoln Center. In the meantime, he studied directing with Lee Strasberg and Harold Clurman, whose techniques were basically traditionalist and fit in with his own needs. Mason worked mostly in theatre-related odd jobs in order to support himself: he got a job as an assistant stage manager at the Phoenix Theatre, which, in his own words, "led nowhere"; acted as treasurer at the Cherry Lane Theatre in Greenwich Village; and worked as an independent electrician.

In 1962, within one year of his arrival in New York, Mason found the Caffé Cino. It was here that Mason sank his roots deep into the soil of the off-off-Broadway movement where, despite scarce audiences and scarcer funds, there was an abundance of experimentation and enthusiasm. Mason had stumbled into the forerunner of the workshops, showcases, and laboratories that would comprise the off-off-Broadway scene. Although by 1975 Marion Fredi Towbin would call off-off-Broadway "the source—the lifeline—of American theatre," in the early sixties it was new and had a low profile. Mason had never heard of the Caffé Cino, which, by the time he got there, had been giving plays since 1958, called itself an "art center," and was already considered an establishment by the *cognoscenti*. Mason immediately availed himself of Joe Cino's generous policies and began directing again.

By the time Thirkield returned from the army and was directed by Mason in Claris Nelson's *Medea* at the Cino, Thirkield was keenly aware of the artistic change in Mason. There was no doubt in Thirkield's assessment that his friend had made the transition from actor to director with a conviction and artistic vision that encompassed not only the immediacy of directing, but also goals for the future. These goals revolved around the company of artists they both had envisioned while working together on what they always referred to as "real plays" at Northwestern.

It was not long before Mason and Thirkield got together with Claris Nelson and Dennis Parichy (fellow graduates of Northwestern University) and organized their first company, appropriately called "Northwestern Productions." Although they worked mainly at the Caffé Cino and Cafe La Mama, they did branch out to off-Broadway. Mason directed Claris Nelson's *The Rue Garden, The Clown,* and *Medea* before directing Ibsen's *Little Eyolf* at the Actors Playhouse. *Little Eyolf* received fairly good reviews from all the critics except Walter Kerr of the *New York Times,* who disliked it intensely. The impact of Kerr's review and the succeeding production of Shaw's *Arms and the Man,* which Mason considered unsuccessful, brought an early end to Northwestern Productions.

At this time the Cino was presenting some one-act plays by a young playwright, Lanford Wilson. Mason had seen him around and was wary of what he perceived to be Wilson's hyperactivity. He remained removed from Wilson, although privately he confessed to Thirkield that he would like to direct one of Wilson's plays. However, apart from one quick, cursory introduction in which each had measured the other in terms of external appearances, Mason and Wilson had still not met. Mason knew little of the playwright except that he had originally come from "some little hick town" out West.

Lanford Wilson

The tiny town of Lebanon is almost dead center on the Ozark plateau that stretches across all of southern Missouri. This massive hill country maintains an untamed wildness about it that has challenged three centuries of man's ingenuity to force it to his personal use. From this Midwestern soil one of our most prolific "New York" writers sprang. Lanford Eugene Wilson was born in Lebanon, Missouri, on April 13, 1937, to Ralph Eugene Wilson and Violetta Careybelle Tate Wilson. He was the only child of what would turn out to be an unhappy and unenduring marriage. As he remembers, they were "very, very poor." The boy was small and thin and his face, with its perennial pallor, was dominated even then by the crystal-clear blue eyes that would always be the first thing one noticed upon meeting him.

Although he lived in Lebanon only until he was five, Wilson vividly and warmly described the little town in an interview with William Sibley forty-two years later:

> It's a very small dusty town with some nice people and some frankly uninteresting "frank" kind of architecture. . . . The roads weren't paved where we lived out in Old Town—the black community. I remember ice trucks going by and kicking up the dust that lasted for hours at a time. I spent some wonderful

> summers in Lebanon as a kid. Gateway to the Ozarks, you
> know. The sign at Claxton's Texaco says, "5,000 Friendly Peo-
> ple Welcome You to Lebanon."[2]

When Wilson was five years old, his parents divorced. Not only was his family suddenly gone, but his entire world was disrupted. Violetta took the boy to Springfield, Missouri, fifty miles south of Lebanon. Ralph Wilson, who had worked as a cobbler, immediately departed for San Diego, California. It would be twelve years before Lanford would see his father again—twelve years that to a small boy would seem like a lifetime.

Even with much of the male population away for the duration of World War II, Springfield in 1942 was a booming metropolis compared to Lebanon. Violetta had little trouble getting a job in a garment factory, one of many menial jobs Lanford watched his mother endure. He even clearly remembers helping her make up beds in a fancy hotel.

The years passed rather quickly at this time with that peculiar combination of isolation and togetherness that is often imposed when a young mother with a young child is forced to support them both.

Between the ages of five and eleven, Lanford lived only with his mother. Then she married Ralph Lenhard, a Wisconsin dairy farmer who brought with him two daughters from a former marriage. Suddenly, after six years alone with his mother, Lanford was surrounded by a full family. Trust and friendship eventually developed between Lanford and his new family, but he was always plagued with a sense of rootlessness. The ambiguity of wanting a family and at the same time not wanting to share his mother created mixed feelings that would be difficult for any eleven-year-old to sort out, especially one of Lanford's sensitivities.

After the marriage, the family moved ten miles south of Springfield to a small rented farm in the tiny Missouri town of Ozark, population 1,500. They were still in the Ozark highlands—still in the dead center of the country and still surrounded by the singularly Midwestern rhythms and sounds that Wilson would one day convey clearly. It was in Ozark that he first saw the large old meandering house that would become the setting for the Talley trilogy years later. The house was up on Harper's Hill overlooking the town. It seemed awesome and full of secrets, so completely inaccessible to the local children that they endowed it with mystery. As Mel Gussow has pointed out in acknowledging the structure's importance: "As an adult, Wilson has begun to populate the structure, the 'Talley house' of his theatrical imagination, with a rich and luxuriant tapestry of people."[3]

Undoubtedly, Wilson began to populate it in his imagination even earlier, long before he had any thought of becoming a playwright. Ozark, the smallest of his hometowns, remained the closest in his conscious memory. The idols of his teen years, all the schoolmates of promise who seemed to have their lives structured with clear plans founded on position and bolstered by wealth, could already have been residents of that early "Talley house." In his mind they were, but years later when he returned to Missouri, it was disillusioning to find out that " . . . these heroes of his youth, the 'hotshots of Ozark,' had had terrible lives filled with divorce, impotence, alcoholism, murder and suicide."[4] The third of the Talley trilogy, *The War in Lebanon,* was planned to honor the memory of these lost heroes, for the heroes of one's youth are not easily dispelled by reality. In Lanford's case it was to be a catharsis by pen. However, the third play in the trilogy became *A Tale Told,* leaving past idols to be put to rest another time.

Wilson, whose personal life is the rich wellspring of all of his work, openly admits to writing into his plays many of the people he has known. His particular ability to capture and orchestrate the feelings and sounds about him makes his stage come alive with his own reality—a reality based on passions deeply felt. Often he reacts to people, and thus to the characters he creates, through his own pain, which makes him particularly sensitive to that of others. "We're so easily hurt by all these damn things," he says, "and yet we come back and we really know what we're doing." It is interesting to note that although he readily admits to the autobiographical source of much of his material, especially *Lemon Sky,* a fairly direct account of his meeting with his father in San Diego, he has "never written his mother." He has, however, used many facets of her in various characters. A washerwoman in *A Tale Told* reflected her many occupations. In the CBS-TV play *The Migrants,* a character cleaned houses for wealthy Talley-type families, much as his mother did during the lean years. That character was even called "Viola," but he has never truly written a Violetta yet, or fully probed her personality or their private relationship in his work.

As the new family settled into the routine of farming, the sense of isolation was camouflaged by the number of people about every day. Although the family remained poor, Lanford remembers these years as relatively happy ones. He continued his education in Ozark's public schools, became a member of the 4-H Club and Future Farmers of America, and even came in among the top three in a cattle-raising competition one year. "I'm really a country boy at heart," he notes. "I learned to milk cows before daybreak."[5]

Unlike Mason, who could not wait to depart from Texas, Wilson developed a profound love of the soil of the Midwest that he would later render into the deep-rooted setting of most of his plays. This love was also obvious in the seriously cultivated garden in the backyard of the old house in Sag Harbor, Long Island, he would one day buy, although he would be quick to point out that part of this appreciation can be attributed to the influence of his maternal grandmother. Part American Indian, she was enormously important to him in his developmental years. It was she who taught him to raise chickens and pick wild greens in the woods while his mother worked. Interestingly, she is another important woman in his life whom he has not yet "written."

Wilson was popular in school. He had a keen interest in sports which led to a position on the track team, and an even keener interest in art which he was sure would translate into a career someday. Although he had always wanted to paint, art was also a conscious way of identifying with his natural father, whom he was told had "a native talent for it." Unlike Mason and Thirkield, who instinctively knew the direction in which they had to shape their destinies from the time they were very young, theatre never once entered into Wilson's plans. However, there was obviously a need in the youth for the fantasy world of make-believe. Like Mason, this need was nourished by films; although the opportunity to see live theatre did not present itself very frequently in Ozark, films were readily accessible. With the encouragement of his high school English teacher, Wilson did some acting in high school and his interest began to be fired by the live stage. However, it was not until Wilson saw a touring company's production of *Brigadoon* that he completely shifted his inner devotion from films to the stage. After the magic of seeing the sleeping little town of Brigadoon come back to life on stage, he happily admitted that films could no longer compete with the excitement of live performances; his heart belonged to the theatre although he still had not the remotest idea that he would one day write for the medium. He was happy enough to continue acting. One of his most memorable roles was that of "Tom" in *The Glass Menagerie*. Little could he imagine that he would one day collaborate with its author, Tennessee Williams, on the CBS-TV play *The Migrants,* and write the libretto for Lee Hoiby's opera of Williams's *Summer and Smoke.*

By the time Wilson had graduated from Ozark High School in 1955 and had completed one unsatisfying term at Southwestern Missouri State College, he was restless. He felt a growing urgency to fill the void that remained when his natural father left, a void felt all the more keenly since he was beginning to flounder badly from lack of a goal. Needing to make contact with this memory, he departed for San Diego. The distance in miles was easier to cross than the distance in years. The reunion turned out to be an unhappy one, difficult for both father and son; it was less a reunion than an introduction to a man who was essentially a stranger. They did not get along at all.

Ralph Wilson had reestablished himself with a new wife and two young sons. Once again, Wilson was on the fringe of an established family circle. He got along well with his stepmother and acted the role of big brother to the two boys with ease, but he often refers to the relationship with his father at this time as a "total disaster." Ralph Wilson worked in an aircraft factory as an engineer with "so much seniority he sat around drinking coffee all day." Apparently it was enough seniority to get young Wilson a job as a riveter. He disliked the work as much as his father disliked the idea of his writing stories. But despite the unspoken objections, Wilson enrolled at San Diego State College (now University) and began writing what to his teachers and classmates seemed like exotic stories about the Ozarks of Missouri. It was here that he discovered his ability to write strong, naturalistic dialogue and an ear for speech patterns he did not even know he possessed.

Wilson remained in San Diego for only one year. The rejection he felt from his father was a bitter disappointment to one who had travelled so far and with such hopes. He later explored and to some extent exorcised these feelings through his play *Lemon Sky,* an autobiographical work about a boy who seeks a reunion with his father after a long separation and finds rejection instead. Despite the fact that familial wounds have healed and father and son now have a workable relationship, it was more than twelve years before Wilson could translate the painful experience into a play.

When Wilson left San Diego, he headed home to the Midwest. On his way he stopped in Chicago to visit a friend for a few days. Immediately taken with the wild independence of the city, Wilson stayed six years. When he arrived in Chicago he was only nineteen and completely on his own for the first time in his life.

Like Mason he was forced to support himself; unlike Mason, who worked in career-related jobs, survival took top priority over career considerations for Wilson. He was fired from his first job, as an office clerk, for tardiness. Then, in succession, he took an apprenticeship at the Fuller, Smith and Ross ad agency to capitalize on his art background, worked at the Artists Guild for several years, and later held a position at a personnel agency for commercial artists—all jobs he disliked intensely. Whenever his job took on a steady daily routine, he returned to writing on a regular basis. Despite the usual rejection slips—not one of his stories has ever been published—he continued to write. It did not matter whether he could earn a living writing; writing itself was his need.

The moment of illumination, when it became clear to Wilson that he was a playwright, occurred while he was working at the ad agency. At first he only answered phones, typed correspondence, and designed boxes. Eventually, as he says, he would paste up photographs and "that sort of thing. But I was writing at the time—short stories. Then I came across one that I thought should be a play and I said, 'What do you know!' Then I discovered that all along my dialogue had been good and the narrative qualities of my stories had been terrible but I didn't know it. Halfway through the first page I said a dozen times, 'What do you know!' By the second page, I knew. This is what I am. This is what I am going to do."

It had never occurred to Wilson in San Diego, when he first became aware that he wrote good dialogue in his short stories, that plays were all dialogue and that if he concentrated on writing plays he would have the advantage of dealing mainly with his strengths. Now Wilson, in the flush of discovery, began telling everyone he met that he was a playwright—even though he had not yet written one scene.

"Once I decided that's what I was going to do," he says, "the frustrating, grinding, awful, horrible feeling of working just for security's sake fell behind me. I eventually took any job as long as it left me free to write. My only goal was to be a really super playwright."

He immediately signed up for a playwriting class at the University of Chicago Downtown Center "and learned what a play was and how to construct it if you wanted to construct it that way," which he did not. From the very beginning he wrote mostly on impulse. He came to the theatre scene through the standard American play and now through the standard playwriting course. But from the beginning he had his own ideas of what theatre should be. He wanted to write plays as though they were a three-ring circus with everyone talking at once, blending together in a manner similar to musical harmony. He immediately broke all the rules of structure, an approach which would serve him well in the open context of such plays as *Balm in Gilead,* which takes place in an all-night cafe and follows the vague existence of many characters, but which would subtly plague him in such works as *The Mound Builders.*

His impatience to surrender to the lure of New York City left Wilson with only enough time to take one writing course in Chicago. It would be the only writing course he would ever take, even though he enjoyed it enormously. Actors from the Goodman Theatre came into class to act out the student's scenes, adding more fuel to an already stimulated young playwright who began directing all of his energies toward writing plays. As he says, "I learned what conflict was and all those things. Fundamentals. And wrote a play that is very bad indeed with all those fundamentals in it. And a one-act that was our final. And as soon as I finished that, I came to New York."

It was the summer of 1962.

"There's magic in the air right over the island," he had said to Alan Wallach. "I was in New York walking all over the Broadway theatre district absolutely gaga, and at the same time bought a typewriter and started writing another one-act play, because I thought I must start right now."[6]

He was sure that New York was where a playwright should be, but despite the "magic," he was keenly aware of the dichotomy of his emotions regarding New York, from wide-eyed awe to abject fear of the streets. Out of work for three months and not having enough money to afford better lodgings, he moved into a seedy hotel on the Upper West Side. In desperation, he lied his way into a variety of jobs, none having to do with theatre, all having to do with survival. By this time he found himself disenchanted with New York City. I realized that no one gave a damn for you in New York," he said to Steven Grover of *The Wall Street Journal,* "and I wasn't sure I had enough strength for it." In addition, echoing Marshall Mason's own feelings upon first viewing theatre in New York, Wilson became quickly disillusioned with what he saw on Broadway. He had saved up his money and had seen everything that he could, since seats were relatively inexpensive in the early sixties. When he came to New York, he was sure he would find plays like O'Neill's *The*

Hairy Ape in one theatre and Williams's *The Glass Menagerie* next door. All of New York would be demonstrating a serious celebration of America's finest playwrights. He was extremely discouraged to find he hated most of what he saw with the possible exception of *A Man for All Seasons,* which Wilson readily admits he did not fully understand at the time. On Broadway the marquees boasted a veritable musical bonanza: *Bye, Bye Birdie; West Side Story; My Fair Lady; The Music Man; La Plume de Ma Tante; Gypsy; Fiorello!* and *Take Me Along* were all playing to capacity audiences in the early sixties. This bonanza, some of which were holdovers from the fifties, may have delighted enthusiasts of one of America's native genres, but it hardly inspired joy in the young playwright.

It was not long before Wilson began gravitating toward Greenwich Village, where a composer he met asked if he would be willing to try a collaboration on a musical revue for Joe Cino. Although the musical revue was written, it was never produced. The important fact was that Wilson went down to the Caffé Cino to see what it was all about and discovered a new world. Like Mason, Wilson had been unaware of the "theatre" which would become off-off-Broadway that was being generated in small coffeehouses, lofts, storefronts, churches, tabernacles, and basements all over the city. He did not even know off-off-Broadway existed. These were the experimental, non-commercial "playhouses" that offered an enormous range of styles that could never be duplicated by any commercial endeavor.

"When I first went to the Caffé Cino, the room was about thirty by twenty. It's still there—an office, but you can't go in there now. I think it's Mafia," Wilson laughs.

> We could crowd thirty people in there. It was just a little coffeeshop, very Italian looking. Blinking Christmas tree lights, layers upon layers of posters and material that Joe thought was nice, stapled to the wall one on top of the other. Glitter all over the floor. Every table was a different height and a different kind of table. All the chairs were different just because he got what he could find. They had pastries and sandwiches that were very good and an espresso machine, and an area set aside that was usually in a different place for each show. His friend John Torrey, who was a lighting designer and had lit the first poetry reading, set the different areas with lights.

Marshall Mason corroborates Wilson's first impressions of the Cino as "romantic, dark, atmospheric, magical, inviting. Like walking into Disneyland." Operating under the same licensing as a restaurant, everything was extremely clean.

The first night Wilson walked in, there were about fifteen or twenty people seated at little tables. He got himself a pastry and a coffee and sat waiting. The "stage" was made out of milk crates covered with pieces of carpets, all of which had been salvaged from the streets.

What he saw that night was a ferocious, pirated version of Ionesco's 1950 play, *The Lesson.* Unlike Mason, who was always a bit annoyed with Ionesco, for Wilson the performance was to be a pivotal experience. By the end of the evening he would know where he wanted to work. "I had never seen an Ionesco play before," he says enthusiastically.

> I don't know if I even knew who he was. My European theatre history was non-existent. I was blown away. It was the funniest thing I had ever seen. Brilliantly done. The actors were incredible. And the most ghastly ending. It was the first theatrical experience I'd had in New York City. That is what I thought theatre was going to be, not Broadway. I didn't *know* that's what I thought theatre was going to be. But it was the first time I was engaged by something and probably the madness of that play influenced my plays at the Cino a little bit — because it was so vivid. Maybe not, maybe so.

Wilson began frequenting the Caffé Cino on a regular basis from that point on.

Joe Cino

Although the beginnings of any movement are always difficult to pinpoint exactly, it is probably safe to say that the off-off-Broadway movement began officially at the Caffé Cino, 31 Cornelia Street, Greenwich Village, New York City, in 1958:

> Joe Cino was an overweight ex-dancer, a homosexual, an alcoholic, a drug taker and a flamboyant Greenwich Village "character." Having given up his stage ambitions in 1958, he opened the Caffé Cino, one of the many coffee houses that sprang up in the Village in the late 1950s. The Caffé Cino quickly became a haven for other outcasts, misfits and failed

would-be performers; the long, narrow storefront cafe had a tiny stage in the middle, where the loving host let his guests live out their fantasies by performing for each other and for any unsuspecting tourists who wandered in. Eventually some of the Cino regulars put on a play and Off-Off-Broadway was born.[7]

Of course, none of the young people who worked at the Cino considered themselves outcasts and misfits. They were poor, but they were separate from the others who merely came to watch to hang around. They had, in essence, found a place to work. Tanya Berezin's recollections of the Caffé Cino were vivid. Berezin, whom Wilson would later describe as having had "the most normal upbringing in Philadelphia," began frequenting the cafe in 1962 when she first came to New York City, long before she met any of the people with whom she would later work so closely, and long before she realized that the Caffé Cino represented quintessential off-off-Broadway.

Looking back, she calls the Cino

> Fabulous. A true artistic haven. Joe Cino was Italian, gay, chubby, generous and caring. He was an ex-ballet dancer and was in awe of all ballet, had no particular power trip or ax to grind as far as theatre was concerned. As a producer, it was just his place. And the theme of the place was, "Just do whatever you have to do." I remember going there before I knew any of these people and asking if I could work there. I was very young and he said to me, "Do whatever you have to do, honey," and me thinking that meant get out of my cafe, not thinking that it was an invitation and an opening, which I realized later that it was. It was up to me to use it or not. He gave you the room. The rest was up to you.[8]

While Mason would only smile and say, "How do you describe the wind?" Wilson's recollections of Joe Cino were much the same as Berezin's. "He was a ballet dancer—or rather wanted to be, and he was ashamed of himself because he was too fat. There was a point at every party when he would start stripping and doing a ballet dance. It was very exciting to see, except that we'd as soon he'd not strip. He was a good dancer but he was too heavy to be a dancer."

Generosity seemed to be an inherent part of Cino's personality. The very fact that he would open up his cafe to let people "do it!" demonstrated the generosity of his heart, if not his discrimination. Very rarely did he actively take a personal interest in the quality of the presentations or even directly involve himself in the productions. He only wanted to make sure that his cafe was available to those who were able "to make things happen" and he wanted those "things," whatever they were, to happen at the Caffé Cino. It was not so much that he was enthralled with theatre or with poetry readings, which is the way his open policy began; rather, as Wilson would point out, "He *was* these people. His enthusiasm and protectiveness and concern, once you were there, was very mother-hen. If you were his — you were golden. Even people who were God-awful bad — the doldrums."

And there were many who were "God-awful bad." The Caffé Cino presented more "non-writes" and more fifteen-minute plays than one could imagine. Some of the actors hung around because they could not get work any place else. According to Wilson, the talented actors at the time mostly would not go near off-off-Broadway because "A) you had to pass the hat around. And B) it had a bad reputation of being real slummy. Amateursville." The desire to work, no matter how highly motivated, did not automatically produce great theatre, nor did shoe-string budgets or experimentation with the rudiments of theatre craft. Much of the work was crude, lacking not only skill but talent. However, when the work was good, the freedom from commercial considerations became an important factor in its development. Financial failure was virtually implicit in the system, and thus accepted without condemnation. Without the burden of commercial success, artistic freedom was a high priority and an important bonus to the talented who truly wished to experiment.

Berkowitz presented much the same conclusions in *New Broadways* when he summed up the Caffé Cino's importance:

> Despite its enormous output (a new play every week or two for almost ten years), the Caffé Cino did not produce many plays or artists of particular merit. Lanford Wilson's *The Madness of Lady Bright,* Sam Shepard's *Icarus' Mother* and Tom Eyen's *The White Whore and the Bit Player* stand out, and director Marshall W. Mason served part of his apprenticeship at the Cino. Generally, though, Joe Cino's determined lack of objective standards — he put on what he liked or what his friends wanted to do, and his tastes and his associates ran to the outlandish and extravagant — made the Caffé Cino one of the more self-indulgently amateurish of Off-Off Broadway venues. Its importance, even at the time, was largely symbolic: it was *there,* and its continued operation in spite of zoning laws,

financial pressures and creative failures seemed to prove that some unquenchable artistic force was present and had chosen Off-Off Broadway as its home. The Cino proved that a theatre of experiment, of violated rules and of personal vision could still exist after Off Broadway had become commercialized; and even its coterie quality allowed for positive interpretation, suggesting that drama and theatre could be a vehicle for communal unity and expression.[9]

"We knew everyone," Wilson says.

We didn't really trust people from the outside, because as soon as they decided to do our play, they'd get a commercial and have to fly down to Tampa to do a shoot on the beach, and we were "going on" in three days. They didn't care. This wasn't something outsiders were really committed to. And also, they couldn't possibly afford to turn anything down. We were only making $16 a week—that was our average. I figured it out by passing the basket and dividing it up amongst the actors and the playwright and the director. Everyone got the same. About $16 a week—which was enough. Joe gave us sandwiches and scrambled eggs and coffee. Most of our meals were on him and we ate all the pastries at the end of the day because he got fresh pastries every day. So we got food. What more do you need? We weren't living very high on the hog but we had some place to work.

Not only had each of the cofounders of the Circle Repertory Company independently found the "place to work" when they discovered the Caffé Cino, but they had also found the supportive environment—often referred to as "the family"—that was important enough to them to later consciously recreate it within the environmental structure of the early Circle Repertory Theatre on 83rd Street. To Marshall Mason the Caffé Cino atmosphere encouraged a sense of comfort. He understood only too well when he first discovered the Cino a year before Wilson saw *The Lesson* that the most important aspects for him were the right to experiment without the pressures of commercial considerations and the right to fail without shame. Only a comfortable "family" environment free of undue criticism could offer such possibilities; there was no money to speak of, no commercial ambience, no financial considerations. There was simply the never-ending support of Joe Cino himself, the by-now-legendary Village character, who kept encouraging Mason to do his work in the no-strings-attached cafe. Mason has often given unqualified commendation to Cino for the artistic freedom his generosity made possible. Whatever the problem, Cino would quite simply say, "Do whatever you have to do." To him theatre was "Magic Time!" and he wanted his cafe to be used to create this magic.

Cino also encouraged the many different groups of people that gathered regularly at the Cino. He needed to surround himself with all the private little cliques that developed independently of one another at the Cino, from the "Andy Warhol crowd" to "Mason's crowd" from Northwestern University. In a sense they were all extensions of Cino's multifaceted interests.

Lanford Wilson recalls the dance group comprised of seven or eight dancers that often came over to the Cino from the Judson Poets. The group would sometimes perform dance shows based on what Wilson considered very "experimental, odd things." He clearly remembered one which involved moving all the people and all the tables to one side of the room and then moving them all back again. "And you had to get up and walk around and move the chairs, and who cares!" he says, getting caught up in the vivid memories of the Cino. Here is what, in essence, turned out to be groundwork for the multilayered fabric that encompassed off-off-Broadway, and Wilson speaks at length, recreating the short-lived bygone world in rich strokes of personal memory:

> I never spoke to any of those dancers—hardly at all. Although I knew Al Carmine and Larry Kornfeld who worked at the Judsons Poet Theatre, I didn't know the dancers. A whole part of that world was Joe's. There was the opera-queen crowd. They would get dressed up once a week and go to the opera—his Italian background. I hated opera with a passion that was undying—so I didn't know any of that opera crowd. There were about fifteen of them. They would sit around and I would just move to another table when they were talking about opera. They could relate. I don't know what Joe did on the way to the opera and on the way back when he was with those opera queens and they were singing all night long until seven in the morning because I didn't see it. There was a sex crowd that I was certainly in on, that was, you know, horny, rub-a-dub-dub and we would close down the place and be there all night. That was more or less my part of the crowd and it was very, very small. And then the realistic, poetical writer thing that Marshall (Mason), Claris (Nelson), David (Starkweather), and Sam (Shepard) were in on. Sam was never really a part of the Cino's.

He had his own crowd. He was part of the Theatre Genesis, but he came around a lot. And Robert Patrick. These were the playwrights and their immediate actors and directors, and Neil Flanagan, and all that. Rob (Thirkield) and Tanya (Berezin) were not a part of it yet. There was Marshall's crowd from Northwestern. Claris was sort of under his wing all the time. There was my crowd at the Cino, and there was—unbeknownst to me and to Marshall and to most of our crowd—there was a rather heavy drug scene that Joe was into. A few people crossed over into that, like Eric ———, who was sort of half into playwriting and half into drugs, although not seriously into drugs.[10]

Besides the different regular groups, there was the usual Village clientele which would buy the espresso, the cappucino, the "great" sandwiches, and to whom the hat was passed after each production.

By the time Tanya Berezin started working at the Cino, it was in full operation. She vividly recalls passing the hat. "That was for the actors," she says. "They weren't paid except from the hat. Joe made money through food and coffee. The playwrights were not usually paid anything. Most of the clientele were people who were involved there—theatre people from everywhere—from all over town. Young people and a few Village beatnik, hippie, cafe-hanger-out type of people. But the reputation spread quickly and people started coming down. And that's where you got to know people."

The Cino was becoming legendary even in the early stages of its operations, and would soon be overtly copied all over the Village. Ellen Stewart's early Cafe La Mama, begun in a basement in 1961, was a frank imitation of the Caffé Cino. By the time the Cafe La Mama became La Mama Experimental Theatre Club, Stewart had developed her own standards for production, but she credits the Cino with paving the way and inspiring much of her own enthusiasm. Ellen Stewart did not hide the fact that she was deeply stimulated by the very *idea* of the Cino. Despite the obvious self-indulgence, Joe Cino was instrumental in capturing and promulgating an irrepressible artistic force that needed the restrictions of a steady environment. It was because people successfully got together to "make something happen," as Joe called it, that the Cino's reputation spread throughout the community as the place where new theatre happened, which had nothing to do with "showcasing" either material or performer for uptowners.

Tanya Berezin is most emphatic on this point. "You did the place to do the plays," she says.

> The whole off-off-Broadway scene in those days was not career or success oriented. People were simply working with people. Marshall had not a penny. Lanford had not a penny. They would build their sets and they would scrape together money and they would borrow money from Rob and get something on and, of course, never pay Rob back. Whoever had the money at lunchtime would pay for lunch. Completely different heads than the world is now and than the theatre is now. You didn't invite agents down to Cino's to see a play. You didn't think of any of that as making contacts. You worked with people because you wanted to do the play.

It was customary in the early days for anyone who was involved theatrically to see everything that was being done. Since there was no charge for any of the productions and the off-off-Broadway fare was still fairly thin, it was possible to take in its entire offering with ease. Much of what Tanya Berezin relates could apply to off-off-Broadway in general and would eventually be an accurate assessment of the early Circle Repertory Company itself, but at this point she is speaking most particularly of the Cino.

"It was really an artistic community," she says enthusiastically.

> It was actors, writers, and directors working together for an event. It was incredibly unselfish. The only selfish thing was the work. People didn't leave rehearsal to go to a commercial audition. They do that now at every off-off-Broadway theatre. It was just a completely different head. There was a sincere artistic commitment to the work that was being done and the work was never seen as a stepping stone to doing O'Neill, for instance. The work was explored and created for itself—truly for itself— as Sam Shepard was doing things at La Mama at the time.

Of the four co-founders of the Circle Repertory Company, no one more openly credited Joe Cino for the stimulation he provided than Wilson. There is no sadness in his reminiscences, only boundless appreciation of Cino's particular gifts. "After I decided I was a writer," he recalls,

> I found Joe Cino at just the right time. And that atmosphere. That uncritical "Do it!" "Put it on!" "Go for it!" He's the one who started "Do your own thing!" That was all from Joe Cino. Joe's came before "Do your own thing." Joe's was, "Do what you have to do!" And this was wildly encouraging—I can't tell

you. He was the only one who matched my energy. He quadrupled it. I can't tell you how huge the man seemed to me. I don't see anyone like that now. There hasn't been anyone like that since. Ellen Stewart had that same madness—that same mad drive—that same mad encouragement. Gertrude Stein said, "Artists don't need criticism, they need approval." That incredible approval was half of the stimulus, and wanting to get something on—wanting to do something else. And being stimulated by all the other things that were being done off-off-Broadway in other places—and all the people we ran into.

A year before Wilson saw *The Lesson,* Marshall Mason had already worked the Caffé Cino. Mason's reputation as a director on the off-off-Broadway grapevine was excellent. He had left Cino's in order to direct Ibsen off-Broadway. Anyone who was able to make the leap from off-off to off-Broadway was considered successful, and Wilson had heard of Mason before he caught his first glimpse of him. However, Wilson's first impressions were less than overwhelming.

"He came in back then. Had the worst teeth in the world," Wilson recalls.

> Tallest, thinnest thing you've ever seen in your life. Bright yellow hair. He had outgrown all of his clothes, and his pants cuffs were halfway up his calves, which was ridiculous. None of his clothes fit. And he wore tight, tight, tight, tight pants. He came in just looking like an idiot, I thought. Very pretentious, very much. I mean—that was my first impression. And I was introduced. *That* was the Marshall Mason who the year before was everything at the Cino.

The contrast between the two of them must have been startling. Although they were both tall and thin almost to the point of being gaunt, Wilson was a mass of energy—"The Mad Aries," as Joe Cino dubbed him. Photographs of him at the time show him to be approximately one hundred twenty-six pounds. He was all eyes, with bursts of bushy eyebrows and huge circles under his eyes. He had an electric energy that apparently frightened some people or made them nervous. Although he never used drugs of any kind, he was often suspected of being "high" because he always spoke very quickly and very loudly. This was not the same Lanford Wilson who had come to New York City such a short time ago. The gangling Missourian now responded in like energy to the hectic rhythm of New York, which was "five times as fast" as anything he had ever seen before, as though the city were "on a different speed—78 instead of 33." The hyperenergy he exuded was a creative response to all the theatrical activity in which he had immersed himself.

Mason, on the other hand, was soft-spoken and appeared to be mild-mannered. While Wilson's eyes darted everywhere, Mason's eyes lingered and missed nothing. One of the interesting things about Mason is that he appears to be always smiling at the very same moment he seems to be always frowning. A magnetic quality about him makes one automatically dismiss everything else in the room and concentrate only on him. It seems necessary to lean in toward him when he speaks, even though he projects clearly. When he speaks it is apparent that his attention is one hundred percent on what he is saying, yet a part of him—revealed by the way he looks across a room or stares into a crack in the floor—is elsewhere. It is easy to believe that there is a "secret Mason," even though on the surface he is open and friendly.

While Mason and Thirkield had been temporarily away from the Caffé Cino with their first company, Northwestern Productions, Wilson had been taking giant steps at the Cino. He was correct in his own self-appraisal that he had found the Cino at precisely the moment in his life when it could make the most impact.

Never satisfied with what has just been done, Wilson is the type of artist who must always strive for something more. It is a testament to this temperament that after a shaky beginning, he has proven to be one of the most fertile of the young writers to come out of the early off-off-Broadway movement. With almost fifty plays to his credit, his volume is matched only perhaps by Sam Shepard's. Part of Wilson's artistic temperament is based upon the fact that he enjoys the intense complication of writing plays. The fact that he was sure he would "never be able to get it right," never be thoroughly "satisfied with his work," meant he had found something to which he could devote his life.

Joe Cino finally told him to forget about the musical review he was working on and write a play instead. No words could have made Wilson happier, since he was already at work on the one-act play *Home Free!* He immediately completed the play and gave it to Cino. Wilson recalls, "Joe almost never reads anything. He didn't read closely or well, but he did read *Home Free!* and he said, 'Lanford, I don't know. All of this bippity-boppity, poo, and this, "Sweetie-this" and the "honey." It's just a little too—it's too precious. I mean it's so sugary. I mean, I can't read plays, so I gave it to a director, Neil Flanagan.' My God!" Wilson says, "that was a star! That was the one I'd see in *The Lesson* and the following week in *Who's Afraid of Edward Albee,* David Starkweather's play—which had been another miracle. By this time I'd seen some really rotten things down at the Caffé Cino, but every third one was a miracle all over again. The others were so bad, you started to look at the door. Neil came in with my play under his arm and said 'Joe, I really don't know how I feel about this play because I'm Catholic and this is the most immoral play I've ever encountered in my life.' Of course, Joe was blown away. He thought it was the sweetest thing in the world—'precious.' The world the characters creates *is* precious in a way. it just happens to be incestuous and private."

Home Free! is a play about an incestuous relationship between a brother and sister in which she gets pregnant. It is a vital, original play with a distinctly different voice from the two one-act plays Wilson had written in Chicago. By this time Wilson had consciously decided that he wanted to capture the sounds of characters in contrapuntal rhythms and was working in a very different manner from the way he had started. Most of what he had written before was the complete fabrication of a youthful and active imagination, but in *Home Free!* he wrote about four people he knew and blended them into the two characters with a specific world of their own. Wilson captured this world which seemed so magical, private, and insular that it did not relate to the outside world at all.

By the time Cino convinced Neil Flanagan to do the play, Wilson had already submitted it to Giancarlo Menotti at the Spoleto Festival. Since the festival only considered unproduced plays, Wilson wanted to wait for Menotti's response. Six months passed before Wilson discovered that Menotti liked the play, but had lost it before he could give it to the judges.

Glenn DuBose, the director who had been working on the musical revue, suggested to Wilson that he write another play for Flanagan. Since he had been working on a little play called *The Bottle Harp* with which he was not pleased, he set it aside, sat down with another idea, and "in five hours flat" wrote *So Long at the Fair.* In a *Wall Street Journal* article in 1979 Wilson described the play as a "silly little comedy," but it would be responsible for his making his New York writing debut in record time. *So Long at the Fair* opened at the Cino in August 1963 to good critical reception. Michael Smith of *The Village Voice* in his review of August 29, 1963, called it a "tense little comedy" and praised the "exactness and inner logic" of the dialogue, "which, at its best, springs half-thought-out from the characters' lips." Unfortunately, there is no existing copy of the script.

Speaking of the early working days at the Cino, words pour out of Wilson almost torrentially.[11] In glowing terms of appreciation, he describes the stimulus, excitement, and energy which produced the ensuing prolific parade of plays, beginning with *Home Free!* Wilson had written the leading role for Michael Warren Powell:

> He was a friend and I wanted to give him something to do. They all liked Michael. An incredibly personable man, but it turned out that the director went through hell with him. I think Michael was "acting" acting. And I had imposed the actor on the director. So I thought I'll write another play for you that you can direct and cast and do anything you want to do. So I wrote *No Trespassing* for Glenn and he hated it with a clean, pure, white loathing. He didn't want to do it at all. Very funny. A play I'd given him with no strings. In the meantime I found out that Spoleto had lost *Home Free!* and the Festival was over. Glenn didn't know *Home Free!* but Neil Flanagan, the original director, loved *No Trespassing*. So *Home Free!* and *No Trespassing* were done simultaneously. One would play the 9:00 slot and the other would play the 11:00 o'clock. Then they would reverse. Like a one-act rep for all the weeks that they ran. *No Trespassing* was a horrible flop but everyone loved *Home Free!* a lot. It moved over to La Mama's because they had a cancellation. And that's the first time I saw La Mama. I had never heard of it before. Ellen saw the play; everyone saw everything in those days. There wasn't that much to see, so everyone went back and forth. So Ellen saw it and said, "Oh, could you bring that over and save me, because I don't have a show. The show that I had was going to move tomorrow but the girl got a job and had to move off somewhere." So we actually got to run it for two weeks—an unheard-of joy. The space was comparable. A funny little stage.
>
> I still had not met Marshall.
>
> One thing stimulated another. In interesting ways. You'd have something on and have it running. You'd go through rehearsal periods as the play was running. You'd get so excited and another idea would come to you, and so you'd write it and in another week you'd start rehearsals. I was very prolific. I was just so stimulated by the entire scene.
>
> By this point I was working at the Americana Hotel on the reservations office where they had a typewriter. I was on the night shift so there weren't many calls, but the typewriter was on all night. So it was very lucky for me.

Contrary to some reports, this is not where he met the model he used for his one-act play *The Madness of Lady Bright*. Wilson says that he does not know how the assumption ever got started:

It isn't true. I don't remember who was on the desk then. How it came about—just to show you impulses—how everything feeds everything; I was still great, close friends with Glenn Du-Bose. I went first to a show and then to his house just to sit and drink. And I had seen Kennedy's play *Funny House of a Negro*. For some reason, it just had not done a thing for me. I don't know why. It should have. Now, of course, I love it. I just didn't in that particular production. It was very removed and cold. That night at Glenn's house, upstairs from him, I'd seen a total queen—tall, thin, aging queen, who was hysterically funny. Always kept me in stitches. I never paid any attention to him at all except that he was hysterically funny—one of the happiest people I'd ever met, always with something cutting or outrageous to say. Always on top of everything. Someone said somebody was going down to the trucks, and this queen said, "I never go down to the trucks, not even for an ice cream. My second husband was killed by a truck." We all screamed with laughter. And he said, "He really was, you know. I'm not making it up." And we just screamed. Then we went into the next room, all except him. Then I went back because I had forgotten a fork and the guy was looking out the window and crying because he was remembering this guy. I sneaked out real quick because it was a very private thing to have invaded.

In the next room, talking about *Funny House of a Negro,* trashing it, seeing this silly black girl flip out in her room was the most uninteresting idea. I'd just as soon see some screaming faggot go mad, and I said, "Wait a minute! What an interesting character." That's when I thought of it. And of course, the guy upstairs didn't know he was being used. He never went to the theatre. I don't think he ever saw a play.

And it wasn't just him. I used people I knew in Chicago; they're much queenier than the queens I knew in New York. Makeup on the street and all—back then, anyway. You didn't see that here.

The next night I went to the Americana Hotel and I knew that the queen broke down completely. I knew it was all about youth and loneliness and losing that "beauty" and facing a future. It started as, "Will somebody please escort Miss Bright to the lounge," which is going to be the last line of the play. That's all I had. It was never changed from the first draft—hardly a word. I wrote the first fifteen lines and I thought, "Oh my God, this is very wild." I called Neil Flanagan and I asked, "Neil, what exactly can we get away with at the Caffé Cino? Can we do anything that enters our head, absolutely anything? And he said, "Like what?" And I said, "Can we have an absolutely screaming, raging queen going hysterically mad on stage right before our eyes? But really, can we show that queen in absolute, no-holds-barred, uncensored—" And he said, "Well, write it and we'll see." I wrote it in two nights, I think, and brought it in. As I said, we were very stimulated. *Home Free!* and *No Trespassing* were still playing. And so, while I watched *Home Free!* Neil and his wife, Jackie, read it.

Neil came back and said, "We have to get absolutely the best director we can possibly find for this." And I said, "Oh . . . I was hoping you'd like it well enough to direct it yourself." And he said, "No. I'm going to play it." And I said, "You're not at all what I had in mind." And he said, "I know. That's why we have got to get the best director we can find for this."

So we got Dennis Deegan. I don't know what happened to him. Sort of drug culture, jet setter. I wonder what happened to him because he was real good and did a stunning production of it. Neil gave a classic portrayal of an aging transvestite. That's when Joe calmly told the next show that he didn't want them there; *The Madness of Lady Bright* was going to run.

It ran for an unprecedented two hundred and fifty-four performances in two separate runs and was credited as being the Caffé Cino's first major success.

Spurred on by the additional stimulus of *Lady Bright*'s unheard-of triumph, Wilson continued to produce one one-act play after another, which were presented at the Cino throughout 1965 and 1966; *Ludlow Fair* is a delightful and completely realistic play of two lonely young women, Agnes and Rachel, one sardonic and down to earth, one romantic and foolish, whose dreams of romance are repeatedly frustrated; *This Is the Rill Speaking,* which has an artistic relationship to *The Rimers of Eldritch* in the same way that *Wandering* has a relationship to *The Family Continues,* is an autobiographical impression of small-town life in the Ozarks. Six performers, playing seventeen characters, enact scenes that Wilson heard in his own kitchen. *Days Ahead,* a play full of fear of the future and lack of trust in commitment, is a middle-aged man's monologue. He speaks throughout to his (absent) wife, whom he abandoned twenty years earlier because he was afraid that if he remained he would spoil their perfect love. *Wandering* is an Ionesco-type short play in which three characters recite the life of one of them and mime his emotions. Starting with *So Long at the Fair, Home Free!* and *The Madness of Lady Bright,* which was one of the first plays about homosexuality, Wilson continued to produce. He did not know it, but he was growing up in the off-off-Broadway movement which received its official name at about this time from Jerry Talmer of *The Village Voice.* It was beginning to feel like a theatre revolution as participants began to sense the creativity and experimentation in what were becoming the precious laboratories of new ways to approach theatre. No one felt that it was meant to be a tributary theatre that would lead to the apex of Broadway. The new movement was definitely a completely alternative theatre which was, as Wilson would tell Emory Lewis, in many ways "a superior theatre."[12] Superior or not, there were nights when nobody came. On those nights, they performed just for Joe.

In 1965, the Caffé Cino presented a revival of *Home Free!* which Mason came to see. Afterwards he came over to the table and was introduced to Wilson. Wilson had rewritten the play and was quite happy with the new version. It was the first time he had ever done a revision on a play that had already been produced. He told Mason he wished he could have seen the original version because he felt that now it was quite exciting.

But Mason said, "I saw it the other way and I think you've ruined it." That was the first thing he ever said to the man with whom he would share a very long collaboration.

Wilson was devastated. "I thought he was absolutely horrible. I thought he was a terrible bitch and just awful and wrong!"

But it did not matter. It was the first step toward a new appraisal of each other.

For several weeks Wilson had been working on a new one-act play about strong family conflicts called *The Sandcastle,* which takes place in San Diego. Mason was now back at the Cino after the demise of Northwestern Productions. He was rehearsing a new Claris Nelson play. The same night Mason and Nelson came into the cafe to take measurements for their production, Wilson was present telling Joe Cino that he had just finished *The Sandcastle* and was anxious to have Cino read it. Typically, Cino insisted Wilson read it aloud to him.

To Wilson's dismay, Cino gathered Mason and Nelson after the evening's show and insisted that they listen to Lanford Wilson's new play. With six people now sitting around a table waiting for him to read aloud, Wilson felt committed to proceed. It took one hour to read the play. After he finished, Wilson looked up and waited. Although Claris Nelson, Joe Cino, Dennis Parichy, and Cino's friend John Torrey were present, Wilson remembers only Mason, because his reaction was so vivid. Mason said that it was the best original play he had ever heard. Still wary of Mason, Wilson asked, "Not to be picky, but how many original plays have you heard?"

"All of mine," Claris Nelson answered for him and Wilson realized that the quiet Texan had loud views and was extremely outspoken when it came to expressing them. It was actually to be a strength in their relationship. One could never be in doubt as to where Mason stood on an issue of theatre.

The two men were beginning to assess each other more realistically now. Wilson had seen Mason's production of Claris Nelson's *Neon in the Night* and admitted to himself that he really appreciated the way Mason had used the cafe; it was solid, a "real piece." Under Mason's detailed direction, the actors were made very conscious of the space and the emotional regions from where they were to come.

Now Mason was beginning to fully appreciate the high degree of personal intensity Wilson injected into his plays. He expressed a strong desire to direct *The Sandcastle,* but Wilson, no longer rankling over the stinging comment on the last version of *Home Free!* offered another play that he would rather have done. It was a full-length play entitled *Balm in Gilead,* which he felt was closer to completion than *The Sandcastle.*

After Mason's reaction to *The Sandcastle,* Wilson was anxious to have him read *Balm in Gilead.* It was late into the night but neither of them could sleep. The mutual stimulation that was to be one of the important factors in the success of their association was already at play. Wilson invited Mason to the two rooms he shared with Michael Powell. Each had a bedroom. There was no living room, no kitchen—just the two bedrooms and a bathroom. Wilson sat in one room while Mason sat in the other and read the slightly unwieldy, fifty-five character play. When Mason finished, thinking it was "the most incredible play" with literally four or five scenes going on at once, he returned it to Wilson saying, "It's going to require a very good director. Thank you for letting me read it, but it's going to require a *very* good director."

And he departed, leaving Wilson to believe that the play had failed completely because only a very good director would be able to make something out of it. He did not realize until Michael Powell accosted

Mason on the street that Mason had not only loved the play, but had also decided that *he* was going to have to direct the play or it would never turn out to be what it was meant to be.

Quickly putting misunderstandings aside and taking full advantage of the swiftness with which decisions were made, they were casting the play within one week.

Mason decided they would rehearse *Gilead* at the Actors Studio and present it at La Mama, which had an opening slot for it. It was the first full-length off-off-Broadway play ever produced; it would be the first off-off-Broadway play ever published. From start to finish, it was an exciting adventure of discovery for everyone concerned.

Rob Thirkield, Claris Nelson, and Michael Powell were in the play with Dennis Parichy's designs, bringing sharp echoes of Northwestern University and Northwestern Productions. Wilson did not argue when Mason cut the characters down to a more manageable thirty-five. His greatest discovery during the play was Marshall Mason himself, once again eliciting ardent streams of vivid recollections.

"When someone asks me how to select a director," Wilson says,

> I've developed this answer: Give him your play, let him read it—respond to it. Then say, please describe my play to me. And if he describes what you've written as you understand it, then you're beginning to reach a relationship—an understanding. Marshall described *Balm in Gilead* to me—every toenail that I tried to put into it. The sociological importance of the play. The whole thing about buying and selling. With different language it would be about Wall Street, which is what I had in mind from the beginning. Of course, he approached things from the Actors Studio kind of acting, and I was enthralled by it. I think I had been up to Actors Studio already but I didn't know what they were talking about until I heard Marshall explain it. On the first day of rehearsal he said he was going to break the play down into beats—fifty-one beats, or something like that. And he did. Every single beat—*my* inner beats. We hadn't talked about this at all. It was just the way he worked. I started looking forward for the next beat position and I couldn't do it fast enough for the next beat division. Every single time, he was right! Every single time, and one of them was right in the middle of a line that I had already decided that was where the change was. And he hit it! It was exactly right. It was phenomenal. That blew me away; I didn't get over it for a week. So I was just his from then on. I sat in awe of what he was doing with some of the actors—exercises he made them do if they were too

phoney and he wanted to "real" them up a bit. Back then the people we could get who would commit to doing a play for three weeks' rehearsal and one week of shows — some of them were not that good. So a lot of rehearsal time was acting lessons — teaching. That's one of the reasons he wanted to develop a company.

Balm in Gilead is an extraordinary revelation of a particular slice of New York sixties' culture. It was written by a young man who had the ability to capture the madness almost without recourse to plot, for there is very little plot in *Balm in Gilead:* a lonely girl comes to New York from Chicago, meets a pusher in an all-night coffee shop, and attaches herself to him until he is killed.

Much of Wilson's earliest life in New York is revealed in this play. Living on the Upper West Side in a cheap hotel crowded with a bizarre assortment of outcasts, he often visited an all-night coffee shop that was the habitat of pimps, prostitutes, pushers, junkies, and the seedier inhabitants of the gay world. These were the night dwellers who came out when the rest of the city slept. Wilson was terrified, but felt almost compelled to record it. "A very vivid memory sitting there in that all night coffee shop below where I lived," he says. "Copying down everything that was said. That's how *Gilead* was written. It was a heavy, heavy drug scene."

It would have been extremely easy — an almost natural progression — to fall into drugs, completely surrounded by them as he was, but mostly Wilson kept himself rigidly free from use and often acted the role of one-man emergency squad.

"I came as a sane person from a very ordinary kind of lower, middle-class upbringing," Wilson remembers.

> I came as an outside observer seeing this — writing my reactions to this craziness. *Balm in Gilead.* I sat there fearing for my life half the time, falling into half the scene very easily but not the drug scene. The drugs scared me to death. I didn't know for six months that there were drugs except that you stepped on a syringe on your way to the bathroom in that hotel. I knew there were prostitutes. That's not difficult to see; they're jingling their change at everyone that goes by. And I knew there were queers and drag queens and dykes because I'd seen that in Chicago. That was nothing new to me except that these were wilder. I found out after six months that they were wilder because they were all on heroin. I started asking questions the way Little Tim

asks questions or the way Darlene did coming from Chicago as an "innocent" dying to be a prostitute like her sister had been. I came so from the outside of that situation that the one time I'd smoked hashish it didn't affect me much. Maybe I'd done it wrong. Everyone else at the party got so stoned that they were turning to ice and not making any sense at all. They were all on very bad trips and having a terrible time and I was the nurse for about six people, giving them tea and telling them it was going to be all right. It was just hashish but they acted very wildly. Later on, when I did have something that made me space out and trip—it frightened me so much that I never went near it again. I was so horrified that I was losing it. I remember crossing the street in traffic. Next thing I knew I was in my hotel room. Then the next thing I knew I was back in the park. I was completely losing control and I said, "Oh honey, no thank you, darling." I like to have control. I'm held together by a thread and don't muck around with that thread, because if that goes, *I* go. . . . I've always felt that.

Balm in Gilead, then, portrayed the tragedy and waste of this netherworld. In a forlorn setting of grime, graffiti, and cigarette butts, the nocturnal community comes to life, just as quickly to death, and finally to acceptance and apathy. The characters seem to be locked into street rituals, the strange loyalties and harsh rules that can bring swift, violent death to anyone with the temerity to break them.

Presented at La Mama, the play caused a sensation. While Ellen Stewart argued at the door with fire marshals who complained of over-crowding and violations, doors had to be locked to keep out the many theatre-goers who could not be accommodated in the little space. The production became a private memory to the relatively few who had seen it in the two weeks of January 1965. It was not to appear again in New York until the extraordinary revival in 1984 by the Circle Repertory Company in conjunction with the Chicago Steppenwolf Company, directed by John Malkovich. Although Mel Gussow, who had only read the play, "never realized the work's hallucinatory energy until seeing it," Rob Thirkield believes that nothing could ever compare with the power and breadth of the production Mason originated, a production to which he brought an acute sensitivity and understanding through his interpretation; it grew directly out of the immediacy of the world just beyond Stewart's locked door. *Gilead* was written in an open, free style that was full of risk-taking and a Wilson style of overlapping dialogue and contrapuntal rhythms that he would continue to develop until his work would often be described in musical terms. Mason understood perfectly the kind of orchestration this instantly recognizable world needed, for while Wilson may have sat at the counters and moved from table to table, "listening to the wistful stories and remembering everything—the writer as shameless spy,"[13] it was Mason who poured the coffee, lit the joints, and burned the hamburgers—the director as creative hierophant.

Mason was not alone in judging *Gilead* to be a landmark production, but despite enthusiastic support it was over almost before it began. The production represented a major transition in the creative lives of both Mason and Wilson, and had finally introduced Wilson and Thirkield into their first working relationship as well. However, it could hardly affect a theatre world that was going through many transitions of its own, most of which could be directly related to the energy and sociological discontent of the mid-sixties.

There was a tremendous surge in absurdist revivals at the time, with characters like "Winnie" submerged in sand up to her breasts in Beckett's *Happy Days,* or peeking out of giant urns as in his *Play.* These plays were being produced with increasing regularity. There were also chronic revivals of Albee's *The Zoo Story* and *The American Dream,* both in the absurd tradition. Albee was becoming increasingly abstract in new plays like *Tiny Alice,* which critics like Robert Brustein called "camp" and led him to question the "author's sincerity." There were also new plays such as William Hanley's *Slow Dance on the Killing Ground* and LeRoi Jones's *The Slave* and *The Toilet,* all of which Brustein found very disconcerting. These were the current plays; these were the playwrights who represented the new young dramatists of the day and were, according to Brustein, "all possessed of a subterranean nihilism."

By 1965 it was obvious that the Repertory Company of Lincoln Center was in a state of collapse. Kazan and Whitehead had resigned and Brustein dreaded, "the nightmare that is coming to take its place. Must we choose between a discredited establishment and a careerist avant-garde?" he asked in *Seasons of Discontent.* "Are the only alternatives to be between the collapsed idealism of the old and the secret cynicism of the new?"[14]

There seemed to be little alternative to the "alternatives."

By this time The Living Theatre had also closed its doors. Its directors, briefly imprisoned, had now expatriated themselves to the "freedom" of Europe, while Poland's Jerzy Grotowski had come to America to expound his minimalist approach to theatre. Grotowski stripped his theatre of all that he considered unessential "where the personal and scenic techniques of the actor is at the core of theatre art."[15]

Not everyone was impressed. John Simon was still intimating as late as 1970 that Grotowski was a theatrical fraud. On seeing Grotowski's adaptation of Juliusz Slowacki's adaptation of Calderón's *The Constant Prince,* he wrote, "The five men and one woman in the cast cavort, contort, skip, wallow, prance and dance about. They shrill or rattle off words unintelligibly even for Poles; they sound like human hurdy-gurdies, whining, shrieking, chanting, howling."[16]

In this case, Mason seemed to be in tune with Simon. However, there were those who were convinced that Grotowski had made an important contribution to a theatre that could absorb a multiplicity of approaches. Joseph Chaikin, for example, was eventually influenced by Grotowski's Open Theatre and broke down the traditional theatrical realism which Mason was creating in such intimate detail in *Gilead.* While Grotowski minimized the importance of language and realism, Mason worked on the extensive monologue Wilson had written for Darlene with a sincere appreciation for the language and the truth of interpretation that seemed almost out of step with the times. There was much about the ambience of *Gilead*'s coffee shop that could have been interpreted in a nonlinguistic manner, but Mason was not a Grotowski enthusiast and took great care to give the overlapping dialogue considered emphasis so as not to lose any of it.

Equally visible at the time were Joseph Papp, who was taking Shakespeare to New York neighborhoods in 1964, and Ellis Rabb's APA, now merged with the Phoenix Theatre and presenting revivals of mostly European imports—Shakespeare, Chekhov, Shaw, Ionesco, Pirandello.

Although the production of *Balm in Gilead* reflected the times, it also reflected Mason's ultrarealistic approach—an insistence upon exactitude in scenic design and an exploration of relationships with an insistence on truth worthy of a psychiatrist. Everything had to create the reality of the total picture. It was more than realistic; it was a naturalistic slice-of-life. Even the coffee smelled stale.

And here, perhaps, is the point—the very thing that separates the artistic direction of the Circle Repertory Company from all the other off-off-Broadway theatres of the late sixties: the style of production was intense realism, here brought to bear on a slightly mad play that had been sliced out of the sixties' drug culture. This at a time when practically everyone else was reverting to the security of revivals from the past, or to wild abstraction and experimentation which, though often theatrically exciting, were bizarre and often had a strong element of nihilistic antitheatre. Mason's style, which would lead directly to the "lyric realism" rubric, made his artistic vision clearly an exception to almost everything else that was happening.

Tanya Berezin

The last human ingredient in the founding of the Circle Repertory Company is Tanya Berezin, who did not really enter into the picture until 1967. In 1965 she had come from Philadelphia to New York City as Harriet Berezin. She immediately entered the impoverished but active world of off-off-Broadway determined to pursue an acting career.

Two years after the production of *Balm in Gilead,* Rob Thirkield went to the Catskills to do a season of summer stock and met the young red-headed actress who was now calling herself Tanya Berezin. They immediately fell in love. "The next play I did was *Rimers of Eldritch,*" Thirkield recalls. "Lanford had written the part of 'Skelly' for me. Marshall wanted a bigger space than La Mama to do it in; it was just upstairs in a little coffee shop with just a bunch of platforms. Lanford wanted to see it on so he directed a small production of it. I knew an actress who could play the role, my girlfriend Tanya. So she came two days before opening. She barely got her lines in two days and screamed them all. She'll tell you today that she was just awful. But that's where she became known to the rest."

"The day that changed my life was the day I met Marshall," she says:

> Rob said he wanted me to meet his friends and had told me all the wonderful experiences he had with *Balm in Gilead.* And it's very funny because he had described this wonderful production in which there were all these people talking onstage at the same time, and there was this real life going on, and how fabulous it was. Then I spoke to a friend of mine who was a director who had gone to see it and he said it was ridiculous, with all these people talking at the same time. So, I thought, who am I to believe? When we got back to town, Rob took me over to Marshall's apartment to meet him. They were at the time doing a play at the Cino of Claris Nelson called *The Clown.* It took place in Renaissance time. So I walk into this apartment— one of these high-rise things. And there was an archway. And Marshall was leaning up against the archway reading *The Hob-*

bitt aloud. The room is filled with all of these playwrights, Lanford, Claris, Ron Link, and they were all in there sewing sequins on these costumes while Marshall read aloud because he couldn't sew. So that was his contribution, to read aloud and keep them entertained. My mouth just dropped open. I didn't know anything like this existed. I didn't know an artistic community existed within the theatre. I was astonished. I fell in love with these people immediately. Lanford and I got along right off the bat. For a long time, Marshall viewed me as Rob's girlfriend and obviously of no value. The first time I worked with either of them was on *Rimers of Eldritch,* the original production which Lanford directed. They had to fire an actress and I stepped in. I was very young and the part was a mother— I'm probably right for her now. I just learned lines, got up there and screamed. *Rimers* is a play where everyone is onstage all the time. So if you make a terrible mistake in your scene, you can't leave the stage to recover. You have to stand there and be humiliated. It ran for two weeks at La Mama and I couldn't wait for it to be over. Then I worked with Lanford again in *This Is the Rill Speaking*—a one-act play. It's a wonderful play. It's part of what later became *Rimers of Eldritch,* but it's a very different play. Then they were doing the second production of *The Sandcastle,* which I adored, and Marshall was going to direct it. And I knew he had no respect for me as an actor. Marshall was all over the place doing different things and I followed him—called him. He wouldn't even return my calls. So I followed him all over the village and waited in doorways outside for him. I finally got him and said I wanted to read for *The Sandcastle.* He said, "Okay, come on," and I said, "Not now. I want to go home and work on it." So we made a date. I read for it and he gave me the part. And we just kept working together.

Tanya remembers the time quite well. Although she is now a leading actress with the Circle Rep and has made a career out of creating new roles, the experience of her first appearance still stings.

It is extraordinary to note that the young actress who hid in doorways and followed Marshall Mason through Greenwich Village in order to audition for him would one day be selected by the Board of Directors to follow in his footsteps in 1987 as Artistic Director of the Circle Rep.

The four people—Marshall Mason, Rob Thirkield, Lanford Wilson, and Tanya Berezin—who would co-found the Circle Repertory Company had finally met and were working together. The year was 1967.

3

The Core of a Company—1965–1969

"**T**HE company started very naturally for all of us—Marshall, Rob, Lanford, and myself," recalls Tanya Berezin, "because we had worked together before off-off-Broadway and had gone to London with some of Lanford's plays. So a company was a natural progression. In a sense it had an artistic core to become a theatre. There was an artistic focus in terms of values—what we were after."

The natural progression began immediately after the production of *Balm in Gilead* and took place in five distinguishable phases: the period following the success of *Gilead* in January 1965; the change in off-off-Broadway's communal thrusts by 1967; the group's first trip to Europe in 1967; the triumphant trip to London with the American Theatre Project in 1968; and Mason's quitting theatre after returning to New York later in 1968.

The four and a half years following *Gilead* witnessed euphoric highs and calamitous lows for the embryonic company. Despite the emotional turmoil of this see-saw existence, Mason and his entourage became a recognizable theatrical presence in the off-off-Broadway environment. In these years, off-off-Broadway increasingly reflected the strong antiwar, antiestablishment sentiments of the rising counterculture, as well as its tolerance for drug use. However, in retrospect, it appears that in a theatre that was increasingly confrontational, Mason, Thirkield, Wilson, and Berezin were holding out for a kind of theatre held together by the tattered threads of lyric realism. They were the local dinosaurs.

Immediately after *Balm in Gilead,* Mason directed Wilson's *Home Free!* at the Cherry Lane Theatre in Greenwich Village. With the interchangeability of personnel on off-off-Broadway, it was not unusual that the bill included *Balls,* a play by Paul Foster, who was president of La Mama, and *Up to Thursday* by Sam Shepard, from Theatre Genesis. Stephanie Gordon, an early Circle Rep member who has remained with the company through the years, was in the Shepard play. The momentum that started with *Balm in Gilead* continued in the summer of 1965 with Mason's production of Wilson's *The Sandcastle.*

Continuing to work with Thirkield, Nelson, and Powell, Marshall Mason also did a series of short plays by Michael Matthias—*Blind Guy, Lethma,* and *The Bottled Room*—quickly followed by Beckett's *Krapp's Last Tape,* David Starkweather's *The Love Pickle,* Tennessee Williams's *The Mutilated,* and another Wilson play, this one the one-act, Ionesco-like *Wandering,* which was actually a short section of *The Rimers of Eldritch.* Working wherever he could find the space, he continued this prolific pace with Donald Kvares's *One Room with Bath* at the tiny 70-seat Thirteenth Street Theatre between Fifth and Sixth avenues. Once again he worked with Claris Nelson, Michael Powell, and other members from the original *Balm in Gilead* cast, which continued to stay together as though unwilling to allow that particular experience to disappear.

It is clear that the roots of the Circle Repertory Company are a direct outgrowth of *Balm in Gilead,* despite its very brief initial run. Not only was it a landmark production for off-off-Broadway itself, it was also a landmark experience for those who had been involved. The ensemble spirit generated was such a strong, positive one that they continued to work together, developing ever stronger social and working relationships that would be at the very foundation of the Circle Rep when it finally formalized into a company in 1969. Although the preference to work with known entities is hardly unique to this particular group of artists, the desire to explore together and grow together as a group, while still encouraging a very strong-minded individualism, is a constant thread throughout the evolutionary process of the company. It was a direct contributing factor in the growth of their ensemble playing—the most important aspect of their work as a group—and it was something that was immediately communicated to an audience. Everything about their commitments to each other as individuals, as artists, as friends, and as lovers contributed to the strong ensemble character that distinguished their work from that of other groups. Such closeness cannot be emphasized too strongly; the ensemble playing would be one of the most important elements in bringing them fame, would be one of the most important aspects in their individual development as artists, and would be at the very core of the Circle Repertory Company's credo when Marshall Mason found it necessary to state one formally. When the ensemble spirit faded in the eighties, due to commercialism and to the very size of a company blown up by its own success, the company experienced major problems.

While the roots of the company were set down at the time of *Gilead* in 1965, Marshall Mason feels that the turning point for its founders began in 1967 during their trips to Europe. Early in 1967, Ellen Stewart invited Mason to accompany her on her first trip to Europe.[1] It was a big event: off-off-Broadway goes to Europe! Stewart was organizing three troupes to go at the same time: the first directed by Tom O'Horgan, the second directed by Alexander Ross, and the third to be directed by Mason. But Mason's methods of working were very different from Stewart's, and since he was busy with projects of his own that interested him more than Stewart's less verbal approach to theatre, Mason turned down her invitation. In light of his refusal, it is interesting that Stewart felt obligated to ask his permission to take four of "his people" with her—Lanford Wilson, Rob Thirkield, Claris Nelson, and Michael Powell. Although they did not have a theatre or a company of their own, they were already recognized in the theatrical community as a contained group with Mason at its head. Mason was quick to encourage Stewart in what could only be a broadening experience for all of them.

The four young artists accepted Ellen Stewart's generous invitation without hesitation. To go with the La Mama troupe seemed like a natural thing to do. It was not unusual for participants in the early days of off-off-Broadway to switch from one group to another. Because of this effortless shuttling back and forth, it is easy to see how the early days of the Circle Rep were deeply interwoven with the Cafe La Mama as well as the Caffé Cino, the Judson Poets Theatre, the New Dramatists, and the Open Theatre, even though loyalties often leaned more toward one group or another. For example, Rob Thirkield's loyalties were deeply involved with Marshall Mason and the original group from Northwestern University no matter where they worked. But teaming up with the La Mama troupe in the early days and working so closely with Tom O'Horgan accelerated the development of Thirkield's avant-garde leaning. Thirkield would eventually play the title role of *Tom Paine* off-Broadway and the role of Father Satz in the original *Futz,* both stage and film versions, all directed by O'Horgan. And as a result, differences between Thirkield and Mason did begin to emerge. Thirkield was less a traditionalist than Mason and more open to the wildly stylistic theatrical interpretations and devices that would mark O'Horgan's controversial career. However, these very differences would eventually prove to be mutually beneficial and broadening for Thirkield and Mason.

While his friends toured Europe, Mason directed a second production of Wilson's *The Sandcastle,* at the Cafe La Mama, in which Tanya Berezin played a major role. The working relationship between Mason and Berezin, which had gotten off to a shaky start, became strongly cemented during this production and has endured to this day.

In time, word got back from Wilson that he was dissatisfied with the course of events in Europe. He had written *Untitled Play* in a lushly antirealistic style specifically for the La Mama troupe in order to take advantage of their particular strengths. But months had passed, and they had not yet begun to work on the play. Wanting Mason and Berezin to join them, Wilson and Thirkield sent them ticket money, and in mid-1967 Mason and Berezin caught up with the travelling troupe in Copenhagen.

Since Mason wanted to see Europe and Wilson was still upset over the lack of commitment to *Untitled Play,* the two of them left the troupe to head for southern Europe. At the time, Wilson was writing the libretto for Lee Hoiby's opera version of Tennessee Williams's *Summer and Smoke.* After travelling to as many major cities as they could on their limited budget, Wilson finally finished the prologue to *Summer and Smoke* in Rome, a wonderfully apt locale for writing about Williams's kneeling angel, surrounded and inspired as they were by an abundance of ancient statuary.

After Rome, they wound up their travels back in London, where the La Mama troupe was enjoying a huge success and adding immeasurably to Stewart's international reputation. The director of the International Theatre Club in London, flush with the triumph of the La Mama Company, suggested to Mason and Wilson that they remain in London in their respective roles as director and playwright to do one of their own plays at the Mercury Theatre. American productions in general were enjoying success and were therefore easy to sell. However, despite their temptation to seize new opportunities, Mason and Wilson could not remain in London on such short notice. Nurturing the possibility of returning the following spring, they returned to New York in the fall of 1967. In a sense, however, the English invitation would turn out to be the genesis of the Circle Repertory Company. The invitation was the beginning.

Back in New York, Mason undertook the direction of *Untitled Play,* which Wilson had originally written for the La Mama troupe. Moving away from the traditional approach he was most attuned to, he mounted a highly experimental production. It was one of the first plays to display total nudity onstage. The play was a departure in genre for both Mason and Wilson, and served as another step in their creative development as artists.

In the spring of 1968, Mason returned to London with plans to produce Wilson's plays *Home Free!* with its strong theme of incest, and *The Madness of Lady Bright* with its gripping portrayal of the emotional disintegration of an aging transvestite. Wilson, who does not fly, chose not to return, and Thirkield, still touring with the La Mama troupe, could not participate in Mason's latest project. But Tanya Berezin did travel to London with Mason, along with Claris Nelson, Charles Stanley, David Groh, and Michael Powell. In March of 1968, the six of them were rehearsing Wilson's *Home Free!* and *The Madness of Lady Bright* aboard the luxurious Queen Elizabeth en route to London. Aware that American actors sometimes had difficulty getting work permits to perform as independents in England, Mason thought it best to "put something American" in their covering name to reassure the British powers that be that they were performing as invited short-term guest artists. They chose to call themselves the American Theatre Project to emphasize the "guest" aspect of their visit and to point out that they were to be perceived as a "working project." The American Theatre Project, coordinated by Mason and Berezin, was the actual forerunner of the company that emerged a year later as the Circle Repertory Company.

Rehearsed amid the silken surroundings of the Queen Elizabeth,

Wilson's two plays opened at the Mercury Theatre in London to outstanding reviews. Not only was the critical reception enthusiastic about the plays themselves, but the critics were equally rhapsodic about the productions. *The New Statesman* hailed their project as "the most brilliant, imaginative and ambitious American company seen so far" and called *Lady Bright* the finest performance to be seen in London.

During their run in London with *Home Free!* and *The Madness of Lady Bright,* the performers first decided, a bit precipitously perhaps, that they were a company in actuality as well as in name and were going to go back to New York to be, as Tanya Berezin says, "this big, big, big hit." However, good reviews in London notwithstanding, they had not set down the principles upon which they would base their efforts. Necessary articulation of their purpose and direction was as yet not forthcoming, not even from Mason, who was too preoccupied with doing the best work he could to really delve into how good work happens. More troubling, later in 1968, the group came back heady with the success they experienced in Europe, only to find painful situations awaiting them in New York. Joe Cino had died. Although Cino's death occurred before the second European trip, it was not until now, in 1968, that his absence was truly felt. With Joe Cino gone, the entire élan vital of off-off-Broadway seemed to have died with him.

The end for Cino had come abruptly at the Caffé Cino in April 1967. "He committed suicide on April 1st," Mason recalls. "Even though he survived for a few days, April 1st was the day he did it because it was his lover, John Torrey's, birthday." The manner of his death was talked about with incredulity for years to come. Joe Cino committed suicide on the stage of the Caffé Cino after-hours — most likely with the lights on — where, during a ritualistic kind of death-dance, he literally slashed himself to death to a recording of Maria Callas singing "Norma."

"It really happened," Tanya Berezin says quietly and unemotionally. "He slashed himself until, I guess, he couldn't slash himself anymore. Why? Pain. Life. Drugs. John Torrey — a lighting designer — went out of town to light a show and was accidentally electrocuted and killed." Despite the mythical proportions in the retelling, there was little romance in the violence of Cino's bizarre suicide. Driven by visions of Torrey's hideous death, unable to cope with the personal loss, and equally driven by drugs, Cino took a knife to himself. It did not seem possible that he could slash himself a hundred times, but he had. "A lot of bad things came down with drugs and nontheatricality and star trips, and things that were going on at the time, and the drug scene was very heavy at Cino's," Berezin adds.

Lanford Wilson admitted that Cino "seemed old to us," but in reality, at the age of thirty-six, he was in the chronological prime of life when he died. Whatever the differences in age, Cino's death had a profound effect on his young friends that is still evidenced today. Wilson, who made a point of saying he did not want to discuss it because the visions were so frightening, finally spoke at some length about his reactions and how the suicide has adversely affected him.

"No such thing ever crossed my mind—suicide," Wilson says thoughtfully. "I didn't know it existed. I didn't know any rational person who would do something like that. I had seen Joe in very bad shape. I knew he was having difficulties and being a little crazy. This was in reaction to Torrey's death and drugs—the amphetamines and the speed. And we were completely devastated. We vowed that the Caffé would go on. Everyone came and said, 'Oh, my.' Everyone went to the hospital and said, 'Oh, my.' Then when he died after we thought that he was going to recover—they got everything working again, they got him all stitched up, and then his heart failed. It was a massive blow. He did himself in—cut himself everywhere. Immediately after, it put suicide in my mind and it's never been out since. I started getting terrified by everything," he continued emotionally. "I don't think I had a phobia about knives before—I do now. I cannot have a knife around me. Scissors, razors, nothing. So it affected me psychologically so deeply that that's why I don't want to talk about it—because those things are there now, and I start talking about them and I want to jump out the window or something. And I'm not joking. I mean I really have strong self-destructive impulses that I never had before. I have no idea if it was Joe's suicide that awakened these impulses in me, and I don't intend to explore it either. I just know it changed me completely, and I hate it. It made it much more difficult to live."

Mason, on the other hand, was one of the few who did not really attribute the suicide to drugs and was unemotional about it, even though he was no stranger to suicide. In the past he had demonstrated a hesitancy to discuss what he considered pathological behavior, having personally known three people who had committed suicide, including his wife, Zita. The third was Jim Tuttle, an acting teacher at Neighborhood

Playhouse who, in working with Circle Rep and in teaching for them, had been very important to them in the first few years.

"How do you deal with something like that?" Mason asks, even though he had obviously absolved himself of any feelings of culpability. "I think in the long run, suicide is a matter of choice. I think it's a mistake for anyone else to feel responsible. If someone decides to kill himself, I think it's very much his decision — I respect it. I don't have any problem with suicide in a sense that it's been around a very long time. The Romans regularly got into a bathtub and slit their wrists. When Joe did it, the revival of *The Madness of Lady Bright* was playing at the Cino. We were in rehearsal to bring back Claris's play *The Clown,* which Joe had requested we do.[2] We were all here when it happened."

Charles Stanley, an early Circle member, tried to keep the cafe open, but without much success. Plagued by financial problems despite benefits by friends to raise money, the cafe was eventually forced to close its doors. It seemed ordained; without Joe Cino there would be no Caffé Cino, despite all good intentions to keep it alive. It was left to playwright Robert Patrick, another early Circle Rep member, to keep the memory fresh with his frequently revived play about the early days at the Cino, *Kennedy's Children.*

According to Mason, Bob Patrick's play encouraged the story that Cino's death was drug-related. Bob Patrick, once a "good-time boy," is a great moralist who became violently antidrugs. Patrick had been acting as host at the Caffé at the time of Cino's suicide and cleaned up Cino's blood in the aftermath. In trying to understand Cino's shocking death, Mason believes, Bob Patrick's moralistic side came forward; only drugs could explain the violence of the incident. But unlike Wilson and Berezin, Mason himself never believed that the drug scene at the Caffé Cino was as extensive as Patrick depicted in *Kennedy's Children.* In his opinion, Joe Cino was not a heroin addict, nor did he use amphetamines. "Speed makes people lose weight," Mason says, "and Joe Cino was very heavy. If anything, it was the psychedelic things. Zita was absolutely convinced that the psychedelic drugs were the salvation of mankind. I was convinced of it too for a while. There were many of us who bought into this idea, including Joe, because of the mind expansion of drugs like LSD." The mind-expanding drugs were believed to be totally different from the addictive drugs like heroin, speed, and cocaine. "The Beatles went through all this," Mason points out. "It was part of the culture. . . . Those drugs allowed one to see the world in a new light. I know so many people who were absolutely uptight about their own sexuality until they experienced these drugs and then accepted their own sexuality, whether heterosexual or homosexual."

It was in directing the film version of Bob Patrick's play for CBS–Cable TV that Mason made his personal views known. First produced in London, *Kennedy's Children* was then brought to Broadway. Mason's film version was shot in the Caffé Cino with Michael Warren Powell. As extras, Mason cast Johnny Dodd, a co-founder and dishwasher at the Cino—"the most important face at the Cino outside of Joe's"—and Kenny Burgess, the artist who had done many of the drawings on the walls of the cafe. Based on his personal knowledge of the man, Mason staged Cino's final moments with as much truth as possible.

"I believe that is pretty much the way it happened," he says. "Joe put on the Callas record. He was alone, but I know Joe quite well and it's very vivid in my mind the sort of thing he would do. It was a very definite decision, a very extravagant suicide. He was a dancer, you know. And I feel quite sure that the stabbing he did of himself, which was repeated, was ritualistic and extended and enjoyed to the fullest. What he would call 'High Kaya.' A mad, crazy thing. It's a term Joe used all the time. He had a whole private language that you can only understand from context. I would really be hard-pressed to define 'Kaya.' A mood of exultation, probably—either positive or negative. The extraordinary transfiguration that one can experience in great artistic performances, for instance. Or, if someone is in high dudgeon, screaming out of his mind, you would say 'He's in High Kaya today.' It's when a person is beyond himself in a high, emotional state."

It is difficult to assess the true impact of Joe Cino's death on off-off-Broadway except in personal terms. As Wilson says, "When your father and boss and preacher kills himself, you find yourself without much to believe in. Everyone—except Joe—knew that he was creating new theatre in America. His excitement was responsible for half of the vitality of off-off-Broadway, and his death heralded the end of free activity. After Joe died, off-off-Broadway got less communal, more competitive."

Marshall Mason agrees. He feels that those who worked with Cino had been through an extraordinary era marked by boundless enthusiasm and energy—qualities difficult to assess in terms of concrete effects. "It was very innocent before Joe died. There were really only the Cino, La Mama's, and Judson Poets Theatre. New Dramatists and Theatre Genesis were there but they were never a powerful force on off-off-Broadway. They were specifically about play development, whereas off-off-Broadway was about the experience of theatre."

After Joe Cino died, La Mama grew larger. More people emulated Ellen Stewart than Joe Cino, but she had imitated Cino. "So Joe was really the beginning of off-off-Broadway," Mason says. "It changed a great deal after he was gone. A great many little groups sprang up all over the place. Off-off-Broadway became more oriented to growth and being discovered by the *New York Times*. Equity became important. Joe had never wanted to get bigger. He had his little place and that was it. When it burned down in 1966, we had a big benefit to rebuild it; I was the artistic director for it. Edward Albee came down and spoke. We had the opportunity to buy the place next door and make it bigger, but Joe didn't want it."

Cino had never taken the time to wonder whether or not he was creating new theatre. He was too busy violating rules, encouraging experimentation, taking care of "his people," insisting upon "Magic Time!" and thumbing his nose at commercial considerations. Cino's death ushered in a new age of competition. The era of free-spirited communal participation was over. This much was clear in 1968, when the members of the American Theatre Project came back to America.

For Mason, there were other, even more personal reasons that would alter the manner in which he perceived his own involvement with off-off-Broadway. Outwardly, the direction of his life seemed to be in an upward swing. In February 1968, he directed Wilson's *The Gingham Dog* at the New Dramatists while the play was still in its early stages of development. It was a strong two-character play about the final hours of an interracial marriage in which the young husband and wife are unable to surmount their differences. Mason's dramaturgical skills during the course of directing the play greatly aided its development before its Broadway premiere in 1969.

Mason sounded bitter as he recounted the next series of crucial events, events that would propel him to give up theatre altogether despite what had begun as an exceptionally productive period in his life, rather than fight any longer against "whatever it is in this country that seems to damn creativity at every turn."

The first play Mason directed in New York under the banner of the American Theatre Project was Billy Hoffman's *Spring Play*. Billy (William) Hoffman was an early Circle Rep resident playwright, whose play *As Is* moved to Broadway in the spring of 1984 after its premiere at the Circle Repertory Theatre. *Spring Play* was a fairly solid piece of work that Mason was anxious to explore. Flush with the success he had enjoyed abroad, Mason approached Jules Irving at the Vivian Beaumont Theatre in Lincoln Center. Convinced that the American Theatre Project was ready to "mainstream," Mason was also fully aware that Irving was sitting with an empty theatre space on his hands. Irving, impressed with Mason's zeal and not unaware of the young company's past history, gave them The Forum, a little downstairs theatre with a small stage. It was a suitable space for the play. But the project turned out to be a disillusioning experience for all of them, most particularly for Mason.

"Jules Irving said we could use the Lincoln Center," he says. "Equity said we could not and prevented us from performing at The Forum. They sent us instead to a theatre across town with three hundred seats, a proscenium and long rows of seats. We were on stage for one and a half hours and couldn't be heard past the sixth row. We had not rehearsed in that kind of space. It was a disaster."

Thirkield, Wilson, and Berezin well remember the frustrating experience. Not only was the production a disaster, but even more discouraging, no one other than they cared one way or the other. Mason was eager for stateside acknowledgment of the value of his work. In order to continue in a profession in which emotional blows are a built-in hazard, some kind of formal recognition was becoming necessary for the healthy functioning of his creative psyche.

Thirkield, on the other hand, was unwilling to concede even a slight measure of defeat. Instead, he was thinking about how to solve the perennial problem of where to perform. It was a problem in the new competitive atmosphere of off-off-Broadway that was becoming more acute and one that would have to be solved if they were to continue functioning.

Wilson had been talking about a place of their own since 1965, but Mason resisted for a long time. "I just wanted to hold them together," Wilson recalls. "I had read the book about the Group Theatre. Marshall didn't want to read it because he was afraid that it would all fall apart. I don't know if he's read it yet. I know I spoke about a company in '67 with *Untitled Play*. Marshall wasn't quite ready yet. I had said it with *Balm in Gilead*. I said it when he was working with the box office at the

Actors Playhouse. I'd come and sit on the steps with him there. And I kept saying, 'Marshall, we've got to start a company that we can work with and that we can depend on all the time.' And Marshall kept moaning, 'I know, I know.' "

But Marshall was struggling with his own private demons. This was not the time to deal with failure. It did not matter so much to him that they had not performed well with *Spring Play.* What mattered more was that there was no understanding of the right to fail as well as the right to succeed. All of the internal, supportive environmental ingredients he was so careful to create for others in production were denied them externally through the rejection of indifference. More than ever Mason was aware of a new set of rules, a bureaucratic set of priorities that had little to do with creativity. The memory of Joe Cino's "Magic Time!" added to his growing conviction that a supportive environment was necessary for the nurturing of creativity.

Although these frustrations would translate into a clear set of working standards for Mason's own company, at the moment he was too frustrated with the experience of *Spring Play*'s demise at the hands of Equity to think in any other terms than that he had had enough. He remembers saying, " 'To hell with it! I don't need a life in the theatre. I'll do something else!' I was really upset and felt that I couldn't keep creating miracle after miracle. I had been doing good work for a long time. I had no money and no one knew us, especially in a material sense. We were better known in England than in New York after four years of hard work here. After *Spring Play,* I said, 'I can't go from place to place and produce great theatre.' "

When the American Theatre Project disbanded in 1969, few people outside of a very small, insular group of direct participants knew about Mason's work. There had been Wilson's plays—*Balm in Gilead, Home Free!, The Sandcastle, The Madness of Lady Bright, The Gingham Dog*—all of which Mason had not only directed but worked on in close collaboration with Wilson. With his particular brand of encouragement and his dramaturgical skills, he had helped enormously in the early development of a young man who would eventually prove to be one of America's more prolific playwrights. There was also Robert Patrick's play *The Haunted Host,* which Mason premiered; and Claris Nelson's plays, *The Rue Garden, The Clown, Medea, Neon in the Night,* and *The Girl on the BBC;* and many other original works that he had directed all over off-off-Broadway. Success or failure had never been the important factors, although he had always been more successful than not and had built an extraordinary following in his own small theatrical world.

Even though Mason pulled back and claimed he was through, he began to think about what it takes to develop a serious company. Pulling back was more than an emotional reaction to disappointment; he needed time to reorganize, rethink, regroup. He knew that the only answer to his own artistic needs, as well as those of all who had remained loyal to him, was a permanent company with a permanent home. He had been resisting such a commitment for a long time. He was keenly aware, for example, that the Group Theatre of the 1930s had disbanded despite its impressive accumulated talent. But little by little, the need to create a theatre company became more important to Mason than his worry that such a company might share the ill fortune of Northwestern Productions and the American Theatre Project.

None of Mason's friends pressured him when he quit the theatre and went into creative isolation for six months. Thirkield knew Mason was rethinking his position, and he himself took the opportunity to think about what the needs of a company would be. It took a little time, but after all the thinking, after giving up the idea of abandoning theatre, after all the discussions, Mason and Thirkield knew they had to go ahead with their recurrent dream of starting their own company. A first formal articulation of artistic purpose was soon forthcoming.

As summarized in an early Circle Repertory Company brochure, those purposes included the following:

> To make the action of the play the experience of the audience.
> To contribute to the future of Theatre Arts through the exploration of our contemporary world by the finest writers of today.
> To preserve the great traditions of the past through a Permanent Repertory Ensemble that embodies the discipline of the classics and the imagination born of experiment.

These principles, of course, could serve as the artistic credo for any number of theatrical groups. What distinguished the Circle Rep more than anything else was the constant reference to the human experience in terms of content and to the *process* of creating an environment that would accomplish the stated artistic goals. The process had to do with getting a group of actors trained in the classics to work on plays of resident playwrights who would write specifically to their particular talents, not once but again and again, with all of the ensuing benefits of mutual familiarity. It had to do with intensive labs and workshops in which actors, directors, playwrights, and designers worked together as a unit, practicing and learning each others' disciplines in order to cultivate better understanding. It had to do with Marshall Mason's strong sense of what he calls "the native American voice" that is inseparable from realism. It was a voice he wanted to reintroduce to an American theatre then permeated with the avant-garde. At the same time, however, realism itself had to be permeated with open-minded experimentation as well as love of language. This, Mason believed, would lead to the rediscovery of lyric realism, thus renewing the native American voice. And most important, perhaps, the process had to do with the careful construction of a working environment in which the artist would feel free enough to experiment, safe enough to fail, and comfortable enough to work in any genre, including the classics.

From its inception, the Circle Repertory Company was to be an ongoing permanent company. There were no other such groups functioning in New York City at the time. Even La Mama, which by now was calling itself the La Mama Experimental Theatre Club, was mainly for playwrights. Even after the impact of Tom O'Horgan, when the emphasis shifted to directing, La Mama was always a place where new plays could be tested, each with a new cast selected on an ad hoc basis to fulfill the requirements of the particular play and then disbanded. La Mama did not have a company, nor did the other groups of the time. The Living Theatre was in Europe, the Association for Performing Artists had folded, and the Open Theatre was an experimental group more than a company. In that sense, the Circle Rep would be the only company in town with articulated, ongoing commitments.

The eventual success of the company would be due to a particular combination of fortuitous circumstances. It helped that the earliest resident playwrights were of the caliber of Robert Patrick, David Starkweather, William Hoffman, Claris Nelson, and most particularly Lanford Wilson, who was and continues to be the company's main resident playwright. It helped that Tanya Berezin was a young actress of great potential who, as a co-founder and a leading company actress, would eventually set a standard of performance for all involved. It helped that Rob Thirkield's enthusiastic embrace of the experimental techniques of such innovators as Grotowski, his disciple Eugenio Barba, and Tom O'Horgan created an ambience encouraging risk-taking in the workshops. It also helped that Thirkield had the money to support the company for well over a year until the grants started coming in. Finally, it helped that Marshall Mason's vision of what a company should be was so unswerving. What would distinguish the Circle Rep from the other groups was not only the idea of a permanent theatre company, but also the presence of Marshall Mason himself.

4

A Company Is Born —July 1969

IN the summer of 1969, Rob Thirkield was a patient of psychiatrist Dr. Harry Lerner, a man of broad interests. A consultant to the World Federation of Mental Health, Lerner also had a keen interest in the arts. He was the executive director of the World Cultural Center and the executive director and founder of the Coordinating Committee for the Utilization of the New York City World's Fair. These positions involved him in the Council for International Recreation, Culture and Lifelong Education — or C.I.R.C.L.E., an ambitious world peace movement meant to bring together many different kinds of people. The formula for doing so included the creation of theatre, dance, and other groups of artists in the belief that the universality of the arts could dispel artificial boundaries between people of different backgrounds.

Thirkield had mentioned to Dr. Lerner that he and Mason, who had also been a patient at one time, were looking for a home in which to finally start their theatrical company. One July afternoon, when Mason, Thirkield, Wilson, and Berezin were together at Rob and Tanya's apartment on Bank Street discussing what they would need in order to go ahead with their plans, Thirkield received a phone call from Lerner. Lerner had come across a space on the upper West Side that he thought might be adaptable to their needs. He invited them to look at it and to consider starting their company under the auspices of C.I.R.C.L.E.

Mason, Thirkield, and Wilson took a taxi uptown and pulled up in front of a rather shabby building on West 83rd Street and Broadway that was old enough to have been declared a landmark and charmless enough to make one wonder why. A theatrical company's home has to be able to fill all, or at least most of, the company's major requirements; unfortunately, everything was wrong with the loft Dr. Lerner had sent them to inspect, including its location. "No one goes that far uptown," Mason said. The loft was on a second floor over a Thom McAn shoe store, and it had a rough external appearance. The building had been through many transitions, each of which had left its mark. At one point it had been a warehouse; at another it housed a men's chapel; it was later used by a pornographic film club; and most recently it had served as a recording studio.

As they stared up at the enormous flat soundboards hanging from the ceiling — remnants from its latest incarnation — Wilson expressed optimism but Mason was already shaking his head. Besides the seediness of the building, the space itself was the wrong size and shape. It was long and narrow and, worst of all, had resounding echoes. Mason was convinced they needed something better, for the loft had too many inherent problems to overcome. But when Mason called Dr. Lerner to tell him they were sorry and not really interested, the doctor told them he had already leased the loft since it was so inexpensive. If they wanted it before he set up his own various offices for C.I.R.C.L.E., all they had to do was take up the lease. They could then produce their theatre under the aegis of C.I.R.C.L.E., which would give them immediate not-for-profit tax benefits as long as Dr. Lerner maintained his position as executive director of the World Cultural Center. For Lerner it would be the first step in the realization of his desire to bring together various arts groups for his world peace movement; for them it would be the first space that was totally their own.

Despite misgivings, Mason finally said, "Oh, the hell with it. Let's do it!" — clearly holding out the option to vacate the loft without recriminations once he found the right place. Rob Thirkield took the lease from Dr. Lerner and began paying the rent out of his own pocket: $300 for the first two months, then $400, and finally $500 per month. Thus began Thirkield's personal financial support of the company on a monthly basis.

Dr. Lerner's influence, then, was considerable. That he was a good friend who believed in them was a very important boost to their confidence. That he took the space, imperfect though it was, without waiting for approval, *forced* them to take their first formal step. That Lerner gave them an immediate ready-made tax umbrella by allowing them to operate under C.I.R.C.L.E. made it possible for them to receive much-needed donations. Because of Dr. Lerner's interest, their company had finally emerged out of the discussion stages. They were now paying rent; they now had to produce.

"Dr. Lerner did two good things for us and one bad," Mason says, quick to acknowledge Lerner's important contributions:

> He found us the place and gave us the tax umbrella. Those were the two good things. The bad thing was that he insisted we change our name to the Circle Theatre. We called ourselves the American Project at the Circle Theatre. Dr. Lerner said that was too confusing. He insisted that if we were going to stay there, we change our name to Circle Theatre. We sort of had a fight over it. I was concerned with the confusion with Circle-in-the-Square. And I didn't really want to name it Circle Theatre especially because it was a "project." We didn't really have any idea we would start out as a full-blown theatre. We were a project—a theatre project that would someday, perhaps, grow into a theatre. But then I said, "What's in a name?" It was not too much of a compromise. So I said, "Okay, let's change it!" We became the Circle Theatre.

Even though they had disbanded the American Theatre Project after *Spring Play,* they were still an informal group of about ten people who had spent the last four or five years working together—Marshall Mason, Rob Thirkield, Lanford Wilson, Tanya Berezin, Stephanie Gordon, Claris Nelson, Jane Lowrey, Michael Powell, David Groh, Charles Stanley, Dennis Parichy, and several others from Northwestern University. Loyalties were enduring. As Mason points out, "Take Dennis Parichy. Not only did he light *Little Eyolf,* the first play I directed in New York, he also did *Balm in Gilead.* This was a period of time when Dennis could not afford to live the life of a Bohemian artist. He had a wife and child. For a period of time—about three of four years—we were out of touch. He was making a living lighting ballets and operas and working in schools. Then he rejoined us once we set [the company] up."

However, they knew they needed to involve more people in order to run the many aspects of a formal theatre within a set plant. They made phone calls to virtually everyone they knew in New York who was connected with theatre. Literally hundreds of calls went out with invitations to attend a combination party/meeting about a "new theatre." Tanya Berezin recalls, "Marshall simply said, 'Whoever wants to come can come. Whoever stays is the company.' "

The big meeting that ensued, which in the retelling has assumed legendary proportions, occurred on July 14, 1969, in the second-story loft on West 83rd Street and Broadway. Many responded to the calls— some seriously interested, some merely curious, and some looking for any excuse to party. Most were in their late twenties or early thirties.

"There was something like sixty-five people at that first meeting," Tanya Berezin remembers, "and Marshall has always been very pie-in-the-sky. His ideas have always been enormous. And he's standing up there, poor as a church mouse with his pants above his ankles, telling people he was going to start a great theatre. And a lot of people laughed at him and didn't come back. Some of us were already a part of him. Some others who were brand new didn't laugh. Some people joined because it was an opportunity to work for free. We never charged anybody. Some people joined because of focus. Some people just hung around. The company was formed out of the people who showed up."

Mason was a startling figure as he announced his intention to start a new theatre. At twenty-nine, he was still extremely thin, with long, slender, bony hands and long, straight hair that hung well below his shoulders. At the first meeting, he spoke and then Thirkield spoke. Next Mason and Thirkield took turns reading passages out of Stanislavsky's *An Actor Prepares.* Then Mason began to outline the public goals they envisioned. It was their intention to begin a theatre in which people could work together in an ensemble and be trained in the classics. Once such a classical ensemble was trained, it could then be made available to a group of new American playwrights who would be in development and in residence to write specifically for the company.

This was a new idea in American theatre, even though permanent resident companies and permanent combination companies had been common in late nineteenth-century America.[1] Some of the earlier companies had manager-dramatists or actor-dramatists who wrote plays to add to the standard repertory fare, which usually consisted of Shakespeare and melodrama. For example, Dion Boucicault (1822–1899), perhaps the most successful dramatist of his day, wrote prolifically for his American company in the years 1853–1860. Augustin Daly (1836–1899), best known for establishing the director as a major force in theatre, owned his own theatre and toured with his company as far as England. Daly wrote many adaptations of European plays for the company he founded in 1869 at the Fifth Avenue Theatre. Steele MacKaye (1842–1894), best known for his scenic inventions and his training programs that led to the American Academy of Dramatic Arts, wrote or adapted nineteen plays for his company in the late nineteenth century. And David Belasco (1853–1931), the most important American producer in the early twentieth century, wrote plays for his company. However, there had never been a *permanent company of professional actors* in the United States that concentrated almost exclusively on original material and worked in a *continuing* process with a *group* of resident playwrights who were carefully developed and who created material specifically for the company actors.

This had not even happened with the Group Theatre of the thirties, where, in an attempt to keep all options open, such an idea had been strongly resisted. Harold Clurman, one of the founders of the Group Theatre, wrote:

> Years ago when I spoke to the governing board of the Theatre Guild about the possibility of developing dramatists for the company that was to become the Group Theatre, I suggested that we make young writers part of the organization—even assign them jobs. The response was something like outrage. "You mean you want dramatists to write with your actors in mind?" I pointed out the Rostand had written *Cyrano de Bergerac* for Coquelin with a by no means deplorable outcome. I might have even more pedantically mentioned that Shakespeare and Molière had written certain roles with particular actors of their permanent companies in mind.[2]

When the Group Theatre was formed in 1931 by Lee Strasberg, Harold Clurman, and Cheryl Crawford, there were no resident playwrights in their group. They produced plays by Paul Green, John Howard Lawson, Dawn Powell, William Saroyan, Maxwell Anderson, Sidney Kingsley, and Eugene O'Neill, none of whom was a Group Theatre member, before they discovered Clifford Odets's *Waiting for Lefty*. Odets was a young actor who had been invited to join the company and then discovered he could write. He became a major voice of the Group Theatre as well as a prominent spokesman for the decade by the accidental combination of talent and opportunity, not by the conceptual design of the company.[3]

But Marshall Mason had a very definite conceptual vision in 1969: the needs of the new company were to be based on the relationship between the actor, the playwright, and the director. A major goal was to create a theatre for the artist. The objective was not only to insure the opportunity to work, although that was certainly a part of it; artists must practice their craft, and Mason wanted to make sure he would always have the chance to direct. Once the company was formed, he was really interested in the kind of work they could all create together. From the beginning, the aim was quality. Of course, as Stanislavsky told Norris Houghton, "no one has ever deliberately tried to found a bad theatre."[4] But for Mason, Thirkield, Wilson, and Berezin, it was more than just doing good theatre. Their goal was to improve as artists. They wanted to become better than they were. They wanted to challenge each other as they had never been challenged before. They wanted to explore the human experience in order to create living theatre.

Mason meant this very seriously. They were young, idealistic, enthusiastic, full of dreams, wanting to startle the world and make an impact, and in so doing startle themselves as well. As Mason pointed out ten years later, "It was, after all, the late sixties and we thought and still feel we could accomplish things together that had never been accomplished."[5] To Mason, the recurring values were independence, unity, and a passion for excellence.

Thus, after much thinking and many discussions, most particularly with Thirkield, Mason could begin to delineate the kind of theatre they envisioned. The common goals were to create a theatre for the artist; to improve and grow as artists; to break down the walls between the various theatre disciplines; to explore the human experience without embarrassment; and to create a theatre event as a living experience for the audience. The methods would be a permanent company managed by the artists; extensive ensemble training, particularly in the classics, through workshops and labs; and playwrights-in-residence writing directly for the company. And the guiding values would be a community-style environment with rights, privileges, and obligations; an ideology based on the self; and a protective, nurturing environment.

In short, this was to be a theatre for the artist to create a theatre event. The theatre event was the "living play" they wanted the audience to experience.

It was to be a way of life.

Although the idea of creating a company is hardly unique, the idea of creating a theatre first and foremost for the artist *is* unique. In 1898, the Moscow Art Theatre—shining example for all who venture into such territories—declared its objective to be the development of a theatre for the educated working populace and the middle-class intelligentsia. In keeping with this, their first theatre was called the People's Art Theatre. The Group Theatre of the thirties had visions of becoming a national theatre, but became instead the political pulse and emotional temper of the times. The short-lived Repertory Company of Lincoln Center of the sixties also had ambitions of becoming a national theatre. With enormous resources of both private and public funds available, it seemed that the realization of these ambitions might have been possible had it not run into such a great deal of critical pressure regarding artistic differences.

The Circle Repertory Company, well aware of its forerunners, was designed primarily to fulfill the day-by-day needs of the working artist. This concept has never changed. Fifteen years later, in a Circle Rep *Showbill* for *Levitation,* Mason would restate this premise:

> The needs of the artist were the last things considered in the commercial theatre. When a production finishes, the scenery is burned, the cast is dispersed, and the commercial theatre starts again in a totally different context. Whatever you might learn happens individually and not collectively. I felt this was like General Motors firing everyone at the end of each year and starting off with new designers.[6]

In a theatre for the artist, the playwright and the playwriting process are treated with extraordinary care. Before the play is ready for a major production, it becomes part of the lifeblood of the company. It is read aloud by and for the company members. It is discussed, reshaped, developed, and given intensive, detailed attention. It might be given a workshop reading with an audience symposium, then rewritten, reshaped, and given another workshop. The playwright is never completely isolated during this period of writing. Such care is given not only because the playwright's contribution is so important, but also because the very nature of his contribution makes him the most vulnerable. His work must be protected in order not to block growth. Mason discussed this point with Paul Gardner of the *New York Times* in 1976:

> Of all the people in the theatre writers are the most tender. They put themselves on the line, sharing their perceptions of reality with us. They are very easily damaged. The American theatre chews up writers, gnashes them badly. Look what happened to Tennessee Williams, our greatest living playwright. His *Red Devil Battery* opened in Boston. It wasn't ready. He was butchered. . . . Clifford Odets, William Inge—they were chewed up. . . . Often it's hard to tell when the production is at fault and not the play. Even the critics can't make the separation. The playwright takes the fall.
>
> Once the play flops on Broadway, it's dead. It's like a disease no one wants. It has been stigmatized. When a playwright is with a rep company he's protected from the hit-flop syndrome. . . . In the commercial theatre, two Broadway flops and you've got not only a couple of dead plays, you've got a dead playwright. No one will finance him and he can't write anymore. He's blocked.[7]

The care given the playwright should be given to each theatre discipline. Ideally, each artist can expect to have the right to be selfish about his creative needs, and to have the community privilege of acceptance, freedom to work, expectation of being treated seriously, and the concomitant obligation to afford the same care to other participating members.

Mason was aware that he was setting up a different ideology, one based on the self. He knew it would be met with wide-spread disagreement, often by the most respected figures in theatre. Critics with the stature of Robert Brustein believed that individual ambition could be fatal to a repertory theatre, since by their very nature repertory companies had to be based on cooperation, selflessness, and humility:

> For if a repertory company is ever to function properly, its members must subordinate their own aspirations to the demands of the company, working in perfect harmony for the sake of a balanced unified whole.[8]

Mason was absolute in his insistence that his had to be a theatre for the benefit of the artist before it could be a theatre for anyone else. It was a courageous stance to adopt in the "togetherness" atmosphere of the sixties, when a strong communal thrust was felt throughout society. The La Mama troupe, for example, as though literally following a credo set out by theatre statesmen like Brustein, ran on an enthusiastic, everybody-for-the-group philosophy. The Circle Repertory Company did the exact opposite; "no self-sacrifice" was its philosophy. Mason declared his own "selfish" objectives and encouraged them in others, "Because if you are insistent on your right and need to grow as an individual artist, then you can truly recognize other people's needs. And from that kind of selfish point of view, we can build something together that we can't build separately. So we never encouraged people to sacrifice themselves to the interest of the group."

This philosophy is in direct opposition to the philosophy of other drama groups. The Group Theatre, for example, following the more conventional approach to the issue of service to the company, had difficulty with its application. Ruth Nelson, an actress with the Group Theatre, claims that the Group actually "wrecked some people's lives" because of its insistence on total service to the company. "We didn't join to serve ourselves; we served the playwright; we served the theatre."[9] This approach can be destructive as well as counterproductive when the individual artist is made to feel insignificant by the insistence that he or she function more as a servant to the needs of other artists than as master of his or her own. Mason wanted his artists to expect that their needs as artists would be continually nourished. It is not only the secret of a successfully functioning artist, he believes, but also the secret of a successfully functioning community. "We have rights, privileges, and obligations to each other that are based on mutual respect for one another and the fact that we share the same goals. Nobody is trying to become a star at the expense of someone else, which is the way it usually is in other groups."

As Brustein warned, individual ambition could be fatal to a repertory company. Perhaps so, *if* it is ambition of the wrong kind. Ambition to become a "star" has no place in a repertory company. But ambition to do the best work one is capable of is to be encouraged, for that kind of uncompromising "selfishness" can be highly beneficial to the entire group.

Wary of the hazards of failure with its depressing aftermaths, and equally wary of the seduction of success with its ever-present threats to artistic integrity, Mason wanted to develop an artistic environment in which both failure and success could be endured. In his company, actors, directors, and playwrights would experiment freely, without fear of rejection.

Evidence of company ideals appeared in the workshops run by Ma-

son and Thirkield; here everyone was expected to participate and everyone's needs were examined. One important goal of the workshop was to
break down walls between the various theatre disciplines. For example,
historically speaking, the play and the playwright have always been all-
important. However, the theatre event can only be created when there is
complete collaboration between the playwright, the actor, the director,
the designer, and others involved in the production.

Such collaboration begins with understanding. It is Mason's conten-
tion, and one guiding much of his handling of the company, that there
has always been too much emphasis on the playwright, especially in
commercial theatre—and that there is a naive belief that if a playwright
comes along with a "great" play, everything else will automatically fall
into place. He is fond of pointing out it was not until Stanislavsky
discovered how to play Chekhov that *The Sea Gull* was appreciated (by
the critics at least, if not by Chekhov himself). *The Sea Gull*'s first
production had been a total failure and almost ended a brilliant playwright's career before it had begun. Mason believes that a full realization
of the playwright's vision requires a symbiotic attachment between the
playwright, the director, and the actor. This is what he set out to achieve
in the Circle Repertory Company.

Fifteen years later, Tanya Berezin would reaffirm Mason's belief:

> The actor who is a member of a company is constantly investi-
> gating what makes a playwright's material work. When
> Marshall says that the Circle Rep does what the Moscow Art
> Theatre did for Chekhov or Burbage did for Shakespeare, it
> sounds very easy. But it is exactly what he is talking about.
> Performing artists—actors, directors—have to learn what Lan-
> ford Wilson is, what John Bishop is, what Milan Stitt is. They
> have to make the play work. For example, Ed Harris and Cathy
> Baker know about *Fool for Love*. They know Sam Shepard. We
> had to have auditions to replace and understudy them. Some of
> the actors who auditioned were off the wall. The wrong-headed-
> ness about the play is astonishing since we now know what the
> play is supposed to be. Now we say, how can they not know it—
> see it? They cannot see it because they are not connected to the
> playwright.

Lanford Wilson agrees: "There are moments when the actors realize
a play far beyond the playwright's most hopeful expectations." Accord-

ing to Wilson, this is the most satisfying kind of collaboration possible. In order to achieve this collaboration, there has to be communication with even the most basic elements of theatre — for example, the technician.

As Mason points out, "It has always been divided into 'Us' versus 'Them.' It happens even in academic theatre in which actors see the technician as someone who's going to get in the way, and the technician sees the actor as someone who breaks props. So there's very little communication. We were determined to undo that. We were also determined to make playwrights understand what actors were about, and actors understand what directing was about, so that everyone could work for the common goal."

If everything falls into place properly, the ultimate goal is what Mason calls "the living experience for the audience." The idea is to create a living script, a harmony between the spoken word and the experience of the audience. Implicit in this is the belief that theatre can uniquely bridge the distance between people by showing the workings of the human spirit through human behavior in the here and now. Theoretically, the process may be described in the following manner: 1) a theatre for the artist results in 2) an atmosphere where the artist's best work is possible, 3) which translates into the all-important theatre event, 4) which culminates in the common goal — a living experience shared with the audience.

Was it all policy fanfare? Was it a search for a home they had somehow personally lacked? Belonging instead of gypsy-acting? Succor instead of criticism? Undiscriminating support instead of truth? Or were they in the process of discovering what Harold Clurman called the fundamental "idea" of theatre?[10]

Questions are always being asked, by critic and scholar alike, about what constitutes a true theatre. Clurman, co-founder of his own company, respected director, and one of the finest critics of his day, was no exception. His critiques, though sometimes devastating, were nonetheless sparked by the generosity of understanding born of the working theatre artist who had broken down the walls between theatre disciplines. Having worn various hats himself, he was sure he knew what constituted a true theatre. In *The Naked Image* he quoted Vachtangov, who, given his work with Stanislavsky and the Moscow Art Theatre, became one of the heroes of the Group Theatre and the Actors Studio.

> The answer, once given by the great Russian director, Vach-
> tangov, was couched in the special jargon of his time and place
> (Moscow, 1919) but it is nonetheless exact: "A theatre is an
> ideologically cemented collective."[11]

Clurman agreed with Vachtangov but took it out of the abstract by
itemizing what he considered four essential ingredients of a true theatre:
1) a true theatre must create an identity; 2) it must produce its own
native playwrights; 3) it must be a creative organism rather than an
interpretive one; and 4) it must have an aesthetic and a philosophical
attitude.

The new Circle Rep fit Clurman's criteria of what constituted a true
theatre. It had created a unique identity in that it was a theatre of the
artist, by the artist, and for the artist. It was dedicated to the development of its own native playwrights, which made it a creative rather than
just an interpretive organism. Despite an open willingness to experiment,
aesthetically it leaned toward realism and the rediscovery of the native
American voice, while its philosophical ideology was dedicated to the
celebration of the human spirit through human behavior.

Enthusiasm was high—so high that Mason was unembarrassed
when he said, "I hate to say something as naive and as obvious as saying
part of the goal was to become a national theatre. But if we were as good
as we hoped we would become, that was inevitably where we were
headed."

Of course, the odds were against a national theatre ever becoming a
reality in America. The most recent effort to create a national theatre,
the Repertory Company of Lincoln Center under the leadership of Elia
Kazan, an early hero of the Circle Rep group, had just died. Beneath all
the heady enthusiasm of dreams was an awareness that their company
was coming directly in the aftermath of the Lincoln Center Repertory
fiasco, in which the board of directors—comprised of lawyers, bankers,
and other nontheatrical people—had just fired its artistic directors, including Kazan.

Mason and Thirkield had looked to the Repertory Theatre of Lincoln Center with great hopes for the American theatre, and in some
respects they wished to emulate it. Its demise was a warning signal to
them, for they believed that the Repertory Theatre of Lincoln Center
had been destroyed by people who thought a working company could

evolve overnight and by people who demanded instant "smash hits."

The attitude of the Circle Rep regarding the demise of the Lincoln Center company was passionately synthesized by Tanya Berezin, for even though the Circle Rep did not have even one small percent of the Lincoln Center company's financial backing, the identification factor between the Circle Rep and the ill-fated older company was powerful. "The Circle Rep didn't pop out of Jupiter's thigh in 1969 and produce a smash," Berezin says. "As Marshall, Lanford, Rob, and I were together, the Lincoln Center had Bobby Lewis, Kazan, [Robert] Whitehead, and Arthur Miller—people who had natural experience in the past, trying to pass that on and share it with young actors and mature actors alike. They had never before worked in a committed way together, but they had a natural artistic affinity from the fifties."

The Circle Rep had a very low profile in the beginning, whereas the Repertory Company of Lincoln Center had been highly visible from its inception. The Repertory Company of Lincoln Center was not permitted either to fail or to experiment. Although critic Robert Brustein condemned its leaders for bringing commercial theatre sensibilities to the Repertory Company of Lincoln Center, the company was nonetheless being judged by the criteria of that same commercial theatre. Either it was a tremendous hit or it was a complete flop—there was no in-between. "They could have been given time to grow," Berezin continues.

> They had lots of money. They had lots of power behind them. They didn't have to succeed immediately. It was just the mentality of the Lincoln Center board that said they had to. They could afford to lose a lot of money. Part of our opportunity was our low profile, because when we failed, and we did, our board of directors was us. When we lost money, we lost $14. But you see, they did not have to make money. That was not what they were there for. They had all the money in the artistic community behind them. They should have been prepared to lose a lot of money. The Royal Shakespeare Company lost money when it started. They all lose money. It's something this country is not prepared to do. I think that given time they would have worked. They were different people from us—other voices, but strong voices.

In *The Naked Image,* Clurman condemns what he called an American characteristic that frustrated the hopes for new theatre—impatience.[12] He had urged patience in regard to the Lincoln Center company and warned against foolish expectations grounded in the impossible hit-flop syndrome that characterized the commercial theatre of Broadway. He was absolutely correct in asserting that the founding of a *theatre* is "not the same as setting up a series of productions."[13] He also insisted that no theatre could look forward to a secure future when it was expected to provide a smash with its initial production. "The theater is not a merchandising business any more than is a library, a museum or a symphony orchestra."[14]

Taking a lesson from experiences of the Repertory Company of Lincoln Center, the Circle Rep group decided that its board of directors would be comprised of the artists themselves. They hoped in this way to avoid the major pitfall of an artistic clash with the differing objective of a board primarily geared toward financial solvency.

The founders of the Circle Rep were also directly influenced by the Actors Studio and inspired by its parent, the Group Theatre.

Speaking of the Group, Mason notes "that even with its extraordinary vision and vast reservoirs of talent it survived only ten years before succumbing to whatever it is in America that seemed to doom every living, artistic thing." He admits that in some ways he was subconsciously emulating the Group, partly because of the romance of their relatively brief but exciting life and partly because the personnel went on to contribute so profoundly to modern theatre: Lee Strasberg, Harold Clurman, Cheryl Crawford, Elia Kazan, Stella Adler, Lee. J. Cobb, John Garfield, Morris Carnovsky, and Franchot Tone. Out of the Group Theatre came the Actors Studio, with its revitalization of realistic American acting, its legacies of Marlon Brando, James Dean, and Montgomery Clift, and its new approach to scenic design.

In Mason's view, Hollywood contributed a great deal to the collapse of the Group Theatre, and here was another danger to avoid. Not only did Hollywood have huge sums of money to entice the Group's major playwright, Clifford Odets, into writing for films, but it also drained the company of many of its best actors, all of whom wound up with excellent careers in films but left the Group bereft of the necessary personnel to continue. Mason felt that a good part of the company's dissolution was due to ambition and greed, and he took another huge lesson from its experience. "We have always encouraged people," he says. "Yes, go out and make the money, and *then come back*. That way everyone will grow and we will all be stronger." Indeed, Christopher Reeve, Judd Hirsch, Beatrice Straight, Richard Thomas, Tony Roberts, Fritz Weaver, and William Hurt—to name a few high-profile Circle Repertory Company members—have all gone on to successful careers in film and television and have periodically returned to work with the company over the years.

Mason and Thirkield were also aware of models from the more distant past and consciously looked to pattern themselves in part after the Moscow Art Theatre. The M.A.T. was originally privately funded; Stanislavsky came from a wealthy family, as did Rob Thirkield. Indeed, Stanislavsky privately supported the M.A.T. at first, as Thirkield supported the early Circle Rep. The interest of the Czar was eventually stimulated by the M.A.T.'s excellence and innovations in acting. It was then that the M.A.T. was subsidized by the government. Mason hoped to achieve the same quality of excellence, so that modern-day "czars" would not be able to overlook their work and would come forward with subsidies and grants.

It is ironic that while they looked to the inspiration of the Moscow Art Theatre—and Stanislavsky, the first director ever to center his work on the actor, in particular—the Moscow Art Theatre met lukewarm critical reception in the United States. In 1964, when the Circle Rep was in its earliest stages of development, the M.A.T. came to America, bringing Mikhail Bulgakov's *Dead Souls* and Chekhov's *The Three Sisters* and *The Cherry Orchard* in repertory. The Stanislavsky acting system, which had revolutionized Western theatre, now seemed a bit musty and old-fashioned to critics more accustomed to the Strasberg method. This Americanized version of Stanislavsky's system, with its intense concentration on naturalistic behavior and psychological truth, often at the expense of articulation, clashed with the open, direct style of the M.A.T. With recognition of the "glories of the past," Roberts Brustein put the Moscow Art Theatre out to pasture and called on America to "break the bonds of naturalistic truth and psychological reality," lest it get mired in the rear guard along with the Moscow Art Theatre.[15] This at a time when Mason's thoughts were headed toward a new realism!

The new Circle Rep was lucky. It did not have the Moscow Art Theatre's glorious past to live up to. It did not have the Group Theatre's fame. It did not have the publicity of the Repertory Company of Lincoln Center. The Circle Rep had no hot spotlight. No one cared whether or not it succeeded except its members themselves. No one demanded instant achievement. No one pointed an accusatory finger at the red ink in the credit column. They had what Clurman would call a strong "Idea" and a definite philosophical point of view. While critics demanded novelty from the M.A.T. and instant fruits from the Lincoln Center Repertory, the Circle Rep had the comfort and time to nurture the environment in which it would grow. It is most fortunate that the Circle Rep did not receive strong public recognition at first. By the time it achieved its "overnight success" in 1973, its founders had been working together for almost ten years.

5

The Early Days

THE Circle Theatre Company made its first home at 2307 Broadway, between 83rd and 84th streets. The company was run by the artists themselves, as planned. Rob Thirkield was the managing director, Marshall W. Mason was the artistic director, Tanya Berezin was the administrative director, and Beverly Landau, an off-Broadway producer, was the executive producer. Although Lanford Wilson was listed as one of the company playwrights — along with Robert Kesser, Helen Duberstein Lipton, Matthew Silverman, David Starkweather, and Doric Wilson — he had very little to do with the actual start of the company, with the exception of a secondary kind of support. He was occupied elsewhere with the production of his plays *Serenading Louie, Lemon Sky,* and *The Gingham Dog.*

The initial company roster consisted of twenty-five members:

Tanya Berezin	Robert Frink
Beth Bowden	Stephanie Gordon
Patricia Carey	Spalding Gray
Mona Crawford	Ellen Gurin
Linda Eskansas	Carl David Jessup
Michael Feisenmeier	Jane Lowry

Sharon Ann Madden   Bob Shields
Marshall W. Mason   Maria Stefann
Henry Mellor   David Stekol
Roddy O'Connor   Tony Tenuto
Bill Oxendine   Rob Thirkield
Burke Pearson   Alice Tweedle
Suzanne Pred

There were also thirteen associate members, plus John Dowling, company artist; John Deans, company architect; and Alonzo Levister, company composer.

The loft on upper Broadway proved to be a decent place to work. It was clean and large enough to accommodate the twenty-five to thirty people who showed up on a regular basis to participate in the workshops that Mason and Thirkield began coordinating. The workshops were broken up into two separate areas—the Methods Workshop, under the direction of Mason, and the Exploration Workshop, under the direction of Thirkield.

The earliest goal of the work was pragmatic—to establish a vocabulary that would be familiar to all. The ultimate aim was an ensemble that had trained together to such a point that it would be impossible to tell where the written word ended and the acting began. Training *together* was the key. Everyone participated in the workshops—actor, director, playwright, and designer alike. In fact, Mason and Thirkield participated in each other's workshops. It was only when the boundaries between the theatre disciplines were truly crossed that the ensemble began to feel real; it was more than mere training in acting. Most of the people who came already had some theatre training in their backgrounds. Now, in sharing experiences, the company created a mutual language. Although Mason would often say that there was no specific method taught, and upon examination this proved to be true, the Circle Rep approach was a way of pulling together many styles in its own unique identity.

The first eight months were spent exclusively in workshop training. Each workshop met three times a week for three hours at a time, so that those who availed themselves of both workshops—and most did—actually found themselves working together every day. Even the Group Theatre had only ten weeks to get to know each other. An eight-month period of training was a luxury in any off-Broadway or off-off-Broadway theatre, let alone the commercial theatre. It had happened only once before in New York. Elia Kazan, Harold Clurman, and Bobby Lewis conducted a solid year of ensemble training with the personnel of the Repertory Company of Lincoln Center before its first production. Mason took much of his inspiration from this distinctive beginning. "That's the way to do it!" he had said. "You take the time to train and *then* go into production." Circle Rep was very much a reaction to the unusual feature of the Lincoln Center's beginnings as well as a reaction to its failure. However, it must be remembered that at this point, Circle Rep's expenses were minimal. There was no wolf howling at the door. They did not have to cover expenses by forcing immediate income-producing productions before they felt ready. Whatever expenses they did have were essentially covered by Thirkield, who believed so deeply in what they were doing that he was willing to finance it completely. His dedication and generosity combined with Mason's strong vision to make their partnership mutually inspiring. They felt they were creating the kind of environment that would nourish their own creative needs — a very important point — as well as those of the company they formed around themselves. It was in their workshops, with their emphasis on individualism, that the seeds for true ensemble interaction were being sown.

From Mason's point of view, the training was done very much in terms of the classics. It was always his intention to reflect the contemporary world: first, through the mirror of the classics, hoping to bring the wisdom of playwrights such as Shakespeare, Chekhov, Ibsen, and Strindberg to illuminate the timeless dilemma of the human condition, and second, through contemporary plays, hoping to attract new playwrights to write plays for the company.

While Mason vigorously trained in the classics, Thirkield spent his workshops in experimental methods. As Mason says, "For a long time that was one of our hallmarks. The experimental alongside the traditional. We didn't recognize any limitations in terms of what we were exploring at this time. We believed whatever works for an individual actor is good."

Most of Mason's training has been in terms of Stanislavsky through Alvina Krause. Krause, who did not approve of Lee Strasberg, took Stanislavsky very literally — "straight from the book" — which Mason believes made her a great teacher. When Mason came to study at the Actors Studio, he already had a profound understanding of Stanislavsky's system, "so I knew when to listen to Lee and when to ignore him." Mason learned mainly through Harold Clurman. However, the Actors Studio does not teach the Stanislavsky system geared to sensory memory. Rather, it concentrates more on the "other branch" of Stanislavsky, according to Mason's observations, which was geared more to the stimulus-response orientation that became the foundation for the Neighborhood Playhouse. Both sensory memory and stimulus-response are interrelated, having a strong common base in the Group Theatre, but the differences between them are evident in the various directions taken by the Group's alumni. Out of the Group Theatre came Lee Strasberg's Actors Studio, Stella Alder's extended approach, and Sanford Meisner's Neighborhood Playhouse. Mason embraced them all:

> Meisner's direction has to do with spontaneous imaginative response to what is actually happening onstage. Stanislavsky called it "doing the physical action," and it really means to bring it down to the here and now basis which the Neighborhood Playhouse concentrated on. More important than the sensory work and the imaginative work that the Actors Studio did was the relaxation, concentration, and imagination in the here and now. But we don't really subscribe to any one theory. All is important. All. I certainly know enough about the Actors Studio to be able to say to Kathy Cortez, who is oriented to their method, things like, "You're not relaxed enough," or, "You need a more personal objective." Or, when I'm working with Trish Hawkins or Tanya Berezin, whose backgrounds are from the Neighborhood Playhouse approach, then we work more in terms of independent activities and objectives, and try to get the action in the here and now.

It was not until Circle Rep began that Mason became fully aware of the distinctions between the three branches of the "method"— Stanislavsky, Strasberg, and Adler. Although most theatre scholars are aware that Strasberg became profoundly fixed on the techniques outlined in *An Actor Prepares,* it is interesting to note how the disputes between Strasberg and Adler affected those, like Mason, who were more involved in pragmatics than theories. Through direct study, Mason evolved his own opinions of the disputes. "Strasberg got hung up on the idea of the use of effective memory," but Mason finds it "useful only for an acting exercise. Adler says Stanislavsky insisted that the action was the most important element," he continues, "but Meisner got Stanislavsky's principles down to the stimulus-response. Doing the action and responding to your partner—what he developed into word games. All of which are Stanislavsky-based except that Meisner took it much further."

The basic difference has to do with Strasberg's devotion to the emotional life of a character and Stanislavsky's, Adler's, and Meisner's devotion to the "action" — what is happening. It is this second branch of the method that Mason eventually adopted, believing that "the emotions will follow what happens." Thus, in the Methods Workshop, Mason taught eclectic Stanislavsky/Strasberg/Adler/Meisner exercises and techniques in a setting reminiscent of a classroom. In addition to the ongoing exercises, the actors prepared individual scenework in out-of-class rehearsal and then presented the scenes within the workshop for evaluation and support. Little by little, during the course of those first eight months, Mason concentrated most of the Methods Workshop on *The Three Sisters,* which turned into extensive background work for the first production he would direct at the new Circle Repertory Theatre.

There was an unplanned but fortuitous balance between Mason's Method Workshop and the Exploration Workshop Thirkield simultaneously ran. In the Exploration Workshop, the goals were a bit less structured than the usual acting systems. Having consciously applied acting techniques to exercises, the goal now became to free the imagination from the conventional techniques in order to develop individual methods of expression through the voice, the body, and the personal psychology of each actor.

Like Mason, Thirkield brought a rich background of acting training into his workshop, from the bedrock traditionalism of Alvina Krause at Eagles Mere and Northwestern to some of the more unconventional styles currently in vogue. This eclectic mixture contributed greatly to the highly experimental nature of his workshop. While touring Europe for two years with the La Mama troupe, he had studied in Denmark with Eugenio Barba, who had been a devoted disciple of Jerzy Grotowski. Thirkield freely used Grotowski's techniques as well as Barba's extensions. Barba was a self-proclaimed psychic who approached acting through an intensely personal, internal view. At the same time, since Grotowski was Barba's base, the minimalist approach was evident. The actor was trained to rely more on the self and the body in motion than on the external accoutrements of set, costume, decor, and even, in some respects, the play.

At opposite ends of the spectrum, Thirkield assimilated the "wildly wonderful movement improvisations" from his dance therapy studies with Blanche Evan, which both he and Mason felt helped the actor develop the elasticity necessary to play a multiplicity of roles. As if this were not eclectic enough, Thirkield also introduced exorcistic-type vocal experimentations reminiscent of Artaud, and even the yogalike body control of headstanding. As he explains it, "The standing on the head was simply to help the body find its own balance. I found that similar to playing a big moment in a play. Instead of getting all tense about it, just do it. Let it happen."

All this might have proved highly confusing except that Thirkield, a strong actor and director, was perhaps a born teacher more than anything else. He had an extraordinary way with people, and he had the ability to inspire trust — one of the most important prerequisites to teaching. The actors would try anything for him.

Thirkield's appreciation of the strengths and weaknesses of the various acting methods gave authority to his eclectic approach. "I've seen many actors from the Actors Studio who have auditioned for me," he recalls. "They were very relaxed, but they also feed themselves very painful memories in order to relive them. Whereas in the Meisner method, the emphasis is on getting *out* of yourself. Certainly you can feed yourself something from your own past to get your emotions cooking, but mainly you get your attention off yourself and onto the other actor and let it rip. When you finish performing, you feel as though you've expressed something from your own experience — it's quite real and very believable, and it's much healthier."

Similarly, many members of the Group Theatre, where Strasberg began relying on effective memory and improvisation to stimulate the actors' feelings, found his technique too painful to endure. Actor Morris Carnovsky eventually dismissed it completely as he found it very harmful. Actress Margaret Barker says she thought she "was going to crack" in being urged to relive her roommate's death repeatedly in order to effectively use her pain. Actress Phoebe Brand claimed that "Lee crippled a lot of people. . . . acting should be joyous, it should be pleasurable and easy if you do it right."[1] And this was exactly Thirkield's philosophy: acting should be enjoyable. He would never waver from this philosophy, whether he was dealing with an acting workshop, an audition, or directing a play.

This philosophy would be an important contributing factor to the wholeness Mason and Thirkield brought to Circle Rep with their individual personalities and different approaches to theatre. "Both Marshall and I believed in the concept of the Circle very strongly," says Thirkield. "We saw the same thing. A good part of that vision came from our work at Northwestern."

But while both of them had the same vision of what an acting company should be, their personal manner of dealing with day-to-day realities acted as an important element in creating a company texture rich in diversity. "Marshall had the 'pure' vision," Thirkield says,

> and was so wonderfully able to write all these things down on paper and send them to the National Endowment to get money. He was just so above everybody—in his personality. He had these great ideas in theatre. For a while he was copying Alvina Krause, who was very queenly; Marshall was very princely. Very. Which made it a bit difficult sometimes for people to talk to him. Whereas I was sort of a humanizer. That was my contribution. I was able to talk to people and get a nice, warm relationship going. I wanted whoever came to work in our theatre to feel welcomed. I wanted them to feel relaxed and at home— enjoying themselves and not worrying. I knew they all wanted to please Marshall because he had such high ideals, and I said, "To hell with all those. Just work with what you have now. Eventually you'll get there." It was a balancing act that Marshall and I did, but the main thrust of the theatre was basically both of us. We approached it differently, that's all. He always was, and still is, a fanatic for details and artistic integrity, where I tend to say, "Relax. Do what you can. Don't work so hard for results."

Although Mason found it a burden at times to know people were intimidated by him, he also believed he needed to be captain of the ship, with the kind of distance that implies. Again, the balance came from the fact that Thirkield was not interested in that kind of position, nor could his temperament support separation. "My thing is, 'No, no, relax!'" he says enthusiastically. "People come to audition for me and I have them do their scene a couple of times, which stuns them. Nobody's ever done that. It's always, 'Next!' I want to tell them they're terrific and that their work is wonderful. I think it comes from my being an actor. Actors have enough rejection as it is."

No one worked harder than Thirkield to develop the togetherness that would be at the very core of the ensemble. His own private needs for interaction translated into encouragement of self-exploration and trust in acting sessions that strongly resembled encounter groups. This, perhaps more than anything else, represented the true legacy of the sixties culture with its concentration on encounter groups, group therapy, marriage encounters, communes, Transcendental Meditation, yoga, and so on—all of which, when brought into the workshops, created an atmosphere where any exploration was possible once the mutual rapport had been established.

In the drug experience going on around them, many barriers were being broken down through chemically induced stimuli. At Circle Rep, barriers were now being broken down through exercises in trust. Thirkield's approach was deliberately geared to getting the actors to such a point of trust that opening up first to each other personally, and then by artistic extension to their scene work, was a natural evolution.

Thirkield's work in the Exploration Workshop eventually led to the first production of the Circle Repertory Theatre Company: *A Practical Ritual to Exorcise Frustration after Five Days of Rain* by David Starkweather, a playwright from the early Caffé Cino days. Rob Thirkield directed, with sets by Lanford Wilson, masks by playwright Doric Wilson, and theatre stages designed by Marshall Mason. Thirkield gives a soft extended scream to the ceiling when he thinks about the first production. Then he grins broadly. "It was actually a wonderful play for the Circle at that point . . . especially because of my workshop. In the workshop I had them all running and jumping and dancing and standing on their heads. This play had a looseness about it that fit."

Actually, the production brought many of the workshop techniques into sharp, pragmatic focus. "The play was about Noah and his sons," Thirkield continues, "and they were on the ark for ages. It took place in the past, but kind of in the present as well. We had all kinds of stuff going on—a radio, rock music—all of these scenes between the sons and their wives. David had these little characters running around doing all kinds of weird things. There was a weatherman (played by Burke Pearson, who is still with the company today) who kept saying that the rain was going to continue, while he walked around with a chart of the human body. It was a very far-out play."

Despite casting problems with Starkweather—"We battled all the way," Thirkield recalls—the play was quite well received. Critics from many West Side newspapers who came to their opening thought the production exciting and began to take notice of the new company on the Upper West Side. Thirkield's favorite story about the production, however, has little to do with the reception or with lofty goals and concepts.

We were about to open Starkweather's play. We had no electricity. We had a lighting board but no electricity. So we said, "How are we going to do this? We don't have any money for electricity in the budget." Sharon Madden, who was in the play, had a friend who was an electrician. He was called in a hurry and he came right in with this huge cable which he ran out of the window and down the side of the building. I thought he plugged it into an outside wire. I didn't think too much about it. The lighting board worked and that's all that mattered. But a year later, when we could afford a better hookup, the electrician said, "Oh, you've been hooked up to Thom McAn downstairs." The big story! Thom McAn supported us for a year without knowing it.

With Thirkield's production of Starkweather's play, all indications seemed to point to what would be a very experimental new theatre group. In some respects this was almost true, for several months later the Circle Rep presented two versions of Chekhov's *The Three Sisters,* both directed by Mason, one of which was highly unorthodox. The two versions, which were presented on alternate nights, came directly out of the work that had been done for the past eight months in Mason's Method Workshop. While Mason directed one version in the traditional manner, he presented the second version in a completely experimental style—no scenery, no props, modern dress, and only two A-frame ladders on stage.
As Mason points out,

If you were traditional, as I am, it was shocking in a way. This was the first experimental Chekhov I'd ever heard of. Shakespeare was experimented with all the time, but I'd never seen it done with Chekhov. As far as I know, we did the first one. Now it's commonplace. But at the time, it was a wild, experimental thing to do, and frankly, I wouldn't have undertaken it if it hadn't been for the fact that we had a wonderful traditional production on alternate nights. You want to see *The Three Sisters* done right? Come see our traditional production. You want to see what Chekhov sings to our times specifically in a kind of sorrowful way? Come see our experimental production.
    The traditional production really was amazing because we were doing it in June–July. We had no air conditioner and the temperatures were above 90 degrees—on a couple of occasions, close to 100 degrees in that space. Our costumes came from the American Costume Company in San Francisco. They were wonderful costumes. Heavy coats and uniforms—authentically

beautiful. Russian bear hats. The play went up at eight and came down at midnight. It was four hours long. The actors were up there "freezing" to death in the Russian winter. We seated a hundred people, sold out every performance and never lost a single person before the final curtain despite the heat. Nobody ever left. We only played twelve performances, but still, it gives you the idea of the power of this production.

Then there was the experimental version. A program note on the production explained:

Chekhov wrote this play in 1900 — twenty-one years after the assassination of a benevolent liberal Czar, Alexander II. He wrote it under the repressive right-wing rule of Nicholas II — the last Russian Czar. He wrote it only five years before the abortive Russian Revolution of 1905. We perform this play today under similar circumstances. The extent of the experiment is to explore the relevance to today's world. To us this has meant simplifying everything in the production to capture the essence of Chekhov's messages and the central void of living in today's world.

Although the Circle Repertory Company was, and still is, essentially apolitical, according to the program note one of the reasons for the experimental approach was "to try to find the parallel between what was happening in Russia during Chekhov's time and what was happening in the United States currently." It was impossible for the group to remain totally unmoved by the tragedies that had befallen the country. Briefly, within a two-month period in 1970, American combat troops had entered Cambodia, a Greenwich Village townhouse on West 11th Street (a cover for a Weatherman bomb factory) was demolished by explosion, four students were killed by the National Guard at Kent State University, and two black students were killed by police gunfire at Jackson State College in Mississippi. In the face of these catastrophes, the feeling was strong at the Circle Rep that if ever there was a need for the arts to make a statement, this was the time. As a group, they joined a 400,000-person march to Washington, D.C., protesting the invasion of Cambodia. Their participation in the march was partly to research the play they were performing and partly a demonstration against the tragedy of the Vietnam War. The experimental production of *The Three Sisters* reflected these events and emotions. As the last line of the program note read,

"The guideline for the experiment was the question: How would Chekhov make use of modern theatre techniques if he had written this play about our own revolutionary times?"

The physical setting for this version established its experimental nature. Opposite the proscenium, they had erected a diamond-shaped thrust. Stretching between the proscenium and the thrust was a long runway that could be put in place when the experimental version was being performed. The audience sat mainly on either side of the runway on pillows, while a few sat on the visible traditional set in the middle of "Prozov's living room" facing the thrust. No one in the young blue-jeans- and-sweat-shirt crowd seemed to mind.

As Thirkield says, "These kids came in from the street — from the neighborhood. They had never seen a play in their lives. We did it very hippie — sort of Woodstock. I don't think they would have watched the traditional version but they watched the entire experimental production."

According to Mason,

> Our Russian army in the play was made up of hippies with tie-dye uniforms. Joe Butler, who was the drummer for The Lovin' Spoonful, played Vershinin. At the moment where Vershinin says, "Just imagine what it would be like, what people would think . . . ," he stepped down on the runway, lit a joint, and passed it around to the kids who were sitting around on the pillows. He talked to them and it was incredible. I vividly remember the moments we used to interpret rock music — the appropriate moments. I remember using Jimi Hendrix's "The Star Spangled Banner." At the closing of the play when Masha and Vershinin are parting,they climb up the A-frame ladder for their last scene. They touch at the top of the ladder; he starts down to leave her and the ladder absolutely parts them. Meanwhile, the soldiers were singing Paul Simon's "Homeward Bound." All that was in the play. The soldiers were singing — the band was playing — the soldiers were marching off to war.

These two simultaneous productions of *The Three Sisters* presented a prophetic view of the future of the neophyte Circle Repertory Company. Although the experimental production created most of the attention with its controversial contemporary explorations, the traditional version was at the heart of the direction they would pursue. The experimental version was done not in place of, but in addition to, the realistic one usually expected with Chekhov. Thus, Circle Rep clearly stated that although experimentation is necessary and freeing, tradition is also essential. Realism has the power to synthesize traditional values into easily recognizable plays with humanistic concepts, and should always be preserved. Although the play used for this demonstration was not new, the same concept would be used with original material as the seasons progressed. In effect, the Circle Repertory Company was saying, "Yes, we rebel; yes, we experiment; yes, we reflect contemporary realities, especially in times of severe strife. But we will not eliminate the beauty and values of tradition. We will not forego the poetry of language no matter how powerful the images of visual theatre can be."

The Circle Repertory Company presented a total of thirty public performances during its first year. Despite such a minimal output, by the end of the season Circle Rep was awarded a grant from the New York State Council on the Arts for the excellence of the work created in the traditional version of *The Three Sisters.* Simultaneously, the Circle Rep received a grant from the Peg Santvoord Foundation for the experimental version. (The Santvoord Foundation, whose sole interest is in experimental theatre, continued to award grants to the Circle Rep for almost a decade in recognition of the persistent experimental thrust in their work.)

The approval demonstrated by this immediate recognition of their efforts not only boosted the confidence of the young company, but made increased production activity financially feasible. Had it not been for these grants, Circle Rep might have followed the course of commercial theatres, all of which were immediately affected by the postwar recession, and raised ticket prices in order to accommodate the ever-increasing costs of production. Higher ticket prices made 1970–1971 one of the highest-grossing commercial seasons ever, but less money was available for production. Less money almost always meant fewer risks were likely to be taken. It is not surprising to note that most of the quality shows on Broadway, such as *Home, The Philanthropist,* and *How the Other Half Lives,* were imports from England with good advance notices and an already proven track record. None of the plays reflected an awareness of the transitional social trends that were beginning to happen in America. Even off-Broadway, usually a barometer of the times, was not reflective of the pulse of change. This was the year of *Miss Reardon Drinks a Little* and *Lenny,* both of which made powerful statements regarding what now seemed the almost antiquated close-mindedness of an earlier era. Even John Guare's *The House of Blue Leaves,* which won the New York and the Los Angeles Drama Critics Circle Award for Best American Play of 1970, was focused on the private and personal interaction within a family structure, and Paul Zindel's 1971 Pulitzer Prize–winning *The Effect of Gamma Rays on Man-in-the-Moon Marigolds* concerned the individual's inability to survive a monstrous family life except in a mutated state. Similarly, the Circle Rep's 1970–1971 slate demonstrated a departure from current American social preoccupations and looked mainly overseas for inspiration. During this ambitious second season they presented six major productions, five of which were written by foreign playwrights: Dylan Thomas's *The Doctor and the Devils,* Witold Gombrowicz's *Princess Ivovna,* Samuel Beckett's *Waiting for Godot,* Ronald Mele's *Paderewski and the Garbage Thieves,* Eugene Ionesco's *The Future Is in the Eggs,* and Molière's *The Doctor in Spite of Himself.*

Not only did this represent a doubling of the major production load of the first season, but a concurrent workshop production program was developed in which four workshops were interspersed with the major productions: Lanford Wilson's one-act *Sextet (Yes);* an experimental version of August Strindberg's *The Ghost Sonata;* an adaptation of Arthur Miller's *Death of a Salesman;* and Helen Durberstein's new play, *Time Shadows.*

The season reflected the desire to work both with classics and with a wide range of genres, from the tender absurdism of Beckett to the nightmarish expressionist fantasy of Strindberg's journey through the subconscious. Very little lyric realism is seen in this ambitious slate; the determination of an identifying trademark was not only unimportant, it was not even a consideration. What was crucial at this time, however, was the growing relationship with the audience. The most important aspect of the first season had seemed to be the preoccupation with finding the actors and creating a common language. Now the emphasis shifted towards sharing the working process with the audience. Although the play selection for the mainstage demonstrates a willingness to experiment in terms of style and form, plays that were being developed in workshop for future projects, such as Duberstein's and Wilson's, show that the relationship with the audience was being encouraged in a participatory capacity. Even at this early stage, the seeds were being sown for the formal play development programs that would later emerge as Projects-in-Progress (PIPS) and Extended Readings (ERS). Equally significant was the fact that the workshop process, which continued at great pace, was being done now with an end product clearly in mind for the next season.

The company worked hard and long hours without complaint and without pay. Individual payment hardly seemed important when so much exciting theatre was happening. Nor was it so unusual for actors not to make money in the post–Vietnam War recession; professional acting was very much affected. According to Equity, only 14 percent of its members had worked during the season with an average income of $2,500.[2]

None of the financial hazards affecting most of the theatres around them seemed to bother the Circle Rep at this time. However, when the company returned from Thirkield's Woodstock retreat to their third season, there were some noticeable changes on the theatrical scene. Black theatre was increasing; the Repertory Company of Lincoln Center was receiving critical acclaim for quality of production, but suffering through tempestuous managerial controversy; and although twenty-six new plays appeared on Broadway, no Pulitzer Prize was awarded at the end of the season. Off-Broadway had fewer productions and lower quality than the previous season, with only forty-six openings and no hits, while off-off-Broadway had its most prolific year, totaling more productions than Broadway and off-Broadway combined.[3]

By this time, Dr. Harry Lerner's role in the Circle Theatre had changed. He and members of C.I.R.C.L.E. had acted like board members of the theatre company, offering suggestions and criticisms of the operations, none of which was taken seriously. Dr. Lerner now stepped back to enjoy the acclaim of the acting company he had helped to launch as part of his world peace movement. The theatre was the only one of the art, music, dance, and theatre groups that had materialized out of Lerner's original dreams. That it was demonstrating signs of endurance was astonishing. Neither Lerner nor his organization had ever been able to raise money to aid the growing company. Financial support came solely from Thirkield, until grants began to enrich his yearly support.

Despite success, by the end of the season there was a good deal of frustration within the group regarding perceptions of the future. Most of the twenty-five members were interested enough in the company and caught up enough in its movement to want it to develop further. The ten productions of the second season had only whetted hungry appetites. With the summer months stretching before them, Thirkield came up with an idea that would eventually develop into a summer tradition for the company. He had once had a house in Woodstock, New York, in a lovely, quiet area away from theatrical mainstreams. It was decided to take the entire company to the same area in Woodstock for a full summer of work and reacquaintance. This was very reminiscent of the Group Theatre's summer at Brookfield Center in Connecticut in 1931, where work, relaxation, lectures, and rehearsals determined the philosophy of the company and integrated the members into a solid working unit.

At his own expense, Thirkield rented a huge ten-bedroom mansion. A cook was hired who prepared steak every night and several company cars were at their disposal. Mason recalls with amusement that a group of "drop-outs" from *Hair* was living down the road from them in a *real* commune at the time that the Circle Rep company was actually living quite well. "Fortunately, Rob Thirkield had the money," Mason says candidly.

The summer was a consolidating experience for the company. The surroundings were luxurious but the work was intense. Residents worked from early morning until late at night on improving themselves as artists. During the day they did exercises out in the sun on the grass. At night, group improvisations indoors sometimes continued into the early hours of the morning.

As Thirkield vividly recalls,

> We had a wonderful experience in Woodstock which I will never forget. We were rehearsing a play in the house. We finally got to the third act at three o'clock in the morning. There was a fire — people from the town to take care of — a doctor. I was playing the doctor. I got Tanya and some whiskey and went down to the basement. Then when the time came, Marshall banged on the floor and I came up and saw all these bodies lying around the living room being bandaged — terribly hurt. And then I went to Irena's room, washed my hands in the sink and started crying. I mean — we were living the role. Then I came down against all these bodies. They kept calling, "Doctor, Doctor. . . . " It was wonderful. An incredible experience. How to recreate that. . . .

Although they rehearsed entire plays, they did not perform in Woodstock at this time. They reworked *The Three Sisters,* a constant source of inspiration. They improvised on *The Ghost Sonata.* The time spent in Woodstock helped to strengthen not only their combined working methods but also their spirits as well. They came back to New York with renewed energy and based their next season on the work they had done in Woodstock.

Experimentation became the catchword, while the classics took a secondary position. Of the four major productions, three were original works by contemporary playwrights. Once again the style within the season varied widely, from strict realism, to farce, to reinterpretations of the classics. The 1971–1972 season presented a new adaptation of Chekhov's *The Three Sisters*; an experimental version of Strindberg's *The Ghost Sonata;* Berilla Kerr's new play, *An Elephant in the House;* and Helen Duberstein's *Time Shadows,* this time as a major production. In addition, they played a varied series of workshops, all of which were open to the public: Richard Steele's two plays, *Denim and Rose* and *Howie;* company member Conchatta Ferrell's *Danny 405,* and Boris Vian's *The Empire Builders.*[4]

With Boris Vian, Mason and the Circle Rep turned again to a modern European writer of the absurdist tradition. Although later than Ionesco and Beckett, Vian is still in the modern French tradition of experimentation in form and style, breaking down the walls of realism both in the theatre and in everyday life. The pattern of turning to modern young European writers seemed to be developing at Circle Rep; the following season, a workshop of Peter Handke's *Offending the Audience* was presented. However, with growing expectations for new American plays, this pattern soon ended. By 1973–1976, the second period of its development, the company began to focus almost exclusively on new plays by American writers. A later return to Europe for plays would be only for the classics.

More so than any previous season, the third season at the Circle Rep was devoted to a combination of classics and new plays. Productions were experimental, traditional, and conservative. The workshops found new plays, and tried old ones in new ways. This was the last year in which the balance of experimentation and traditional presentation was so complete in both the mainstage and workshop season. Significantly, it was also the last season that the Circle Rep did not have heavy critical attention. During the following two seasons, 1972–1973 and 1973–1974, the Circle Rep began to appear in the critical consciousness with increasing frequency and scrutiny.

It is in this context that the importance of the final workshop presented during 1971–1972 is noted—a revival of Lanford Wilson's one-act *Ludlow Fair.* For Wilson, suffering from severe writer's block, had finally come uptown to the loft to "hang around."

6

The Turning Point
— 1973

LANFORD WILSON, who had enthusiastically supported the concept of a company and had often prodded Marshall Mason toward such a goal, was not involved in the actual setting up of the new company. At the time that the Circle Rep was forming, Wilson, then 32 years old, had three major full-length plays in production: *The Gingham Dog, Lemon Sky,* and *Serenading Louie.* It was a very productive period for Wilson in terms of exposure, but a devastating one in terms of success.

The Gingham Dog, about the marital breakup of a black social worker and a white lawyer, had its premiere performance at the Washington, D.C., Theatre Club in 1968. The play originally showcased under Mason's direction at the New Dramatists in New York.

Coming out of Wilson's work at the Actors Studio, where he was keenly aware of the polarizations between whites and blacks, *The Gingham Dog* starred George Grizzard and Diana Sands, both of whom were commended for the sensitivity of their portrayals. The excitement of having it picked up for his first Broadway experience, however, was quickly dispelled when it closed after only five performances at the John Golden Theatre following unfavorable notices in March 1969.

Lemon Sky, Wilson's autobiographical account of the reunion with his father, opened at the Studio Arena Theatre in Buffalo before it was brought to the off-Broadway Stage Arena a year later in March 1970. Although Clive Barnes, then with the *New York Times,* reviewed the New York production favorably, it too closed quickly after only seven performances. Sensitive performances—Christopher Walken as the son and Charles Durning as the father—could not save the play. Its failure was particularly painful for Wilson since it had been a difficult play to write. It had taken him ten years to sort out the unhappy early experiences with his father. *Lemon Sky* had drawn criticism earlier. When the play opened at the Studio in Buffalo, it elicited an outraged letter from a woman who was appalled at the "smut" being screamed from the stage. It is easy to pretend this kind of attack can be dismissed. Although the artist may defend himself as Wilson did in "Dammit [sic] Lady," a magazine article, he heard every word. Something had moved the "Dammit Lady" enough to sit down and write a letter. Wilson himself interpreted her complaint as a longing for a theatre that "reflected the aspirations of our pioneer fathers and how we have embodied and made manifest those high dreams." Nevertheless, her open letter stung enough to elicit Wilson's defensive response: "Dammit Lady, that's all I ever try to do."[1]

Wilson could find nothing positive to glean out of the failure of *Lemon Sky*. There seemed to be little, if any, support from the producers. What Wilson did not fully realize at the time was that working in commercial theatre was a very different experience from working in places like the Caffé Cino or La Mama, where money was never a major factor outside of operating necessities. Also, even in the best of circumstances, the sense of non-participation that occurs when a playwright hands his material over to a producer was a new experience for Wilson, who had been in the habit of constant and complete communication with his directors and casts.

Nor was the experience any better with *Serenading Louie*. It opened at the Arena Stage in Washington, D.C., in May 1970, two months after *Lemon Sky*. Once again Wilson was shut out of the kind of participation theatre that so nourished him, as he watched rehearsals from the back of the theatre with little input. *Serenading Louie* is a chilling four-character play about the collapse of two marriages and the resulting murder in one. It successfully straddled the fence between realism and theatricalism, something Wilson was experimenting with, and in this sense was an artistic achievement. However, it did not approach the commercial success it would achieve in its 1983 revival in New York. For Wilson, at this time, it represented another failure — three in quick succession, even though there was an obvious development in the plays of a recognizable Wilson style. Both *The Gingham Dog* and *Lemon Sky* displayed the simultaneous action and dialogue that has come to characterize a good deal of his work. Tensions mounting almost to the point of hysteria are created in both plays with this collage technique, moving back and forth between past and present. As Mel Gussow described *Lemon Sky*:

> . . . counterpointing conversations, directly addressing the audience in the middle of scenes so that the play became a mood-filled overlapping sea of impressions.[2]

But four years of hard work had come to an ignominious end despite some positive reviews. The pain was all the more keen since Wilson had been consciously attempting new directions. Not since *Balm in Gilead* had he concentrated on the full-length format. Never before had he deliberately tried for such important plot thrusts in his work or made such a serious attempt to delve deeper into his characters. Most of his plays had dealt with characters deeply embedded in the atmosphere of their environment. Now he wanted them to be intensely delineated within the atmosphere of the lyrical mosaics he was creating. By the time he started writing *The Gingham Dog,* he felt that his work was becoming too facile and that he was not developing his characters as thoroughly as he might. Too many characters — *Gilead* had started out with fifty-five — limited the possibility of deep investigation. In *The Gingham Dog* he deliberately dealt with fewer characters. The moment he did this, the sets became more realistic and the play became more literal.

Wilson felt that even *Lemon Sky* was "sort of a throwback. I already had the plot and the story. I just hadn't been able to write it. I was very reluctant to go back to that kind of style because I felt it wouldn't develop. So it straddles the fence — half realistic, half theatricalized." This style was artistically more exciting, although not exactly what he was striving for. In recognition of this, he deliberately strove for another fence-straddler in *Serenading Louie.* Its long scenes take place in a realistic set. Yet there is a continued musicality to the movement of the dialogue, which is often directed at the audience, removing the play from the realm of total realism with the sudden disappearance of the fourth wall.

Throughout Wilson's work, however, the one common element is the beauty of the language. Developed from the inner rhythms of the characters, this lyricalization of dialogue creates the effect of a heightened form of realism — more in terms of a poetic aura rather than in terms of specific lines.

The Gingham Dog, Lemon Sky, and *Serenading Louie* are the intense efforts of a growing artist. Since all three plays were produced in immediate succession, Wilson found himself in one rehearsal period after another with little time to recoup losses or reflect on the reasons why. His efforts were met first with the heady success of production — including one on Broadway — followed immediately by commercial box-office failure and, paradoxically, by the kind of critical acclaim which is laced with enormous expectations.

"There were all the reviews for *Lemon Sky* saying all of these incredible things," Wilson recalls. "Saying all 'this gift,' all this everything. And it was absolutely clear that the next thing I had to do was write the great American play. It was a setup. 'Watch this person!' I could just put a piece of paper in the typewriter and write 'The Great American Play' by Lanford Wilson. As soon as it was set up like that, I couldn't write a word. I had not an idea in my head after *Lemon Sky* in 1970. It came from the 'Oh my God, we can't wait for his *next* play' kind of thing. What a kiss of death!"

And it was. Not since the early days in Chicago, when he did not know what to do with his life, had Wilson floundered so badly. The writing block was total; he felt crushed.

It was at this time that he began "hanging around" the new theatre company his friends had started uptown. At first he offered only encouragement. Then he began participating in the workshops like everyone else. He sat in on rehearsals, helped with the box office, scrubbed floors and walls, and answered the phone. Then, taking advantage of the six years he had worked in an artistic capacity in Chicago, he designed posters and helped paint and even design sets. All of this busy work was in keeping with the early spirit of the group in which everyone chipped in and did whatever had to be done. "Doing everything" was a legacy left over from the participation theatre of the Cino days, in part because everyone was young and enthusiastic and wanted total involvement, and in part because they could not afford to hire outsiders.

After several months, Mason decided to produce two one-act plays by Wilson that he had never directed before: *The Great Nebula in Orion* and *Ikke, Ikke, Nye, Nye, Nye.* They were to constitute the fifth major production of the Circle Theatre's third season. *The Great Nebula in Orion* is a melancholy reunion of two Bryn Mawr college friends, one of whom is a lesbian who has just been jilted. *Ikke, Ikke, Nye, Nye, Nye,* about a secret telephone breather, is in Wilson's own estimation a "silly little farce—but great fun." The bill featuring the two short, bittersweet plays was complementary, but together they did not constitute a full evening.

"Marshall decided to do those two because he had the right actors for them," Wilson recalls, "but others in the company won't have anything to do, I thought, so I wrote an acting exercise for them, *The Family Continues,* to fill out the evening."

It was so similar to an acting improvisation that Wilson did not realize it was the beginning of the crack in his two-year writing block. "In writing *The Family Continues,*" he says, "I did the same thing I'd done for *Wandering,* so I didn't have to worry about format at all. I just wrote this round and it was more like a problem of how to get all these lines to answer each other correctly because it's almost like a group sing-along. It's just ridiculous. It goes back into itself again. So it's just a problem. And it's very, very short. And I wrote it straight out like a puzzle and I gave it to Marshall, and he said, 'Oh what fun!' I didn't even know I'd written a play."

Mason sensed that Wilson's writing constriction was coming to an end even before Wilson did. Participating once again in the familiar group ambience was the stimulating factor. Mason immediately announced to the company that the Circle Theatre was going to produce a new full-length Lanford Wilson play the following season. With a production date in sight, it suddenly seemed possible for Wilson to write plays again.

He started work on *The Negro Plot,* a play which had been in the back of his mind for a long time. It was based on a true incident that took place in 1740, in which 150 Negro slaves in New York were killed— mostly burned at the stake—following suspicions of rebellion and potential uprising. Although Wilson felt the "black theme" was pertinent to contemporary America, before long he began distrusting his own motives for writing the play for this same reason. He abandoned the project, feeling that he was attempting *The Negro Plot* because it was very popular to write a black play at this particular time.

Now, ironically, Wilson was anxious and ready to write but had no actual project in mind. Once again Mason was present and influential at an important moment in Wilson's life. "So on that famous night that Marshall and I were painting the risers and getting high—we were using shellac and getting so high on the fumes," Wilson laughs, "we had to go out of the theatre every five minutes into the office or faint. I was never on drugs, but that night I did sniff glue or shellac. In between the fumes, I was telling Marshall that I was a train freak—not one of those who knows the name and time schedule of every train and what the conductor's name is. There are people who really know all that."

The new play was beginning to form. One of the people would be the seventeen-year-old call girl, a resident of what had once been an elegant hotel. The girl was already in Wilson's mind—not as a realized character yet, but more as an inner part of himself that he was sharing that night. "I am a train freak because I'm afraid of flying," Wilson says. "I like going from city to city on a train, seeing all of these old buildings because I'm an architect freak also, especially of antique homes and buildings. And you'd see some of the best buildings in a city abandoned—beautiful old train stations. They would stand abandoned while newly erected little ones stood in front, which were awful. I walked through any number of empty old stations. One could get in and wander through them—or maybe basements were still used and the entire upstairs was abandoned."

While Marshall and Lanford continued to paint the risers, an old song came on the radio, "The City of New Orleans," coincidentally a song about riding on a train. "And I said, 'Oh my God, I've been thinking of doing a play—a long aching lament for the lost railroads.' And Marshall said, 'Write that then if you're not getting anywhere with the other one.' I said, 'The play would take place in a hotel near a train station, and there would be this train freak and this engineer.' And Marshall said, 'Write it. Start it.' So I said, 'Okay. I'll work on that.' And I started working on it. I was using the hotel I used to live in, the *Balm in Gilead* hotel."

Wilson wanted the new play to follow the pattern of *Gilead,* but with the addition of all the sado-masochism he had left out of *Gilead.* "I was going to write a real hard-hitting play about that, which I did not understand at all," he continues,

> but thought I did. I had this guy kicking the coke machine and trying to get something out of it. . . . And this railroad engi-

neer comes in. He had been out flagging the train all night but he was really retired and wasn't supposed to be there anyway. He just does it to stay in practice. . . . And he's frozen and they give him coffee. . . . And then they go off and someone else came down . . . and it went on like that. Then "Milly" comes on and it goes on for a while. Then "April," the big fat whore, comes in. And I said, good, that'll be fun. She comes on saying, "Come on, what the f— is this?" And I knew the whore, and I said, I know this play. I'd been floundering around but as soon as "April" came in I knew! It's a whore's hotel. I was going to write this fifteen years ago when I was in Chicago, about the hotel that was shared half by whores and half by elderly people. And I said, "Got it!" Then "Mr. Morse" comes automatically and "Milly" has a reason to be there. But I didn't really know what the play was about until "April" said, "What the f— is going on now? Last night the boiler broke. The night before that. . . ." You know! Got it! Got it! And then it just started to fly through."

While Wilson was working on the play he went out to Sag Harbor, an old town on Long Island where he had bought an aging house that had been previously owned by a whaling captain. The house had four apartments, three of which were occupied with tenants. Wilson moved into the other apartment, but did not have the heart to ask the tenants he had inherited to move out. Ironically, he wanted them all to move because he could not bring himself to collect the rent. It seemed to him that he had not done a thing to earn the money. "It was the most awful, grubby feeling I've had in my life. And the first time the guy asked me to write a receipt for the rent, I almost said that they could live rent free. I couldn't deal with it." Wilson was being paid solely because of ownership, and not because he had earned the money by "digging" or "sweating," and he "hated it!"

"I'm a late riser," he continues.

There is a crazy guy—one of the three bums who had the upstairs back apartment. I had seen him and then he vanished. He was probably thirty but he looked very old. One of the guys was about sixty-five, and the other was the hugest, fattest guy in the world; he was about fifty. His name was Ace and they all lived in the upstairs back apartment. One morning, I'm awakened by this little white-haired woman who is a vacuum cleaner salesman in Sag Harbor—door to door. She's Ace's mother. I'm awakened by this "knock, knock, knock," and then she's sitting

at the foot of my bed. I don't wake easily. I tried to focus on
her. And she's saying, "Mr. Wilson, you're not going to kick
Ace out, are you? I've got a thing from a psychiatrist that says
he's practically normal. And you're not going to kick him out,
are you?" And she went on and on and I just wrote it straight
down the next day. Ace's name became "Horse" and she became
Mrs. Bellotti. I was taking anything and everything that happened. . . . So much of my life.

It took Wilson only three months to write *The Hot l Baltimore.* As
in *Balm in Gilead,* the dramatized incidents comprise an atmosphere
rather than a plot. The dramatic action is presented as a series of thematic motifs returning in variations which create a certain musicality
reminiscent of a sonata within the structure. The play takes place on
Memorial Day in the lobby of the once-fashionable Hotel Baltimore.
There is very little, if any, reduction in time. It is a sad hotel that has seen
prouder days — days before the "e" in the "Hotel" sign had disappeared
into the abyss of neglect — days before the caliber of the tenants, once
elite, was reduced to prostitutes, drifters, and the impoverished elderly.
Hanging over the building is the prospect of demolition; the Pioneer
Hotel up the street is currently under the ball of the wrecking crews.
Nineteenth-century "palaces" such as these were fated to disappear into
the world of nostalgic memories, like the trains whose whistles were still
occasionally heard in the distance. It is this — the end of an era — that is
the major theme of the play. Although a bittersweet nostalgia permeates
The Hot l Baltimore, Wilson celebrates that which is forever lost at the
same time that he mourns it.

Wilson's characters are very personally drawn. They are people who
made up his own world, not only when he lived in shabby hotels in the
Midwest, but also when he first came to New York and was forced to live
in even seedier hotels on the Upper West Side. There were the elderly
pensioners — from "Milly," who claims she can sense the presence of
ghosts, to senile "Mr. Morse," who sings at the top of his voice on his
"doctor's orders." Then there are the prostitutes. A seventeen-year-old
"Girl" identifies distant trains by their whistles and bemoans their coming obsolescence in an air age. She has a great desire to make everyone
happy and to meet Milly's "ghosts": "I want to see them and talk to
them — something like that! Some miracle! Something huge! I want some
major miracle in my lifetime." Then there is "April," a brassy, down-to-
earth prostitute who has seen better days. And "Suzy," who looks like a

Jewish Marilyn Monroe and always seems to have her head in the air. She inadvertently states the theme of displacement in the play when she wonders what will occupy the space that is currently filled by her room once the hotel is torn down.

What story line there is comes through "Paul Granger III" (who has come to look for his grandfather, a former tenant of the hotel), and the tough-talking "Jackie." Jackie is deluded enough by her great need to have something that belongs to her and her mildly retarded brother "Jamie" that she buys a "farm" through a radio ad. She wants to grow garlic organically so that it can be used as a natural pesticide.

At the end of the first act, Wilson uses his technique of overlapping dialogue like lines of music in counterpoint. All of the characters are basically reiterating their positions. Now they swell together like a harmonic chorus toward the act's climax. The technique is reminiscent of the second act of Chekhov's *The Three Sisters,* as each character speaks of the subject that is most on his mind. Although their monologues do not overlap, neither Vershinin, Masha, Tusenbach, nor Irina hears what the other is saying. In this sense a verbal counterpoint is created that has a similar kind of musicality.

In variations Wilson has presented the same theme throughout the first act — things die, vanish, or decay: the Pioneer Hotel is swallowed up by progress; ghosts from the Hotel Baltimore are presented as documentation of those who have come, gone, and left only a spirit of themselves. Like a musical motif, the trains also represent a variation on the theme of what is passing into obscurity. Now the once-elegant Hotel Baltimore is joining the list of things that are fading into the past — and so are its current inhabitants.

By the third act the tenants are packing up their belongings and leaving one by one. There is little to indicate that they will be moving on to a better life — rather the reverse — but there is no bemoaning their fate. They look to the future as though it holds bright promise for them. Suzy goes on to a "new life" with a pimp, blindly clutching great expectations of happiness. Milly senses that Paul's grandfather is still alive. The girl refuses to give up the search for him. "It's really chicken not to believe in anything," she says, though Paul has lost interest. Jamie is learning to dance with April, who insists that it doesn't matter how well he dances as long as he "moves."

As the future ghosts of the Hotel Baltimore, these characters should be filled with terror. Had they been written by Chekhov, they might have been charged with a sense of futility. Had they been written by Tennessee Williams, they might have been overcome with a sense of doom. As written by Wilson, they simply refuse to give up. Yet with his special tenderness for lost causes and unwanted people—the quietly alienated, the psychically wounded—and with his skill for orchestrating multiple scenes and evoking intense nostalgia for a way of life that is fading into the past, Wilson appears to be a spiritual heir to the poeticised realism that sparked such individuality in Chekhov and Williams. Despite major differences, there are many thematic and stylistic similarities worthy of exploration.

There is very little plot in *The Hot l Baltimore,* and what little there is, is drawn very loosely. The story lies in the idiosyncracies of the tenants of the hotel—their dreams, their foolishness, their hopefulness. Chekhov also dealt more in character and mood than in plot; often his characters' lifestyles were on the threshold of fading into the past. Similarly, Wilson deals with the dispossessed and the dreamers who live in a world that is quickly vanishing and who should have little reason to hope. However, whereas Chekhov dealt mostly with Russian gentry who had lived off the land and could not cope with the changing times that were making them a class of the dispossessed, Wilson deals with the more common elements of society in a fading urban setting—prostitutes who live off themselves, and the drifters and the elderly who have even fewer resources. With these differences, however, there are still strong parallels in the evocation of mood as well as in theme.

Mostly, Chekhov depicted the life of the landed Russian gentry who were being dispossessed because they could not adjust to changing times and new lifestyles. Steeped in memories of lost grandeur, they could only look ahead to a bleak and frightening future. Despite his lyricism, Chekhov's plays thus unveil a profound, though understated, feeling that the inevitable destiny of man is a tragic one. *Ivanov* presents the idle and ineffectual life of a landowner ruined by changing times and debt. *The Sea Gull* depicts the underlying theme of loneliness and isolation as each character fails to achieve his private dream. *Uncle Vanya* communicates a very subtle form of dispossession; the tragedy of the individual, as personified in the unrequited love all the characters feel for one another, is a palpable one. *The Three Sisters'* underlying current is, once again, dispossession, this time a material one. The characters live in a sterile, empty, changing world, continuously talking but never listening to each other. In the absorption of their own thoughts, they manage not to hear anyone else. And finally, *The Cherry Orchard* shows an entire generation turned out, dispossessed by a changing world that no longer has any room for them. The preoccupied characters helplessly witness the passing of a graceful era and the disintegration of their world. They talk and talk, but never do anything. The dramatic action is established at once: to wait. As the passing gentry, doomed to the inevitability of an oncoming revolution, clutch a heavily mortgaged estate, we see that theirs is a world of illusion. All of these plays convey Chekhov's deep sense of the tragic destiny of man.

It is easy to see why Wilson is often compared with Chekhov. Not only is Wilson similar to Chekhov in his general plotlessness, but also in terms of the content and themes he chooses to dramatize. Wilson too speaks of the dispossessed, the disenfranchised, and the lost, even though his characters have been imbued with a different breath of life. Chekhov's characters essentially do nothing, while Wilson's characters are always doing something. Although they too talk and talk, they just do not seem to get anywhere. But where Chekhov's characters demonstrate childlike responses to their situations, either bursting into tears or bursting into laughter while their world disintegrates about them, Wilson's characters are as busy as ever, unrealistically planning their futures—a garlic farm in the desert—while their world disintegrates around them. In Chekhov's plays, the characters' illusion that somehow something will happen only adds futility to an already stagnant environment. Not so for Wilson's characters, notably those in *The Hot l Baltimore;* the inhabitants of the hotel are survivors. They do not even sense their stagnation.

Another interesting comparison can be made between Wilson and Tennessee Williams, the true poet of lost causes. His preoccupations have always been society's fugitives—those who are psychologically maimed, such as Blanche in *A Streetcar Named Desire,* or the physically deformed, like Laura in *The Glass Menagerie,* to the point that their view of the world is often filled with terror. Williams spoke from a sense of the mores of the forties and fifties, often attacking in disguised form the underlying hypocrisy he perceived. Homosexual themes such as the subtle undercurrent of *Cat on a Hot Tin Roof* were never stated openly. Williams's own homosexuality was kept a secret for a long time. Wilson, on the other had, had no such restrictions placed upon either his personal life or upon the lives of the characters he created. Wilson's characters have the no-holds-barred freedom that came directly out of the sixties' culture. Despite underlying lyricism, many of Wilson's most memorable characters are foul-mouthed, and could even be considered the dregs of society—pimps, prostitutes, junkies, and pushers.

In Williams's plays, one character usually stands aside from the rest. By virtue of being different, he can see the world with a clarity (and often a horror) reserved only for him. This character never quite belongs wherever he is and appears to have the soul, if not the occupation, of an artist. Wilson's plays, on the other hand, have no characters who stand aside from the rest. Except for individual idiosyncracies, they are almost indistinguishable from one another. As threads of the same fabric, it is *together* that they comprise a communal difference from the rest of the world. Unlike the horror behind the perceptions of Williams's characters, their vision has a bizarre hopefulness with its own clarity, investing them with a deep-seated ability to survive despite the most awesome obstacles.

The most striking similarity between the three playwrights is lyricism overriding realism, and the ability to create the entire fabric of a particular moment in time with an exquisitely painful sense of truth. Each presents masterful pictures of nostalgic moods, although Wilson's pictures—perhaps because of their contemporary quality—are considerably less delicate than those of his forebears.

Not only would *The Hot l Baltimore* break Wilson's writing block, but it would also prove to be the critical turning point in the fortunes of the Circle Repertory Theatre as well. The transition for the company from relative obscurity to the spotlight of public attention came in 1973, almost four years after the company had begun its operations. *The Hot l Baltimore* was critically and publically received so well that after its brief initial run at the loft, producers Kermit Bloomgarden and Roger Ailes transferred the play to the downtown, off-Broadway Circle-in-the-Square on Bleeker Street, on March 22, 1973.

Rob Thirkield sums up how the extent of *Hot l*'s success took them all by surprise. "Lanford, who hadn't been able to write anything except these one-act plays for two years, just sat down and—shoom!—wrote *Hot l Baltimore* for the company. So we did it and it was very strange; we just weren't sure. Lanford's agent came in and *he* wasn't sure. Then some critics came and said, 'You're going to move this to Broadway, aren't you?' And we said, 'Sure, I guess so.' So we took it to the Circle-in-the-Square with the original cast. It took the entire cast to move the play downtown."

Once again, it was directed by Mason, with sets by Ronald Radice, costumes by Dina Costa, and sound by Chuck London.[3]

The play had been written for company members. This was not the first time Wilson had written roles with particular actors in mind (e.g., he had written the role of "Scully" in *Rimers of Eldritch* for Rob Thirkield). However, this production would establish him as a playwright-in-residence at the Circle Rep in actuality as well as on paper. From the beginning his name had been in the Circle Rep's programs as one of their playwrights, although he had not written anything for the company until now. From this point on, however, writing for specific members of the company became an established part of Wilson's creative thinking.

The original cast was as follows:

BILL LEWIS	Judd Hirsch
GIRL	Trish Hawkins
MILLY	Helen Stenborg
MRS. BELLOTTI	Henrietta Bagley
APRIL GREEN	Conchatta Ferrell
MR. MORRIS	Rob Thirkield
JACKIE	Mari Gorman
JAMIE	Zane Lasky
MR. KATZ	Antony Tenuta
SUZY	Stephanie Gordon
SUZY'S JOHN	Burke Pearson
PAUL GRANGER III	Jonathan Hogan
MRS. OXENHAM	Louise Clay
CAB DRIVER	Peter Tripp
DELIVERY BOY	Marcial Gonzales

Only Tanya Berezin of the original founding four did not participate directly in this production; as Mrs. Rob Thirkield, she was on maternity leave.

For Wilson after three successive commercial failures and a devastating slump, the success of *The Hot l Baltimore* had, in his own words, "saved his life." He would always be grateful to the Circle Rep and company, but most especially to its artistic director, Marshall Mason, whose encouragement was so instrumental in causing the breakthrough.

"The Hot l Baltimore was a big event," Mason says, recalling the production with genuine pride. "It could still be argued that it became the longest-running American play in the history of off-Broadway at the time. *Vanities,* which actually played longer, had an interruption in its run, and normally when there's an interruption in a run, it is not considered to be the same run when it comes back. For some reason, with *Vanities* it was still counted as one run. But *Hot l* was the longest *consistent* run, about 1,200 performances. Clive Barnes wrote a review of *Hot l* in the *New York Times,* claiming that it was "the herald of a new era."

Clive Barnes's reference was to the fact that the play originated off-off-Broadway. It was unusual, not only for a play of its genre to have originated off-off-Broadway, but also for such a play to have successfully upgraded to off-Broadway. After it transferred to the Circle-in-the-Square for its extended run, Barnes wrote:

> One interesting economic point. This play was first produced Off-Off-Broadway where it had considerable success with both critics and audience. Now it is moving to Off Broadway as a tried and proved product. It has a cast of fifteen people. I do not for one moment believe that even with Mr. Wilson's considerable reputation behind it the play could have been staged in New York without this kind of Off-Off-Broadway try-out first. Here could be a herald of new patterns.[4]

Mason, never one to hide his feelings where theatre is concerned, says that although the reference to the off-off-Broadway "try-out" for the play was true, "I was offended by Barnes's attitude toward it because he was seeing it as an historical thing—an economic phenomenon. I was saying the hell with economics! Look at the work. Harold Clurman was pointing out that this was a real theatre company with a real ensemble. I was looking for people to look at the Circle artistically."

Marshall had no need to be impatient. The reviews were generally excellent. And even though the Circle Rep was never conceived as a production house, it is of interest historically that it was perceived as an in-town tryout for off-Broadway, as well as for Broadway, in place of the more common out-of-town tryout. In retrospect, it can be seen that the in-town tryout of new plays was indeed unusual enough to warrant comment by critics like Barnes, and with a successful precedent set, would become a common occurrence by the eighties.

The new company was in the vanguard of the off-off-Broadway

movement that was being perceived as a growing force in New York, much as the off-Broadway movement had grown to critical prominence in the early fifties. Until the establishment of the Circle Theatre and, several years later, Playwrights Horizons, the only off-off-Broadway theatre had been the Cino—now gone—along with La Mama and the Judson Poets Theatre. The Circle Rep was the first major off-off-Broadway theatre to attract prominent critics by providing new American plays for off-Broadway after their premieres at the loft.

The reviews for *The Hot l Baltimore* were almost unanimously good. Michael Smith and John Lahr of *The Village Voice*; Mel Gussow, Walter Kerr, Guy Flatley, and Clive Barnes, all of the *New York Times*; Jeff Street and Alan Wallach of *Newsday*; and Martin Gottfried of *Women's Wear Daily* all gave positive reviews, not only of the play but also of Mason's direction and the ensemble playing of the company as well. No longer was the Circle Rep being reviewed only by the little neighborhood newspapers, as had been the case when they first opened their doors to the public with David Starkweather's play in 1969. Now all the major reviewers were making the trek uptown to see what was going on in the little loft space that held no more than one hundred seats.

The Hot l Baltimore created landmark changes in the phenomenon that was off-off-Broadway, as is evident in the discernible upgrading of the Circle Rep's own status. After the success of *Hot l,* subsequent productions at the Circle Rep were viewed with a new seriousness and awaited with great expectations. Anticipations were raised regarding all future work, not only of Wilson's plays but also of the Circle Rep's role in theatre as well. It was a role that the critics would guide more and more in the direction of play development. Now, however, the most important change was that after four years the Circle Rep company was finally being taken seriously as artists by the most influential critics in New York—a change which they welcomed with confidence. It is doubtful that the Circle Rep could have withstood this kind of intense scrutiny and attention if it had not already had a solid base of work as a unified company which stretched back to 1965.

Two other important developments can be traced to *Hot l.* For the first time there was an awareness of the way of life the Circle Rep tried to create for its artists and the effect such an environment could have on play development. The principle had been stated clearly four years earlier by Mason: playwrights-in-residence would write directly for the company in a community-style environment with all of the protection and nurturing implicit in such an arrangement. Emory Lewis of the *Long Island Record* recognized the value of this arrangement, noting that Wilson was once again writing in the element that was most conducive to his particular talents:

> Lanford Wilson is now playwright-in-residence at the Circle Theatre and that is good news indeed. He writes plays that have real resonance and dimension. Here he can work with a large and experienced cast without the hit-flop pressures of Broadway.[5]

The second development was the enthusiasm with which the critics recognized and responded to what was in essence a reintroduction of realism into American theatre. Realism itself is neither new nor surprising. However, to reviewers steeped in expectations of the avant-garde, the bizarre, the highly experimental, or the blatantly confrontational every time they set foot in a non-Broadway house, it was certainly a surprise to see realism not only alive, but exciting and vibrantly alive in one of the most unlikely places to find it — off-off-Broadway. Alan Wallach of *Newsday* singled out the Circle Rep for its work in a realistic genre. Of Wilson as a contemporary playwright willing to explore realism again, Wallach wrote:

> One of the qualities that distinguishes Lanford Wilson from the other young playwrights to emerge from the Off-Off-Broadway scene in the last decade is his willingness to work within a conventional framework exploring relationships between recognizable people in believable situations.[6]

The Hot l Baltimore won the first in a long list of awards that would come to the Circle Rep and its members over the ensuing years of production. Wilson as playwright won the 1973 Outer Critics Circle Award, the 1973 Obie for Best Play, the 1973 New York Drama Critics Award for Best American Play, and *The Hot l Baltimore* was included in the *Ten Best Plays* annual of 1973.

Marshall W. Mason won the 1973 Obie for Distinguished Direction. Mari Gorman won the 1973 Obie for "Distinguished Performance," the 1973 Drama Desk Award for Best Performance, the Theatre World Award, and the Clarence Derwent Award for Best Performance. Trish Hawkins won the 1973 Drama Desk Award for Most Promising Performance, and the Theatre World Award.

As evidenced by the fourth- and fifth-season slates, the company was entering the mainstream; by the end of 1974, they were firmly placed within the context of New York theatre.

1972–1973 SEASON:

Three New Plays by Lanford Wilson – Major Production (last year's workshop)

A Road Where the Wolves Run – Claris Nelson – Major Production

Canvas – David Roskowski (later, David Ives) Workshop

The Hot l Baltimore – Lanford Wilson – Major Production

Icarus Nine – Bruce Serlen – Workshop

Peace at Hand – Richard Wolf – Workshop

When We Dead Awaken – Henrik Ibsen – Major Production

Offending the Audience – Peter Handke – Workshop

The Tragedy of Thomas Andros – Ron Wilcox – Major Production

Mrs. Tydings Mason-Dixon Medicine Man – John Heuer – Workshop

Smith Here – Ed Greenberg – Workshop

Snow Angel – Lewis John Carlino – Workshop

When You Comin' Back, Red Ryder? – Mark Medoff – Workshop

1973–1974 SEASON:

When You Comin' Back, Red Ryder? – Mark Medoff – Major Production (last year's workshop)

Straights of Messina – David Starkweather – Workshop

Prodigal – Richard Lortz – Major Production

The Amazing Activity of Charlie Contrare and the Ninety-Eighth Street Gang – Roy London – Major Production

Hothouse – Megan Terry – Workshop

The Sea Horse – Edward J. Moore – Major Production

him – e.e. cummings – Major Production

The Persians – Aeschylus – Major Production

One Person – Robert Patrick – Workshop

When Everything Becomes the City's Music – Lance Belville – Workshop

Not Enough Rope – Elaine May – Workshop

The Summer Solstice – Doug Dyer – Workshop

Busy Dyin' – Sheila Quillen – Workshop

All of this activity kept Circle Rep actors very busy at a time when 75 percent of Equity actors were chronically unemployed, only 22 of 95 Broadway productions presented over the two-year period survived their openings, and the Repertory Company of Lincoln Center gave its farewell performance (1972–1973).[7]

The twenty-six presentations by Circle Rep over the same two-year period demonstrated a willingness to explore many different types of plays — original, revival, American, foreign — and in so doing explore a wide variety of theatrical genres. Plays ranged from the somewhat realistic *A Road Where the Wolves Run* and the highly impressionist *Canvas* to the classical tragedy *The Persians,* the avant-garde *him,* and the social realism of *When We Dead Awaken.* The many and varied workshops, although remaining with the contemporary, followed the same pattern of diversity and also demonstrated a continued encouragement of member expression — all of this at a time when economic factors made 1973–1974 the year of revivals on Broadway.[8]

However, even though one play such as *Hot l Baltimore* might suddenly be able to raise critical consciousness to a theatre's existence and even establish its reputation, one play alone could not maintain a theatre's standing for very long.

Fortunately, the success of *Hot l* at the Circle-in-the-Square was quickly followed by the very successful *When You Comin' Back, Red Ryder?* by Mark Medoff, and the equally well-received *The Sea Horse* by Edward J. Moore. With three successive hits the Circle Rep was now officially on the map. Awards, recognition, public acclaim, grants, and — not insignificantly — the ability to produce two highly successful additional plays in immediate succession established the theatre as a significant presence on the New York theatrical scene.

When You Comin' Back, Red Ryder? was directed by Gene Frankel who, having staged Mark Medoff's *The Wager* at the Cubiculo Theatre in New York City in 1972, was an established associate of Medoff's. Continuity of artistic association was encouraged by the Circle Rep whenever realistically possible. The play takes place in New Mexico in a run-down diner on a lonely desert highway. While it raises an interesting contemporary question — where have all the heroes gone? — it thematically deals with the manner in which people handle their fears when they are confronted by violence and intimidation.

Moore's *The Sea Horse,* a two-character play, was presented under Mason's direction. It is about Harry, an engine-room seaman back from the sea, who is determined to marry his huge, tough-talking girlfriend, Gertrude, who runs a waterfront bar. Gertrude, unwilling to risk tenderness, is equally determined to throw Harry out. Under Mason's direction, whatever sentimentality might be in the script is skillfully turned into believable vulnerability and conviction as the two lovers reach out to each other.

Red Ryder and *The Sea Horse* were important in establishing that Circle Rep's success with *Hot l* was not a fluke. In fact, they added to the list of awards the Circle Rep was accumulating: the 1974 Outer Critics Circle Award to Medoff's *When You Comin' Back, Red Ryder?* for Distinguished Play, the 1974 Drama Desk Award to Medoff as Outstanding New Playwright, and inclusion of *When You Comin' Back, Red Ryder?* in *The Ten Best Plays* of 1974.

Other awards included the 1974 Obie for Distinguished Performance and the Drama Desk Award for Outstanding Performance to Kevin Conway for *Red Ryder,* the 1974 Obie for Outstanding Performance, the Drama Desk Award, and the Theatre World Award to Conchatta Ferrell for *The Sea Horse,* and the 1974 Obie for Distinguished Performance and the 1974 Drama Desk Award for Outstanding Performance to Elizabeth Sturges for *Red Ryder.*

By the time the off-off-Broadway Circle Repertory Theatre received the 1974 Drama Desk Award and the Vernon Rice Award for Outstanding Contribution to *off*-Broadway (italics mine), Clive Barnes's observation about the off-off-Broadway Circle Repertory Theatre Company providing new plays for off-Broadway seemed prophetic. Both *When You Comin' Back, Red Ryder?* and *The Sea Horse* followed *The Hot l Baltimore*'s lead and made the move to off-Broadway after their brief premiere runs at the uptown loft. *Red Ryder* opened at the Eastside Playhouse, 334 East 74th Street, in March, and *The Sea Horse* opened at the Westside Theatre, 407 West 43rd Street, in April.

Thus, within a twelve-month period, Circle Rep had three new American plays upgraded to off-Broadway houses. In retrospect one can see the presentation of these plays not only as a phenomenal achievement by the tiny Circle Rep company, but also as events which reintroduced realism as a viable contemporary genre and caused the reevaluation of off- and off-off-Broadway designations as well.

Reviewing *The Sea Horse,* Edwin Wilson of the *Wall Street Journal* summarized the development of off-Broadway as an answer to the increasing costs of Broadway productions. When off-Broadway became a victim of its own success and was "beset by the same problems of steep production costs which it had been created to solve," it spawned off-off-Broadway, which developed to fulfill the function off-Broadway once filled. In speaking of off-off-Broadway's offerings, Wilson wrote:

> As might be expected, the quality ranges from the stimulating and exciting to the awful. As for the types of offerings, they generally fall into one of two categories. The first are revivals, including everything from Medieval mysteries to Molière to Somerset Maugham. The second category included avant-garde or experimental works which by definition thrive best in the informal atmosphere of coffee houses or converted warehouses. . . . An exception to these general practices of off-off-Broadway is the Circle Theatre, a group which has come to prominence in the last two years for plays which are neither revivals nor experiments but new works in the solid, realistic mold so popular earlier in this century. Three plays which received enough critical and popular acclaim to move successfully to longer runs Off-Broadway.

Realism suddenly, and quite unexpectedly, became a prominent feature of off-off-Broadway. Although the off-off-Broadway movement dated back only to the early sixties, there had been no realistic theatre to speak of. Edwin Wilson closed his review with the following:

> Realistic theatre has been the predominant mode in the Western world for the last 100 years, but there have been times when it seemed to be in eclipse. Just at such a moment, a theatre like the Circle demonstrates that realism still makes a strong claim on theatre audiences even as we approach the last quarter of the 20th Century.[9]

The most interesting aspect of Edwin Wilson's view is his recognition of the Circle Rep as an *exception* to the usual fare produced off-off-Broadway.

It is from this time that the Circle Rep became labeled as the sole consistent purveyor of "lyric realism"—a realistic style of play and production which nevertheless is distinguished by its lyricism and poetry. It is a term that has clung tenaciously. The critics were beginning to speak of a Circle Rep "style," which they identified in these three productions. However, Mason is quick to point out, "We didn't choose this style. We didn't say, well, we're going to do American realism. These were our roots. These were the plays that interested us. Our style, the lyric real-ism, comes from growing up on Tennessee Williams, Arthur Miller, Robert Anderson."

Even so, this was hardly all they did. As Tanya Berezin insists,

> In the beginning we did a lot of experimentation, a lot of test-ing. There were no set boundaries. We didn't have a term like lyric realism at that point. That's a PR term. We do not func-tion with it. We never functioned out of it. There were no limi-tations. There are no limitations now except money. Lyric real-ism is a term that is used to describe us. It is not something that we seek to be. And then, it had to do with artistic excellence. The first play we did was *A Practical Ritual* by David Starkweather, who was a very abstract playwright and very alle-gorical. I don't think we set out for a style. What we set out to be was a company capable and available to a playwright's imag-ination. The plays that were successful defined whatever style they thought we were. But we did all sorts of different things in all sorts of different styles.

However, lyric realism would be what Circle Rep would be most famous for, even though, as Berezin justifiably points out, there had already been a history of experimentation in many of their productions, espe-cially in the highly eclectic training the company members received in the workshops under Mason's and Thirkield's tutelage.

But, like it or not, the high-profile hit plays which happened to be of the lyric realism genre brought them recognition. Without the hits, the Circle Rep would not have received the attention which eventually brought it to prominence. Although much well-deserved praise was lavished upon such production aspects as Mason's extraordinarily de-tailed direction, the tight ensemble acting, and the set designs, the critics were mostly responding to the new plays—and to their lyric realism.

It is not usually a company of actors that brings a critic into the theatre, unless it is a highly publicized or controversial one like Jerzy Grotowski's Polish Laboratory Theatre. It is not even the concept of a new company that draws a critic, unless that idea is something like the Repertory Company of Lincoln Center with its enormous advance press expectations. Apparently what most interests the critic is the play itself. The excitement becomes great indeed when a new play is reviewed posi-tively, since really good plays are rare.

In speaking of the new plays, it is important to remember that one of the reasons for the attention heaped upon the Circle Repertory Theatre Company was that critics recognized the return of a native American voice to the American theatre. After a plethora of abstract, absurdist, and direct confrontational theatre in the sixties, *The Hot l Baltimore, When You Comin' Back, Red Ryder,* and *The Sea Horse* seemed to indicate a welcome resurgence of the kind of realism associated with O'Neill, Odets, and Williams. It was as though the heirs of these playwrights had finally matured. The critical reception to the Circle Rep's new offerings seemed to indicate not only an appreciation of the quality of the plays themselves but also the recognition that it had been a long, dry spell of antirealism. The timing seemed right for plays that could successfully fill that void.

By May 1974, Mel Gussow acknowledged the sudden successful reappearance of realism on the New York scene. In "Suddenly Real Plays About Real People," Gussow wrote a lengthy article in the *New York Times* about the tiny off-off-Broadway company that had "given birth to three of the best plays in town." The article is an important recognition of the Circle Rep's artistic achievements as well as an important step in the acceptance of the company as a group of serious artists. Gussow also pronounced the introduction of new plays to be a major consideration and a primary expectation in his concept of the group:

> The Circle Repertory Theatre Company in a second floor walkup theatre on Broadway and 83rd Street (geographically about as Off Off Broadway as you can get) has in the past year become the *chief provider of new American plays to the New York commercial theatre.* (italics mine)[10]

The expectation that it would continue to provide this supply would evolve into a major developmental concern of the Circle Repertory Company Theatre as the years progressed. Although new plays had always been important, and from the earliest concepts the company was to be available to playwrights-in-residence, new plays had never been Mason's and Thirkield's primary concern. The major emphasis in the beginning had always been on the actors. Only much later did workshops geared specifically to the development of playwrights begin.

The turning point for Circle Rep, then, not only brought it recognition but also was about to dictate a new direction—the nurturing and development of playwrights who would supply the new plays that were suddenly expected by critics and audiences alike. There was to be a subtle shift in emphasis from the actor to the playwright. It is difficult to escape the sudden enormous importance placed on the plays, despite the fact that the actors have always been crucially important to the success of any play. At the Circle Rep, in particular, the actors' contributions were highly significant, not only in the actual production, but often in the developmental process as well; the entire ensemble concept of the company was based on mutuality of development and contribution. However, Circle Rep's future depended on continued seasons of well-received *plays*.

The pressure on Circle Rep fostered by its own success, though subtle at first, was nonetheless significant. To be labeled the "chief provider of new American plays" aroused major expectations. To be thus labeled at a time when American society was rapidly changing added an additional dimension to the pressure, for America in the seventies was changing in a great many ways—politically, socially, and economically— and contemporary artists were increasingly challenged to explore the new societal trends. It was inevitable that the "chief provider of new American plays" would be expected to set some of the new patterns, if not the entire pace.

A decade had passed since the enthusiastic young artists who founded the Circle Repertory Theatre Company began working together in 1965. *The Hot l Baltimore, When You Comin' Back, Red Ryder,* and *The Sea Horse* were a far cry from the explosion of experimentation and confrontational theatre that had identified much of off- and off-off-Broadway in the troubled sixties. Even then Circle Rep had reflected a comparatively conservative style—if not always conservative choices in subject matter—having been partially conceived in reaction to the less realistic presentational formats of the sixties. Mason had felt that all too often, only ideas were being presented, not experiences that happened in the present tense with the audience as witness and participant. With the kind of attention and critical approbation of such articles as Gussow's "Suddenly Real Plays About Real People," it was becoming increasingly clear that Circle Rep had found its artistic stride. Though a bit out of step with the times during the sixties, Circle Rep now revitalized the realistic genre for which the theatrical community was apparently hungry. It had succeeded in carving out a niche for itself in the mass of New York theatrical presentation. It was the home of realism in New York.

7

Changing Times, a Changing Rep, and Unlimited Growth

THE seventies were just as remarkable as the sixties in terms of the changes which created troubling new approaches to everyday life in America. Hardly anyone remained untouched or aloof. America's theatre, off-off-Broadway in particular, recorded the emotional pulse of the times with journalistic vigor. Politically, the nation was in great flux. There had finally come an end to the most divisive foreign war in the history of the nation, but the American soldier returned to silence rather than to ticker-tape parades.

The end of the war also helped to bring about a deep economic recession which, in turn, led to a stabilization of sexual mores. Concurrently, one of the most idealistic generations in the history of America had suddenly transformed into the "me generation" of the seventies. The make-love-not-war philosophy became the philosophy of self-fulfillment first. Living for others was now seen as a trap. The underlying bitterness inherent in the philosophy of "taking care of number one" was shrouding everyday business interactions as well as personal ones. According to sociologist Daniel Yankelovich, living for the self became part of the self-fulfillment ethic that had been confined to the college campuses during the late sixties, but had spread to society at large by the seventies.

The seventies also witnessed the rise of the women's movement, with all of the broad ramifications implicit in the sudden prominence of an entire population which had previously been in a subservient role.

Changes were occurring in other American institutions, most notably the presidency of the United States. With Watergate's sensational daily media coverage, the wiretaps, the Senate hearings, the "President is not a crook" speech, and the ultimate resignation of the president of the United States, there seemed to be little that could restore the faith of the newly disillusioned.

Ironically, it was in this unsettled, transitional atmosphere that the Circle Theatre, now in existence for five years, would find its artistic voice. Rather than being swept away by social and political changes, Circle Rep reflected and took advantage of the general swing toward conservatism. The subtle undercurrents of realism in much of the company's training, even when they were at their most experimental, were beginning to be looked upon with a new appreciation by outsiders. As previously noted, it was almost as though the audience's need for something "real" had finally caught up with what had always been at the artistic core of the company's explorations.

In reviewing Circle Rep's first fifteen years, there are four major stages in the company's development:

1. 1969 to 1973 — the period of greatest experimentation before the company became well known;
2. 1973 to 1976 — the period in which the company found its artistic stride and began to gain acceptance by the critics as well as the public;
3. 1976 to 1980 — the period of expansion and growth that maintained and secured the theatre's reputation as the home of new American plays;
4. 1980 to 1984 — the period in which artistic as well as financial problems became paramount.

During the first period one of the external factors that influenced Circle Rep's operations was the 1972 founding of the Off-Off-Broadway Alliance (OOBA) as a central service office. Not only did OOBA encourage the exchange of information and ideas among its two hundred member theatres, it also lent credibility and accessibility to off-off-Broadway as a united entity with a definite position and voice of its own.

During the second period several important factors affected Circle Rep, not the least of which were increased expectations from both public and critics. The constant critical analysis of the health of the off-Broadway theatre with its soaring costs, diminishing number of productions, and even fewer hits, created a great deal of speculation as to whether or not off-Broadway was "dead."[1] Concomitantly there were continuing observations that off-off-Broadway was growing in leaps and bounds and was replacing off-Broadway as the arena for vital experimentation and growth. The atmosphere for serious critical attention to and discovery of off-off-Broadway was never more ripe.

One definite sign of off-off-Broadway's growth was Equity's increasing interest in its activities. A staggering number of plays were produced — 548 in approximately 150 theatres — during the 1974–1975 season alone. Mel Gussow claimed that with at least fifty shows per weekend, it was becoming impossible for a critic to review everything that was happening.[2] Off-off-Broadway was the new hotbed of creativity; the sheer bulk of it was its highest recommendation. It also led to a highly controversial new Equity Showcase Code for off-off-Broadway issued on August 4, 1975. Jerry Arrow, executive director of Circle Rep at the time, felt that had the code been in effect in 1969, Circle Rep would not have been in existence in 1975. "By trying to make Off-Off-Broadway a closed shop," he said, "when it is not even commercial is silly as well as destructive."[3]

At the center of the dispute was the conviction of playwrights, directors, and even actors that not only was the revised code unrealistic and impractical but that it would kill the vital experimentation that distinguished the off-off-Broadway movement. Interestingly, while Equity was negotiating with the OOBA for what essentially amounted to control, Kevin McCarthy, who played the leading role in Circle Rep's *Harry Outside,* spoke in an interview with Tom Buckley of receiving a bare $5 per day for rehearsal and $12 per performance, which he willingly accepted in order to do the play. McCarthy felt that it was only on off-off-Broadway that a play such as this was possible. Commercial theatre would not be able to take the risk.[4]

One of the major battles erupted over the new provisions that called for 1) the mandatory use of Equity actors and stage managers, 2) minimum reimbursements for travel, and 3) setting aside part of the box-office receipts to defray additional expenses. William Lieberson, a playwright with the tiny Quaigh Theatre, claimed that the code could not possibly work for them. Despite the fact that their 64-seat theatre was filled to capacity every night when they produced the Pulitzer Prize–

winning *Street Scene,* they still found themselves $600 in the red after paying the rent. They would not be able to exist if they had to add the additional five or six hundred dollars to their expenses that the new code would mean.[5] Even more controversial in the new code was "a proviso that all members who rehearsed four weeks or less in a showcase production would automatically become owners of 2% of the present and future rights of the show, this share to rise to 8% under certain conditions."[6] Robert Moss, director of Playwrights Horizons and president of the Off-Off-Broadway Alliance, was quoted at the August 25, 1975, meeting as saying that the code was "turning off-off-Broadway, which is a developmental situation, into a horse race where you bet on winners,"[7] while Terrence McNally, author of the then-current *Bad Habits,* which had made the long transition from off-off-Broadway to off-Broadway to Broadway, argued that it would be the playwright who would have to share future profits; this would force many playwrights to use non-Equity members during the early stages of a play's development.

Donald Grody, executive secretary of Equity, did not believe that the new code could ruin off-off-Broadway as so many claimed. He felt that the financial stimulus of grants changed the economic structure of off-off-Broadway by making much more money available. This was arguable since production costs for off-off-Broadway were rising at the same rate as off-Broadway and the projected inflationary trends of the Carter administration were causing corporate funding to diminish to such an extent that the Off-Off-Broadway Alliance was trying to raise working funds collectively. Collective fund raising was an innovative idea. So, too, was the possible creation of an emergency fund to rescue the theatres that were already in imminent danger of closing down.[8] However, crucial to Donald Grody's position was the belief that the actor made an important contribution to the success of a play, and should have a piece of the pie if a nonprofit play became a hit. This was a highly inflammatory issue and would become a major battleground in the playwright's boycott of the code in 1980–1981.

Six months after the new code was presented, the controversial issues remained unresolved. Amidst proposals and counterproposals for modifications pending further investigation, the new code had been voted down by Equity members.

However, the issue of the Showcase Code for off-off-Broadway eventually became a moot point for the Circle Repertory Company. In 1976, Circle Rep signed a Mini-Equity Contract and moved up to off-

Broadway status, marking the beginning of their greatest period of expansion and growth, 1976 to 1980.

By the time of *The Hot l Baltimore* in 1973 more than half of the company, which now numbered twenty, had been with Circle Rep since the beginning. Loyalties seemed to be enduring in both directions, but the time had come for some basic changes within the structure of the company. Mason and Thirkield wanted to set out in the new directions opening up to them with a renewed sense of freedom. It was at this time that they decided to buy out the C.I.R.C.L.E. Their independence cost a great deal of money, but Rob Thirkield felt that it was worth it. However, it took four years before they decided to end their commitment to the C.I.R.C.L.E. In 1973 they became a separate corporation under the name of The Circle Repertory Company, Inc.

But an even more basic change was imminent, one that would affect every phase of their operations. The five-year lease on the loft theatre was due for renewal in June 1974. Despite the success of *The Hot l Baltimore,* Thirkield remembers that they "just kind of hung on there. We had two more plays to do and no actors, so we grabbed people from the street and put them into the next couple of plays."

Success was creating some unwanted attention as well as desired critical regard. "By then we were in our fifth year," Thirkield continues. "A clothing store was downstairs and since *Hot l* was doing well, the owners were saying, 'Okay, your rent is now a thousand dollars. And, also, you have to make it a legal theatre with the right fire exits'—things we had never bothered with. At this point, a big decision had to be made. Do we stay or leave? I decided we should move downtown to the square. The rent was $2,000 a month but it was a real theatre and a nice location. So we moved downtown."

Thirkield, in his usual easy manner, makes the decision to move sound simple, but it was hardly that. Circle Rep knew that it was becoming too big to continue in such a small, out-of-the-way theatre; the Upper West Side had never been a theatrical haven even for a theatre classified off-off-Broadway. However, there were inherent risks in a move at this critical point in their development. The commercial theatre world was beckoning; producers were coming to scrutinize each new Circle Rep presentation for additional commercial "moves." *The Hot l Baltimore* was being filmed as a situation comedy by Norman Lear, and already TV had stolen Mari Gorman and Conchatta Ferrell from the original Circle Rep production.

In the face of such open scrutiny, the company had to decide if it could maintain the personal sense of identity that had always been a part of its credo. On a pragmatic note, the group had to consider if they could survive the move as a company. First of all, physical upheaval could be dangerous to their comfortable sense of ensemble at a time when outside interest and commercial lures made the necessity of tightening up the ranks more important then ever. Second, they had to consider whether or not a move downtown would cost them the audience it had taken five years to create.

These were all important considerations, but philosophical discussions eventually had to be put aside, risks taken, and a decision made. Perhaps the only thing they could directly analyze was their audience. A great deal of time was spent going over subscription lists before the decision to move was finalized only one and a half weeks before the opening of the first play — Tennessee Williams's *Battle of Angels* — was presented at Sheridan Square. Inevitably, there were some defections by subscribers who lived on the Upper West Side. According to Mason, "A few people did not want to come 'all the way down to the Village.' But . . . only about a fourth of them lived in the West 70s and 80s. The others were from all over. Even from Upstate and New Jersey. There were many Villagers who ventured 'all the way uptown' to see us."[9] Eventually, it was obvious that the defections were more than balanced by new subscribers and that the advantages of a move back to the Village far outweighed any negative possibilities. On October 23, 1974, Thirkield signed a ten-year lease on the Sheridan Square Playhouse.

The building they were to transform into the Circle Repertory Company home had been built in 1919 in what has now become a historic landmark district. It had originally been built as a garage. In the late 1920s it became famous as Billy Rose's "Nut Club" (although the club was actually owned by Meyer Horowitz and later by Bernard Bernardi; Billy Rose was only one of the frequent patrons). After the heyday of the Nut Club, the building was refurbished as the Sheridan Square Playhouse. When the Circle Repertory Company took over the theatre in 1974, they exercised great care in handling the much-needed renovations, always mindful of its importance as a historic landmark. The facade of the building had taken on the grimy appearance of more than fifty years' accumulation of New York City soot. At a restoration cost of at least $3000, they sandblasted down to the original brick, discovering in the process the original blue mosaic rectangle sign over the door which read "Garage." Reminiscent in its design of Florentine house numbers, it can still be seen behind the huge red Circle Rep banner that waves outside the building. The seating capacity was 160, with flexible seating options possible. The playing area was equally flexible (e.g., proscenium, thrust, round). Unlike the loft, Thirkield remembers that the theatre, which was air-conditioned, looked pretty much the same when they moved in as it does today, except for cosmetic refurbishings. The beauty of the theatre was that with such flexible seating, the stage could be placed anywhere in the theatre. Eventually, the stage near the dressing rooms seemed to be the most convenient, so it has remained there for the most part.

For a brief time, there were offices behind the theatre. Later, they were moved to 111 8th Avenue for several years because of the need for additional space, and then in 1976 to 161 Avenue of the Americas, where they have remained. The separation of the administrative offices and the theatre created unexpected problems. As Rob Thirkield remembers, "What was so wonderful about being uptown at the loft was that you could come in and say 'Hi!' to the people in your office and go directly into the theatre. The separation made a great many strangers within the company." With physical separation the sense of "family" began to suffer, or at least change.

The company was no longer a little unknown family of artists; at the height of creativity, they were beginning to attract many people. At this time Tennessee Williams and William Hurt came to work with the group. With the beginning of the 1974 season, the move to Sheridan Square, and the placement of the company in the larger context of theatre through the attention of the critics and the production of *Battle of Angels,* the Circle Rep was entering the theatrical mainstream. Now they were working directly with, and as equals to, one of the greatest playwrights the American theatre has known. Working directly with Tennessee Williams — an early personal idol of the four founders — was a major accreditation of themselves as artists that not even the critics could match. The Circle Repertory Company left their theatrical adolescence firmly behind them as they planned the 1974–1975 season:

Battle of Angels – Tennessee Williams – Major Production
Innocent Thoughts, Harmless Intentions – John Heuer – Workshop
Fire in the Mindhouse – Lance Mulcahy, Arnold Borget, and Dion
    McGregor – Workshop

St. Freud – David Roskowski – Workshop
The Mound Builders – Lanford Wilson – Major Production
*Down by the River Where the Waterlilies Are Disfigured Every
    Day* – Julie Bovasso – Major Production
Scandalous Memories – Harvey Perr – Workshop
Afternoon Tea – Harvey Perr – Workshop
Harry Outside – Corinne Jacker – Major Production
Spring Awakening – Frank Wedekind – Workshop
Not to Worry – A. E. Santaniello – Major Production

Battle of Angels was the first play presented at Sheridan Square.
One of his earliest full-length plays, it had been written by Williams in
the autumn of 1939, and had originally been produced in Boston in 1940
by the Theatre Guild. The play had starred Miriam Hopkins with direction by Margaret Webster, and ran for only two weeks before closing. On
March 21, 1957, completely revised and presented under the direction of
Harold Clurman, it was brought into New York's Martin Beck Theatre
under the title *Orpheus Descending*. The next version was a 1960 film
directed by Sidney Lumet and titled *The Fugitive Kind*. It starred Anna
Magnani, Marlon Brando, Joanne Woodward, and Victor Jory. The
original *Battle of Angels* was a much lighter play than the two versions
that followed. In its original form, it received its New York premiere at
the Circle Repertory Company on November 3, 1974. Marshall W. Mason directed, with set design by John Lee Beatty, lighting design by
Dennis Parichy, costumes by Jennifer von Mayrhauser, and music by
Norman L. Berman.

During the rehearsal period it apparently was difficult to maintain
an ongoing relationship with Williams. He seemed a frightened man to
Tanya Berezin, who admits she could not get to know him very well
personally. It is not surprising that a great deal of care went into working
with him, not only because of the stature of his talent and reputation,
but also because his sensitivity and fear made him so vulnerable. Although Williams seemed to enjoy working within the supportive environment which was Circle Rep's trademark, and even permitted a Friday reading of some of his work, he did not have a great deal of trust for
anyone. His past intruded on his ability to accept completely the kind of
working relationship that was being offered to him. Although he was
formerly listed as a resident playwright for several years at his own
request and he worked with the group several times, he was never for-

mally a playwright-in-residence at Circle Rep; he was not expected to participate in the playwriting process that a resident playwright would ordinarily undergo in the open environment of the company. It was difficult, therefore, to assess how much value, or even enjoyment, Williams actually got out of the minimal Circle Rep process he would permit himself to accept.[10]

One person who did manage to get fairly close to Williams was young Daniel Irvine, who was acting as Marshall Mason's directorial assistant on *Battle of Angels*. Irvine, who is now in charge of the labs at Circle Rep, was only twenty years old at the time. He had been a visual artist who made the transition to theatre when he volunteered his services to the young company on 83rd Street and found himself hired instead. It was Irvine who became actively involved with Tennessee Williams during *Battle of Angels*. Irvine recalls that one of his first assignments as directorial assistant to Mason was to keep Tennessee Williams company.

"It was quite wonderful," Irvine recalls. "Williams would go from one bar to another and I had to make sure his mink coat was not ripped off. And the man still owes me money! He played a lot of pinball and never had any change. Quite wonderful for me. So many prominent theatre people, including Tennessee Williams himself, in so short a time in New York."[11]

The reviews for *Battle of Angels* were uniformly good, although not ecstatic. The production was also noted for the Circle Rep's customary attention to detail. Just as one sensed that the bar in *The Sea Horse* could actually have served drinks, the "Terrence Mercantile Store" in *Battle of Angels* "was reproduced down to the jukebox, pinball machines and shoeboxes filled with dowdy shoes."[12] The Circle Rep was applauded not only for the rediscovery of a Williams play that deserved attention but also for the newly restored little playhouse on Sheridan Square—a welcome addition to the off-off-Broadway theatrical scene.

Besides being the first production at Sheridan Square, and the first Circle Rep collaboration with Tennessee Williams, *Battle of Angels* also introduced a key element in the continuing artistic evolution of the company: set designer John Lee Beatty, whose ability to create the poetry of Mason's visual concept of *Battle of Angels* began another mutually inspiring theatrical marriage. From the moment he joined the theatre, John Lee Beatty was the one who took the Circle Rep's concept of making the audience visually and environmentally part of the theatre experience, and made it work. Mason considers Beatty's entrance into the company one of the major artistic events in the evolution of the theatre, since one of the truly innovative concepts of the Circle Rep has always been making the action of the play become the participatory experience of the audience. In *Hot l Baltimore,* for example, the audience had to cross the lobby of the old "Hotel Baltimore" in order to get to their seats. In a wildly experimental version of Molière's *The Doctor in Spite of Himself,* the audience sat in the middle of the room with the "stage" surrounding it, so that when Tanya Berezin floated in to the sound of "Lucy in the Sky with Diamonds" with helium balloons attached to her fingers, the audience was literally in the middle of the action. But it was not until John Lee Beatty took the same kind of environmental impulses and brilliantly expanded and capitalized upon them that the company began to be critically noted for its superb set designs and attention to detail, as John Lee Beatty won an Obie that year for *Battle of Angels* and *Harry Outside.*

Battle of Angels could only seat approximately 75 to 100 people because so much of the space was used for the three rooms of the Terrence Mercantile Store. No one was unduly worried, however; there were not a lot of subscribers at the time of the company move downtown. As Thirkield jokingly said, echoing the Cino days, "This is going to be a very experimental production. There will be no audience. We'll do it just for the room." But the members of the audience who *were* there felt they were an intimate part of the store and thus of the play itself.

Battle of Angels was only the beginning of five consecutive years of environmental experimentation.

"Let me start with *In the Recovery Lounge,*" Mason says enthusiastically.

> For the entrance into the theatre, John Lee designed the hallway of a hospital with a tile floor. The audience's experience began immediately as it walked into an area with highly glossed walls. There was an elevator as you turn left of where the tickets are taken. There was a low ceiling overhead that was all frosted plexiglass with electric lights above it so that it was a lighted corridor. There were red plastic signs for visitors. The audience had to walk through a wide set of swinging doors (for hospital beds) with the little cross hatches on the doors, into the "recovery lounge," before it could take its seat. Completely en-

vironmental. When we did *Ulysses in Traction,* which takes place in a school where a play was being rehearsed, it was designed as a three-quarter arena. The audience again came down a school corridor, making the audience a part of the academic atmosphere from the moment it entered the theatre. When we did *Harry Outside,* it was done completely in the round with muddy hills and mounds. It was something new every time. The really glorious years—the first five years beginning with *Battle of Angels*—the theatre was changed with every production. John Lee brought us into this space in a new way each time. But after we'd done that for five years, I said, we know we can change the theatre around making it absolutely right for each play, but it's exhausting us. Let's settle in one place and only vary from it when we really must. Let's take that as a limitation: can we create wonderful things keeping it in one place in a proscenium arrangement?[13]

Beatty became a very important influence on Mason and on the whole Circle Rep sensibility. As Thirkield eventually receded as an artistic influence over the next several years, Beatty's artistic sensibility became more and more important, filling the significant void Thirkield's lessening participation created. Thirkield and Beatty had totally different functions, but each had a powerful effect on Mason. The first five years Mason was tremendously influenced by Thirkield's sense of warmth, generosity, and experimentation. When he found another partner in Beatty, Mason's feelings about the theatre as an experience for the audience finally became completely practical. In a sense, Thirkield's participation became less central after the company moved to Sheridan Square. His greatest contribution was in the first five years on 83rd Street, not only financially but also very much artistically. Mason was the intellectual vision of the Circle Rep, but Thirkield in many ways was the soul, the beating heart, the warmth, the generosity. No one acknowledges this more readily than Mason. Thirkield was the one who insisted on the concept of an artist's "right to fail" as an integral part of artistic growth—a concept that eventually would turn into a major irony for him.

As noted, by the end of 1974 Circle Rep was being hailed in the *New York Times* as one of the "chief providers of new American plays," not only for its original major productions, the most important of which were *The Mound Builders* and *Harry Outside,* but this time also for its series of three consecutive original workshops that each played for two weeks: *Innocent Thoughts, Harmless Intentions; Fire in the Mindhouse;* and *St. Freud.*[14]

It was a good time. Once again a set of fortuitous circumstances gave Circle Rep an edge during this important transitional period in its development. At the time that they were trying to decide whether or not to expand their operations, the business of theatre had been picking up throughout New York City. The computerized box-office system known as Ticketron created almost one hundred new outlets for selling theatre tickets, not only in New York but in New Jersey and Connecticut as well; new and younger theatregoers were standing in line at the outdoor box office on Times Square. Despite the fact that the top ticket price had reached an all-time high of $15, sales were surprisingly brisk. According to John Willis, the season which began June 1, 1974, and ended May 31, 1975, was suddenly so active that it experienced

> . . . the first booking jam in several years, and made it necessary for some productions to wait for others to close. In the deepest national and economic recession in 30 years, the theatre experienced an increase in financial and artistic success that was a surprise to almost everyone.[15]

Many theatregoers were turning to the alternative theatres as well, not merely to take advantage of the less expensive prices, but because in this arena new American plays could be seen. Broadway was producing mostly imports, revivals, and musicals, along with popular and critical successes such as *Equus, The Wiz, Shenandoah,* and *Gypsy,* and an occasional commercial hit like *Same Time, Next Year.* Although off-Broadway was a bit of a disappointment to the critics this season, there were the notable exceptions of the Public Theatre's *A Chorus Line,* the Roundabout Theatre's *What Every Woman Knows,* and the Circle Repertory Company's *Battle of Angels.* The center of creative experiment, however, was perceived to have shifted to off-off-Broadway, with its increasing number of original productions.

It was inevitable that the Circle Rep's next season would reflect the growing critical attention given to play development. A staggering total of twenty-three separate productions was presented at Circle Rep: seven Major Productions, three Special Events, ten Workshops, and three Af-

ter Pieces.[16] Company concerns were radically changing to accommodate the growing demand for new plays, as the sheer bulk and diversity
of the new season's offerings show:

1975–1976 SEASON:
  The Elephant in the House – Berilla Kerr – Major Production
     (revival)
  The Loveliest Afternoon of the Year – John Guare – Special Event
  Overruled – George Bernard Shaw – Special Event
  Dancing for the Kaiser – Andrew Colmar – Major Production
  Knock, Knock – Jules Feiffer – Major Production
  Who Killed Richard Cory – A. R. Gurney, Jr. – Major Production
  Cavern of the Jewels – John Heuer – Major Production – Children's
     Show
  Serenading Louie – Lanford Wilson – Major Production
  The Lesson of the Master – Richard Howard – After Piece
  When I Dyed My Hair in Venice – Helen Duberstein – Workshop
  Solo for Two – Juliette Bowles – Workshop
  The Magic Formula – Sidney Morris – Workshop
  Terminal – Corinne Jacker – Workshop
  Night Thoughts – Corinne Jacker – Workshop
  The Confirmation – Howard Ashman – Workshop
  Prague Spring – Lee Kalcheim – Special Event
  Fog and Mismanagement – Jeff Wanshel – Workshop
  Home Free – Lanford Wilson – Workshop
  Winners – Brian Friel – Workshop
  Wildflowers – Richard Howard – After Piece
  Dark Room – David Epstein – Workshop
  Mrs. Murray's Farm – Roy London – Major Production
  Listen Please – Robert Abrami – After Piece

   The little Circle Rep Theatre was an extraordinary beehive of activity, energy, and drive. During this season the workshop program was
expanded and named the PIPS, an acronym for Projects-in-Progress.
During the PIPS, new plays would be read or partially staged for the
Circle Rep audiences in order to garner their reactions. In their roles as
participators in the play development process, the audience was expected
to work; many enjoyed the responsibility. According to Daniel Irvine,
lab director, the PIPS originally had been designed to give experience to

talented new directors. Eventually, however, the directors also found themselves placed in the position of concentrating more particularly on developing the material itself.

Reviews for the season's products were varied, although they showed an appreciation of Circle Rep's heavy concentration on new materials. In reviewing *Elephant in the House,* Michael Feingold of the *Village Voice* noted with appreciation that the Circle Rep had first struggled with European plays, classics, and difficult new American plays before finding its "style in Lanford Wilson's work." Although Feingold made much of the sensitive nuances and shading in Mason's direction of Kerr's play, he now felt that the Circle Rep had to "go on to greater writers rather than backward to small imitations." He berated the Circle Rep for not exploring "great playwrights," although the Circle Rep was now a leading force in that effort.[17] Feingold's observations are even more puzzling since practically everything about the 1975–1976 season had to do with new dimensions and a new focus dedicated to new works. *Elephant in the House* was the only revival presented and it had been reworked and reexplored for production. *Newsday*'s Alan Wallach understood the importance of the developmental process and its importance to the playwright in his review of *Dancing for the Kaiser.* Although he felt the play was too melodramatic to be significant, he recognized the playwright's potential and believed that the play deserved production if only to aid the playwright's development, an extraordinary position for a critic to take in a society usually geared toward the end result. He praised Circle Rep as one of the most ardent pursuers of that "most elusive quarry, the important new American play," knowing full well that such a goal could only be sought in a situation in which financial and critical considerations were not the determining factors of a company's viability.[18] Although other reviewers did not necessarily stress the developmental aspects of the company, they too directed their attention predominantly to the original works. In reviewing A. R. Gurney, Jr.'s *Who Killed Richard Cory,* Emory Lewis called the Circle Rep the "home of hits,"[19] even though he felt that the play did not measure up, while Howard Kissel stressed that the stylized nature of the writing and acting helped to add another "intelligent new American play to the Circle's already impressive roster."[20]

At this point in the Circle Rep's own developmental process, the pursuit itself was more important than the outer success of the end product. Developing the *process for discovery* was the most important issue at this time. Certainly there was great joy when a play was well-received, but whether it was or not, the financial structure of the company was not affected; subscription monies were already received, an audience was assured, and plays were not expected to continue beyond the normal one-week preview, six-week run. This was an excellent arrangement for any company geared to experimenting with new plays, even though an assured audience did not account for enough revenue to survive.

Regardless of the fact that audiences were finally assured, critical enthusiasm was an important factor in the continuing success of the company. Clearly, the critics can play a significant role in determining the direction in which a company will grow despite all arguments to the contrary. Without critical acceptance, any nonprofit group or company which is institutional in nature can survive only if it has an unlimited source of private funds and can spend monies to create its own private audience.

Without an unlimited source of private funds, a company has to depend for a major portion of its subsistence on public or corporate grants and fellowships which grow or diminish in proportion to the prevailing economy. In this context, the critic can perform the important function of pointing out the quality of the company's work and the importance of its contribution within the context of American theatre. The critic helps to lay the foundation for future funding and external financial support.

Although Robert Brustein may have called it an "obsessive preoccupation with money," the fact of the matter was that existence or nonexistence was almost always determined by the amount of public or corporate subsidies a group could net. The search for federal or private funding was never-ending, since the professional noncommercial theatre's "activities were beginning to outstrip their subsidies" at an extraordinary rate of growth and diversity.[21] Therefore, since the critics not only played a part in affecting immediate solvency but future funding as well, playing to their expectations became part of the game that all funded theatres such as La Mama, Manhattan Theatre Club, and the Public Theatre were forced to play. Fortunately, despite contrasting tastes the critics were unanimously enthusiastic regarding the type of product, if not always the quality, of the Circle Rep's work; they found it refreshing to see such an extensive concentration on new plays and new playwrights.

At Circle Rep, the shift to a focus on plays and playwrights began to affect much of the company's operations. Although the original hope had been for a full-fledged repertory acting company, a true repertory style of playing was not always feasible. There was little room for storage at the small theatre, and the very nature of the heavily detailed physical productions they presented made repertory playing impractical. The first five years of Circle Rep's existence had been focused on the acting; most of the major emphasis within the group had always gone to the development of the actors' craft. Now there seemed to be little doubt that the emphasis would have to shift to the plays. Even though the ensemble acting was almost always unanimously applauded as excellent, the major portion of critical attention given the company was clearly to the plays. This shift in emphasis was evidenced by the fact that almost every mention of the Circle Repertory Company at this time pointed to the role they were playing in bringing new plays to the theatre. For example, on January 15, 1975, in announcing the opening of Wilson's new play, *The Mound Builders,* the *New York Times* stamped the Circle Rep as a "major producer of new American plays."[22] On March 13, 1975, in reviewing *Harry Outside,* Mel Gussow also referred to Circle Rep's new role as producer of new plays. He wrote that on the strength of the first season at the former Sheridan Square Playhouse, "and on its previous work, the Circle is a match for any institutional (and more highly funded) theatre in the country."[23]

The increased attention changed the Circle Rep's status. They felt obligated to meet the growing expectations, but off-Broadway expenses were much greater than off-off-Broadway expenses had been, and were also soaring in the current inflationary economy. Now Circle Rep was finding itself in the position of being in constant serious financial peril; public recognition had brought expensive demands in its wake. It would not be long before the "business" of theatre would emphasize the constant struggle between the integrity of a play versus commercial considerations.

It is clear to see that with the advent of business priorities, many who had participated within the original structure of the company might become disenchanted with its institutionalization. Rob Thirkield, for example, was clearly worried. Once the closeness of family feeling began to erode, a definite lack of enthusiasm was becoming apparent. For someone of Thirkield's disposition in particular, theatre was more a place to celebrate an event than a place to make money. To him, theatre was more than a play or acting; it was communion with an audience. Commercializing the process took away a great deal of the joy, and although the intimate creation of a shared event may sound idealistic, this had been the driving force behind the original concept of the group. Now with such heavy critical concentration on the product, the company itself was unwittingly becoming part of the disposable society that characterized much of the seventies. The joy of creation and exploration was no longer enough; now the plays had to be produced to please the critics in order to keep the company alive fiscally.

Of course, the company was producing work that was good enough to warrant a great deal of critical attention. However, there was another side to the coin of success that threatened to spoil the process that had created their success. They had approached the fine line where they could no longer be permitted to fail. Pragmatic considerations became primary ones in order to offset higher rent and escalating production costs. Such a situation immediately reduces experimentation, which in turn drastically alters the creative environment. Once the environment changes into one in which hits are being sought, like it or not, the company has been forced into the hit-flop syndrome of commercial theatre.

Continuous financial peril had never compelled the Circle Rep's board of directors actively to promote its plays to Broadway, even though doing so is often an extremely viable way to survive. For example, *Ain't Misbehavin'* became a substantial subsidy for the Manhattan Theatre Club (MTC) for several years, and *A Chorus Line* and *The Pirates of Penzance* have proven to be enormous endowments for Joseph Papp. Now taking a cue from the MTC and the Public Theatre, when a play at the Circle Rep had a large critical response, the question arose of either transferring to Broadway, a larger off-Broadway house, a tour, or sometimes even television. As a result, Jules Feiffer's *Knock, Knock,* which was perceived as a "kooky, laugh-saturated miracle play in the absurdist tradition," played by a "splendid cast," and propelled at a "rocketing pace" by Mason, was moved intact to Broadway immediately following its brief initial run at the Circle Rep.[24] It opened on February 24, 1976, in time for the Tony nominations. Marshall Mason was nominated for his first Tony Award for direction. The committee also nominated Jules Feiffer for Best Play and Daniel Seltzer for Best Actor. At the same time, Judd Hirsch won the Drama Desk Award for Best Supporting Actor as *Knock, Knock*'s "Wiseman." For all intents and purposes the successful off-Broadway Circle Rep production had transferred to Broadway with critical acceptance from within the industry as well as excellent reviews. And then came one of the more astonishing incidents in the history of American theatre. The prevailing story had it that

> . . . two new-breed producers moved the successful Circle production of "Knock, Knock" to Broadway where, with Feiffer's consent, they hired a new director and cast, including a glamorous star, and, overnight, turned the downtown hit into an uptown flop.[25]

Mason bristles a bit when he hears this version of the story repeated, since he feels it is inaccurate. The transferred Circle Rep production, complete with original cast, was hardly a flop. It ran on Broadway successfully for five full months during which time it received its Tony nominations, certainly an indication of its continued energy and effectiveness. However, Mason says,

> After the Tony Awards were over, the producers said we were not sustaining the play. With the notices we were getting, we should be selling out. Instead we were doing approximately 70 percent capacity. The producers said they would not continue with the play unless we consented to replace the actors with stars. The playwright came to me and made this demand, and I said, "In no way am I going to replace this successful production with stars." I urged Jules not to listen to them. I was confident that the play would run, that it was going to do very well, especially after the Tony nominations. But he would not listen to me. He went along with the producers. So I said, "Then you will have to find another director to do it." So I became the only director, as far as I know, in the history of the American theatre who was replaced after receiving the Tony Award nomination for Best Director.

The producers brought in director Jose Quintero and a new cast headed by Lynn Redgrave. It was the new version that failed; it ran for two weeks and closed.

Although Mason felt the producers were wrong, he did not seem bitter about the experience. Nor did he change any of his basic concepts of theatre. If anything, the experience only emphasized his beliefs in company values, not the least of which was the ensemble acting. Mason continued to stress the experience of what is happening for actors as well as audiences as happening in the present tense—a good depiction of directorial lyric realism. He continued to stress the importance of the treatment of the writer in order to nourish his creativity. As testimony to this philosophy, the current commercial season introduced several talented new playwrights, all of whom had been developed through regional companies: Michael Cristofer (*The Shadow Box*); Preston Jones (*The Texas Trilogy*); David Mamet (*American Buffalo*); and Albert Innaurato (*Gemini*). *The Shadow Box, American Buffalo,* and *Gemini* all went on to commercial productions. That *The 5th of July, Talley's Folly,* and *Serenading Louie* were all created within a company setting only stressed Lanford Wilson's own belief that the future of playwriting was within the structure of a company. By October of 1978, an editorial in *Other Stages* discussed the advantages and pitfalls of moving plays from off-off-Broadway and off-Broadway to Broadway. All indications seemed to be that Broadway was relying more and more on the noncommercial theatre to supply plays that had already broken the ice with the critics. Obviously, as evidenced by *Knock, Knock,* making the move was not always completely productive.

The experience of *Knock, Knock* also cemented Mason's belief that the collaborative ensemble of directing and acting could make or break a play even though it is often the "playwright who takes the fall" with the critics, and "the key to ensemble acting is that the actors have to share the same goal—the play." As Paul Gardner wrote shortly afterwards:

> [The] Circle won't be changing its style to accommodate commercial success or its new position as one of Off-Broadway's leading theatres. "Good reviews give us more artistic freedom," Mason said, "and, sure, I'd like to see another play of ours move to Broadway. But when I start directing that's never in my mind. If somebody wanted to move us uptown permanently, I wouldn't take the offer."[26]

However much artistic integrity may sometimes be at odds with commercial considerations, the fact remained that Circle Rep's budget was growing enormously. By the 1976–1977 season, the company's budget for six productions had reached $300,000. The price to a subscriber was a modest $27.50 for a full season of six plays, plus workshops, while commercial theatre had reached an all-time high of $20 per ticket. With such a budget, fund raising had now become a full-time preoccupation at the same time that concentration on play development expanded. The two seemingly disparate pursuits were becoming increasingly inseparable.

1976–1977 SEASON:

The Farm – David Storey – Major Production

A Tribute to Lili Lamont – Arthur White – Major Production

My Life – Corinne Jacker – Major Production

The Passing of Corky Brewster – Jerry L. Crawford – After Piece

Gemini – Albert Innaurato – Major Production

For Love or Money – Jay Jeffries and Jason McAuliffe – After Piece

Suicide in Bᵇ – Sam Shepard – Play-in-Progress

Allegra – Allan Bates – Play-in-Progress

To the Land – Claris Nelson – Play-in-Progress

Exiles – James Joyce – Major Production

Fat Chances – Charlie Peters – Play-in-Progress

Cabaret/New York Times: A Review – James Tobin – After Piece

What the Babe Said – Martin Halpern – After Piece

Mrs. Tydings Mason-Dixon Medicine Man – John Heuer – Play-in-Progress

Celebrations Off River Street – James Tobin – Play-in-Progress

The Brixton Recovery – Jack Gilhooley – Play-in-Progress

Unsung Cole – Cole Porter and Norman Berman – Major Production

During the 1976–1977 season there were six Major Productions, four After Pieces, and seven Plays-in-Progress (PIPS). Only two of the Major Productions were written by company playwrights, Corinne Jacker and Albert Innaurato, neither of whom was seriously active within the structure of the company (Innaurato spent most of his developmental process with Playwrights Horizons). The search for new plays was extending beyond the limits of the existing company list of resident playwrights to a greater degree than ever before.

Although the 1976–1977 season would see the last of the After Pieces (which would emerge the following year as Late Show series), the new Play-in-Progress series was introduced as a very important part of the developmental process that was emerging almost organically at the Circle Rep. The PIPS were staged readings of plays by resident playwrights such as John Heuer, or visiting playwrights such as Sam Shepard, that were not felt to be completely ready for production, but eminently ready for the acid test of audience reaction. Of the six Major Productions, four were new American works and one, *Gemini,* moved on to Broadway, creating instant recognition for author Albert Innaurato. The Circle Rep can readily claim *Gemini* as one of its own, even though its first workshop production had been given at Playwrights Horizons, an off-off-Broadway house. However, it was not until Innaurato brought the play to the Circle Rep with several important cast changes along the way that the comedy achieved its full potential.

The Farm initiated a season that was not only full of new works but also studded with actors who were growing in national recognition. The cast of Corinne Jacker's *My Life* had William Hurt, Christopher Reeve, Jeff Daniels, Tanya Berezin, Roger Chapman, Douglass Watson, Jo Henderson, Nancy Snyder, and Claire Malis. *A Tribute to Lily Lamont* was noteworthy mostly because Mason had assembled an excellent cast in Leueen McGrath, William Hindman, Helen Stenborg, and Burke Pearson. Not only was Mason an actor's director, it was also much to his credit that *The Farm,* by English playwright David Storey, inspired critical celebrations. With its terse but poetic language covering the quiet inertia in which the characters live, *The Farm* was directed with the rich sensibilities that Mason brought to a play with such a Chekhovian spirit.

The beginning of the 1977–1978 season was notable because of a funding breakthrough in which three major New York off-Broadway theatres—the Circle Repertory Company, Manhattan Theatre Club, and Playwrights Horizons—received Ford Foundation grants for the express purpose of producing new American plays. Of the three theatres, only the Circle Rep was an acting company with resident actors and resident playwrights. However, knowing that the bulk of foundation money was being channeled only toward the encouragement of new American plays, Marshall Mason banded together with Lynne Meadows of the Manhattan Theatre Club and Robert Moss of Playwrights Horizons to break through the barrier of corporate funding with astounding success. A total of $1.4 million was granted to theatres doing new American plays.[27] This was an extraordinary financial boon to all three groups. For the Circle Rep it was also a confirmation of the direction in which they had been heading. There could be no more doubt that their major concern had to be the development of the new American plays that attracted necessary funding, even though, as we shall see, there are still company members who deny that this is so.

By the 1977–1978 season, the Late Show series had been developed; it was the brainchild of Daniel Irvine, Mason's assistant. In 1973–1974, Irvine had been doing a little bit of everything, including acting as head of the informal literary department. It was in logging and reading many of the unsolicited manuscripts that he first thought of taking advantage of this wealth of material. Many of the manuscripts were one-act plays, not the form usually presented at Circle Rep. The thought occurred to Irvine to present original one-act plays as late-night events, adapting the existing set of a play already in production and presenting the new work as the reverse of a curtain raiser. Mason, always in tune with new ideas, encouraged Irvine to work out the details. Assembling a staff of designers with the creativity necessary to adapt a new play to an existing set with minimum modifications, Irvine initiated and directed the first "After Piece." *The Passing of Corky Brewster* by Jerry Crawford was presented on the set of Corinne Jacker's *Harry Outside,* the current Major Production. It was the beginning of four continuous years of presenting premieres of hour-long new one-act plays on a very modest production budget of $150 each. The plays started after the main production ended; sometimes the audience took a break and returned, sometimes the one-act play attracted a totally new audience. By the next season, the name had formally been changed to the Late Show series. It was not long before the series of original works attracted major critics like Clive Barnes, Mel Gussow, and Douglas Watt. The Late Show series was welcomed as an important and innovative addition to the New York theatrical scene, as critic Mel Gussow noted:

> One of the most laudable aspects of the Circle Repertory Company's series of late-night productions of one-act plays is that the plays—at least the first two in the series, Lanford Wilson's "Brontosaurus" and John Bishop's "Cabin 12"—really are one-acts. These are not unfinished full-length plays or close-ups from a larger canvas, they are the theatrical equivalent of short stories or character sketches.[28]

Both company actors and company playwrights became excited about the project. Lanford Wilson wrote *Brontosaurus* especially for the first Late Show, to be played by Tanya Berezin, Jeff Daniels, and Sharon Madden; it was presented in the "silo" from the *Feedlot* set. Resident playwright John Bishop's *Cabin 12* was written for and played by Edward Seamon and Jonathan Hogan. Resident playwright Robert

Patrick created *My Cup Runneth Over* for Nancy Snyder and Amy Wright.

There is little doubt that the addition of the Late Show series was in keeping with Circle Rep's growing image as a house of original plays, whether full length, one-act, mainstage, workshop, PIPS, After Pieces, or Special Events. As can be seen, in critical expectations the emphasis had now changed almost completely from the actor to the playwright. As long as the grants kept coming for the new plays and as long as the critics continued to cheer only when the new plays were hits, the Circle Rep was forced to follow the lead of these expectations. The group of actors was still there and still available to playwrights; they helped to realize the new plays, with the maintenance of the playwright's vision and integrity a primary concern. This concept had not changed. What had changed was that the plays became more important than anything else, since it was the plays that brought in the subsidies. Inevitably, the "individual" was beginning to be lost in the currents of the mainstreaming process. Although on one level there was great joy among the founders at the company's good fortune, on a deeper level the personal response, expressed privately, was that some of the original enthusiasm was beginning to ebb. The original spirit of the company was in danger of being compromised, as some of the results of the next season demonstrated.

The 1977–1978 season presented only ten events:

Feedlot – Patrick Meyers – Main Production
Brontosaurus – Lanford Wilson – Late Show
Ulysses in Traction – Albert Innaurato – Major Production
Cabin 12 – John Bishop – Late Show
Lulu – Frank Wedekind – Major Production
Two from the Late Show – Lanford Wilson, John Bishop – Major
    Production
The 5th of July – Lanford Wilson – Major Production
The Living Hand – Mark Stevenson – Special Event
My Cup Runneth Over – Robert Patrick – Late Show
Pushing 30 – Jonathan Hadary – Late Show

The artistic failure of the production of Frank Wedekind's seventy-year-old naturalist/expressionist drama *Lulu* seemed almost prophetic in the current atmosphere of searching for the new. Wedekind had adapted

Lulu from his *Earth Spirit,* written in 1893 and produced in 1898, and from his *Pandora's Box,* written in 1903 and privately produced in Vienna in 1905. The sexually honest, erotic tale by the early twentieth-century pioneer of German Expressionism does not always fare well in a translated production. Ironically, its failure at the Circle Rep served to point out an important developmental concern within the company. Never before had the Circle Rep received such blistering attacks by the critics. The production, adapted from 180 pages of text, incurred all of the negative eloquence of the critics. Condemnations ran heavy, most particularly aimed at Rob Thirkield, the play's director. Only once before was it recorded that *Lulu* had been performed in New York — ironically enough on the same site, the Former Sheridan Square Playhouse — and it had opened and closed in one night, March 27, 1970. Few recognized the courage in Thirkield's attempt to revive the difficult play, mistaken though the production might have been. Experiencing such heavy critical disapproval served to point out an important difference from the early days at the uptown loft: the freedom to fail at the Circle Repertory Company was over. In particular, the freedom to fail and still be able to walk away with a sense of accomplishment in a difficult artistic attempt would not return. Failure was no longer acceptable in an atmosphere thick with critical scrutiny. The Circle Repertory Company now had a position to maintain, a position that was at complete odds with the original philosophy of the company.

The failure of *Lulu* proved to be the beginning of the end of Rob Thirkield's direct participation in the company. *Lulu* was produced shortly after his divorce from Tanya Berezin. As he remembers it,

> Something strange happened then. I wasn't that happy with the production, but it was wonderful for the company. The actors were all exceptional in it, and the audiences were completely freaked out. It turned out to have the best box office of any play that year, which was surprising considering the reviews were so terrible. But that was the year the Circle ran out of money, which was the main reason we closed the play. It had so many people in the cast we couldn't afford it. But it was a weird point for me. I felt I didn't do very well. And all the actors in it felt, well, I guess Rob wasn't that good a director. I waited for the next thing to come along to direct, and nothing came.

The heaviest irony was that no one had had more to do with creating the Circle Rep's comfortable, pressure-free environment than had

Thirkield. It was he who had constantly supported the actors through all the ego-shattering growing pains that were so often an integral part of development; it was he who had preached that there was no such thing as total failure, that even a box-office or commercial failure could have its value in terms of growth. But in Thirkield's wounded state, the same support did not seem to be forthcoming for him.

"It was a sort of turning point for the theatre," he continues thoughtfully. "They started saying we ought to be a little more careful about the plays we do from now on. They started doing small plays with a limited number of characters. *Lulu* was the last large cast until the revival of *Gilead*. I felt myself out in the cold a bit."

Lanford Wilson's *The 5th of July* stood out as the one major critical event of a particularly uneventful season, except for the addition of the Late Show series. While reviewers like Rex Reed were beside themselves with "genius raves" for all involved, on a more sedate level critics like Harold Clurman, Edith Oliver, and Mel Gussow were enthusiastic, but more careful in the use of superlatives. More and more the collaborative nature of Mason's directorial work with Wilson's plays was being recognized; the smoothed plot seams from an earlier version, the clarified character relationships, a calming of the play's overly comic aspects, all lent a more Chekhovian air to the current version and were directly attributed to the freedom of the company atmosphere and to the long-standing working relationship between Wilson and Mason. In addition to the recognition of this important collaboration, the ensemble acting was being perceived as inseparable from the play, so much so that when Mason says, "It is the company that has inspired Lanford," his meaning becomes more apparent. "One of the reasons Lanford is here writing is because he is inspired by the actors to investigate particular things. If he were off writing by himself alone, as he did earlier—and I'm not taking anything away from him when I say this; he's a wonderful playwright—but the balance gets so off."

The true essence of the nature of collaboration in theatre is explored in this manner—doing it, working it, feeling it, seeing it come to life, and not being isolated in a creative vacuum. The inspirational exchange between actors and writer is very stimulating, and an aspect not generally appreciated by the public regarding an acting company with resident playwrights. As Mason points out, "Harold Clurman said it so well about *Hot l*. He said you could not tell where the writing ends and the acting begins. I've literally experienced this with *Hot l* when returning from seeing a production of it in California to seeing our own production again in New York. People came downstairs and wandered about. And Chatty Ferrell was so big and fat, and she'd slide over a chair and sit down because she looked like she couldn't stand anymore. I had no connection that I'd told her to do that. It was the same thing with the lines. They came spontaneously. You never had the sense that they were written down. That's what happens to plays that are successful. You lose the sense of the script. What Clurman calls the true play." The same sense of interrelationship occurred with the production of *The 5th of July*. Although the play always belongs to the playwright, the coauthorship of the *production* becomes obvious when the script has intermeshed with the directed creation of the actors to the degree that something totally three dimensional is born.

In 1974, the Circle Rep had been presented the Drama Desk Award for Outstanding Contribution to the Off-Broadway Theatre. Now, Circle Rep was presented with the Margo Jones Award for Most Significant Contribution to the American Theatre, 1977; and the Outer Critics Circle–Joseph Kaye Award for Distinguished Contribution to the American Theatre, 1978.

Beginning its tenth season in the fall of 1978, Mason wrote an open letter to the company:

> Circle Repertory will continue its leadership in continued commitment to the discovery and nurturing of the American writer. Circle Repertory is the only permanent professional New York acting company since the Group Theatre to work with a resident ensemble of artists placed at the service of America's major playwrights, eleven of whom are in residence. Based on the concept that the *action* of the play should be the *experience* of the audience, Circle Rep attempts to bring this concept to life through the imaginative interaction of the ensemble of actors with the resident playwrights. . . . Circle Repertory remains the standard bearer for the new American play.

To date, the Circle Rep had presented sixty-nine world premieres.
The company playwrights included

John Bishop	Martin Halpern
Julie Bovasso	Albert Innaurato
James Farrell	Berilla Kerr

Roy London   Milan Stitt
Patrick Meyers   Lanford Wilson
Claris Nelson

The ensemble of actors included

Michael Ayr   Marion Levine
Tanya Berezin   Bobo Lewis
Roger Chapman   Sharon Madden
Jeff Daniels   Debra Mooney
Jack Davidson   Edward J. Moore
Brad Dourif   Burke Pearson
Conchatta Ferrell   Joyce Reehling
Neil Flanagan   Edward Seamon
Stephanie Gordon   Timothy Shelton
Mari Gorman   Nancy Snyder
Bruce Gray   June Stein
Trish Hawkins   Helen Stenborg
Judd Hirsch   Danton Stone
Jonathan Hogan   Elizabeth Sturges
William Hurt   Douglass Watson
Nancy Kilmer   Jimmie Ray Weeks
Ken Kliban   Amy Wright
Zane Lasky

The company directors were

Neil Flanagan   Marshall Ogelsby
Daniel Irvine   Terry Schreiber
Marshall W. Mason   Rob Thirkield

The company designers (including sound and music) were

John Lee Beatty   Charles London
Laura Crow   Norman L. Berman
Dennis Parichy

Whether or not company participation directly influenced the
1978–1979 season, one of Circle Rep's most golden years, is difficult to
assess, but it would seem that everything in the way of expectation and

development had at least been pointing in the direction of encouraging increased writing activity.

1978–1979 SEASON:

Glorious Morning – Patrick Meyers – Major Production

Stargazing – Tom Cone – Late Show

In the Recovery Lounge – James Farrell – Major Production

In Three Easy Lessons – John Calene – Project-in-Progress

Total Recall – Martin Halpern – Late Show

The Runner Stumbles – Milan Stitt – Major Production

The Human Voice – Jean Cocteau – Late Show

Minnesota Moon – John Olive – Late Show

Winter Signs – John Bishop – Project-in-Progress

Winter Signs – John Bishop – Major Production

The Deserter – Norman Beim – Late Show

Perched on a Gabardine Cloud – Steven Braunstein – Project-in-Progress

Talley's Folly – Lanford Wilson – Major Production

Life and/or Death – Herb Gardner – Late Show

Van Zandt Ellis Piano Recital – Special Event

A Woman's Life in the Theatre – Rita Gardner – Special Event

Gertrude Stein, Gertrude Stein, Gertrude Stein – Marty Martin – Special Event

Buried Child – Sam Shepard – Summer Major Production

Gertrude Stein, Gertrude Stein, Gertrude Stein – Marty Martin – Major Production

Of the seven Major Productions, five were enormously successful, while two were brought in to mixed reception. *Glorious Morning* opened the season happily. Though the play strained credulity with its bizarre characters, it was the quality of the production that brought the melodramatic aspects of the play up to the quality of the "rattling good dialogue" that John Simon applauded.[29] There was the frightened but feisty mother who was dying of cancer, played to such perfection by Tanya Berezin that Tich Dace wrote, "such performances demand to be seen and relished and treasured,"[30] while Howard Kissel wrote, "her characterization is so complete it does not seem to begin or end with the play; every gesture seems drawn from a whole life."[31] The Circle Rep was credited with giving Meyers's play a nearly perfect production, "and even if the situations and motivations are apt to be unconvincing, the characters have a thumping theatricality that keeps us steadily interested, even if only intermittently involved."[32]

In the Recovery Lounge, by James Farrell, is a play about a nurse and her patients for which the Circle Rep production was again rated superior to the play itself, most particularly for Tom Lynch's hospital setting, but this did not save the play. Only Clive Barnes, now with the *New York Post,* was "outrageously amused by this hospital farce" with its "unusually witty script" with which director Marshall Mason "has done a great job of placing the play right inside the audience."[33] Even Barnes felt that the playwright was helped by an exceptional production, but he was alone in his positive critique of the play.

However, the poorly received play was immediately obscured by a revival of Milan Stitt's powerful courtroom drama *The Runner Stumbles,* about a Catholic priest on trial for the murder of a young nun of his parish. A moral and psychological study, *The Runner Stumbles* was an extraordinarily successful revival of the very successful 1976 Broadway production that had been directed by Austin Pendleton. Besides being so well received, this production was important because it introduced Milan Stitt directly to the Circle Rep audiences. Stitt, who at Mason's invitation had just joined the Circle Rep as its official playwright-dramaturg, was to contribute substantially to the Circle Rep's playwriting development over the next several years. The play was also directly responsible for bringing B. Rodney Marriott into the company. Stitt had discovered several changes while writing the screenplay for Stanley Kramer's film version of the script that he wanted to incorporate into the revival. When Austin Pendleton did not wish to create another version that would necessarily force comparisons with his original production on Broadway, Stitt thought of Marriott, who had successfully directed a production of *The Runner Stumbles* at Yale University, and asked him to direct the new version. In Marriott's own words, "The experience was one that was rich and wonderful for me."[34] He came from Exeter College, where he had been teaching, to direct the second New York production of an established play, and was thrown into working with some of the best actors in New York, including William Hurt.

The desire to find another work forced the premature production of the fourth Major Production, *Winter Signs,* by John Bishop, which was not well received. It is possible that the Circle Rep may have gotten too excited about this talented writer whose plays *The Trip Back Down* and *Cabin 12* had shown such merit and originality. Martin Gottfried was one of the few who recognized that the company may have produced Bishop's play *Winter Signs* prematurely, thereby aborting the necessary development it required. Gottfried's observation is quite astute, since *Winter Signs* was surprisingly produced immediately after it had been give a PIP. Usually a PIP received a longer period of gestation before it moved on to a Major Production, no matter how promising the play may have appeared in workshop.

Then came the major event of the Circle Rep's season, another Lanford Wilson play—the two-character *Talley's Folly*. The simplest, most lyrical of all of Wilson's plays now emerged as part of a trilogy about the Talley family of Lebanon, Missouri, which Wilson had begun the previous year with *The 5th of July*. The character Aunt Sally of *The 5th of July*, who carried her beloved Matt's ashes around, is now seen as Sally Talley in 1944. Thirty-three years younger, she is being courted by the same Matt Friedman. The midwestern spinster determined to hold herself in strict reserve against the persistent charm and humor of the Jewish accountant from New York City determined to win her are two seemingly disparate souls whose human affinities eventually erase all external barriers. Faultlessly directed by Mason and beautifully played by Judd Hirsch and Trish Hawkins, the play was extremely well received by all the major New York critics, including Clive Barnes, Walter Kerr, Mel Gussow, Jonathan Beaufort, Harold Clurman, and even John Simon, who wrote, "Wilson is the only playwright I can think of who is steadily growing, improving, paring himself down to essentials."[35]

Capping off a rich season were two summer productions, Sam Shepard's 1979 Pulitzer Prize–winning *Buried Child* and Marty Martin's one-woman play, *Gertrude Stein, Gertrude Stein, Gertrude Stein*, featuring Pat Carroll's tour-de-force performance. Like *Gemini* and *The Runner Stumbles*, both plays had been developed elsewhere. *Buried Child* had originated at San Francisco's Magic Theatre under the aegis of director Robert Woodruff, who worked with Shepard in a manner similar to that of Mason with Wilson. *Buried Child* had a brief run at the Theatre for The New City on Second Avenue before moving to a major summer production at the Circle Rep. It is not surprising that the Circle Rep would produce one of Shepard's plays, particularly such a powerful one. Shepard, a quintessentially American playwright with midwestern roots, was an old friend from the early days at the Cino; he still considered the Circle Rep his New York home. Circle Rep would continue to produce Shepard's New York productions, including *Fool for Love* in 1984.

It was a little more surprising that Circle Rep would present a play by Marty Martin, a twenty-six-year-old playwright from Austin, Texas, who had no connection at all to the company. *Gertrude Stein, Gertrude Stein, Gertrude Stein* was a completely independent production. Produced by Mary Ellyn Devery for The Sea-Ker, Inc., with Milton Moss as director, it was sought for summer presentation in its entirety by the Circle Rep, fitting in only with Circle Rep's image as the home of new plays. Since there were many resident and Lab playwrights available with less tested material, it is possible that the burden of the hit-flop syndrome was beginning to have its effect on nonprofit theatre. It was the old story that risks were not likely to be taken when the stakes were too high. Noncommercial theatres like Circle Rep previously could afford to nurture the playwright and take the chances, but more and more pressure was placed on them to find new plays to move to Broadway, making them more like experimental production houses rather than an alternative theatre. This situation was creating an interesting dichotomy; the demand for the new was never ending, while the arenas to create the new were shriveling under the heat of the hit-flop syndrome.

Unfortunately, the need for that which is new could create myopic visions of the very nature of theatre itself, as witnessed by Martin Duberman's indictment of the American theatre in the May 1978 issue of *Harper's*. Duberman felt that the bicentennial celebration had led to the golden age of American plays. However, according to him, American drama had been pretty thin and mostly terrible. In the sixties, he contended, it seemed possible that theatre might "get better; black theatre had some hope." The physical theatres of the sixties—the Open Theatre, the Living Theatre—were good, but now they were all gone. The writers of the sixties, such as John Guare and Sam Shepard, had not lived up to expectations. Duberman felt it was all "facile theatrics," and that the newest trio, Babe, Innaurato, and Mamet, were also thin and facile. Only the Circle Repertory Theatre was labeled as "the theatre with the most distinguished record for new plays." Although this was a form of praise for Circle Rep, it was becoming increasingly and alarmingly clear that, in many views, not only were new plays sought, but unless a theatre produced *great* new plays it was considered insignificant.[36] Unfortunately, too many people believe that if a play is not "great" it does not deserve to exist. In England, at least, it is almost expected that a new play will not be great because the measure is so extraordinarily Olympian; Shakespeare is difficult to match. Therefore, the light can be dimmer and still cast a glow. In this country, even though our heritage is English theatre, we do not have an Olympian backlog. Perhaps we are still looking for the American equivalent of Shakespeare; anything less produces cranky critics.

Arguments like Duberman's applied subtle pressure and made it appear as though the sole aim of theatre was to create new plays. Such a concept is an almost total negation of one of the primary reasons for theatre, the event itself — the performance, the audience involvement, the celebration, the sheer enjoyment of spectacle, and the religiosity of it, which is at the root of theatre's earliest origins. Although new and original work is of extreme importance — each generation needing to stamp its identity on the broad context of theatre history — sometimes it is forgotten that the entire experience of theatre can occur even with a two-thousand-year-old play. The only acting company in town that had started out in celebration of both classic and contemporary theatre had just about relinquished the classics by 1979, relegating them to perhaps one a season. Although Circle Rep had always acknowledged the importance of encouraging new works, they had become caught up almost exclusively in the search for the new. To this end the Literary Department was created.

8

The Literary Department and Institutionalization

THE formal creation of the Literary Department of the Circle Repertory Company occurred in 1977, eight years after the company began. It was created to formalize procedures and programs that had already been informally established. For example, Workshop productions had been presented since 1969, but were not part of a consistent developmental program; readings of new plays were held frequently, but with no formal or regular scheduling; unsolicited manuscripts were accepted without restrictions, but were read only when someone in the company managed to "get around" to them. The growth of the Literary Department was a major step in the institutionalization of the company; the resulting increase in activity made the smooth operation of the company more difficult, yet absolutely essential.

The aspirations of the Literary Department were always far-reaching and idealistic. At the heart of the department was an optimism which seems always to have been embodied by the people who worked in it, as though it were a prerequisite for the job. There seemed to be an undying love of process, of development, and of growth for growth's sake. In the world of theatre there are many groups dedicated to the development of professional playwrights, but Circle Rep's desire to create a nurturing and comfortable environment in which artists can develop theatre literature has been unequaled anywhere in its humaneness. Furthermore, there are few groups which have demonstrated such dedication to the unknown artist. Particularly in this context of service to unknown playwrights, the uniqueness of the Circle Repertory's Literary Department is apparent. Thousands of unsolicited manuscripts were received every year by the department, yet each person who submitted a manuscript received a well-thought-out personalized letter of critique and encouragement.

Literary departments, literary managers, and dramaturges are a new breed in American theatre, even newer than the professional director, who has been in existence approximately 110 years. The first formal dramaturg in theatre history, Gotthold Ephraim Lessing, worked for the Hamburg National Theatre in the late 1700s, and was also a resident playwright. He began the tradition of having a playwright fill a staff position called "dramaturg" or "literary manager," a tradition that continues to this day. Literally, a dramaturg means a "maker of plays," or playwright. As a writer-in-residence at the Hamburg National Theatre, Lessing had a large role in the theatre's management. To this day it is in Germany that the role of the dramaturg has the most importance. The theatre company is split between the director, who controls the actual production, and the dramaturg, who controls play selection. In addition, it is the dramaturg who provides the artistic and theoretical overview for the company. As a playwright, critic, theoretician, and scholar, Lessing initiated the era of dramaturgy.[1]

In the English-speaking theatre, Kenneth Tynan convinced Laurence Olivier that there should be a critic in residence at the founding of the National Theatre in England. However, unlike in the German model, in that role Tynan does not seem to have had any artistic control. He did not control the play selection process, nor did he have any great effect upon the artistic vision of the theatre. Instead, he assisted those writers who were rewriting, and he provided a great deal of research for the ongoing productions. This configuration is more in keeping with the American version of the position of dramaturg, particularly as defined by the Circle Repertory Company.

Although dramaturgy was a priority function of the Literary Department at Circle Rep, there were many aspects that fell far afield from pure dramaturgy. A summary of the Literary Department's role at Circle Rep shows that it was in charge of all scripts — solicited, unsolicited, in-house, out-of-house, in development, already completed, classics, and so forth. "In charge of" means running the processes, the evaluations, the photocopying of mainstage scripts for the actors, buying copies of classics that are to be done, or researching script material.

The literary manager was in charge of the developmental processes for scripts, including Script Evaluation Service, Friday Reading, Projects-in-Progress (PIPS), Extended Readings, Playwrights Lab, play selection for all developmental programs, reading scripts and holding script conferences with writers, attending outside readings and productions, maintaining supportive contact with member writers, and finding new writers. The ultimate goal of these tasks was to develop a series of plays that were then put on the menu, from which selections were made for mainstage presentation. The most basic of all day-to-day tasks of the literary manager, however, involved the process of evaluating the more than two thousand unsolicited manuscripts which were received by the company each year. This task involved prioritizing the reading process, finding outside readers, reading plays and holding script conferences with selected writers, contacting agents, and writing letters of critique.

As a member of the artistic staff, the literary manager had direct input into the decision-making process. Unlike persons in other management staff positions, only the literary manager was able to remain solely artistic in temperament. Because the department was not concerned with fund raising or with a product that was to be judged immediately by an outside audience, the artistic voice of the literary manager could remain "pure," an extremely important stance. Often, it meant that the literary manager became the "loyal opposition," to use a parliamentary term; that is, the literary manager could point out that a particular policy was not in keeping with the artistic goals and philosophy of the company. Thus, ideally, the literary manager at all times questions, advises, and cajoles. On this adversary level, the task of the literary manager was to keep the company "honest."

From its founding, the role of the playwright has been central to the development of the company. Lanford Wilson often filled the same role for the Circle Rep as Lessing did for the Hamburg National Theatre. As a resident playwright, and to all intents and purposes a co-founder, he found himself acting in the capacity of advisor in all matters pertaining to playwriting. This self-initiated involvement in plays that were not his own was a natural evolutionary step. It came directly out of the participation theatre traditionally begun with Joe Cino's famous "It's Magic Time!" When Wilson became active at the Circle Rep, he brought not only the same kind of infectious energy that had sparked the early days at the Caffé Cino, but also the same habit of filling in and doing whatever had to be done. According to Mason, Wilson was often present during the rehearsal process of any play being readied for the mainstage. It would be Wilson who would take aside the author of the play and discuss possible revisions based upon his own reactions to the rehearsal. Toward the end of the rehearsal process, Wilson would also assist by talking to Mason about the direction of the play. Almost all of these functions are traditionally filled by the dramaturg of a theatre company. At the time, however, it was an unofficial position that Wilson assumed when he perceived such needs within the company.

It was only when Marshall Mason returned from a State Department tour of Germany in 1977, where he saw dramaturgs in action, that he felt the need for a formal staff position to encourage and promote play development. Although it was obvious to him that Lanford Wilson had been usefully performing many of the functions of a dramaturg, it was also obvious that it would be more productive to have a staff person involved in such matters on an ongoing basis with responsibility not only to see the procedures through to the end, but also to create new opportunities for play development on a regular basis. The next step in stabilizing the theatre was to create a formal play development program in the form of a literary department with a dramaturg at its head.

In the summer of 1977, then, Mason invited playwright Milan Stitt to be Circle Rep's dramaturg. After giving Stitt some scripts to read, Mason realized that he had found not only a kindred spirit in terms of taste, but also a man who was skilled in the techniques and structure of writing realism. The choice was an obvious one; in September 1977 Stitt became the official dramaturg of Circle Rep.

Originally, Mason envisioned Stitt working very much as Wilson had, spending most of his time in the rehearsal hall. But Stitt did not devote a great deal of attention to rehearsals for mainstage productions, relying instead on the continuing tradition of the director acting as dramaturg on his own productions. Rather, Stitt looked upon the appointment as an opportunity to expand the company's existing work with playwrights. He devoted most of his attention in the beginning to formalizing the existing play development program with consistent expectations and schedules. Inevitably, Stitt would find it increasingly difficult to be both a full-time dramaturg and an active playwright.

At this time Porter Van Zandt was brought into the company as managing director. Van Zandt, who entered this position in the midst of all the increased activity, felt that in order to solidify the institutional groundwork that had recently been laid, it would be necessary to hire a full-time managerial staff. In an echo of this move, Stitt convinced Mason to hire a professional literary management staff. In 1979 B. Rodney Marriott, who had been brought into the company to direct the revival of *The Runner Stumbles,* was asked to take over the duties of literary manager, while Milan Stitt was retained as the company's official dramaturg.

At this point the two positions of dramaturg and literary manager became institutionally divided, each with specifically defined individual duties. The position of dramaturg at Circle Rep was to be filled by a senior member of the playwriting company such as Milan Stitt or John Bishop (who replaced Stitt from 1981 to 1984), and became a position on the artistic staff. In John Bishop's words, "The dramaturg is a member of the artistic decision-making staff, who provides a long-term overview of the goals of playwriting at Circle Rep." In other words, the dramaturg is the member of the artistic staff who makes sure that the playwrights' needs are taken into consideration when a policy decision is being made. The senior dramaturg also presumably collaborates on mainstage productions. On the other hand, the position of literary manager as defined by Circle Rep involved the day-to-day work of running the many and varied functions of the department. Eventually the separation between dramaturgy and literary management would translate into an isolation of the Literary Department that placed it in an ivory tower of theory and of play development purely for the sake of play development.

As things evolved, it was the dramaturg, usually a mainstage playwright himself, who directly participated in mainstage work. When dramaturgical expansions began in 1982, Literary Department personnel, such as assistants or interns, were assigned dramaturgical responsibilities to PIPS and Extended Readings (nonmainstage activities), as much to train the personnel in dramaturgy as to assist in development of the works in progress. Thus, although the Literary Department worked completely to feed the mainstage, it actually had very little practical participation in the mainstage production aspects of the company. This separation was far from the original intentions of hiring a dramaturg, even though theoretical considerations were inherent in the position.

Mason had said that his goal was to create a company of national renown that would perform classics as well as new plays written for and developed by company members in a true rotating repertory. The programs developed by Stitt went a long way toward realizing this goal. Just as a constant reevaluation and reinterpretation by each succeeding generation of artists is required for the classics, so too is it required for new plays after their initial runs. It was strongly believed that there can be a life for a new play even after its initial production, and this is where Stitt came in. He felt that a play should be produced again and again, applying fresh insight and interpretation to it each time. To this end, Mason and Stitt agreed to the idea of producing not only one classic and four new plays each year, but also one revival of a recent American play. The concept was that theatre literature is a living thing — a resource to be drawn upon for the expression of human truths through exploration with actors, involving both classics *and* new plays, with contemporary plays receiving the same treatment as classics.

At approximately this same time Porter Van Zandt began to reorganize the company into a well-staffed, smoothly functioning business organization, and to influence Marshall Mason to focus the company's direction toward a mainstream position of commercially viable material. It was probably to this end that Mason selected Stitt's own *The Runner Stumbles* as the first entry in the contemporary revival program, even though it had not been developed at Circle Rep. *The Runner Stumbles* had already been successfully produced on Broadway and had additionally been made into a Stanley Kramer film. For a variety of reasons, mostly to do with critical expectations and the insistence upon discovering new American plays, *The Runner Stumbles* remained the only entry in this program until the 1984 revival of Lanford Wilson's *Balm in Gilead* was presented in coproduction with Chicago's Steppenwolf Theatre.

Another idea was to keep the Circle Repertory work alive by having a series of productions of Circle Rep's own "classic" plays in strict rotating repertory at one theatre while the mainstage season of new plays and regular classics was continued at another. The plan was for productions such as *The Hot l Baltimore, When You Comin' Back, Red Ryder?, The Seahorse,* and *Talley's Folly,* the plays which had made Circle Rep's reputation, to have a continued life in the manner of a more traditional system of repertory playing. Although continuing the perennial search for the new, the theatre was now to be firmly concerned with existing theatre literature while at the same time trying to add to it. This plan was not Stitt's only philosophical contribution, although it was probably his most successful; it would be a perennial undercurrent of Circle Rep's production concept despite the fact that the plan to revive their own classics had yet to come to full fruition.

What can be said of Stitt's tenure as dramaturg is that he made sense of what had been an extremely haphazard developmental system. The formalization of existing programs and the innovations Stitt instituted had far-reaching effects. He created and maintained programs and systems that were specifically designed to help playwrights develop their skills as well as their plays. All playwrights who were associated with the company went through the process to some extent, from Lanford Wilson with his solid company foundation, and Tennessee Williams with his worldwide reputation, to the most innocent beginner.

Script Evaluation Service

One of the first things Stitt did during his tenure as official dramaturg was to take on a group of people to act as readers and to help sort out the mountains of scripts that had been sent to Circle Rep by hopeful writers. Stitt's hiring of readers led to one of Circle Rep's most unusual and unique offerings: the "Script Evaluation Service." Each script was read and evaluated by a member of the literary staff. Unless completely hopeless, each play was given a written, in-depth analysis and commentary by a staff member. Although the literary manager's name was at the bottom of each letter, the letters were actually a collaborative effort, starting with the reactions of the first readers and ending with those of the literary manager, always taking care to complete the process as humanely as possible. The feeling was that even if the news was bad, the written comments often gave the writer a sense that someone had indeed read the play and taken the time to think seriously about it; the letter would often be the impetus for a revision.

Most theatre groups, most particularly those in New York, do not accept unsolicited manuscripts, let alone critique them, and when replies are sent to the playwright, they are usually sent through printed form letters. In the beginning, before the process flowered into the Script Evaluation Service for which Circle Rep was to become famous, form letters were also the case at Circle Rep; any play that was not being considered for development was returned to the playwright with a terse, polite note over Milan Stitt's signature. By 1984, however, when B. Rodney Marriott was acting artistic director, he was emphatic in his desire to provide American playwrights with a personal response to their work despite the tremendous amount of time, thought, and money involved in critiquing each play. When a play was considered particularly promising, a staff member met with the playwright to offer suggestions for further development. As B. Rodney Marriott says in *Playwrights Don't Grow on Trees,* a Circle Rep Brochure:

> No script can be written adequately if the author feels he is writing in a "vacuum." Our script evaluation process is designed to give all playwrights who submit their work a reaction from the Circle Rep.

This dedication to the playwright and to the craft of playwriting was the core of Circle Rep's Literary Department, and illustrates Circle Rep's concern for artists, even for those it did not know and whose work would most likely never be done by the company. At least one third of all scripts received had some merit and were to be encouraged. Only a handful, approximately twenty per year, would actually become part of a developmental program such as the readings or the PIPS. Most readings and PIPS came from in-house writers, whose work was given priority treatment.

Finally, it must also be pointed out that statistically, the unsolicited manuscript process actually had limited success in terms of immediate result and product. During the five years of the Literary Department's heyday, only two unsolicited manuscripts ever made it all the way to mainstage production. These were *Threads,* by Jonathan Bolt, submitted in 1979 and produced in 1982, and *Levitation,* by Timothy Mason, submitted in 1982 and produced in 1984.

Friday Readings

According to Stitt, much of what he wanted already existed informally at Circle Rep when he took on the position of dramaturg in 1977. For example, Wilson had been writing for the company for nine years. Although it had been an informal process — such as waylaying whoever happened to be in the hallway to hear how a particular speech sounded—Wilson had been receiving from the company the trusted, affectionate, and hard criticism he needed. As a playwright himself, Stitt understood only too well the value of live readings of works-in-progress. As he said in *Playwrights Don't Grow on Trees*:

> Until I hear the actors for whom I'm writing speak the words, it feels as if I'm writing in the air. After a Friday reading of a first draft, the work becomes concrete, somehow more real, and the possibilities and enthusiasm for a rewrite expand.

A top priority was to make the readings accessible and scheduled with a high degree of dependability. As Stitt further pointed out,

> The process involved having company members do readings of rewrites; and finally seeing his work realized in full production by the actors for whom he had written. . . . Formalizing Wilson's informal process, I introduced Friday morning readings as a regular part of the acting company's work.

Company playwrights had always been able to organize a reading of their own plays as the need arose. Now the readings were turned into a regularly scheduled Friday morning event in the presence of the artistic staff, company members, and often the administrative staff as well. The idea was to insulate the process as much as possible so that although there might be critical reaction to the piece, it would be from a supportive community. The New York theatrical community was often quite eager to hear the readings, and at first it was invited to attend in order to swell the ranks. However, to insulate the process further, the readings were closed to the public in 1982.

Since the readings were of full plays, the ten to fifteen playwrights-in-residence could not possibly supply enough plays to fill a weekly schedule. Many outside playwrights were brought in to have their plays read to the company by Circle Rep actors at the Friday Readings. Sometimes the playwrights were invited on the basis of an unsolicited manuscript, sometimes on recommendation, occasionally on the suggestion of an agent. For outside playwrights, it was a fortunate expansion of Circle Rep's play development program. The readings were essentially unrehearsed, but a few plays and playwrights were being discovered through this process.

In theoretical terms, the Friday Readings were intended to be a kind of two-way street. On one side, the reading process was structured to help the playwright in every way possible, most particularly with direct input from company playwrights to determine how best to serve their own needs. On the other side, *every* project developed by Circle Rep began with this program. For the period between 1978 and 1983, there were no exceptions to this rule.

Company input to the readings was felt to be vital, so much so that until 1982, the policy was that no company rehearsal was to be held during the readings so that all company actors, playwrights, and directors would be able to attend. Additionally, the readings were an important weekly gathering place for a company that more and more was being scattered about the city trying to find additional theatrical work.

In the first year and a half of Stitt's unofficial—"unofficial" since the expected grant funds to pay Stitt did not materialize—but active tenure as dramaturg, thirty-seven playwrights in addition to Circle Rep's core of eleven resident playwrights heard their work read. By 1979, both Marshall Mason and B. Rodney Marriott felt that the Friday Readings were at the heart of what the Circle Rep did, and occupied much of their day-to-day planning. The first developmental step for any play of interest, whether member-authored or unsolicited, was a company reading. *No* play was ever considered to be ready for production until it had been fully tested through the various developmental stages. Whether this process was instituted more because it was felt to be impossible for a play that was fresh from a typewriter to be "right," or whether it was a serious attempt to minimize the risks of failure in a highly critical, commercial atmosphere, it served both purposes.

Although until 1984 a nominal fee of $5.00 was paid to each participating actor, actors were quite willing to take part in the series. They were always cast very carefully, first by the literary manager, and later by Tanya Berezin when she was hired as associate artistic director in charge of casting in 1982. A difficult balance had to be found; the playwright had to be given a good, clean, clear, intelligent reading which would insure the play's integrity and come close to realizing what he intended his play to be, while the actors constantly had to be given new challenges to explore their talents. Within the structure of the company the Friday Readings became one of the few places where the actors were not being overtly judged, so there was a greater sense of freedom in taking risks and in experimenting. Obviously, at the heart of the Friday Readings was the central philosophy of Circle Rep itself—the importance of nurturing its artists, whether playwright or actor.[2]

The ultimate goal of the program—to introduce plays to the company that could be selected for production—succeeded. Of 150 plays read between 1979 and 1983, twenty were produced by Circle Rep on the mainstage; this number equals more than three full seasons' worth of plays.

Projects-in-Progress

Another important part of the developmental program is the Projects-in-Progress series, or PIPS, held at the mainstage theatre, usually with script in hand. This is the only stage of the developmental process open to theatre subscribers and the public in general. The PIPS have been an established part of the developmental process at the Circle Rep for some time, but from 1977 the process took on a definite structure, as explained in a company brochure:

> When a play's growth requires in-depth workshop development with a director and cast, a Project-in-Progress may be scheduled. The PIPS program gives the playwright the benefit of a brief rehearsal period and audience reactions to the project. The play is first performed twice with each performance followed by an open discussion led by a member of the artistic staff.
>
> The playwright is then encouraged to make revisions before the play is again performed in a final week of PIPS.

The PIPS are also the most widely advertised of Circle Rep's activities. At the bottom of the program for each PIP, a short paragraph reads:

> The Projects-in-Progress series is an essential part of the play development process at Circle Rep. PIPS are rehearsed for two weeks, and are presented with minimal props and scenic elements. The PIPS program is designed to provide the playwright, director, and cast with information that can be garnered only with the help of an interested, critical and supportive audience.

The original idea was to have the audience participate in the post-performance discussions very much in the same manner as the Friday Readings. Again, as with the Friday Readings, there are two reasons for giving a play a PIP: the first is to develop the writer by affording him the opportunity to work on his play in depth; the second is to develop the play for full mainstage production.

At the PIP stage, Circle Rep is beginning to invest money in the material. The average Friday Reading costs $50, whereas the average PIP costs $2,000. Therefore, for a play to receive a PIP, ideally it should be under serious mainstage consideration. For example, John Bishop's *Winter Signs* was presented as a PIP in 1978, and then almost immediately remounted as a mainstage production when audience reaction was good, despite the fact that the play could have benefited from further development. More than likely, this precipitous push to formal presentation, which resulted in a poorly received mainstage production, occurred because there was then no program for play development.

Upon close examination, the PIPS demonstrated the best and the worst of the institutionalization processes which occurred at Circle Rep in its search for supportive ways to find new plays and new playwrights. An examination of how the PIPS were first received by the audiences and then perceived by the major participants reveals the working structure of the Circle Repertory Company itself in microcosm. Both the enormous benefits of working in a company environment and the persistent problems surrounding creativity in such a setting can be seen.

Within a short time after formalization of the process, the PIPS became a major problem in the substructure of the company. The fact that the audience for the PIPS was made up of 90 percent Circle Rep subscribers added a pressure to the series which the Friday Reading did not have and the PIPS were never intended to have. Subscribers began to realize that by attending the PIPS they could get a preview of the plays under consideration for the following mainstage season. The PIPS were the only point in the relationship between subscriber and theatre company where the audience could give direct feedback to the people responsible for presentations. However, in the heady process of participation, audiences sometimes forgot that the series was essentially a research-and-development program; their comments were often too harsh, sometimes destructive, and always judgmental. At the same time, unlike the professional theatre people who attended the Friday Readings, the audiences were not always knowledgeable. Yet the playwrights whose work was produced in the PIPS readily admit that the concept is a valid one. Playwright John Bishop candidly pointed out that one of the most valuable aspects of the PIPS was merely placing a play in front of an audience without necessarily paying attention to anything it had to say.

"They already come with a decision in their minds that they're coming to 'fix the play,'" he says.

> So their perception is different. I never stay for the discussions
> of my plays. I have always found the PIPS valuable to do but,
> on the other hand, most of the conversations afterwards are
> ridiculous. Let the director stay, or the dramaturg. I don't want
> to hear what they have to say. It's too destructive to me. A
> playwright is hard on himself anyway. I only hear the negative
> things, so I have to protect that. That's why I don't go. The
> important part of the PIPS is getting it read in front of an
> audience and hearing your play through an audience. You can
> hear everything that's wrong with it. Usually I get confirmation
> of problems. You can just sit there and watch them. You don't
> have to hear their comments. You can look at them when it's
> being read and you can see where it's not working.[3]

Ari Roth confirms Bishop's statements with his own observations during
his tenure as both associate literary manager and literary manager.
"PIPS please no one," Roth says.

> They don't please the actors because they are basically readings;
> the actors don't get to do much work. They are like guinea pigs
> for the playwright. The playwright likes PIPS because he can
> do some revisions, but he certainly doesn't get to see his play
> mounted or staged one bit, and the Circle is not making a
> commitment to produce the play. So in artistic terms, the PIPS
> are in the middle ground. It's even more frustrating for the
> director. We're not doing real theatre with them, just a little bit
> of script work, but it's not as intense as most people would
> want right now. It has become a safe kind of program. It's a
> placating device for people we owe things to; in a way, people
> we want to string along. This is a backlash. It never, ever was
> intended to be this way.[4]

As in any institutional setting, political considerations also arise. In
the case of the PIPS, the Literary Department would get caught in the
middle. There are many writers who wait their turn—writers to whom
the department owes favors—and although the Literary Department was
committed to performing ten PIPS a year, this number was often cut
down to six or seven due to financial considerations. There is never a
way to satisfy all the hunger. Many plays were PIPed even though they
would never be considered for mainstage, simply to repay obligations.

Obviously, Circle Rep's philosophy of nurturing was not always successful for everyone.

The fact that there was no real commitment behind the PIPS was an even more serious problem, one that created deep erosions in the very concept of family and company. There is still little doubt that what was perceived as a lack of commitment was antagonizing a good many of the playwrights. However, there is equally little doubt that commitment to a family of writers and commitment to the very best play are two quite different things. As Ari Roth said, "We created this expensive developmental machine to find the great American voice. Therefore, the Literary Department has gone off in one direction with its very conscientious and idealistic reports while the company ideology, as it panned out, has gone off in a somewhat different direction. Or, at least, they are not walking in step with each other."

Another negative aspect of the Circle Rep system was that there were always a great many plays that were ready enough for production consideration but too few available slots in which to place them. Because of this situation, the playwrights were often kept waiting an inordinate amount of time before production was possible. At the same time, the nature of the theatrical business was such that the Circle Rep was unwilling officially to release their plays. Even plays that appeared to be set for either PIP or production would often fall through at the last minute for a variety of frustrating reasons. To strike a balance, the Literary Department in the 1981–1982 season created what was tantamount to a PIP contract. More of a letter of agreement than a contract, the most interesting clause was that Circle Rep had one month following the date of the last PIP performance to inform the playwright in writing of its choice of one of the following options: 1) to produce the play in a specific season, 2) to request a further revision while maintaining an expressed interest in the play, or 3) to express no further interest in the material and release it. In this manner, as long as the play was being PIPed, Circle Rep was assured of first option without feeling pressured. Too often in the past a play not under contract would be snapped up by an outside producer, so that the money invested in the PIP by Circle Rep would be lost.

One such case was *Spookhouse,* by Harvey Fierstein, which was given a PIP toward the end of the 1981–1982 season. At about the same time, Fierstein was beginning to experience some success with *Torch Song Trilogy,* which moved to off-Broadway and then to Broadway while

Spookhouse was at Circle Rep. After its PIP, Circle Rep expressed interest in the play, but it was clear at this point that Fierstein had a commercial future. He and his agent refused Circle Rep the rights to the play, which subsequently opened on off-Broadway in a commercial production in 1984 starring Anne Meara.

As the seasons progressed, the subscribers' attendance was so regular that an entire four-performance PIP run could easily be sold out almost as soon as the seats became available, thus leaving little room for the company to attend. It also became policy by 1983 that company members were seated on a second priority basis. This policy meant that the company's participation in the selection of PIPS-to-mainstage was minimal. By the 1982–1983 season, ten PIPS were scheduled; even in an ideal season, only five of these would be able to make it to mainstage. But in fact the 1982–1983 season had already been selected from the previous season's PIPS. Also, the 1983–1984 season was being filled very quickly with a number of special projects: Sam Shepard's *Fool for Love* was imported from San Francisco; *The Sea Gull* was selected as the season's classic; *Full Hookup,* by Conrad Bishop and Elizabeth Fuller (to be directed by Mason), had already been produced in Louisville and did not need to be PIPed; *Levitation,* by Timothy Mason, had already been PIPed in the 1982–1983 season; John Bishop's new play, *The Harvesting,* was PIPed before the 1983 season began; Wilson's *Balm in Gilead* was selected as a revival production in conjunction with Chicago's Steppenwolf Theatre; and Marsha Norman's *The Winter Shakers,* which had been written on commission, was chosen (but did not materialize during that season).

Thus the nine PIP slots would be for plays that would have to have mainstage consideration postponed for a full season at the very least, by which time it was pretty obvious that other special projects would be developed, thus jeopardizing their possibilities for mainstage production even further. It is easy to see why enthusiasm for the PIP series began seriously to lag. This lagging enthusiasm spelled the beginning of the end of the Literary Department's heyday.

Extended Readings

Extended Readings, the newest aspect of the developmental programs, was never clearly defined; as a result, its success has been difficult to evaluate. During Marriott's tenure as literary manager, it became increasingly obvious that further revisions might be necessary on a play even after it had received a PIP. The company might require further time to review the material, particularly if radical changes had been made. To address this growing concern, Mason and Marriott created the Extended Readings. They were structured with one week of rehearsal for director and cast, but unlike the PIPS, revisions were not encouraged during the rehearsal process. Initially, this program had been designed as an intermediary step between the informal Friday Readings and the more formal PIPS; in such a capacity the program could have served as a clearing house for plays of marginal interest to the company. In fact, the first two plays given Extended Readings were *Gas Station,* by Shelby Buford, Jr. (a company playwright), and *The Bone Garden,* by Peter Maeck (a lab playwright), both plays admittedly of borderline possibility for the mainstage since they were wildly different from the lyric realism style that had come to be associated with Circle Rep. Marriott felt, however, that both plays were well written and he wanted an opportunity to hear them read aloud before a decision was made whether or not to give them a workshop production. Ultimately, neither play was done in workshop, although both went on to full productions in other theatres.

Soon, however, Mason decided that the Extended Readings program could be used to greater benefit. If it were defined as an intermediate step between a PIP and a mainstage production, a number of tasks could be performed: a play could be given an Extended Reading if the company wanted one last look at the play before deciding whether or not to produce it, or if it was clear that the play was going to be a mainstage production, but the author wanted a chance to hear a new draft one more time before production. To avoid possible pitfalls, Rob Meiksins, assistant literary manager, successfully argued that the program should be utilized only when needed. Thus, although specific times were set aside within the season for Extended Readings, and up to seven were budgeted, they would be used only when directly needed.

The success of this program is almost impossible to judge. Each Extended Reading, with up to twenty hours of rehearsal, would be presented only once for an audience made up entirely of Circle Rep company, staff, and friends (approximately fifty people), who would, as always, remain for a discussion. Probably the greatest shortcoming of the program was that it was neither a cold reading nor was it rehearsed enough to give it an adequate representation. The actors were usually anxious to get on their feet to stage some of the action, thereby finding the seats a constraint. The author was not permitted to revise the play during this period, so that if problems became obvious during the rehearsal, he was not encouraged to deal with them. The danger then was that the discussion after the play would only confirm problems that the author already knew existed. From this point of view the process was not highly productive.

For Circle Rep's purposes, however, the program was undoubtedly of great value. It gave management the opportunity to hear a play one more time before decisions had to be made. The Extended Readings demonstrated one of the few times that pragmatic production considerations were considered more important than the needs of the artists.

Playwrights Workshop/Playwrights Lab

Continuing the process of formalizing existing programs, in the fall of 1978 Stitt formed a Playwrights Workshop for those writers he considered to be the most promising and talented. The workshop has continued to grow, numbering in 1986 at least twenty who meet biweekly with the literary manager and the company's resident playwrights. Of the writers who participated in Stitt's original workshop, most have successfully progressed to productions either at Circle Rep or at other New York theatres. The initial group included James Farrell, whose play *In the Recovery Lounge* was produced by the Circle Repertory Company in 1978, and who was commissioned by the company in 1984 to write *Bing and Walker;* Mick Casale, whose play *Elm Circle* won the FDG/CBS Award in 1984 and was produced by Playwrights Horizons in May of 1984; Ralph Pape, who had a long-running off-Broadway hit with *Say Goodnight, Gracie;* Joseph Pintauro, who has had two novels published to critical acclaim, and whose play *Snow Orchid* was produced by Circle Rep to poor reviews after an extraordinarily well-received PIP presentation; and Joseph Mathewson, who also had two novels published and an off-Broadway production of his play *Man Proposing* during the 1984 season. Of this group, James Farrell and Joseph Pintauro have become members of the Circle Rep Playwriting Company. Another Stitt discovery, although not a part of this early group, was Bill C. Davis, whose play *Mass Appeal* had originally been given a Projects-in-Progress production at the Circle Rep and went on to become an off-Broadway as well as a Broadway success.

The Playwrights Lab, as it is now called, is by far the most popular and effective of all the developmental programs run by the Literary Department. It was created by Stitt as a way of developing and grooming talented writers for potential membership in the playwriting company. The Lab writers under Marriott and Meiksins were mostly younger writers whose future was of interest to the company. Most were found through the unsolicited manuscript process. In general, the theory behind the Lab was that a writer who had talent, even though unrefined, would still be a valuable member of the theatre, if not of Circle Rep. By making the playwright a member of the Lab it would be possible to keep a close, interested watch on his or her work. Also, a Lab playwright would more likely give the company top priority on all new work, an inexpensive way for Circle Rep to find good plays and good writers.

Workshops for playwrights have a long history and almost always reflect well on the company that creates them. Obviously, the success of the workshops is determined by the talent of the writers who participate. One famous workshop was run by the Royal Court Theatre in London in the late 1960s. The members of the Royal Court Theatre Writers Workshop went on to considerable renown, even in America, including David Edgar (*Nicholas Nickleby*), David Hare (*Plenty*), Stephen Poliakoff (*American Days*), and many others. Most of these writers now make up the leading playwrights of the English theatre. It is too soon to tell whether or not Circle Rep Lab playwrights will enjoy the same celebrity as their English counterparts. So far, the members have had a certain amount of success both with productions at Circle Rep and at other theatres around the country.

Originally called the Playwrights Workshop, the structure of the Lab has remained intact since it began in 1977. The idea is to provide an isolated, insulated forum to which writers can bring their work, however long, short, or in process. In three-hour sessions held every two weeks, the pieces are read aloud by member writers and discussed. Here, however, the attempt to protect the writer is not as strong as at a Friday Reading or a PIP. The Lab reading is perhaps the only place at Circle Rep where a writer might be told that his piece quite simply does not work and perhaps should not even be written. The Lab is a community of writers who are theoretically not in competition with each other, even though some are established and some are beginners. It was reorganized to provide writers with a sense of belonging to a theatrical community. The value is in receiving the comments of their peers in an insulated environment that permits only playwrights and a member of the literary staff.

As the years have progressed, the membership of the workshop has grown from the original five under Milan Stitt to twenty-five under Rob Meiksins. This size makes it increasingly difficult to accommodate the needs of all who wish to have their work read. To relieve the pressure, only small pieces are worked on during the sessions. To be able to read full-length plays, however, a series of weekend retreats throughout the year was created. There are at least three or four such weekend retreats, most of which are held on Long Island at Sag Harbor, which is where Lanford Wilson, Tanya Berezin, and many other friends and members of Circle Rep live. Approximately thirty-five people can easily be housed in the various homes. These weekends may last for three days with three or four plays featured every day. At these meetings full-length drafts are read to acquaint the Lab members with the plays that are then worked on in sections during the biweekly meetings. Attendance by the more established playwrights has been somewhat erratic, but many have participated and most use the workshop and the weekend retreats as a resource for the development of their own work. The benefit for the young writers, obviously, is the opportunity to have their plays critiqued by some of the more famous and established writers in the company. For the most part the process has been perceived as morale boosting. Julie Bovasso has been very active in this regard, constantly reaffirming the playwrights' sense of pride in being artists, and always insisting upon maintaining the integrity of the individual artist's work amid all the critical analysis. The other company playwright who has been most active in this capacity is Lanford Wilson, who has brought his own work periodically to the workshop, but for the most part provides a great deal of critical input and encouragement.

As has been noted, the Literary Department is the keenest example of the conflict within Circle Rep between support for the artist and the search for new plays. It is undeniable that the amount of work covered in its five years was extraordinary, including more than ten thousand unsolicited manuscripts read and evaluated with letters of critique returned on each one; more then two hundred plays given readings; and approximately forty plays given PIPs. It is difficult to see how this kind of work could be accomplished without the Literary Department. Yet this was the first department to suffer extensively from the budgetary cuts of 1984. By its very nature, the Literary Department has been an investment in the future. Without the research and development it represents, the company may suffer from lack of the explorative efforts for which it has become well known.

But according to many people within the company, a severe credibility gap had developed within the department as it pertained to the operating structure of Circle Rep as a production house. The beginning of this gap was in the very origins of the Literary Department in 1977, when it became clear that what had originally been expected of Milan Stitt — focus on productions in rehearsal — and what he actually focused on — development of new playwrights — were two quite different things. It seemed to have been painfully obvious to everyone involved that the Literary Department had been cut off from the mainstage almost entirely. This was, and is, a serious problem. Mainstage play selection has always been handled by the artistic director who, by definition, is responsible for the artistic content of the company. Thus, the focus of the Literary Department became only to "put plays on the menu," a background type of functioning which is difficult to justify considering the activity of the developmental system itself. A great many plays were being directly affected in that they were being developed by a department that could not fulfill the promise inherent in a development program. There was, rather, only the vague hope that Mason (or later Marriott) would like a play well enough to produce it. But from the playwright's point of view, the play was being developed by the department with the goal of production. The only way to bridge this gap would have been for the department to fulfill its original role by acting as dramaturg for the mainstage. However, most of the Literary Department personnel, except for Marriott, had difficulty getting into the mainstage arena of activity.

Ironically, then, the department which was perhaps the truest expression of the nurturing aspects of Circle Rep became so involved in nurturing that it became isolated from the mainstage. While isolation was exactly what was needed to create the kind of environment that would best allow for the nurturing, isolation also meant that the department had no input into play selection or into development of the final product — in a sense leaving its work to be solely theoretical.

Thus in an odd turn of events, the department that was the most popular with the outside world was the first to be cut when a financial crisis hit. Playwrights loved it because it gave them good, caring feedback about their work; audiences loved it because it afforded them a rare opportunity to participate in the process of play development; actors loved it because it gave them the chance to work on many different kinds of plays and roles, thus enhancing their personal artistic growth. But in the final analysis, the department was not sufficiently product-oriented to warrant the financial investment it required to remain fully operational. As a result it was substantially cut and rendered almost impotent.

Beginning with the winter of 1984, the position of literary manager will eventually be phased out altogether. Along with the position of literary manager, the process of reading, evaluating, and returning unsolicited manuscripts with personalized commentary will be phased out as part of the budget-cutting process. Until the phasing is completed, the department will still look at all the scripts that are sent in. Any that are of inherent interest (revisions of encouraged plays, or plays of authors that are well known to Circle Rep, or plays submitted by an accredited agent) will be read in the usual manner. All unsolicited manuscripts will be returned to the author unread with a cover letter explaining the financial difficulties that make it unfeasible to continue the costly process. Also, as of the winter of 1984, it would seem that Mason intends to cut the Playwriting Company down to approximately five writers per year who will be commissioned to write for the company.[5]

The rationale behind this severe reorganization was that Circle Rep had become such a highly visible institution over the years, and that the New York theatre scene was so critically competitive, it was no longer possible for the company to produce a writer for the first time. Too much had come to be expected, and any writer being premiered at the Circle Rep would automatically be reviewed harshly by the critics, a situation ultimately hurting rather than helping the development of the writer. Thus, although Circle Rep will continue to produce new plays, it will no longer be the function of the Literary Department to discover *new* playwrights, a major change in the company's philosophy and operations.

The future of the Playwrights Lab is also uncertain. It is possible that it will continue to exist as it has since 1977. It is also possible that, because of the strong family feelings within the Lab, it will continue as it stands now, but as an independent writers' workshop outside the bounds of Circle Rep. It is difficult to determine its future with any certainty; one cannot second guess what Mason's ultimate decisions will be. As Ari Roth has said, "The message that has come down from on high is, 'You guys have done a great job in the past but the past is over. We're going in a different direction.' "

Throughout its history, Mason deliberately set out to establish Circle Rep as a major force in American theatre. He did so systematically and, it seemed, quite logically. However, Mason did not control the growth of his company and permitted it to expand under a management staff that was isolated from the artistic content of the company. The company's talents seemed to be spread too thin and subsequently the quality of the product declined. Frequently, Circle Rep was gently reproached by those who had always been its greatest champions. Peter Buckley, in a May 1980 article in *Horizon,* worried whether the Circle Rep was becoming a victim of its own success. On March 14, 1982, Jeremy Gerard wrote an extensive article in the *New York Times,* "Will Success Spoil Circle Rep?" Although he itemized much of the obvious increased activity from the Circle Rep's classics (*Hamlet, Mary Stuart, Richard II*) to the Young Playwrights Festival, he worried that all the activity might be diluting the company's effectiveness since the 1982 season had been uneven despite some of "the most prolific talent around." He pointed out that *Threads* by Jonathan Bolt had been well liked by subscribers, but had perplexed the critics. Patrick Meyer's *K2* was dropped. It was to have been coproduced with the Phoenix Theatre, but the two companies were unable to work out a fiscally equitable way of dealing with a $60,000 set, two subscription lists, and a limited run. Dropping the production, however, left holes in both groups. Gerard continued his assessment by accusing Circle Rep of filling in with a tepid evening of one-acts to accommodate its subscribers.

Mason, however, as quoted by Gerard, defended the company's position:

> Over the thirteen years, it's been a matter of expanding and contracting a number of times. At the moment, I guess you could say we're expanding. It may be too much. The larger you are, the bigger the problems. Maybe I've forgotten how difficult it is when nobody knows you, but I don't believe anything gets easier. I must say I don't think we're doing badly. Our production of *Richard II* definitely demonstrates that we're out there taking risks.

Gerard never answered the question posed by the title of his article, but he did recognize that the company activity reflected Mason's enthusiasm for trying new things.

Although the company had grown almost organically, it had been caught up in the mechanism of institutionalization almost beyond its desires and, more particularly, beyond the realm of its original concepts.[6] It could no longer continue without drastic changes in operation — changes that would be keenly felt in the Literary Department. The big budget cuts of 1984 included 1) phasing out the position of literary manager, 2) returning unsolicited manuscripts unread, 3) relinquishing the active search to discover new playwrights, 4) cutting the reading and evaluating of plays almost entirely, and 5) phasing out the Playwrights Lab during the 1984–1985 season.

The year 1984 was not one of great success and stability. Instead, the fifteenth anniversary year of Circle Rep marked the beginning of radical and sweeping changes in the company, all designed to bring back the success and vitality that had been so obvious during the late seventies. For the company which was suffering one of the worst financial crises of its existence and also meeting with critical dissatisfaction, 1984 was a disappointing year all around.

Circle Rep seemed to be suffering not only a budget deficit but an artistic deficit as well, even though from 1974 to 1984 the Circle Rep grew both in size and reputation. During that time, the company's number of subscribers reached as many as six thousand; the number of artists who called it home quadrupled; the number of projects being developed at one time increased; and the management staff more than trebled. In this sense, the decade was an exciting and productive one, but it was also a period in which the product was simply not meeting the standards that critics had come to demand of the Circle Rep. Thus, with Mason's attempt to create a living theatre of major importance, he eventually found that artistic quality had indeed been sacrificed. This is the double-edged sword of growth and deficit Circle Rep felt. A major transition in company policy resulted, beginning with the extensive budget cuts in 1984 which decimated the Literary Department programs and personnel. The Literary Department had been created essentially to fulfill an idealistic goal. Because of that optimism, it did not have the political effect it could have had within the company. Although it had been created to participate in the mainstage, it never met that goal. It became, in last analysis, dispensable.

Lanford Wilson and Marshall W. Mason in 1969.

The first productions
at the loft: Chekhov's
The Three Sisters
(1969–1970 season).

Rob Thirkield (l.), Zane Lasky (c.), and Conchatta Ferrell (r.) in Lanford Wilson's *The Hot l Baltimore,* directed by Marshall Mason (1972–1973 season) (photograph by Ken Howard).

Mark Medoff's *When You Comin' Back, Red Ryder?* (1973–1974 season) (photograph by Robert E. Wasserman).

Tennessee Williams and Marshall Mason at opening night party of Williams's *Battle of Angels* (1974–1975 season) (photograph by Ken Howard).

Tanya Berezin (l.) and Conchatta Ferrell (r.) in Tennessee Williams's *Battle of Angels,* the first production at the new theatre (photograph by Ken Howard).

Rob Thirkield (l.) and
Bradford Dourif (r.) in
Not to Worry, directed
by Lanford Wilson
(1974–1975 season)
(photograph by
Michael Zettler).

Wilson and Mason in 1974
(photograph by Ken Howard).

Jules Felffer with Mason, who directed Feiffer's *Knock, Knock* (1975–1976 season) (photograph by Herbert Migdoll).

Judd Hirsch in Jules Feiffer's *Knock, Knock* (photograph by Herbert Migdoll).

Frank Wedekind's *Lulu* (1977–1978 season).

Christopher Reeve
and Jeff Daniels in
Lanford Wilson's *The
5th of July*, directed by
Marshall Mason
(1977–1978 season)
(photograph by Ken
Howard).

William Hurt with Bobo
Lewis and Joyce
Reehling in Milan
Stitt's *The Runner
Stumbles* (1978–1979
season) (photograph
by Ken Howard).

Judd Hirsch and Trish
Hawkins in Lanford
Wilson's *Talley's Folly*,
directed by Marshall
Mason (1978–1979
season) (photograph
by Gerry Goodstein).

William Hurt and Bea-
trice Straight in William
Shakespeare's *Hamlet*
(1979–1980 season)
(photograph by Gerry
Goodstein).

Tanya Berezin with Stephanie Gordon and Timothy Shelton in Friedrich von Schiller's *Mary Stuart* (1979–1980 season) (photograph by Gerry Goodstein).

Wilson and Mason (photograph by Ken Howard).

Wilson autographing
The Mound Builders
(photograph by Ken
Howard).

Wilson and Mason
in 1987 (photograph
by Jay Thompson).

The four founders in 1984, the fifteenth anniversary year: Rob Thirkield and Mason, standing; Wilson and Tanya Berezin, sitting (photograph by Ken Howard).

9

Transitions and the Changing Climate of the Eighties

DESPITE the severe problems that befell the company in 1984, the tally sheet still looked positive at the end of 1983. By that time, fifteen years after Circle Rep organized as a company on 84th Street and upper Broadway, the company had experienced considerable and continual success. For one thing, it had accumulated an impressive record of awards: the Pulitzer Prize, two Tony awards, two New York Drama Critics awards, twelve Drama Desk awards, twenty-seven Obie awards, seven inclusions in *Ten Best Plays* annual, four Theatre World awards, five Outer Critics Circle awards, two Clarence Derwent awards, thirteen Villager awards, the Vernon Rice Award, and the Margo Jones Award.

The list of successful plays was equally impressive, including such works as *Talley's Folly, The 5th of July,* and *A Tale Told* (revised and produced again in 1985 as *Talley and Son*), which make up Lanford Wilson's Talley Trilogy; Wilson's *The Hot l Baltimore, The Mound Builders,* and *Serenading Louie;* Mark Medoff's *When You Comin' Back, Red Ryder?;* Edward J. Moore's *The Sea Horse;* Jim Leonard's *The Diviners;* Sam Shepard's *Buried Child* and *Fool for Love;* Milan Stitt's *The Runner Stumbles* and *Back in the Race;* Marsha Norman's *'night Mother, The Holdup,* and *The Winter Shakers;* John Bishop's *The*

Great Grandson of Jedediah Kohler, Winter Signs, and *The Harvesting;* Albert Innaurato's *Gemini,* and *Ulysses in Traction;* and Jules Feiffer's *Knock, Knock,* to name just a few of the outstanding plays.

In addition, by 1983 the company had an expanded roster of serious theatre artists with the kind of impressive professional credits that would make an old-time studio proud.[1]

Still, despite what was phenomenal success for a company with a tiny 160-seat theatre in an industry fraught with artistic and financial hazards, major upheavals were imminent. Many of the company's activities were being reassessed for their appropriateness to the goals that were still important to the CRC. Conflicts within the leadership had placed Circle Rep at a crossroads. Everyone felt the necessity for change in the face of problems which had multiplied with success and growth. Ari Roth expressed his feeling that "any artistic divergence or crossing of paths that have happened within the last few years, I think, come from conflicts in the masterminds at Circle; what they see as the guiding artistic force. By that I mean, we are committed to both an idea of family and one of excellence. We are committed to the idea of putting on the best possible play. That's one of the reasons we have a Literary Department; to continue looking for the great American voice."

Yet with the institutional growth of the theatre much of what had been considered valuable—particularly the intimacy—was gone. As John Bishop pointed out, "I think those of us who were there very early and those of us who came during the real growth period—which was the late 70s—see the Circle more as an institution now and sort of mourn the passing of the smaller theatre."

Equally important, the direct approach of the early days had been dispersed into an all-inclusive shotgun effect that concentrated heavily on "the plays" without fully determining which plays were the most important ones to develop. As Richard Frankel, general manager, noted, "We are still trying to figure out what we want to be doing and what is important to us. Are all new plays important to us? Are only American plays important to us? Or new plays by new playwrights? Or is it new plays by our resident playwrights that are important to us? Do we do only classic classics like Chekhov and Shakespeare? Or, what about our own classics? Do we do *Hot l Baltimore?* Would that be just regurgitating old stuff or do we have a legitimate responsibility to our own legacy?"[2]

Marshall Mason, however, pinpointed without hesitation what to him was still the most important aspect of the Circle Rep—the excellence that could earn it the position of a national theatre. "I would be less than candid if I didn't admit that from the very beginning, the idea was to create a theatre of such startling excellence that sooner or later, by way of acclamation, the world, as it were, would come to us and say, you will be our theatre in the United States—a National Theatre. I would love to be deserving of having accomplished enough of importance to be considered the best America has to offer. We have not accomplished that yet. When I started in the beginning, I said it would take twenty years to build such a theatre—to build a great theatre. What I meant was the kind of theatre whose excellence is so clear that it would become a leader to everyone else."

Now, at the end of the Circle Repertory Company's fifteenth year, the company was in the process of a reorganization that would result in a major operational transition. It would be a change that, in many ways, would take the company back to its original concepts, most particularly those of ensemble and revolving repertory. Despite original intentions, after the first two seasons on 84th Street the company has only sporadically played in repertory before slipping into a regular play-by-play subscription season: *Hamlet* and *Mary Stuart* were played in revolving repertory (1979–1980), as was *Twelfth Night* with *The Beavercoat* (1980–1981), and *The Great Grandson of Jedediah Kohler* with *Richard II* (1981–1982). Now fifteen years old, Circle Rep will cut out a small, select group of actors and playwrights from the 100-member existing company and revitalize not only its dream of playing in revolving rep but also the original ensemble concept.[3] In 1983, the National Endowment for the Arts (NEA) announced a $1,000,000 major grant to be awarded to five ensemble theatre groups in the country. It was a grant that Zelda Fichandler of Arena Stage called the most important made in the history of the National Endowment. The grant Circle Rep received from the National Endowment totalled $260,000 for the first year of a five-year program beginning with the 1985–1986 season. The first-year grant covered 75 percent of Circle Rep's annual budget. The next year the National Endowment would supply 50 percent of the money, and following year 25 percent, and so on.

The company's transition to this new phase of operations is philosophical as well as organizational in nature. Mason outlined his goals and beliefs in the Artistic Director's Statement made to the NEA in his application for the grant:

> As Artistic Director, I am eager to engage our staff in redefining their own motivations for working in the theatre, and to eliminate what I have perceived as a drift away from sensitivity to the principles on which we are founded.

As has been pointed out, in creating an institution to protect the creative process, the emphasis shifted dramatically from the actor to the writer. In the process of discovering and nurturing the new writer, the company became "increasingly dispirited at being relegated to a secondary position,"[4] even though much new and exciting work was either developed or discovered. After fifteen years, there was a strong feeling that change was needed to preserve the company's original objectives, sustain the group's ensemble image, and insure the company's health in an unrelentingly hazardous environment.

After countless discussions regarding fiscal possibilities as well as a need for reaffirmation of artistic commitments, it was decided that part of the CRC's yearly functioning would finally operate as an ensemble in a true repertory system. The scale of this operation was determined by the generous National Endowment grant. It was the second largest of eight grants made to nurture distinguished ensembles throughout the country, the largest going to the Arena Stage in Washington.[5] The plan called for Circle Rep's new operations to center around a limited season of twenty-five weeks at another theatre of larger capacity and greater storage area than the Sheridan Square Playhouse. This separate season consists of twenty-five actors and four resident playwrights, all of whom are expected to participate in daily exercise, communication, development, and production. Without the usual rush to production, the ensemble can develop classics as well as new works written for them by the resident playwrights. For this total commitment, each participant is paid $500 per week. As Mason pointed out in his grant proposal:

> We need developmental time with our major artists at levels of remuneration that reflect the dignity of their artistic commitment. We need the NEA support to buy us the time to build a genuine repertoire that we can sustain over a period of years, instead of wastefully releasing our creations to commercial managements who exploit the harvest with no thought of enriching the artistic soil from which it came.

Always striving toward the excellence he cherishes, Mason continued:

In the process, the Circle Lab will continue to explore for the discovery of new playwrights, actors and directors, while the Circle Rep Company will focus on the mature artists—a company that shares the goal of leading the American theatre to new heights of excellence.

The actors are engaged seasonally, as in the Royal Shakespeare Company, performing all roles in a three-play repertoire which includes a classic, a revival of a previously produced Circle Rep play which was considered exceptional at the time it was initially produced, and a new play that will be written especially for this select company. The three productions play in nightly rotation, with each actor playing a variety of roles, challenging all to stretch beyond the types demanded by commercial casting. In addition, according to Marshall Mason in his grant proposal, roles are assigned to be performed by more than one actor, endowing each performance with a "freshness and vitality unimagined" in the limited runs that have been the norm of theatrical tradition in the United States.

The remainder of the existing company continues operations as usual. Out of the developmental processes, it is responsible for supplying the two "bookend" productions which, although not performing in repertory, round out the season.

The new project made possible by the National Endowment is very reminiscent of the early days of the company when the family of artists numbered thirty actors and five resident playwrights. It is also reminiscent of when the New York State Council on the Arts in 1978 provided Circle Rep with enough funds to attempt a similar experiment on a smaller scale: at that time the CRC was able to designate sixteen actors for a limited twenty-week season. The resident company members were paid a bare $150 per week for a full-time commitment, but included an impressive array of talent: Michael Ayr, Tanya Berezin, Joyce Reehling, Jeff Daniels, Jack Davidson, Jake Dengel, Stephanie Gordon, Trish Hawkins, Jonathan Hogan, William Hurt, Ken Kliban, Sharon Madden, Burke Pearson, Nancy Snyder, Danton Stone, and Jimmie Ray Weeks.

Despite strong indications of success and even stronger feeling that this was a solid direction in which to move, the 1978 project was dismantled after two years due to the perennial problem of lack of funds. However, it had produced some important results, as the grant proposal documented:

In the two years of this experiment of solidifying the ensemble, we created *5th of July*, Patrick Meyers' *Feedlot*, Albert Innaurato's *Ulysses in Traction* (which prompted Walter Kerr to wonder if a production can be too good for a play) and *Talley's Folly* which received the Pulitzer Prize. Artistically very exciting, this experiment culminated in the rotating repertory of *Mary Stuart* and William Hurt's *Hamlet*. But because the stipend was so small, the actors elected to return to the "by-production" remunerative system. The meager paycheck too strongly resembled the dole, and the actors preferred the dignity of a higher salary for short engagements to smaller pay for a guaranteed period of time. Nevertheless, this experiment whetted the aesthetic appetite of the Company in a way that none of our commercial successes have. It created a hunger for sustained working conditions that would stimulate the creative spirit of collaboration in this artistic community.

The funding provided by the National Endowment was exactly what was needed to continue in the tradition of the 1978 project. Now it can no longer be called "an experiment," but rather a proven method of company functioning in which their best work seems to emerge. Although there was some insecurity on the part of the actors as to the selection of the newly designated ensemble, there was a great deal of enthusiasm for the artistic concept of the "new" operation. In idealistic terms, it is possible to perceive the philosophical aspects of the latest transition not only as the conclusion of one era leading to a new beginning, but also as a retrospective observation that all of the past operations have been a prologue to the new moment. The CRC was originally created as an ongoing ensemble of actors who from the start shared the common vision of creating a new aesthetic together—the complete integration of text and performance into a living play. The achievement of this goal was realized within the fourth year of operations when the company produced Lanford Wilson's *The Hot l Baltimore,* confirmed by the New York theatre critics as an achievement of the company's basic artistic goal. Now, at the end of the Circle Rep's fifteenth year in operation, the NEA Ensemble Grant has given Circle Rep the monies that will make the continuation of this aesthetic goal an ongoing reality.

Clearly, attempting once again to operate in a true revolving repertory system demonstrates that the ideals from the sixties have remained the same over the years. The theatre may have been mainstreamed as plays were produced for commercial reasons alone, even outward appearances may have changed—clothing being more conservative, hair-styles long since retreating from shoulder length to the more conventional cuts of the eighties—and yet, despite both theatrical and personal mainstreaming, the dreams have never changed. The only difference is that now, for the first time in the company's history, there might be sufficient funds to keep the dreams solvent.

In the new NEA program (#2, The Ensemble Project):

> The four playwrights will be commissioned to develop new plays specifically for members of the ensemble to perform. They will each receive the same amount as an actor, totalling $12,500 for each commission. The writers will attend working sessions with the acting ensemble, and will develop plays for the following season.
>
> While we might expect considerable continuity in the composition of the resident ensemble from one season to the next, there will also be an opportunity for change, allowing other members of the Circle Rep to participate from year to year. Four different playwrights will be commissioned each season, which should result in a rich fund of material available for our repertoire—20 new plays will be commissioned over the period of the grant.
>
> In addition to the 80 actors designated as members of the Circle Repertory Company, we will also have the potential to attract other artists who share our vision of theatre and who are able to commit to a residency for a six-month season.

It remains to be seen whether or not twenty new commissioned plays will add up to twenty of the best plays the CRC could possibly find, and whether or not the elitist procedure of designating performers in the existing company or hiring outside guest artists will add to the sense of dispirit that plagued the company during the last few years of its operations.

There were many reasons for Circle Rep's application to the NEA. The company had been mainstreamed, socialized, and institutionalized, but the most important reason had to do with finances. At the fifteen-year mark of operations, Circle Rep's budgets had increased enormously. Within the five years previous to the grant application, the operating budget had escalated an astonishing 400 to 450 percent, despite the fact that company members do not receive compensation unless directly involved in a production. Part of the increase was inflationary in nature—

everything cost more in 1983 than it did in 1978 — but part of it was also due to Circle Rep's increased activity. The larger budgetary needs were met by a variety of means. In 1978 subscription revenues were approximately $22,000. The substantial increase to $504,000 by 1983 was directly attributable to an increase in subscriber membership from 700 to 6,000. Higher revenues could also be traced to an increase in nonsubscription individual ticket prices from $7.00 in 1978 to $22.50 in 1983. Although these figures may indicate substantially higher revenue, what did not change over the years was the fact that the money coming into the company has always been slightly less than the money going out. Proportionally, a debt of $30,000 ten years ago was just as crippling as a $400,000 debt in 1983. According to General Manager Richard Frankel, the only thing that ever changed was the decimal point. As Frankel candidly points out,

> The desperation is continual. We have a plan to try to pay down the debt systematically. To keep our expenses below our output. One thing that's good about us now is that larger amounts of money are generated. If something works we may make thirty, forty, or fifty thousand dollars on it. There are opportunities to take large chunks out of it. We're committed to doing it. We have to do it. We cannot function carrying this kind of debt. . . . To me, it's continual peril. It's a very perilous business. We have debts, and we have change in artistic needs, and we have change in people, and people who are now 45 instead of 28, who want to live differently now than they did back then and do different kinds of work and make more money. The artist doesn't make much money here.

Not only is it time consuming and energy sapping to continually juggle financial obligations, but with accumulating interest payments and penalties for being in arrears, it is also very expensive to be poor. Perhaps even more important to continued operations, Frankel says, "People become reluctant to give you money." Donations and grant monies have always had to be a part of the company's subsistence. In the past, most of it had been seed monies. However, by the 1980s, it had become virtually inconceivable to structure a solvent, nonprofit theatrical existence without some kind of major outside support money. The NEA's announcement of its $1,000,000 grant forced Circle Rep to act upon the major changes it had already perceived as necessary to its continued artistic and financial survival. It was time to put on a well-cut three-piece suit and "do lunch" with the establishment.

The Arena Stage in Washington and Circle Repertory Company, the two largest grantees, have demonstrated considerable longevity in the face of the wide-sweeping social, economic, and political changes since their beginnings in the sixties. Idealistically speaking, it is almost a wonder that Circle Rep applied for the federal money at all, but the CRC has always followed the money—not a small component in its longevity. Although money was always important, in many respects it did not matter in the minds of individual company members who cared more deeply about their artistic integrity. Money was important because it bought independence from financial pressures. Fulfilling a social function and fulfilling their own needs as artists without compromise were difficult goals to correlate effectively. Once again it creates an almost schizophrenic company personality, one which is enhanced by an environment that not only is "hostile to the arts," as Mason believes, but also is becoming more and more expensive. However, following the money, no matter how necessary, could be interpreted as evidence that a great deal of lip service was given to "artistry versus commerciality" while the company quietly sought the established route of the system. On the other hand, Mason genuinely believes everything that he says regarding the issue of artistry versus commerciality. In a sense, he has one foot in the world of the establishment and the other in the counterculture soil that first supported his ambitions. Perhaps this split-personality aspect of the company is exactly what is necessary to maintain viability in an artistic world where aesthetic principles often have to give way to conventional commerciality.

In order to win the grant from the existing social and political system of the eighties, Mason had to prove that the company was fulfilling a useful function to society and was indeed operating as a full-fledged ensemble. Much of the Ensemble Grant proposal had to do with the extraordinary number of hit plays the company had developed during the past fifteen years. It is a sign of the company's chameleon adaptability that when the Ford Foundation grant was available for the development of new American plays, Circle Rep could easily apply. Much of their developmental program was for exactly such purposes: when the New York State Council on the Arts grant was available for traditional material, a good deal of the Circle's major work was perfectly suitable for qualification; when the Peg Santvoord grant was offered to encourage experimental works, the Circle could accept with equal equanimity, legitimately holding up much of its experimental work for inspection. It would not be inappropriate to state that if a grant were made available to companies that dealt in classics, or companies that nurtured new actors, the Circle Rep could just as easily fulfill those, too. Now, with the National Endowment giving supporting grants for ensembles, Circle Rep could apply, pointing once again with complete justification to its own ensemble origins. Such adaptability is a strong testament to the company's durability in the face of statistically stacked odds against survival.

When the CRC's ensemble evolved at the end of the sixties, the day-to-day aspect of its operations was more that of a commune growing out of a sixties rejection of the nuclear family. Now in the eighties, the chameleon factor is still operative; the company has changed colors by throwing aside the institutional element and once again embracing the more intimate ensemble aspects of the company. The ensemble is, and basically has always been, the very foundation of the company's existence. The development of new American plays and new American writers was always meant to be a side product. "Nowhere in our original credo did we say we wanted to discover new playwrights or the next big star or any such thing," says Mason. "We wanted to establish an environment for the nurturing, growth, and maturation primarily of the actor."

Now in the mainstream theatre community, Circle Rep became very conservative in its approach to theatre. Whether the CRC was merely reflecting changes or was in the vanguard of them is difficult to assess.

The eighties represented the reawakening of individualism, capitalism and conservative attitudes in general. The CRC seemed to be articulating aspects of the larger environment, if not in the actual plays it presented, at least in its relationship to the environment. The very act of turning to a government institution like the NEA for funding can be interpreted as a politically conservative action, reflecting an increasing concern with money. There has been the growing sense that it is perfectly legitimate to deal with money openly, even to go after it aggressively. In the sixties nobody at Circle Rep ever worried about money, but they were younger then. Yet, it is not only that company members are older now and want more, but also that the communal attitudes of the sixties have disappeared along with the end of the Vietnam era. As Lanford Wilson said of the sixties when Joe Cino generously supplied sandwiches and left-over pastries every day, what more did they need? At that time, not much; but times change. Circle Rep has changed with the times, not only knowing which political levers to push or pull in order to effect changes, but also demonstrating a willingness to use them. In his proposal to the NEA, Mason "demanded" the right to continue the work the Circle Rep had begun in 1969. However, the transition back to the original concepts of the company was not due only to the available funding of the eighties. There were other factors that affected it, including idealism versus the realities of pragmatism. Financially, the grant represents a respite from desperation and a return to the idealism of youth, as well as a coming of age. Going after this money is part and parcel of being mature artists in their forties who can no longer live on the dole. Coming of age implies an advance from adolescence and an acceptance of adulthood with some of its more dour aspects; there still is the need to give an apologetic accounting for the admission of at least needing, if not necessarily liking, money.

Circle Rep has now fully become a part of the system by the very act of applying for the NEA grant. Their image has changed. Just as one of Ronald Reagan's stated priorities has been to "restore" America's image, Circle Rep's marketing director, Tom Thompson, openly admitted that he was interested in "improving Circle Rep's image"[6] and bringing it to as mainstream a position as possible—a very eighties attitude. At the company's origins, it stood far outside of the establishment. Now, ironically, the only way it could go back to its origins was to become a part of the establishment. Even though it is now the day of "individualism" again, the day of the rugged individualist is over. Now it is more valuable to survival to learn how to play the system, the political game—a position which states a great deal about how theatre survives in America and how Circle Rep, in particular, is held together. Talent is not enough, the bottom line is money. The CRC has finally learned how to play the political game to its maximum effectiveness. It never had trouble with the artistic one. Periodically the CRC has come up with the winners, but the political money game is the one that is going to keep them alive, not the artistic one. This conclusion may be a sad commentary on the arts in America, but it is a valid assessment. Their adolescence is over; they have stopped rebelling against the establishment and have become a solid part of it. As Marshall Mason says, "This grant is such an important thing in my life because it's the biggest, most solid and substantial commitment in history of an artistic idea in this country; the idea of creating theatre through ensembles. By the time we add together the $260,000 we get from the government, the $135,000 that comes from the regular government program, and about $125,000 from the State Council of the Arts, it's over $500,000 that they've given to this tiny little theatre with 160 seats to realize our artistic dreams. They are saying, 'Okay, you say you can do this. Do it.' I think the challenge is tremendous."

One of the major goals of this new direction will be to try to remove Circle Rep from the tyranny of the hit-flop syndrome that plagues so much theatre in New York. As Mason says, "It's not just here in New York City under the scrutiny of the major critics because that is both a strength and a weakness. But it's also the American culture which wants something new without revering and nurturing what is valuable about yesterday. We are really a disposable society. . . . Finding a management and a structure that will help us to grow in that environment is very difficult. People are attracted to plays that will transfer to Broadway."

Do grants like the NEA signify a strengthening of the theatrical fabric in America? Does the transition itself signify a decline or a step forward for the Circle Repertory Company? It is more than likely that it will turn out to be beneficial for Circle Rep, but not a factor for theatre in general. Important here is what the grant represents to Circle Rep in terms of freedom to pursue original objectives, freedom to maintain artistic integrity in a commercial environment, and most important perhaps, freedom from financial pressures—at least temporarily. It might be an oversimplification to look upon the transition in terms of either advance or decline. Circle Rep seems to be turning back to its original concepts which, from an artistic point of view, is positive. The original concept of a unified ensemble behind the resident playwrights often resulted in their best plays, performed at an achievement of peak acting through cohesive ensemble interaction for an audience that seemed to be starved for what the Circle Rep was offering.

While the elitist group of twenty-five actors began its twenty-five weeks of intimacy, the remainder of the company ostensibly continued in the manner in which Circle Rep had been operating for the past years, despite the fact that much of the functioning company, as it had been known, would be phased out. The new group would move on to a recreation of the original concepts of the company. A decline? A move forward? Only time can be the final judge. Despite the 1978 precedent which, in effect, succeeded but had to be abandoned, the new 1985 project is still an experiment. But it is an experiment that is being tackled with great enthusiasm. Company members feel that the only way new theatre with the "experience in the now," as they call it, can be created is through a true company setting where the very environment is conducive to creation. There is no such thing as "one person creates theatre." It is definitely a collaborative art; when the collaborative parts are in a unit functioning together in a controlled environment, the best work is done. It is this controlled environment which they are attempting to recreate. In it they feel the acting gets more forceful, the writing grows in strength and perception, the intensity of participation becomes more palpable, the focus becomes sharper. There is a communion which takes place like that of the early days, when the company members were idealistic, poverty-stricken hippies.

But back in the sixties, the ensemble happened as a natural evolutionary process born of the chaotic and hungry times. Now in the eighties, they are forcing the togetherness an ensemble implies. Neither the same spirit nor the same hunger moves them. Nor, no matter how much money they are awarded, can they ever have the same artistic freedom they had in the beginning when they were unknown and unencumbered by financial or critical considerations. It could very well happen that the new plays, now commissioned rather than naturally evolving out of the communal ensemble environment as they did in the sixties, will turn out to be duds.

One of the strong points in the new project's favor, however, is that Marshall Mason is enthusiastic about it. His enthusiasm lends a great deal of weight to the project's potential success, since Mason has always been the guiding force at Circle Rep. It is amazing how, over the years, his fundamental vision has not altered regarding theatre or his feelings about the ensemble itself. Personal considerations and controversy within the company destroyed the joy of it for him for a while, and he departed on a two-year sabbatical. But he returned to the company in 1984 with renewed vigor and reaffirmed vision. The entire concept of taking the company back to its stated origins without financial pressures has given Mason a strong boost; he is greatly stimulated by the challenge and the vote of confidence the NEA grant signifies.

On the other side of the ledger, however, there is always the danger of trying to place a plastic bubble around the group in order to preserve what has made it special. The attempt to recreate what had originally been done — in a sense to make it hallowed — could be an exercise in frustration as well as a giant step backwards. But there is some justification in the cry that for years critical expectations more or less demanded that the company withdraw from its primary ensemble focus. This time they are not simply following the dollar; they are genuinely trying to get back on a course they feel they have somehow lost.

The NEA grant and the transition it will provoke stimulates the need to emphasize one more important point: CRC's continuing ability to survive. The Circle Rep's current position is not quite as simple as the image of the beautiful, unified organism they first created now (with the advent of the grant) able to go back to its roots after a period of wandering off course. Theatre groups go under when they define their roles too rigidly. When the role begins to be seriously out of step with the times, there are few ways to survive. Maybe one of the ways is for a theatre to have extremely broad missions. Circle Rep's mission could be interpreted as an emphasis on acting, an emphasis on playwriting, an emphasis on experimentation, and an emphasis on ensemble — each individually rich enough to sustain a theatre company's entire philosophy. Together they represent an elasticity that has been implicit in the company's very longevity. It is a broad range of adaptable goals. Thus if NEA was bestowing grants for developing in-house plays, Circle Rep could justifiably apply and qualify: "That's where our roots are. That's what we started out doing. That's exactly what we have been all about all this time." It seems that they have been "all about" a great many things and for a variety of reasons have been very successful, all of which adds up to a very talented group symbolized by the image of an animal adept at surviving even in a hostile environment. Part of being a successful company is the ability to become part of its environment. That quality of adaptability is one of the strongest reasons why Circle Rep has survived fifteen years. What is required is not a rigid over-definition of what the company is about, but something more elastic and much richer.

The transition, then, does not seem to be either a decline or an advance. It is too soon to tell, but if analysis were necessary, it appears more to be merely another chapter in the continuing effort to survive, and to survive with all the things one normally needs to survive; not necessarily by maintaining the highest level of idealism.

In retrospect, it is obvious that there were many reasons for the change in company operations. Within the company itself, there have been many subtle clues that a change was necessary as well as imminent.

In a broad sense, development stopped when the Friday Readings and the Projects-in-Progress lost their impact. The trappings were still there, but the actual development was not. The hunger was gone. Once the hunger and that spirit of excitement were gone, the work became a job, and a great deal of the company's impetus diminished.

The Circle Rep had been mainstreamed into the establishment; socialization processes were having an effect as members expected more for their devotion and commitment. Institutionalization itself had taken away much of the family feeling which had been such an integral part of the entire developmental process. The constant battle between idealism and commercialism took its toll in the heavy emphasis to produce hits. Lack of operating funds placed the company in a constant struggle for survival, and the National Endowment Grant for Ensembles finally *forced* the perennial issue of needed change to a point of decision.

10

Strengths and Faults

IN the face of the National Endowment grant and the transition to new but old dimensions, the important question becomes whether or not the Circle Repertory Company can continue to succeed with old ideas and renewed ideals in a new structure. The answer depends on the force of Circle Rep's strengths and the extent of its faults, both of which it carries forward. How serious have been the problems in the past, and how serious will the problems be in the future? It is important to try to understand the company's strongest and weakest points as they have materialized and evolved over the history of its first fifteen years.

One of the great strengths of the CRC is the combination of Marshall Mason, the director with integrity and vision, and Lanford Wilson, the playwright whose plays have brought so much attention to the company. On the other hand, Circle Rep has never adequately progressed beyond those successes, and has even been unable to rid itself of the confining label of "lyric realism." Critics have perceived Circle Rep as a bastion of lyric realism despite the fact that experimental theatre has always been an integral part of the company. While lyric realism has certainly been one of the company's strengths, to speak of lyric realism is really to speak of Wilson's plays and the interpreting style of Mason.

Paradoxically, the very strengths of the company can translate into weaknesses, sometimes in the least expected manner; a case could be made that one of the Circle Rep's faults is that it is *too* much Lanford Wilson and Marshall Mason.

Yet Mason's working relationship with Wilson is one of those miraculous creative marriages that produces exceptional work. Elia Kazan had that kind of relationship with both Arthur Miller and Tennessee Williams, creating in critical retrospect what can safely be judged as some of the best work they ever produced. Mason has the same working intimacy with Wilson, having directed more than twenty of his plays. No one understands Wilson's ear for the music of language better than Mason. There is little doubt that one of the major strengths of Circle Rep has been the creative association between them, but there is also a negative factor. Mason developed *a* way of working with *a* playwright that did not necessarily work with other playwrights. It is conceivable that the company may have become an institution of broader scope and variety if there had been more resident playwrights in the early days when creative muscles were in their greatest period of development. Having many playwrights at Circle Rep is a relatively recent phenomenon. Originally, there were only three, two of whom were not high profile. Milan Stitt has suggested that "if the other two had been stronger, it would have helped Marshall; he would have developed even more muscle. So maybe the theatre would have been better without Lanford." Since Stitt has worked very seriously and selflessly with Wilson, this statement should be interpreted solely as a sober contemplative assessment regarding the strength of the theatre company as a unit, rather than in terms of any one individual artist.

Would the Circle Rep have been stronger in the beginning with more playwrights of Wilson's strengths but different sensibilities? The answer has to be, of course, that any company would benefit from such abundance. But extraordinary talents such as Wilson's are difficult to find and to develop. Would Circle Rep have been stronger without Wilson? An intriguing question, but it is doubtful that the company would exist with the same degree of visibility without him. Much of the theatre's success has been identified with the work of Wilson; much of the critical interest in Circle Rep has been the interest in his work. Even with all of his success, there are expectations that he is still growing and probably has not yet written his masterpiece. Without Wilson, Circle Rep would still be one of the premiere acting companies in America; in Marshall

Mason it would still have one of the nation's finest naturalistic directors, but it would lose much of its artistic vibrancy.

However, Circle Rep has been operating in a critical ambience in which "the play" is given unparalleled importance. Even though the resonance of Wilson's work has been the backbone of the company writing, Circle Rep's overall strength results from a combination of factors. Mostly success has been due to Marshall Mason's artistic concept; to a great extent it has also come from persistence and hard work. And, while accident and luck have played a part, the genius factor has been crucial both in writing and in interpretation.

Unfortunately, however, as noted, in many ways the CRC has not gone beyond Lanford Wilson, and not surprisingly as a result the theatre is virtually controlled by his works. Such control can be a severely limiting feature even though Wilson seems to be greatly respected by the other company playwrights. John Bishop, for example, was quick in pointing out with the sensibilities of a playwright his belief that "the most important contribution the Circle Rep has made [to theatre] is Lanford Wilson. I don't think it would exist without Lanford," he says, "even though it is Marshall's theatre. I think it was a perfect coming together of two people—Lanford and Marshall. But still without Lanford—without the words. . . ."

Bishop felt that what Wilson does, he does better than any other playwright now living. It is not surprising, therefore, that Circle Rep tends to select plays that are heavily influenced by the style of Wilson's work. *The Sea Horse, The Diviners,* and *Levitation* all had a familiar overlay of lyricism as a stylistic component. It is a company joke that at least once every season there will be one, if not two, sets that will have a front porch, a swing, and a kitchen sink that works. Despite denials, there is an undercurrent of enthusiasm and eagerness to have all the plays follow in the direction of lyric realism. This tendency can be considered a major fault even though, as B. Rodney Marriott points out, with seventy actors, twenty playwrights and twenty more in the Lab, there are more than 100 artists with voices going in many directions. However, there is little doubt that lyric realism is the fundamental core of Circle Rep. The "kitchen-sink" argument is defensible and can be construed as a fault in that this facet of the Circle Rep style is still very much in tune with William Inge, a playwright who dates back to the fifties, rather than with Tennessee Williams, the playwright with whom the company prefers to identify. These could be reasons why people like

Peter Buckley, who although championing the Circle Rep in many ways, nevertheless feel that in "New York alone, Circle has been outstripped in writing . . . by Playwrights Horizons and Manhattan Theatre Club (even by the late Phoenix)."[1]

Intimately involved with the Circle Rep style is regionality. The plays of both Chekhov and Williams were also strongly regionally oriented to a place and time when the rural setting was beginning to decay along with the lifestyle associated with it. Capturing the locale in all its idiosyncratic distinctiveness seemed to have greatly encouraged the action within the plays, whether the plays took place in Chekhov's rural Russia, Williams's decaying South, or Wilson's disappearing mid-America, almost as though finding the right location in a state of transition is a primary prerequisite for the overlay of nostalgia so prevalent in lyric realism. The plays that are the most successful happen to be strongly regional. It is difficult to assess whether or not the theatrical regionality imposed by the individual strengths of Circle Rep's four founders is also one of the company's strengths; it is certainly one of their peculiarities. The mostly midwestern roots of the founders have found fertile soil in New York City, where audiences, despite their cosmopolitanism, respond to the strong nostalgia factor in the regionality of the plays.

While Circle Rep is still one of the few actual companies in the country dedicated to presenting new American plays (a very decided strength), it is still doing a great deal of the kind of work that made them "experimental" in the sixties — traditional, regionally oriented kitchen-sink realism. Now, oddly enough, the strength of the sixties might be one of the weaknesses of the eighties; one of the problems with this kind of theatre is that it is not always very theatrical, nor is this genre best developed on the stage. This kind of realism can be achieved with far greater effect and immediacy through the medium of film. Its theatricality keeps live theatre vibrant and exciting. Becoming mired in the realistic mold, with the fourth wall, living room, kitchen, or one-set concept, as Circle Rep has done almost exclusively, can be a serious problem from the point of view of advancing what *live* theatre is all about. Whether or not one appreciates Peter Schaffer's *Equus,* for example, it is a highly theatrical play. When the tall "horses" on stage stomp their hooves and begin prancing about, it is an astonishing theatrical moment that is totally lost in the realism of films. The point can be clearly seen if one substitutes the musical theatre as a live example of theatricality. Musical theatre is probably the most overtly theatrical of the genres. Because of its high degree of theatricality and the built-in audience response it evokes, musical theatre has continued to exist despite the enormous commercial perils of the modern American musical stage. It is easy to examine the argument by reversing the logic; many musicals lose a great deal of their charm when transferred to film.[2] The screen robs them of much of their magic and immediacy. On the other hand, with its vast scope and close-up explorative camera, film can give realism a great deal more detail, nuance, and ambience than the stage can with its perennial "long shot." Thus all realism, including lyric realism, is better served by film treatment. This would indicate a weakness in the style Circle Rep has become associated with if that style were not also coupled with content.

Probably the most important part of Ari Roth's definition of the "Circle Rep style" spoke to content:

> We want the play to be about people first and foremost, but also about the world. What kind of a statement is it making about the human condition? In some ways that's the archetypal good American play. It's a Tennessee Williams play. If you have to take a founding father for Circle, I'd say it would have to be Tennessee Williams. And that's because Lanford Wilson and Marshall Mason came out of that ilk. That's the kind of theatre that they would most want to emulate—what lyric realism would be. Those are the concrete things we look for in a script. We want to be transported to that world and become involved, and care and find it meaningful to be with them. And it comes to mean something in terms of what life is about. A full experience. That's what's great about the theatre. You become involved in a very personal way. I can tell you quite honestly, that's what gets people excited here.

Once again, the most important element is the content. The kind of play which Roth described both in terms of ambience and content was the readily identifiable "Circle style." Without the fully experienced human content and the profound explorations of the universal human condition, there is no Circle style.

Until 1985, when Circle Rep began its revived ensemble company, it could not seem to establish a consistent policy regarding play development. The company had not been able to determine whether they wanted to use the elaborate developmental system they had achieved to develop new American plays by their resident playwrights, as well as new American plays by established non–Circle Rep playwrights (such as Sam Shepard or Jules Feiffer), and new American plays by burgeoning Circle Lab playwrights, or whether to search throughout the entire nation to find the as-yet-unheard "new American voice." Although it is good artistic policy to keep the doors open to new artists, when it comes to creating new theatre this shotgun approach can debilitate the entire process. One of the Circle Rep's major faults is just this dissipation of control, too wide a sweep of objectives without the time to fully develop existing talents. This approach also creates much dissension within the ranks of both resident playwrights and (most particularly) Lab playwrights who feel they have Circle Rep's commitment up to, but not including, actual production.

It is obvious that the most important aspect of Circle Rep as perceived by the members is the company itself, the "ensemble." Maybe Circle Rep had exaggerated one side of development for a long time — that of finding a play and putting in on — but the combination of play development and ensemble performance made Circle Rep the group it is, and the ensemble process had to feed on something. None of the company's major successes resulted from the classics or a second- or third-rate play. The successes have always been the result of a first-rate new play. But the perfect play simply does not emerge out of the typewriter. The company input very often adds the additional ingredients necessary to full realization. At times there even seemed to be a sense of developing a play "in committee," but as long as it worked, it did not matter; the play always came first. This point was stressed in the Directors Lab as well as the Writers Lab, although the importance of the play, as noted, was certainly not the major focus of attention at the original creation of the group. Now it has evolved to such an extent that new members like Ted Sod, who joined Circle Rep in June 1983, feel that play development is important above all other company considerations.

However, the ensemble draws the greatest support from the members. This support is nowhere more clearly seen than through the eyes of the members themselves who view the ensemble from a variety of personal viewpoints. The insecurity of a profession that can subject its artists to the degradation of "cattle call" auditions and continual rejection in the face of the overwhelming numbers of actors waiting to fill the relatively few professional jobs available, is softened greatly by the sense of belonging.

Repeatedly Circle Rep was seen by its members as a home base with the inherent security that implies—a familiar, comfortable locale in which to work with intimate and trusted comembers. In this context, Circle Rep was repeatedly referred to as a family. For example, actress Mari Gorman wrote glowingly of what a positive experience working with the Circle Repertory Company has been for her both professionally and personally. Even while living in Los Angeles, she was still made to feel a part of the company.

> It is a family. I know of no other "company" that constantly lives up to that appellation. Working at Circle Rep is a luxury in this business in that the atmosphere is completely stimulating, intersupportive and totally focused on the work.
> The "system" of the Circle is just that by their constant communications to the members it is possible to see the system functioning as well as feel a part of it.
> I believe this rare loyalty which the Circle has is one of the reasons why those who now have considerable success elsewhere feel loyal towards the Circle in return.
> I have learned a great deal as an actor in the process of working with the Circle, perhaps, as I have said, because of the purely artistic atmosphere. This too is always a draw for *any*one with *any* degree of success *any*where![3]

Actor Ken Kliban stressed the value of the familiarity factor within a home base structure. Getting to know and work with the same people over a period of time stimulated the foundation for a true ensemble. "People who know and like each other learn to understand how to work together most productively,"[4] he wrote, while actor Richard Seff noted along the same lines that the base from which to work was something very few actors in this country have:

> On a much less lucrative scale, it must be something like what actors felt when they had contracts with the major studios— except we're not exclusively committed to the Circle, and we are free to accept engagements elsewhere.[5]

All of the actors indicated that they felt stimulated by the advantage of daily developmental programs which led to taking greater risks in a greater variety of characterizations. All actors need the constant growth process. They correlate the lack of growth to stagnation, which is perceived as detrimental to craft and art. That their personal growth and development as actors has been greatly advanced through the wide variety of roles encouraged by a company environment cannot be over-stressed and was best exemplified by Bruce Gray:

> It was an honor to be a part of the company. Marshall Mason and the other founders were very creative and supportive, and truly important members of the theatrical scene. What turned out to be so marvelous, on top of all the classes and readings and camaraderie, was the diversity of roles that I was given to do. Over the years I played a Shavian Englishman, an Elizabethan fop, an alcoholic teacher, a burnt-out writer, the ghost of a recently deceased choreographer, an English officer circa 1776, a terminally ill cancer patient, Oscar Wilde, Richard Cory (based on the well-known poem), etc. Now I usually play middle of the road leading men (mostly on daytime TV, a few in films) and it was a wonderful stretch for me to play this myriad of characters. It extended the boundaries of the characters I usually play.[6]

One of the most important aspects of this interactive style referred to by actor members is actor involvement in the development of new Circle Rep plays. Certainly acting is the foremost component of the ensemble's success, but there is another developmental aspect of the working ensemble that is above and beyond performing. At Circle Rep, only rarely is a script considered "frozen" at the time of production; the production itself is part of the developmental process, which in turn adds additional importance to the performance as part of that process also. Most often, however, the developmental process includes the actors' work before actual production. During intensive analytical discussions following company readings, the knowledgeable, artistic input of the ensemble becomes a profound aspect of development. The selflessness of this creative input is a living demonstration of Mason's words, "We have no egos here. Whatever is good for the play is good." Such selflessness may seem idealistic, but when this aspect of development is working at its best, the best work is produced. It does not matter who makes the suggestion for improvement. Just as part of the success of the acting ensemble is the training together which creates the rapport and familiarity so necessary to establishing the sense of ensemble on stage, the same process occurs with the writing during play development. The writing is actually fed by the acting during the long, developmental process — readings, PIPS, Extended Readings — and is one of the advantages of writing for specific actors. The soul and talent of the actor helps to define the stretches of the character the playwright creates.

This process can provide a great sense of joy and accomplishment for the actor. As Richard Seff points out:

> I've spent months in a workshop with Jules Feiffer helping him develop material that was embryonic with him when he came to us asking for help. The Circle offers a great many resources/ outlets for work and development to the artists if the artists are willing to take advantage of them. The family of artists comes together more than once in their lives to do a play. Everyone wants to make the play work. We have been bound by the philosophy that the play comes first.[7]

This philosophy is a compelling company component for member playwrights. The advantages to them of working within a company situation are significant, since the company often acts as a stimulus and source of inspiration. Wilson would be the first to point out the myriad benefits, not the least of which was to know that his work would be performed, read, appreciated; that he no longer had to send scripts to an unknown producer and wait months for a response; that, upon acceptance, he did not have to turn over his material to a producer and sit back while his work was taken over and interpreted — often without consultation — by "strangers." Most writers in the company would agree. Few playwrights have the luxury of a company setting to take the "stranger" out of the process of production, with the exception perhaps of Sam Shepard, with his Magic Theatre, and David Mamet, who keeps returning periodically to his Chicago home base.

In summary, the plus side of member evaluation included strong responses to

1. a home base
2. a sense of family
3. a variety and diversity of roles
4. personal growth and development as actors
5. participation in the development of new plays
6. actors acting as a stimulation and inspiration to playwrights

However, despite seemingly unanimous praise for member-evaluation, there were some very real dangers creeping in to jeopardize the security of the insular little company. The negative side of member-evaluations encompassed some very real disadvantages of working within a company milieu. It was often felt that being a member was *too* safe. One of the major disadvantages was the strong possibility of parochialism, the fear that despite diversity of creation, the overall developmental scope had become too narrow and even provincial. Also, there is a feeling that perhaps not all plays were best developed "in committee." Even Mason would admit that there was a serious problem in members feeling "too safe."

"One becomes isolated from the real world in certain cases," he admits.

> The vicissitudes of being an artist in America, the difficulties of our lives as such, which as artists, is based largely on insecurity. And suddenly with a company, there gets to be a kind of laziness that comes from the security of, "Oh well, I've been a member of the Circle Rep company for ten years; they wouldn't dare kick me out." As a result, there can be the attitude, "Somebody has written this play for me and so I don't have to reach or explore or discover anything new." If it gets too closed, too intimate, too self-involved, it becomes a real danger. I try to keep this stored up by, first of all, constantly returning to the classics to sharpen the instruments. No one can become complacent regarding the classics — they are almost impossible to "master." Also, by bringing in new people from time to time, and by encouraging people to go on to other places.

On a consistent basis, Circle Rep invites its people to leave periodically to work elsewhere, whether in films, on Broadway, in television, or in regional theatre. No one has been able to earn a living working exclusively at the Rep, a reality which makes outside work essential. Additionally, and just as important to the artist, the broadening aspects of artistic diversification have been a primary ingredient in helping keep relationships within the company fresh.

Circle Rep's need for financial stability, which unfortunately determines much of the company's artistic and managerial policies, is the very same need that insidiously creates a star system about which many of the actors complained. Although often hotly denied by management, the star system appears to have subtly altered the policy of displaying casts in alphabetical order. The need for the big name to insure a big box office has been perceived by some as creating a "New Rep" in place of the "Old Rep." It seems to be indisputable that in many ways Circle Rep had indeed fallen into the star system. However, it does not appear to be big names from the outside that have been sought, but actors from within the company who have become well enough known to carry abundant star value on their own — William Hurt, Judd Hirsch, Christopher Reeve, Tony Roberts, Fritz Weaver, Barnard Hughes, Lindsay Crouse, and Beatrice Straight, to name a few. Although each has gone on to considerable success, most of them still consider themselves part of the company. At the same time, the company wishes to maintain their high-profile names on company rosters.

However, many actors in the company who have been with Circle Rep a long time do not necessarily become stars and therein lies part of the internal problem a star system ignites. The issue is always heavy at company meetings. Not one actor spoke harshly about the Rep; not one seriously complained about his treatment. However, there were grievances and the major one was the difference between the Old Rep and the New Rep as it fell into the star syndrome; some of the old guard felt left behind and deeply insecure regarding their status within the company.

It is no doubt true that the casting machinations seem to be striving for a mainstream image as well as monetary considerations — mainstream implying a high degree of visibility. When Circle Rep produced *Hamlet,* it was definitely stated that it was not selected as a star vehicle for Bill Hurt. Yet when the posters were designed for the production, Hurt's name was isolated from the remainder of the company for the first time in the company's history. Ordinarily, the entire company would be listed alphabetically under Mason's direction. This time, it was decided that Bill Hurt's name had to be displayed prominently since it could easily be overlooked if it were placed in its alphabetical place with the entire company.

Lab director Daniel Irvine, who often worked closely with Tanya Berezin as cocasting director, admitted that the star system was true at least on one level, if "not on all levels." Irvine says: "We did a benefit last year (1982) that I produced, called 'The First Annual Playwrights Festival.' I directed one of the pieces as well as produced. I had a real problem with management wanting only stars to do' the plays. Eventually I did get Judd Hirsch, Chris Reeve, Swoozie Kurtz, and Barnard Hughes. Our play-to-play subscription season does not have to depend on stars. But I'm now producing the fifteenth-year benefit. What's the first thing management says? Get the stars involved. Get them in it. But the star system is not necessarily true for all productions. We cast the best actors and these people with names are good actors. We helped build their careers. Bill Hurt and Chris Reeve were both in a play that launched their careers, Corinne Jacker's *My Life* (1977). When people came to see the play it was felt that they were witnessing the birth of two major stars. Bill is a great actor and Chris is very good. He has personality. Chris knows what we offer and he's back here with us. He knows he needs to work and come back to the stage — but now we have a built-in problem because he's such a big name. What do we find for him to do?"

This is an interesting point. Hurt returned to play the roles of Hamlet and Richard II. There has not been anything suitable for Chris Reeve since he became internationally known through films such as *Superman*. But as Irvine points out, "If you put Chris in something that is not suitable, he is going to be ripped to pieces."

As noted, the stars referred to are the stars who came from Circle Rep itself. Even though they are company members in the deepest sense of the word, company members who work at Circle Rep on a day-to-day basis feel the heavy weight of insecurity in that they have "not arrived" yet and fear that the company will hire the successful, well-known actors before hiring them. Their feeling is not due solely to insecurity.

That their assessment is accurate is once again confirmed by Irvine:

> We are doing a play now, *Full Hookup,* and you offer it to Bill Hurt first because he's an incredible actor. Now if he will come back and do it, great, because then we are assured of a really good actor. We are also assured of interest and publicity. We don't *need* stars since we have a built in subscription membership and cannot even get people into the theatre sometimes because of subscribers. But you go with the best actors first — so you ask Bill, but in doing that you have alienated the company for "going after the stars." What they do not understand is that the Circle Rep has helped to create them and they still belong to us and should still have a loyalty to come back and work on the stage. That's what it's all about. Marshall says, "Go out and then come back. We'll all be better for it." So in our day-to-day, play-by-play system, we cast the best actors and get the best directors we can. But on a benefit, they want to make a lot of money. So we go after the names that will bring the people in. And so it goes on.

It is a very interesting problem. In many cases, actors go beyond the Rep and never return. But there are a significant number of well-known actors who choose to return repeatedly. The reasons are varied, but the underlying core of values always encompasses the sense of family, the security of a home base, and the integrity of the work. When the well-known actors do return, the regular company members suffer the pangs of being forced into a subsidiary position. Repeatedly they see the choicest acting roles offered to the returning stars, making fear and alienation a certainty for members who work almost exclusively within the company. The official posture regarding this delicate issue was stated clearly in the program for *Levitation*:

> By the late 1970's Circle could no longer be considered an un-known, poverty-stricken company, but a well-respected theatre that was having growing pains. One of the Circle's main prob-lems, Mason declares, involves scheduling since so many of its "star" actors like Hirsch, Hurt, Crouse, and Reeve have moved on to Hollywood films.
>
> One reason why the Group Theatre did not last beyond 1941, a span of ten years, stemmed from the fact that its actors longed for recognition and a salary that only Hollywood could satisfy. Realizing this, Mason tells Circle actors, "The way you can do the best for the theatre is to do the best for yourself. If you demand your own right to grow as an individual artist, you'll benefit the theatre."
>
> And these Hollywood actors do return to Circle as Judd Hirsch and Richard Thomas demonstrated in the company's opening presentation of its 1983–84 season, Chekhov's *The Sea Gull*. "They keep coming back because of what we do, not to make money," Mason asserts.[8]

Since play production is such an integral part of the Circle Rep's existence, it is important to determine exactly how tied to Broadway nonprofit theatre companies like Circle Rep are, since many of the ex-pectations for the future of American theatre rest upon them. What do these companies need to continue in such a transitory milieu as New York theatre with its "here today, gone tomorrow" syndrome?

Commercialism separates New York theatre from all other theatre in the nation. There is little, if any, commercial theatre in Chicago or Los Angeles, for example, whereas in New York it is a multi-million-dollar industry influencing theatre all across America. Many playwrights prefer to open their plays regionally, which permits the plays enough life to earn their authors a living before being moved to New York City. Even-tually, however, most have to endure the impact of New York City critics in order to qualify in a highly competitive milieu as bonafide play-wrights. The commercialism of the New York theatre industry applies great pressure to nonprofit theatres like the Circle Rep by forcing them to operate under the same rules and critical influences as the Broadway system. No less than one hundred and twenty critics previewed *The 5th of July,* despite the fact that it was an off-Broadway offering under a not-for-profit charter.

As Tom Thompson says, "The public has no interest in plays that are not commercial in one way or another. So New York has to be very careful and savvy about the commercialism of theatre. We at Circle Rep have had to take a really close look at what we do to make ends meet."

Circle Rep is forced to deal with the commercialism of the city in which it operates not only to survive financially, but also in order to take its place in a theatrical hierarchy into which it was absorbed almost unwittingly. More and more frequently, little companies within the city itself are becoming the testing grounds for Broadway. Some plays meant for the commercial stage begin out of town, but out-of-town tryouts are not as common as they used to be. To move shows is exorbitantly expensive; often now, new plays have lengthy previews within the city limits. Companies like Circle Rep are expected to provide new material for Broadway almost in the capacity of an in-town, tryout production house. As soon as Frank Rich of the *New York Times* said to B. Rodney Marriott, then acting artistic director, that he was not fulfilling his function at the Circle Rep to "feed" Broadway—that he was, in essence, "killing" Broadway by insisting on doing plays that were not Broadway material—intimidation was an absolute, since Frank Rich has the power to sink any play produced on or off Broadway. Although the CRC was chartered as a not-for-profit, professional *alternative* theatre, not an in-town, tryout production house for the glorious invalid that is Broadway, Rich is realistic in one way with his demands: by feeding Broadway a theatre such as the CRC is more likely to get funding through grants and private donations.

"That is what is happening to this kind of theatre (CRC)," Milan Stitt points out. "In a way it *is* our job to feed Broadway. We receive more funding when we've had a *Talley's Folly* on Broadway the season before. Private donations are greater also, even though the company needs less when it has a hit running on B'way."

Too much emphasis by the press also creates expectations that are too heavy and unrealistic; an environment is created in which fear is a debilitating factor and artistic problems are created. The commercial theatre has never been Circle Rep's goal, nor was a profit motivation ever written into its charter. When the company started to feel the pressure that one of its functions — if not the major one — was to feed the commercial theatre, and that doing so was a direct line to the grant monies it desperately needed to survive, the broad scope of the work changed. Circle Rep began looking for hits.

Although artistically speaking looking for hits may occasionally prove to be a weakness, from a pragmatic point of view it is a strength to be able to recognize and deal effectively with the commerciality of theatre despite the real danger of being in the center of a commercial environment. If too many powerful critics such as Rich, Brustein, or Simon imply that Circle Rep is not living up to its promise, the resulting damage could be great. In the beginning, before fame set it up to such critical attention, no one really cared what the Circle Repertory Company did. It had the freedom to fail, the independence to experiment, the opportunity to grow, and the courage to lose the little money it had. Now the stakes have changed dramatically; there are enormous amounts of money involved. Mason agrees that this is a highly significant component in the future of the company.

"You hit upon it," he says emphatically. "The money that's at stake. That's the other potential failure. I can tell you for sure, despite all the ideals, we have not been able to match the artistic vision in this theatre ever. As a result, we carry a $450,000 deficit. The sheer weight of the money gap could be the thing that destroys us in the long run. The Moscow Art Theatre would never have become the Moscow Art Theatre if it hadn't been for the government throwing millions of rubles into that company."

To expect the Circle Rep to remain idealistically pure in the face of such pressure is naive. Yet although no one else would insist on purity, it seems to be an expectation of the company. When reviews from the commercial world devastate some of its artistic efforts, internal reevaluations become exhaustive.

The fifteenth-anniversary year that created so much reevaluation resulted mainly from poor reviews of *Full Hookup* and *The Sea Gull*. (*Full Hookup,* by Conrad Bishop and Elizabeth Fuller, was directed by Marshall Mason. Chekhov's *The Sea Gull* was directed by Elinor

Renfield.) These reviews, added to an already enervated company spirit, created a serious crisis of faith. It is therefore important to recognize how intricately commercialism is woven into Circle Rep's daily operations, despite it nonprofit charter.

The CRC opens its new productions to an international press, creating an emphasis on results. This pressure can easily be perceived as a serious problem translating into an operating fault, in that it does an immense disservice to the playwrights the CRC has dedicated itself to serve. The lack of balance between emphasis on end product and the needs of the playwrights is an issue that has never been satisfactorily resolved. Opening to the press sometimes occurs after only three weeks of rehearsal, an impossible situation according to Milan Stitt.

"Marshall doesn't like previews," Stitt says. "We used to open to the critics on the first Sunday which was the company opening. We'd play Thursday, Friday, Saturday and open on Sunday. Marshall still likes that. I fought to extend the preview time for a number of reasons. Now that we have subscribers who buy tickets in advance, I don't know why we open so fast. We're always opening shows when we've only just frozen the script and the actors aren't even sure if something is still there or not. We have to find a way that we don't have critics. We have to find a way that a critic will never see a show at the Rep. And occasionally, as Joe Papp does, they're invited. Which is one of the plans with the new repertory system."

Milan Stitt and Tom Thompson were the only ones who openly admitted that there was also a secret desire to do plays that made money. In the perennial struggle between idealism and commercialism, this admission was almost heretical. However, it was cloaked in truth, as witnessed by the change in company philosophy after *5th of July.* Immediately after the play's success, Circle Rep turned into a company that was trying to create hits. After every show, the big questions at company meetings became, "Will it move?" "Can it move?" "What will Frank Rich say?" "Can we raise money to move this to Broadway?" More talk seemed to go into that aspect of production than any other, despite denials — and there were many. General manager Richard Frankel, for example, denied that there was a search for plays that would make money. Trying to do so was, in his opinion, "stupid." The only feasible and acceptable method of play selection was to go for the best play possible.

"First of all, nobody really knows what will work," Frankel argues.

> The only thing you know is that you have to be true to yourself
> and just do the best work you can and the best theatre you can.
> And if something works commercially, fine. But to go try and
> second guess the public and the critics and do something you
> don't really believe in because you think it will be a hit is not
> only not the way we want to lead our lives, it is also ineffective.
> It doesn't work. What works is to be true to yourself. It is
> basically art, and good art is the best that the artist can pro-
> duce. And artists don't produce the best work when what they
> are chasing is profit. You chase art and the profit will come—
> maybe. You figure out a way to live whether the profit comes or
> not. We don't think the way to work in the theatre is to chase
> profit. That's what they do uptown and it doesn't always work.

Despite denials, however, every playwright wants his play to move
to Broadway; to wish for anything else would be unnatural and untrue.
The best of the work that has been produced by CRC had always moved
to Broadway for a further professional run. However, Frankel's point is
well taken. It is true that trying to do something strictly for success may
not always work. *Full Hookup* was a perfect example. It was exactly the
search for hits that prompted Circle Rep to produce *Full Hookup* in the
first place, but it turned out to be one of the 1984–1985 season's major
disappointments. *Full Hookup* was the primary hit of Louisville's season
in the Great American Play Contest. Even though it was a director's
piece and Mason obviously believed in the play, there was much dissension within the company regarding its production, starting with the fact
that it was not a Circle Rep play and ending with the opinion of some
members of the Literary Department staff that it was not even a very
good play. However, even though Mason had a few problems with *Full
Hookup,* it presented many interesting directorial challenges, had a high
degree of theatricality in its production aspects, and provided good roles
for the company actors—a major consideration.

Critics applauded the production but disliked the play. Although it
was not in Mason's usual repertoire, the direction was greatly appreciated. However, there was violence on stage and a social message implicit in the violence which might have stirred an impressionable collegi-
ate audience, but did little for a secure New York audience. The
audience, like the critics, resisted what two or three years earlier might

have appeared breathtaking on stage. As Ari Roth points out, "The Great American Play Contest of Louisville had been riding on top of the wave with a new version of violent theatre in which you could do rapes and wife beatings on stage."

While on-stage violence may raise moral issues, it is theatrically very exciting. But on-stage violence was becoming commonplace. In the case of *Full Hookup,* it was difficult to care about violence that emanated from characters for whom one had little basic sympathy. By 1984, content and fullness of character were more important than the excitement value of witnessing violence on stage. Additionally, in many ways the premise of *Full Hookup* ran counter to everything Circle Rep stood for, from the fact that it was developed elsewhere, to the recognition that it was unlike other Circle Rep plays. A very dark play, its premise and non-realistic expressionist form ran counter to Circle Rep style. The characters were fundamentally operating out of a negative impulse—that the underlying bedrock of life was misery. That the play was different in style and content, of course, did not necessarily negate its value as theatre. As Ari Roth justifiable points out, the experience could be refreshing "if the company is aware that that's why they're doing something. "That they're exploring something within themselves—including our identity as a company—that we are exploring the underside. Not everything has to be searching for that positive dream. Not every conflict has to come out of love between a mother and daughter."

But Roth was just as quick to point out that the company was not closely knit anymore. Not everybody was involved in the decision-making process which brought the play to Circle Rep—a full company decision which could have cemented their support of the play as an artistic challenge.

However, even with the disappointment of *Full Hookup,* the crisis of faith would not have occurred had the following production of *The Sea Gull* done well, broken even, or reaffirmed the Circle Repertory Company as a living theatre of fine ensemble acting. The negative critical reaction was a shock since the production had done extremely well in its run at Saratoga, New York, its own out-of-town tryout. Ari Roth recalls, "Everyone was upset. We knew when we saw the company opening with Judd Hirsch doing this strange little accent that it was lacking immediacy. It was sweet—a little slow. It wasn't electric theatre but it was good work. Everybody was shocked when people came down so hard on it. Universally so."

New York is quintessentially an American city where only the brightest star is sought even though it is ultimately thrown away, victim of the disposable society syndrome that is part of the hostile environment to which Mason frequently refers. Being "thrown away" often happens to movie stars and rock stars. It happened to Arthur Miller and even Tennessee Williams to some extent. It even happens to new ideas and political and social trends in America as well, unlike in Europe, where there is a certain bedrock continuity of underlying values, ideas, or aspirations passed on from generation to generation. Even critics themselves can be victims in this system. "Mel Gussow as a reviewer seems to be a lot nicer," Roth says, "a lot more supportive and less effusive in a way. He seems to be a little more fair, and yet he remains a second stringer with the *New York Times* maybe because of it. He doesn't feel the star factor. It's hype but it's also pursued for the 'great' American play."

And Roth may have a point. What is America if it cannot produce the greatest, the biggest, the most successful? No one wants to see a revival of *The Sea Gull* if it is only "good"; they want to see it only if it is superlative. Not only is there so much to choose from in New York City, but the high ticket prices make one less likely to accept anything that does not fall close to the glowing category of superlatives, particularly with a classic. But superlative productions are few and far between. It was Harold Clurman who said that most productions are neither "great" nor "terrible"; most fall somewhere in the vast between.[9]

Part of the problem, ironically enough, is Circle Rep's own commitment to excellence. "We didn't get Richard Thomas and Judd Hirsch for *The Sea Gull* just for their 'star' value," Roth candidly admits. "We didn't get them for the money. We wanted to do it because it would be spectacular. We could have hired anybody from our company. We have the 'stars' just as much as anybody else. We have this ambition to be excellent — to stand out — and we want to get tremendous reviews."

But Frank Rich did not like Circle Rep's production of *The Sea Gull* and no matter how a review may be truncated for promotional purposes, the public always knows the underlying truth. *The Sea Gull* was victim of the very commercialism Circle Rep has always tried to negate. It might not have been on the block of the hit-flop syndrome if it had been promoted as art for art's sake, and had opened in a loft or Circle Rep's own tiny Sheridan Square Playhouse. Instead, it opened at the American Place Theatre, a 300-seat space. To open at the American Place Theatre with high-profile stars like Judd Hirsch and Richard Thomas was a deliberate marketing strategy. It proved to be a risk that backfired, demonstrating how often theatrical success or failure depends on untheatrical matters.

"It [*The Sea Gull*] was revved up too much," Roth continues.

> If it had been done in a loft and the press happened to stumble onto it, it might have been a different story. As it was, the expectations were too much. It had been a success at Saratoga. We thought it was a good production and that it could make a lot of money. It wasn't a commercial success. It wasn't an artistic failure. But with all the advance publicity, the critics held the production up against heavy artistic standards regarding a classic. We were hoping to make money on it. That's why we got a bigger theatre space. We got American Place Theatre, which turned out to be a disaster. We had a lot of problems with the theatre itself. It was in the basement — had a restaurant on top that hadn't used a grease trap in twelve years. They were flushing the grease down the toilet. We had to cancel performances because one day the pipe ruptured and sewage spilled all over the stage. It was not as intimate as our theatre space. Perhaps it would have been a different kind of production if it had been. But we were hoping to make money. It was a 300-seat theatre and we booked it for twice the normal run (ten to twelve weeks). Because of the catastrophe of the pipe — what we did wrong, we had to delay the opening until Thanksgiving, until the very last day of the subscriber run. We basically had four weeks of previews and our built-in audience was used up before the reviews came out. So everything was pending on the reviews. If the opening had been two weeks earlier when we still had the cushion of the subscribers and word of mouth, we would have been able to run. But instead we said we were playing from the 31st of December, which is a long time for people to wait to buy their tickets. We didn't say "Limited engagement." Then the reviews came out. Some were complimentary of some aspects. Basically, they thought it was a mediocre-to-good production of a classic that all critics think deserves to be great, and if it's not great, why bother seeing it. Because you can see mediocre Chekhov anytime. So there was no reason to come see it. Word of mouth was not bad. The audiences did not hate it. But it was not true ensemble work. The blame here was shouldered by the director. She didn't really hold things together. Didn't really create an ensemble. Didn't communicate the vision of the play. Someone always gets blamed.

The Sea Gull lost a great deal of money. This loss was one of the primary causes of the huge cutbacks during January and February 1984 which precipitated the serious crisis of faith within the company and the evolving transition back to ensemble origins. Not only were many secretarial and clerical positions terminated (the work being relegated totally to unpaid interns), but even Tanya Berezin, the company godmother, was temporarily relieved of a salaried position. As previously noted, most of the cutbacks, however, occurred within the Literary Department, despite the fact that the department had always controlled play development, one of the company's most important functions. Rob Meiksins, literary manager, was laid off and, although Ari Roth became associate literary manager, Meiksins essentially was not replaced. It was not long before Ari Roth also was let go. During the resulting reorganization, the search for hits continued. Intimately involved in this search was the search for star playwrights. Playwrights like David Mamet and Sam Shepard were brought in. Such a policy will undoubtedly continue even though neither playwright has a genuine desire to write specifically for the company. Instead, Circle Rep brought in their productions from other theatres and called them their own (*Buried Child, Fool for Love*), but Sam Shepard is not a collaborative artist to begin with, nor does he have a particular allegiance to the Circle Repertory Company despite ties of friendship that date back to the Cino days.

Although courting high-profile, successful playwrights is good business, the ensemble spirit gets seriously distorted when there are stars, whether they are star actors or star playwrights. However, the need for hits is an absolute in a modern day economy and therefore the search for star playwrights will continue. Richard Frankel was very candid regarding how the managerial approach has changed. It has become far more sophisticated regarding deals with playwrights, since in the past contract deals were very unprofitable for Circle Rep.

"The plays went on and we didn't make very much," Frankel says.

> Now if the plays are successful, we do very well. The playwrights' contract is now twenty-seven pages. It used to be three. If there are European disc sales we've allowed for that. There never are so it doesn't make any difference. We made a lot of money from *Fool for Love*. We made more from that than anything else. *5th of July* ran for a year and a half on Broadway. We made more from *Fool for Love,* although that's an odd example. We made more because we own it. It's capitalism with

the others—when you're taking a royalty from the originating party but other people put up the capital. In America, people who put up the money earn the profits. We put up the money for *Fool for Love*. It was a very small play and it was doing well. We put up the money to move it and run it, so we made the profits. Plays can be more profitable off-Broadway than on Broadway. It's very hard for a play to be profitable on Broadway. When a play is profitable it may make $100,000 a week profit, but more likely it makes five, loses two, loses ten, makes three depending on the week. Off-Broadway you can consistently make several thousand dollars a week for a long period of time, plus your investment. You don't have to pay back a half a million dollars that's been invested. It's more like $40,000. So in many ways off-Broadway is much more commercially attractive to us than Broadway. I would much rather have a hit off-Broadway than on Broadway—well, I would much rather have a hit off-Broadway than a move and a possible hit on Broadway. Commercially, we're better off.

Conflicts between idealism and needs, whether commercial or personal, have never been adequately resolved during the long process of institutionalization, and in Mason's own estimation are a key to the CRC's faults. "I can tell you right away where the flaws are," Mason says frankly.

I don't think it is in the ideals. The conflict between the institutionalization of those ideas and need for constant personal involvement is one of the basic conflicts that if not resolved will ultimately destroy everything that we are trying to accomplish. That's the key thing. We can look at the Group Theatre and say that greed destroyed them. I don't think greed is going to destroy us, but ironically, I think a theatre that is humanistic and sensitive to everybody's needs—it may be that very sensitivity and responsiveness, in the long run, that wears people down to the extent that they become insensitive and intolerant. It's peculiar. I wonder if the trap isn't there.

Being worn down may be one of the traps, but an even greater trap may be the fact that many of the established resident playwrights feel that the company has been lost to its own success. After Circle Rep went through its early stages of adolescence during the sixties and travelled the cycle to full maturity in the eighties, it is astonishing to hear that many of the resident playwrights feel that they are serving a company that no longer exists, given all that the Circle Rep stands for. However, it is an important and interesting point to explore through the surprising litany of complaints: not only does the company "not exist" anymore, but the actors who are available to the playwrights are the ones no one really wants; many of the actors who remain are the ones who "did not make it"; the CRC has become a company of supporting actors (which works very well only for Lanford Wilson's large-cast shows); the actors who have the charisma to carry a play, for the most part, are gone; the company stars are seldom available. When they are, they are reserved for special projects such as Bill Hurt's being saved for *Hamlet* rather than being asked to be in *Back in the Race* by Milan Stitt, which was written especially for him after *The Runner Stumbles*.

While this long list of negative observations might be "sour grapes" from some playwrights who ride a distant second to Lanford Wilson, much of their criticism is founded in truth. Some even feel that it would be better if the entire company process itself *were* lost, either to success or otherwise, in order for the CRC to move forward artistically. Peter Buckley has come to feel that the insularity of the

> . . . family atmosphere is not necessarily the best thing for producing exciting art, and has led the Circle Rep into a bit of a self-congratulatory position. They tend to use the same friends over and over again, often to the disservice of the production.

Buckley feels that this position leads to a rigidity of approach, that the company has become too comfortable with their well-publicized "lyric-naturalism," which often makes them seem "stuck in another generation. . . . Circle Rep has become a bit stodgy, the old maid of the group" of New York theatres. These observations come from the man who, in the same letter, suggested Circle Rep do only true, blue Americana. It may seem contradictory and perhaps it is. But on the other hand, Buckley also believes that all Circle Rep needs is "fresh blood, fresh wind, and a fresh breeze to lift aloft its lyric-naturalism since it *is* America's foremost exponent of this type of theatre and it is a form of theatre with which we desperately need to keep in contact."[10]

Perhaps the Circle Rep does need "fresh breezes," but there is still much to be said for the "Circle Rep idea."

11
The Circle Idea

CIRCLE REP has many characteristics which distinguish it from other theatre groups in New York as well as the nation, the most important of which is that it is a cohesive, ongoing *company* of actors who specialize in an ensemble approach to theatre. Another equally distinctive characteristic is the way Circle Rep is perceived by critics in relation to the kind of theatre for which the ensemble is noted. In a May 1980 article for *Horizon,* Peter Buckley called Circle Rep the most important regional theatre in America.[1] He claimed that the numbers of plays generated by the Circle Rep established it as the primary producer of lyric realism. At the time, Buckley noted that Circle Rep was the only institutional theatre in the country with resident playwrights creating for resident actors. In retrospect, when Circle Rep started in 1969 it was in the vanguard of the search for the new American play. Concomitant with this search was an intense interest in the revival of the native American voice interpreted by Circle Rep as realism which, in turn, was brought to the plane of lyric realism through the work of its major playwright, Lanford Wilson.

The critical emphasis brought to bear on the significance of the company as the primary generator of lyric realism, as well as its importance in searching for new American plays, would make it appear that the company existed primarily to serve and nurture the playwright. However, Circle Rep was also in the avant-garde in its devotion to the idea of the company of actors itself, so that while the playwright wrote for the specific actors, the relationship was symbiotic in that they were all trained to work together for a common goal: the theatre event and the audience experience. Familiarity between playwright and actor made the writing more intense as it was attuned to the individuality of each performer. Familiarity also made the actor's direct contribution unique in his knowledge of the nuances of the playwright, thus completing the symbiosis. As Mason notes, "Circle Rep has demonstrated again and again that you can have a pretty decent theatre experience with a play that if it were not done brilliantly would be just a so-so experience. How it is done, plus what happens between the actors and the audience is also terribly important." Mason feels that the emphasis is too much on the playwright in commercial theatre. This emphasis creates the illusion that if someone comes along with a great play, the rest simply falls into place without adequate acknowledgment of the immense contribution of actors, directors, and designers to the total experience of the theatre event.

Circle Rep's most distinctive characteristic, however, is that there has been no other American acting company dedicated to the creation of new American plays since the Group Theatre of the thirties. Other theatre groups across the nation offer their own artistic product, but none is a company devoted particularly to the American play. The City Stage Company (CSC) in New York, for example, is a full-fledged company, but it is oriented almost exclusively to the classics. The Association of Producing Artists (APA), which disbanded in 1970, also had a company which performed classics. The Actors Theatre of Louisville sponsors a yearly festival of new plays for which it hires a company, but it disperses at the end of the festival. As previously noted, although playwright Sam Shepard uses the Magic Theatre in San Francisco to premiere his work, the Magic Theatre does not have a resident company. La Mama no longer exists as a company as it did in the sixties when it emulated Cino's Caffé with its small family of artists who were so consistently on hand that their allegiance to the Caffé resembled a company. La Mama presents a variety of new American plays, but it also presents new European and Asian plays. Without a doubt these plays should have a hearing. However, exclusivity and patriotism often play a jealous role in the bestowal of grants. According to Mason, a good friend of Ellen Stewart, La Mama lost some of its federal funding when it came under criticism by the National Endowment for not concentrating on American work. Playwrights Horizons, Manhattan Theatre Club, and the Public Theatre, all of which which are heavily involved in the development of new playwrights, do not have ongoing companies. Although they often deal with the same people who are brought together for a particular production, when it is over the artists go their separate ways. Any company that is put together on an ad hoc basis essentially deals with actors who are forced to make their lives available to the extent that it is safe for them to do so at a given moment. A director who is working within such a situation is essentially constantly training his actors to work with the same artistic goals. Mason is quick to point out the great advantages of a true company situation and is fond of the following analogy: "When you have a company, it is like owning a Stradivarius violin that has been made by hand and crafted specifically for your use. The people become so attuned to the nuances, not only of the director's work, sharing the same vocabulary, but also to the playwright's work. They understand the music, for example, of the language that Lanford writes and I think they are able to give it to him in a way that strangers simply could not do."

They also become attuned to each other as actors, having worked together and trained together over an extended period of time. It is analogous to the difference between musicians who congregate for the first time to play and musicians who have been rehearsing and playing together for a long period of time. There is no comparison with the comfort and sense of belonging, the sharing of dynamics and almost instinctive anticipation of each other's swells and shading.

A number of extraordinary playwrights are associated with theatres like Manhattan Theatre Club and Playwrights Horizons, such as Christopher Durang, Pete Gurney, Albert Innaurato, and David Rabe, some of whom had also been associated with Circle Rep. Mason also points out that when Pete Gurney writes a play for the Circle Rep, the CRC does it; when Gurney writes one that is not for Circle Rep, Playwrights Horizons presents it. It need not be a play that is written for Playwrights Horizons, "merely one that is not written for the Circle Rep company of actors," says Mason.

Joseph Papp at the Public Theatre also has extraordinary playwrights and an extraordinary mechanism for supporting their work. Thomas Babe and David Rabe are two in whose work he intensely believes. Papp has successfully produced a series of their plays, but there is no company as part of his producing mechanism. Although all artists continually call upon past associations out of loyalty and familiarity as well as an inner sense of continuity that most admittedly need, each product that is presented at the Public in essence has to begin production work from step one.

The question is whether or not Circle Rep is substantially more creative because it is a cohesive acting company. Gerald Berkowitz in *New Broadways* has suggested that much of the success of Wilson's plays, for example, comes from his close connection with Circle Rep as a company. Not only has he the luxury of writing with particular actors in mind whose work he knows intimately, but also Circle Rep's special strength lies in ensemble playing, which can be attributed to a closely knit company with it synchronous understanding and ability to perform the "quietly evocative romanticism"[2] that Wilson's plays demand.

Historically, writing directly for ongoing ensembles is not unusual. In both the near and distant past, some of the acknowledged great playwrights operated in ensemble settings. Shakespeare, Molière, Chekhov, and Odets each had the luxury of writing for full-fledged companies of actors. To some extent, even Eugene O'Neill experienced the same sense of continuity with the Provincetown Players, a small, intimate, private group. While Wilson's association with Circle Rep has been essential to the company's success, conversely, a large measure of Wilson's success can be attributed to the company, according to Mason. "The reason we have a Lanford Wilson is because we have a company. And I *really* think that's the distinction." Wilson would be the first to agree. He has often attributed his artistic life to the very existence of the Circle Repertory Company, in whose nurturing atmosphere he moved beyond a debilitating writing block to write prolifically.

As previously noted, historically Circle Rep is reminiscent of both the Group Theatre and the Moscow Art Theatre in its company orientation. In terms of thematic content it is safe to say that Circle Rep leans heavily toward the humanist Chekhovian influences — another distinctive characteristic in today's modern world. However, the similarities with the two older companies end abruptly when one compares Circle Rep's apolitical posture with the Group Theatre's political orientations, or compares Circle Rep's constant financial perils with the Moscow Art Theatre's heavy financial subsidy by its government.

The idea of a company is hardly unique. It has, however, gained in credibility and feasibility due to the success of Circle Rep. According to

Mason, who has kept an ongoing association with many theatre groups around the nation, the Empty Space in Seattle was influenced by the idea of a company; the Cricket Theatre in Minneapolis has looked to Circle Rep and actually voiced the thought that it might be time to consider forming a company of its own instead of merely doing plays; even Joseph Papp, with his considerable success at the Public, has admitted to Mason that he is thinking in terms of a company. Besides established groups considering a change, new companies with similar goals are now opening throughout the country. The Steppenwolf Theatre in Chicago is a prime example. Their devotion to ensemble work, their level of artistry, and their standards of excellence in terms of what they are trying to accomplish are extremely reminiscent of Circle Rep's banner. Mason was so impressed with the Steppenwolf Theatre during a visit to Chicago that he called it "a real echo of Circle Rep's heart," and brought John Malkovitch's production of Wilson's *Balm in Gilead* to the Circle Repertory's Sheridan Square Playhouse in 1984.

Then there are the new companies which openly admit to emulating the Circle Rep. Former company member Jordan Charney's association with Circle Rep helped to formulate the direction which he wanted his new theatre in Sherman Oaks, California, to take. In speaking of his dedication to providing opportunities for actor-members of the company to stretch their artistic muscles through classes, labs, and workshops in addition to public performances, he spoke of making a concerted effort to attract new writers to the theatre in order to "establish a creative marriage between us. Only through an arduous process involving much labor pains can we hope for the continued birth of new and meaningful drama."[3] Charney's entire theatre philosophy could be considered a restatement of Circle Rep's own philosophy. His devotion to CRC ideals is one of the more obvious examples of Circle Rep's influence on other theatres.

It is not really surprising that those who were familiar with Circle Rep's company process often tried to duplicate it. The "Circle idea," as playwright Milan Stitt called it, was one of the distinctive characteristics that separated it from other groups. Not only are other theatre groups consciously trying to emulate it, but Circle Rep itself is trying to recreate its own original premise from which it has deviated over the last several years, leaving in its wake a company suffering from fundamental dissatisfactions and debilitating enervation. The most astonishing conclusion is that, in many ways, Circle Rep is no longer an environment in which to work since it became a production house looking for hits. Now, half of the members do not know each other. Most who attend the Friday Readings are Lab members and interns rather than company members; company members no longer attend regularly, if at all. Tony Roberts, for example, is listed as a company member, but it is doubtful that he would recognize 95 percent of the company members if he ran into them on the street. The sense of company no longer exists in 1985 except in name and desire. The Circle idea has been lost to its own success. Stitt felt that Circle Rep had a "great idea" that had been achieved twice. It had been achieved the first time when the original company worked essentially for nothing and, out of the hardships, developed the sense of camaraderie and ensemble spirit that has been the bedrock for everything that has happened since. The company achieved it the second time in 1978 when, due to the New York State Council on the Arts grant, a small, select group of company members was paid $50 to $150 per week each and could once again fully operate within the company concept — or the "Circle idea." On both occasions, Circle Rep was a truly functioning company under Mason and Thirkield which met consistently; with the spirit of communal exercises and mutual nurturing, the company came to prominence. According to Stitt, that communal spirit disappeared during the eighties: "If we can regain that and learn from the mistakes we've made, and continue to grow, then I think we can once again be an important theatre."

In retrospect, it can be seen that Stitt's assessment can be substantiated with a fair degree of accuracy. Each time the Circle idea was fully operational, the abundant energy and infectious enthusiasm which were generated lasted for several years. There was an appreciable rise in the quality of the work during these periods. When the company idea was working at its peak, the theatre produced some of its most important works, such as *The Hot l Baltimore; The Sea Horse; When You Comin' Back, Red Ryder?; The Mound Builders; Knock, Knock; Serenading Louie; 5th of July; Gemini; The Runner Stumbles; Talley's Folley; The Woolgatherer; The Diviners; A Tale Told; The Great Grandson of Jedediah Kohler; Angels Fall;* and *'night Mother.* It should be noted that of the sixteen plays mentioned, seven were written by Lanford Wilson who, perhaps more than any other resident playwright, operates so well within the Circle idea.

Stitt feels very strongly that Circle Rep has to get "back to the core." He believes there is a great need for reaffirmation of a living theatre ensemble. It is impossible not to wonder whether or not the company should go back to its tiny concerns. A small company interested in serving its own needs can easily be seen as selfish. Or is being "selfish" the only way to maintain true artistic integrity and thereby best serve the needs of drama and theatre itself? There was a certain strength and vitality during the original days of the CRC which could probably be attributed to a confluence of artistic, social, economic, and political forces emanating from the turmoil of the sixties. It might do well to try to recapture that vitality. Although in its artistic content Circle Rep was swimming against the philosophical tide, there is little doubt that its development as a company sprang directly from the powerful communal feelings of the sixties. It is not likely that the company could have emerged from the forties with wartime attitudes creating such strong patriotic and social bonds throughout the nation. Nor could it have wholly come out of the fifties with its surface innocence and growing middle-class affluence, even though it was out of these times that the *idealism* of the founders had been born—an idealism that was imbedded deeply in the company's psyche. In combination, an interesting mix of forces—idealism from the forties and fifties, communal behavioral patterns from the Greenwich Village of the sixties.

Interestingly, Circle Rep's development as a company shows a strong parallel with the Group Theatre of the thirties. The CRC developed at a particularly difficult historical period, just as the Group Theatre developed out of a similarly difficult period and stood against it with the same ideological intensity. The CRC's relationship to the sixties, with its rebellious antiwar, antiestablishment spirit, paralleled the intensity of the Group Theatre's strong relationship to the hard times of the Great Depression, but with different results. The Group Theatre was actively seeking to change the political establishment of its day with such plays as Clifford Odets's *Waiting for Lefty* and *Paradise Lost*. Circle Rep, on the other hand, although participating in civil rights and antiwar demonstrations, was basically apolitical in its play content from the very start. Mason does not believe in the Brechtian didacticism the Group Theatre's ideology represented:

> I have always believed that the artist should steer clear of seeking mere political solutions to problems inherent in the human condition, and I still believe that the theatre is not the most

effective way to instigate activity or sponsor political theory. Essays, demonstrations, marches, speeches, voting—these are more direct means of achieving action in the political arena for policies that address the needs of our society. When the artist turns to politics, he or she is often being used to promote the limited aims of propaganda.[4]

What arouses Mason's interest and sense of responsibility are the plays that raise questions of concern and value in terms of the human experience—plays that delve deeply and ask tough questions that do not necessarily have answers. This tendency, along with the emphasis on the ensemble and on the actors, is another distinctive characteristic of the Circle Rep idea. Quite possibly one of the reasons the company survived was that it was not political in content. The Group Theatre became too political and dissipated; this is not to suggest that that was why the Group Theatre dissolved, but the time did come when its voice was no longer the voice of the depressed times. The Living Theatre became too politically and socially controversial; it self-destructed by creating too much political controversy to be permitted to continue functioning unharrassed by political considerations. When a theatre identifies too much with any one particular point of view, its longevity and very existence become seriously jeopardized. Mason's humanistic approach, on the other hand, includes a multiplicity of viewpoints, thereby cloaking itself in a universality that encourages longevity. Certainly, part of the company's ability to survive was its ability to attract funding, but a good part of its durability was the ideological implications behind much of their work.

Interestingly, most of Circle Rep's plays are not about New York. The plays are not about life on the Upper East Side, or what it is like to be single in New York, or suddenly to have a building convert to co-op, leaving one with the decision either to buy or be evicted. It does not deal with New York issues or New York life as, for example, the New York Yiddish Theatre did in its heyday (it was later the Entermedia Theatre on Second Avenue and 12th Street, and is now the Second Avenue Theatre). Circle Rep was not even conceived or created by New Yorkers. Maybe what was needed to create it as well as sustain it was the psychological undercurrent of wide-eyed innocents coming into the city to conquer the town. It takes courage to leave home, to leave all that is familiar, whether happy or not, and to do it literally on a shoestring. It also takes a tremendous desire and hunger for greater things. Yet like the immigrants who came to a new land and started afresh with nothing but a promise of better things and their own great needs to sustain them, the founders retained their backgrounds under the surface of new sophistications. Dealing mostly with what they knew personally, the founders of CRC brought much of their mid-American style with them — not a style superimposed over a New York setting, but a style with its own regional flavors kept intact. It obviously appealed, even to people in New York.

There is always a different cycle and type of play that the public and artist want to see at any one time. Plays reflect the times. Sometimes it might take longer for art to raise the banner of consciousness; sometimes it precedes all of the variables that serve as catalysts. But art is not only concerned with lofty ideas; it also reflects the concerns of average people. However, it can be argued that American lyricalism as practiced by Circle Rep is *too* exclusively concerned with interpersonal relationships, so much so that it does not seem to handle the big tragic themes or the great issues of the day. Yet, Circle Rep has always dealt with plays about real people and real issues which intimately address contemporary times. The only difference is that Circle Rep's emphasis is on the human and personal side of these issues.

To illustrate this point, consider William Hoffman's *As Is,* under the direction of Marshall Mason. In *As Is,* Hoffman and Mason were not dealing with the issue of AIDS as a negative social force, nor were they dealing with the fact that homosexuals have been the primary victims of the syndrome, or that there has been a decided lack of public and political support for research. They were not dealing with any of the burning issues which surround the disease. *As Is* is a play that offers no solutions; instead, it focuses on a human need — how to deal with death, whether it comes from the bubonic plague in the fourteenth century, or the AIDS epidemic today. *As Is* presents the human issues involved with the sudden recognition of terminal illness, the horror, the impact of how two lovers deal with the realization that death will soon take one away. It is a story of conditional love turned unconditional when the finality of death reduces all other personal considerations to obscurity by comparison.

It is typical of Circle Rep to let others fight the sociological battles. They are more interested in what the disease means in basic human terms. In such a way, the issue of facing death can be universally applied to any disease and any situation in which two people, whether homosexual, heterosexual, married, lovers, relatives, or simply friends, face the

painful prospect of terminal separation, and how they come to terms
with it.

In order to appreciate fully the possible future direction of the company, it is necessary briefly to reexamine its initial goals. The key to
Circle Rep has always been in its attempt to create a lasting theatre by
and for theatre artists. It was created in reaction to two major themes on
the New York theatrical scene of the sixties: the hit-flop syndrome, and
the undirected and self-destructive experimentation of off-off-Broadway.
The company started as "experimental" because it insisted upon a traditional approach in a densely untraditional off-off-Broadway world. As
was to be expected, there was success and failure within each season; the
success was applauded, the failure was not only tolerated but accepted as
an almost necessary part of the process.

In light of the critical attention given to the company, Mason and
Thirkield proved correct in their assessment that traditional realistic theatre—their own realism superimposed over the "experience of the
now"—was still eminently viable, and in fact was what the public seemed
to want.

In the ever-vigilant eyes of the critics, by the late seventies Circle
Rep began to have an obligation to produce new American plays. Added
to this new obligation was the Rep's own internal obligation to produce a
certain high quality of play. It began living up to the first obligation
perhaps, but not to the second. Quality had too often been sacrificed to
commerce and the courtship of critical approval.

By 1979–1980 the CRC's existence was no longer a reaction to commerciality, but had become the very establishment it had circumvented
for so long. Through Porter Van Zandt's influence, institutionalization
of the theatre gave it critical standing and expanded the scope of the
work. It had also helped to keep Circle Rep alive and stable. However,
institutionalization took the hunger away. Circle Rep ceased to experiment and grow; it merely produced more and more of the same instead
of continuing to learn, develop, and expand. Critical pressure would not
allow experimentation on the mainstage, while stabilization led to the
loss of the workshop stage in which to experiment. The catchword became "caution." Experimentation was replaced by the PIPS, which although they were called Projects-in-Progress, in actuality were not
workshops at all, but had become auditions for the mainstage. Whatever
the negative aspects of high exposure, the resulting critical attention and

stabilization made it possible for the theatre to survive, but now expectations have been laid out with a new set of inflexible rules. Failure, one of the measures by which success is determined, is no longer acceptable or tolerated on any level. Even Rob Thirkield, one of the original founders and a person without whom the theatre would probably never have endured financially past the first year, was practically out of the picture after he directed the eminently worthwhile but critically unsuccessful *Lulu* in 1978.

Thirkield's absence raises an interesting question: where does the company's responsibility actually lie as "people to people" in a nurturing environment? Circle Rep probably would have gone the sad route of many enthusiastic but underfinanced theatrical endeavors and been forced to close, if it had not been for Thirkield's generosity. There can be no underestimating the extent of the support he gave to the group, not only in the beginning, but throughout the years.[5] Yet, Thirkield was no longer actively functioning with the company in an artistic capacity. He was still active on the Board of Directors at Circle Rep, but he had not been directly involved in Circle production since the last role Lanford Wilson had written for him, that of the old man in *The Mound Builders,* a role Thirkield did not particularly like.

It was not that Thirkield had given up theatre. On the contrary, he remained very active with River Arts Repertory, a new company he helped to create in Woodstock, New York.[6] It is difficult to pin down his dissatisfactions. Simply, Thirkield had slowly come to feel left out of the Circle Repertory Company. While it seems that he lost interest due to the same kind of well-articulated dissatisfactions of many of the members, it might be more accurate to say that he lost heart. After spending years in a nurturing-teaching role, personally helping many of the members over the difficult creative times, the "right to fail" as a normal part of artistic life seemed to apply to everyone but him. One of the important criteria that had been set up by Circle Rep was the right to fail as part of the growth and experimental process. However, from the time of *Lulu,* Thirkield was looked upon askance. This treatment of a man who had contributed so much of his energy, as well as his money, could be considered grossly unfair; he was an energetic, vital, warm, and highly competent teacher as well as a very talented actor. The virtual discarding of Thirkield as an active member could be considered a tremendous human fault on the part of a company that prides itself on its supportive philosophy. Perhaps Thirkield should have received the same support and nurture in his difficult times as he had doled out throughout his extensive involvement with the company actors. But the experimental attitude which adopted the "if we fail, we'll try again" ideology is gone, lost to the pressures of money and commerciality, as well as lost to its own success—that of being a high-profile organization whose work is put under the microscope and sometimes mercilessly scrutinized by critics, each of whom has his own personal set of expectations. Nevertheless, to be able to experiment and even have the right to fail is a very important part of Circle Rep's artistic credo.

Although it was always possible that Thirkield might return (and indeed broached the subject of directing again at Circle Rep to Mason, which Mason viewed positively), it was Thirkield himself who ultimately cut his own losses with the company and chose to concentrate on River Arts Repertory in Woodstock. Personalities and diverse lifestyles may have been deeply involved in the decision as well. Thirkield was heterosexual. This orientation could have put him a bit on the outside of the inner circle, an assessment difficult to support with evidence. However, Thirkield was one of the few interviewed who insisted that homosexuality within the company should be dealt with in any analysis of the group since it was a factor that often affected who was admitted into the group and who remained.[7]

One of the recurring problems of a company is the human aspect of day-to-day involvement in such an intimate profession. A good argument can be made against what some anonymously refer to as the "pretend, phoney, family stuff." Perhaps even Mason fools himself when he says there is a common artistic goal. It has been said that the only time the company members really mesh is the important time when they are working on a show. At the Circle Rep there is a tendency to believe that it is important to the creative process for everyone to feel a beloved part of the "family." As one writer who disagreed says, "I don't think I should feel a part of the family. I don't think they should either. It's our work. We work together to accomplish it. To a degree the socializing and buying houses next to each other in Sag Harbor may contribute to it but it's not an important part of it. They used to always have Christmas together with a big Christmas party. Marshall would be Santa Claus. But that's all just gilding. If you need it, it's nice. Some people do need it and that's fine. That's good. But it's not what makes a company work. It's super-talented people moving, even *abrasively,* with each other towards the goal of putting on the best possible production. That's what makes a company work."[8]

Under the intensely personal currents of involvement, Marshall Mason and Rob Thirkield went about creating one of the most important off-Broadway theatres of the past fifteen years, and although they succeeded in creating a stable institution which can grow, and indeed has grown, there was much to be sacrificed during expansion which was not expected. The sacrifice was sometimes artistic quality and often the freedom to experiment, the two most fundamental qualities for which the company was originally formed in order *not* to ever have to sacrifice.

At first, critical reception of the Circle Rep was very positive and supportive — "a chief provider of American plays," "real plays about real people," "one of our best theatres." Unfortunately, the theatre was in a constant waltz with the critics in order to remain fiscally solvent. Critical expectations remained high and demanding, but the critics were not getting what they wanted. The theatre began to spread itself too thin in an attempt to gain approval. Mason departed on a two-year sabbatical at the end of 1982, following a season of high activity and little commercial success. Although it has been suggested that Mason left because of mounting personal and emotional problems (indeed, his sabbatical was even privately construed by some as a way of "easing" him out of the company), it is more likely that Mason left in order to regroup and reassess the entire process of the Circle idea. He returned in 1984 obviously refreshed, full of vigor, and ready to tackle the company problems with reaffirmation of his original concepts. This time he would have to do it alone — Rob Thirkield was pretty much out of the active picture — and in a totally different social environment.[9]

One of the differences between the sixties, when it all started, and the eighties is the kind of people who are attracted to New York. In the sixties there were many who could "make do" on the fringes, earning a living in marginal kinds of ways, passing out pamphlets, posing for artists, and so on. Part of survivability was the youth factor. Every age has its young people who make do until they grow older and say, "I want more." Increasingly now, there seem to be fewer people who come to New York with the attitude that "making do" is sufficient. They are the mid-twenties to mid-thirties generation of Yuppies. They make their living by cleverly figuring out the eighties system and doing something that the system recognizes and rewards. In many ways that is exactly what the *new* Circle Rep is doing. Circle Rep began as something very distinctive. It went through a long period of adolescence when it was more than willing to "make do." The inchoate organization — the Caffé Cino with its togetherness and ensemble spirit, its experimenting and smoking marijuana with the audience — is gone now, transformed into something which could easily be recognized by a society geared to the establishment; now they could almost be called "the Yuppies of the theatre." Circle Rep's way of making money and sustaining itself has changed. It is no longer part of the makeshift, make-do, fly-by-the-seat-of-the-pants, hand-to-mouth times of the romantic Cino days. Circle Rep is a different kind of financial survivor now, definitely part of the mainstream, and increasingly looking to the establishment for continued funding as its natural due. It is not only that money is now seen as essential in order to remain in the business of theatre, but also the change is increasingly obvious in the manner in which they figure out how to obtain it. The company has demonstrated an ability to transform itself into something which can appeal to whomever has the money.

What Mason and Thirkield developed with Berezin and Wilson over the years was tantamount to an unacknowledged mininational theatre. Circle Rep has become one of many such theatres in the country which have existed partially on private funding, including the Arena Stage in Washington, the Tyrone Guthrie Theatre in Minneapolis, the Alley Theatre in Houston, and the American Conservatory Theatre and the Actors' Workshop, both in San Francisco. These are unsubsidized, underfinanced American theatres, sometimes resident, often regional, which on their own ideologically assume the national responsibility for new American drama as well as preservation of the old. The Repertory Theatre of Lincoln Center was the closest thing to a national theatre in New York City during the sixties; one of their mistakes was beginning operations with overt expectations of becoming *the* national theatre.

Mason has always had the desire for Circle Rep to become a national theatre. From the very beginning it has been an articulated dream, if not an actual goal, to have Circle Rep earn the right, through recognition of its excellence, to be declared one of the national theatres in the United States. Status as a national theatre would mean the guarantee of a yearly government subsidy (federal, state, city, or a combination), with a resulting lessening of financial pressures. The arts, in the truest sense of the word, have to be patronized; they usually cannot exist for very long otherwise. But the United States population is not very homogeneous; different theatre appeals to different people, without even touching the many layers of ethnic diversity. Such diversity makes it questionable whether there can be a national theatre at all, despite, perhaps, the artistic need for one. On the other hand, since a national theatre does not have to support itself, it does not have to please the largest audience in order to remain solvent. However, the problem is not what a national theatre should be, should produce, or should represent. The problem is that everyone usually thinks in terms of *a* national theatre. Because of that, there is hardly any agreement as to what it should be or what kinds of works should be presented. But if the idea of national *theatres* were spread out across the land representing different regional elements and different creative aspects of this country, it would be a different story. Ideally, the national theatres of America would be located in the great urban centers — New York City, Los Angeles, San Francisco, Washington, Houston, Chicago, Atlanta — each subsidized by city, state, and federal monies to spread the growing abundance of American work which should be preserved and toured throughout the nation and throughout the world as the culturally rich expressions of a multifaceted nation. Into this ideal Circle Rep wants to fit as one of America's national theatres.

There cannot be only one national theatre in America — using the criteria of government subsidy to qualify as a national theatre — just as there is not only one in England or France or Germany, for example, even though they are small countries compared with the expanse of the United States, with more nationally homogeneous concerns and attitudes than the United States. London alone has three subsidized theatres: the National Theatre of Great Britain, the Royal Shakespeare Company, and the English Stage Company (often referred to as the Royal Court). France boasts the Comédie Française (Théâtre Français) and the Théâtre National Populaire, among others. In Germany, although the most theatrically active centers are in Berlin, Munich, and Hamburg, virtually every town of any size has a state subsidized theatre. Italy has eight major resident national theatres in such cities as Milan, Genoa, and Turin. In Moscow, there are three well-known nationally subsidized theatres, ranging from the museum-like Moscow Art Theatre with its heavy emphasis on preservation and scenic design, to the less stylized Contemporary Theatre and the Moscow Theatre of Drama and Comedy (Taganka). In Czechoslovakia, besides the Prague National Theatre, the government created the State Theatre in 1962, a studio designed specifically to assist experimental groups.

As noted, in the United States there are too many major regional forces and too much fundamental diversity to support one theatrical view. However, our theatre is still young, as Harold Clurman so often pointed out:

> If it is correct to speak of our theatre as having been "born" forty-five years ago, we must agree that compared to the French neo-classical stages, the recently founded British National Theatre, our theatre is in its infancy.[10]

It is not surprising that America is still in its theatrical infancy, since so much of its early sociology was determined by the Puritan ethic and theatre was looked upon as sinful by the Puritans. Thus, the European legacy of theatre was slow in developing in America, and there is, therefore, not as rich a dramatic literature in America as in Europe. As Clurman noted:

> Countries which have long theatrical histories may maintain theatres especially designed to preserve those traditions. This is the chief purpose of the Comédie Française, and to some extent this was and is the purpose of the Old Vic and of the Shakespeare Theatre at Stratford-on-Avon. It is largely true of the various state or municipal theatres in Germany. Most European countries have produced dramatic literatures rich enough to sustain such theatres over the years.
> America has not.[11]

It might still be early in its theatrical evolution for the United States to have a national theatre at all, particularly if it follows the snail-like pattern of its English predecessor. Despite an ample theatrical heritage in England which spanned centuries, it was not until after World War II, in the late forties, that Parliament finally approved funding for a National Theatre of Great Britain. Even so, it was not implemented until 1963, when the Old Vic company was disbanded and the new troupe established. With Laurence Olivier as artistic director to a company of fifty-one and Kenneth Tynan as literary advisor, they presented an eclectic choice of plays and production styles; Great Britain finally had its national theatre. America has yet to follow.

Circle Rep now has behind it the NEA Ensemble Grant which represents a respite from the financial concerns which plague all theatre in the nation. The goals five years into the future have not been articulated. The five-year grant will culminate the twenty years Mason has always said it would take to build a great theatre company. At the end of this period, if the work proves to be substantial enough, they will more than likely want to continue in the ensemble manner with a revolving repertory system of performing as described. However, it will be just as impossible for Circle Rep to sustain itself financially through repertory without continued financing—not a uniquely American problem. The National Theatre in Great Britain, for example, works in repertory as does the Royal Shakespeare Company. They are competitive and richly praised. But it is the high degree of government subsidy, and only that, which keeps both companies fiscally intact. As drama critic Stanley Kauffmann points out,

> There is no question as to whether repertory can pay its way in Great Britain: it can't. Both of these companies and others (like the rep theatres of the continent) are kept going by government subsidy far beyond anything the United States has ever given to the theatre. Still, they have had considerable public support and have additionally, become tourist attractions.[12]

American national theatres would need just as much financial support as their European counterparts, as well as critical encouragement. But who will decide which companies should be so designated? There is a kind of commercial attitude in this country which permits the market to decide who will survive and who will succumb. There is no authority vested in a group or organization which will determine which companies might be representative national theatres. Using England again as an example, the establishment decides the national concerns, the establishment consisting perhaps of a combination of people who have been through the private school system, a contingent of Oxford dons, Shakespearean scholars, and politicians operating in a class system defined by heritage and education. In America it is the critics who would have to declare a company's worth in order for the federal government to subsidize continued work, since everyone is going to want to be declared a national theatre.

An American national theatre would have to do American "classics," not European classics, as, for example, the Royal Shakespeare Company supports the work of Shakespeare as only they can, and the

Comédie Française does similar preservation of Molière. There is no American national theatre which preserves the best of American drama, even though as Clurman says, "there are more American plays worth revival than we suppose."[13] But in our disposable society, many fine plays are given a six-week run and then disappear. They are not financially lucrative enough to be performed in commercial theatre and therefore not available to the public. Few individuals, groups, or organizations, whether public or private, are doing anything tangible to make sure these plays are preserved. Perhaps one of the points of the NEA grants was to encourage American theatre groups to try to build a network of national theatres across the country. Perhaps it is also a way of building and training audiences around the country; the public has to be taught to appreciate plays other than those of Neil Simon. This comment is not meant snidely; Simon is a prolific genius in his own way—the Molière of his day who has mastered the American well-made play as few others have. But since we are still in the process of building up a theatrical heritage, an American national theatre would also need to concentrate heavily on new drama and the new artist. This kind of concentration takes time, money, and patience, although it is the money that will say it all.

To some extent the bestowal of the grant monies is political. The National Endowment itself is open to congressional pressures, which lead many to cynically feel that federal money could never create a national theatre—that the politics and special interests would create too much of a problem, with money being distributed through a maze of backtrading behind the scenes. Is NEA giving more to the East or the Southwest? Is the South being cheated of its fair share ("fair" implying equality in accounts above quality in product)? The regional special interests in such arguments could be one of the reasons America does not have a national theatre; all of the private-interest considerations make the nature of distribution difficult to cope with. But problems are inherent in any system involving federal monies to the arts, all of which are starving for recognition. Taking a cue from Europe, one can see that the concept *can* be made to work, despite problems. In France, for example, there was much dissatisfaction with the way the government was distributing subsidies to the many theatrical factions in state theatres and cultural centers—most particularly about what was considered the state's arbitrary assignment of directors and subsidies. Problems were also rampant in Germany, where in West Germany alone there are more than two hundred state-subsidized theatres. In Germany, one of the major problems was the unlimited power to make decisions given to *intendanten,* the state-appointed theatre managers.[14] Nevertheless, for better or worse, the system *does* work. It is doubtful that anyone in Europe would ever wish to return to a box-office support system. Fear of these kinds of problems alongside political pressures lead some to believe that only private money can truly subsidize the arts with freedom. Too much state involvement goes against Circle Rep's original concept of a theatre of "artists for artists," which was carefully created in reaction to the dismissal of Whitehead and Kazan from the Repertory Theatre of Lincoln Center. But only when theatre is federally funded will a national theatre truly work, taking it out of the realm of the entertainment market and putting it squarely within the scope of art for art's sake. However, since there is no national theatre in America at present, companies like Circle Rep still have to make it mostly on their own and must institutionalize in order to do so.

We have already discussed what in means to be a company; it does not have so much to do with success or failure as it has to do with sociological factors. Does it take one genius to hold it together? It is doubtful that Lanford Wilson would be able to hold the company together; he is a writer interested in his own concerns. Does it take a vision? Can one person like Mason keep making it real, keep articulating how it can be made to work and where? How important is the organizational influence of someone like Porter Van Zandt, who insists that only by institutionalizing the ideals can they be protected? Does it have to do with size or with location? All of these factors have to do with what it means to be a company. But sociological factors and the particular set of circumstances that played into the creation of the company notwithstanding, it is the particular combination of *people* that made it all possible. The individual strengths of the four founders when blended together created a unified strength for the theatre. As Lanford Wilson says, "It's difficult to say where it would be without any one of us because we *are* the company. It's not as though we were hired. It's me and Marshall and Tanya and Rob. Marshall has always taken care of the actors' growth, and Tanya the truth, and me the writing, and Rob the teaching. It's Marshall's eye for physical details that gives us that incredibly professional, detailed, finished look that we have."

But each would agree that it is Mason who has been the greatest strength behind the theatre. Throughout the years he has never altered his vision though he has grown and matured and accepted the establishment. His basic fundamental vision of what he wants to do, where he wants to go, what it all means has never changed. A company has to have a certain kind of vision that is strong and permeating. If Marshall Mason were to leave Circle Rep tomorrow for good, and the company advertised in the *New York Times* for a new artistic director, there is little doubt that Circle Rep would continue its operations as an institution. It is an institution that has the ability to support a season and produce plays on a regular basis. But it would not be the same place. A new director would come in with his own vision, his own preference for plays, his own style of directing. It might still be a successful company, but it would be a different one.

And yet, even so, Circle Rep has been more than one person. The ideas grow and take on a separate life of their own beyond those who dream them, until they stand on their own. It looks as though Circle Rep will continue to thrive and still has a long way to go. But there are many danger signals that are beginning to flash. For example, the company can be seen as moving backwards to original concerns rather than moving forward, no matter what rationales are applied. The loss of Rob Thirkield's experimental nature can be keenly felt in an underlying stodginess that creeps into play selection at times. The greatest value and impact of the company has been the discovery of all the new plays. Although this will continue, at least for a while, there is a genuine danger in cutting back the Literary Department, which essentially handles research and development for the future. Cutbacks in this department in particular arc troubling many within thc company as well as outside. Peter Buckley, in a letter to the author, addressed this very issue without being aware of how jeopardized the Literary Department actually was:

> The true impact of a company such as the Circle Rep is that it *does* concern itself with new plays, something on the order of 500 a year, that are seriously read—often out loud and in staged readings—and evaluated, and passed on. Its opinions are sought and respected; it encourages and suggests, even when it is not further involved: and it does produce—albeit sometimes badly—new works that might otherwise be lost. Without companies such as the Circle Rep—and there are dozens of them around the country that must not be discounted—the American

theatre would be in even worse shape than it is, and it's in pretty bad shape as far as new works. But then why should a writer work for a year on a play for $5,000, when he/she can do a movie-of-the-week for $50,000? Because that same writer can, and does, do a couple of movie-of-the-weeks for the bucks and then returns of Off Broadway (or to the regionals) with that subsidy and to a place like the Circle Rep (or Playwrights Horizons or the Manhattan Theatre Club or the Arena Stage or the ART) for the *play*. But without *that* place to place the *play* he/she might very well stay in the mire of television. Without these companies, all of which are underfunded, the spoken word would really disappear; now, it's only in temporary trouble.

We do, of course, need a national repertory theatre of the highest quality—and with the *highest* budget—based in *Manhattan* . . . but with touring companies throughout the country. Until we finally get that, we're still theatrical novices. But as for now, the Philistines are hammering at the gate, but so far we've held them at bay, and it's companies like Circle Rep—perhaps the leading American company at Philistine-beating-back—that have kept us *slightly* civilized. Now, however, it is time to move forward.[15]

And move forward the Circle Rep has, despite the necessary heavy institutionalization of its dreams. The institutionalization process had been going on since 1974, but really began in earnest in 1978–1979 when Porter Van Zandt brought in specialists to head the various departments. It was at that point—the ten-year mark—that Mason, Thirkield, Wilson, and Berezin started to be relieved of the actual running of the theatre. Now the major issue has become how to support the company's operations. As Richard Frankel says, "Right now, in terms of transitions, we are in the middle of what is a ten-year process of institutionalization. I would think that in another five years, we will either be an organization that will survive the people who started it, or it will be closed. That is my guess. That process is going to take a full ten years. Right now, we have the structure, the machine that can produce plays—crank them out. We can produce four, five, or six at a time here. There are many plans and projects for the future but we don't have the financial resources to support it at this point. Either we're going to build a financial structure to support it or we're not." Circle Rep may survive the people who started it. However, there is little doubt that without Marshall Mason, it would be a decidedly different place. There are few who are involved with the company who would disagree. Tanya Berezin, so intimately involved with the entire operation from its beginning, has always felt that the Circle Rep *was* Marshall Mason. It was Tanya Berezin who stressed:

> Circle Rep as an institution, as a theatre, *is* Marshall. It was his vision. And the thing I've always admired most about Marshall, and the thing that has the greatest effect on the theatre, is that not only does he have convictions, but he has the courage of his convictions. He always goes back to his relationship to the work. And all decisions eventually are made from what we set out to do. So that he has never lost his artistic impulse. And I think he has kept it alive. And as much as he likes success, and he does as much as anybody else—he will go anywhere to accept an award—I have never seen him truly compromise himself and his integrity to what he believes is true to the art of the theatre. He's unswerving. We've all made mistakes here and there, but he's unswerving.

From the general manager to the most eager intern, everyone seemed to agree.

In Mason's "Observations from the Sabbatical," he wrote, "I remind myself that when we started the Circle Rep, I predicted that it would require twenty years to build a great theatre. I recommit myself to the twenty years it will have taken."

In the theatre that Mason knew in the late fifties when he first came to New York, Elia Kazan had been his model. "Kazan probed deeply into the human experience and revealed things to me through Brando's and Dean's acting and the Actors Studio and the Stanislavski approach," Mason recalls.

> They were the lifelines that I had towards accomplishing the kinds of goals that I had in mind, but the theatre that I saw around me was a theatre that was quite external and superficial and sentimental. I would put in that category, Inge, the preachiness of Odets, the glibness of Broadway comedy at that point— *Under the Yum Yum Tree* and *The Moon Is Blue* are my favorite targets. I wouldn't be in the theatre if that's what I would have to do. But these goals about illuminating humanity, lofty as they are . . . how do you do that? I felt that maybe that's where I could make my contribution. I'm still struggling with that. How do I put into words the principles that I have learned about directing so that others may use them? I believe that is a major duty—to find that out. In the meantime, for a while, we're going back to where we started. For a while my main

contribution was in directing. I now feel it's going to be in creating a theatre that will allow many other artists to make similar kinds of contributions. So, I guess to answer the question now — simplistic as it is — I want to leave the theatre a better place than I found it. I want it to be a deeper place, a truer place, a more entertaining place and a more celebrated place than when I found it. I'm spending my life doing that.

The most astonishing thing is that Mason has never changed. So many people start off in wonderful directions and then for whatever reason — ordinary need, artistic changes, commercial considerations, or greed — they deviate. Perhaps the principles were never that strong to begin with, or the idealism dissipated through the difficulties of daily life. Mason has grown, but he has never changed. The most difficult courses to stay on are the idealistic ones. Mason has made it very clear that he has a profound conviction that idealism is worthless unless it becomes action: "Once you begin to accomplish your ideals in terms of your day-to-day life and the things that you do, it doesn't do any good to believe that it's harmful to kill people if you don't do something about it. Even if it's only to vote."

The past as prelude and prologue. Mason nods thoughtfully and says, "It's hard to know. I do feel on a new threshold."

Epilogue

In July 1986, Rob Thirkield committed suicide.

In September 1986, Marshall W. Mason announced his resignation as Artistic Director of the Circle Repertory Company. His resignation became effective May 1987, at which time he moved to California.

In March 1987, Tanya Berezin became Acting Artistic Director of the company. In August 1987, CRC's Board of Directors announced Tanya Berezin's appointment as Artistic Director, effective immediately.

Lanford Wilson is still the Circle Repertory Company's most prominent playwright-in-residence.

Afterword BY MARSHALL W. MASON

I returned from my two-year sabbatical renewed and recommitted. I felt the future of Circle Rep depended on fulfilling the destiny we had invented for ourselves: a mature company of artists annually employed to perform an entire season of rotating repertory. We had been rehearsing this destiny for years. It was as though the first fifteen years had been the preparation for what was to come.

To support this vision, we had applied for a grant from the National Endowment for the Arts (NEA), which had just launched a program of support for sustaining the efforts of permanent, ongoing ensembles. The timing seemed fortuitous, and we spent much of the sixteenth season laying the groundwork for the actual realization of the Resident Ensemble Program (REP). In the meantime, our major production season careened from flop to hit to disaster to triumph, like most American theaters.

The NEA remained very concerned about our fiscal health, and we were told it was essential that we show improvement in this area or we wouldn't get the grant. Ever since *Talley's Folly* we had outgrown our tiny space on Sheridan Square. We had more audience than we had seats. As a result we often had to produce part of our season in an additional theater space, which entailed costs that led to a series of annual deficits in our operation. The past several seasons had produced a sizable accumulated deficit under the management of Richard Frankel. The NEA strongly hinted that we needed new leadership in retiring that deficit in order to be considered for the ensemble grant. And so my first duty upon returning was to replace Richard.

It was a most unpleasant chore because I really liked him and had always enjoyed working with him. But it seemed clear that while Richard had a remarkable talent as an entrepreneur, his skill in leading a board of directors to solve the deficit problems of a nonprofit institution left considerable room for improvement. His subsequent success as a commercial theater producer would seem to confirm this assessment.

After a considerable search, I found a talented young woman who had dazzled her teachers at Yale and who seemed perfect for the job at hand. And so Suzanne Sato became Circle Rep's new managing director. Richard stayed on a number of months to ease the transition, but he was greatly dispirited by the turn of events. I'm sure that I seemed especially ungrateful for all he had done for us, and he left with some bitterness, in spite of a very favorable severance package that allowed him to leave with dignity. Still, I understood his disappointment, and I was sorry to lose him. He had been a real supporter of my vision and a good partner.

Many of the artistic decisions for the sixteenth year had been made during my absence, and the first three production had already been decided upon before my return. The company continued to pursue a goal of learning to perform classic theater with the grace and talent we were able to achieve in our contemporary work. With this in mind, we hired a British director, Toby Robertson, to direct the company in a Shakespearean comedy, *Love's Labors Lost*. Whenever we have attempted the classics, Circle Rep has been criticized for lacking the diction and training to do them justice. An avant-garde director of the classics like Toby seemed sure to stimulate us in the right direction. The flaw in this plan lay in Toby's choice of plays. As a director, he was attracted to disastrous plays where his vision might overcome the playwright's failure. *Love's Labors Lost* is about as poor a play as Shakespeare ever concocted: stiff, artificial, and trivial. Unfortunately, our production lacked any focus or style, costumed in some vague period of the early '30s (for no apparent reason). So once again, in attempting Shakespeare, we revealed more about our ambition than our strength.

This was followed by a play we had developed in our PIP process, James Farrell's *Bing and Walker*. It had enjoyed a successful production at the South Coast Rep in California, and I thought the major problems of the script had been worked out. I paired the author with a young director who had shown signs of brilliance in our Director's Lab, Dan Bonnell. This proved a mistake. It was Dan's first experience with a new play in a major production and he kept urging the author to make further revisions in the script. The entire cast joined in with suggestions for improvements, with the result that the playwright lost sight of what he was writing, and the script soon degenerated into a hodgepodge. It is very important for a writer to know when the play is finished. If it's not broken, don't fix it.

The third production also had been developed in our PIP process. The very talented Patrick Meyers had written a fantastical piece called *Dysan,* and my associate artistic director, B. Rodney Marriott, had directed the PIP the previous year. In the PIP, the play seemed a delightful exercise in metaphysical speculation that assumed reincarnation as a fact, and followed four human beings through several lives as they continued to intertwine on their karmic journeys. I think it annoyed audiences and critics more than anything we have ever done. I still like the play, and our production was spectacular. But it was a bit too "California-nut-fringe" for our subscribers. After the third failure in a row, the subscribers were ready to mutiny.

Nevertheless, I decided to follow these with a new play that William M. Hoffman had developed in our Lab about the dreadful, new, mysterious disease called AIDS. Bill had started writing the play in our Playwrights Lab, and after a PIP production in the fall, I began working with the author on revisions. I knew this play would make the first important statement on AIDS. Across town, Joe Papp was producing Larry Kramer's *The Normal Heart,* and for a time it was unclear which play would open first. I assembled an outstanding ensemble of actors, led by Jonathan Hogan and Jonathan Hadary, and our production of *As Is* opened to stunning reviews. John Glines had helped in the development of the play through his gay-oriented theater, The Glines, and he offered to co-produce the play with us, using the profits from the immensely successful *Torch Song Trilogy.* Our new managing director, Suzanne Sato, was eager to share expenses, thereby saving money that would result in reducing the deficit. The play was immensely successful with our audiences. It was a wise, warm, and even funny play—far ahead of its time. It educated and entertained as few plays do. There was immediate demand to move the play to Broadway to help revive a dreadful commercial season. Suzanne sold Circle Rep's rights to the play to John Glines, who produced it along with Lucille Lortel and the Shubert organization. It moved to the Lyceum Theater, where it was nominated for three Tony Awards and won a couple of Obies and the Drama Desk Award as Best Play of 1985. Suddenly, the season had turned a dramatic corner toward success.

This proved very temporary. For ten years, we had been developing a play with Julie Bovasso called *Angelo's Wedding*. It had about it the "feel" of a great play, Bovasso's masterwork. But Julie was so close to the characters in the play that it seemed to obscure her sense of reality. The rehearsals were difficult, but the work of the actors was brilliant. It seemed that if we could only survive the rehearsals and the daily tantrums of our writer, we might give birth to a remarkable breakthrough in the contemporary theater. The work of Scott Glenn, Cliff Gorman, Bill Hickey, and Mari Gorman comprised some of the best acting I have ever seen. But the play remained an unwieldy length, and the promised cuts were not forthcoming. It seemed as if Julie were hell-bent on a self-destructive course. By the time we were previewing, tension backstage had risen to an unbearable level. Because of the physical layout of the Circle Rep theater, the author had easy access to the actors' dressing rooms and the entire backstage area. As they prepared to go onstage, the actors felt constantly imperiled by the unpredictable playwright, who would often harangue them about their incompetence in realizing her play just as they were preparing for an entrance.

Finally, in an outburst apparently fortified by vodka, Julie Bovasso took the stage at intermission, shouting to the audience that she wanted them go home. In such circumstances, it was no surprise that Scott Glenn felt he could no longer continue, so there seemed little alternative to abandoning the production. The subscribers were offered a chance to see *'night, Mother* (which we had developed in our PIP process) on Broadway to fulfill our subscription obligations. Unfortunately the abandonment of *Angelo's Wedding* cost all the money we had gained from the success of *As Is,* but we still ended the season in the black. We all looked forward to the coming season, when our dream of becoming a true repertory company would finally be realized.

Right on the heels of the debacle of *Angelo's Wedding,* Circle Repertory Company became the first American theater to perform in English at Japan's National Theater in Tokyo. We mounted a rather eccentric, abstract production of Edward Albee's *Who's Afraid of Virginia*

Woolf? to great acclaim, and Edward seemed pleased by the success, if somewhat bemused by the production. We also toured our production of Sam Shepard's *Fool for Love* throughout Japan. In this foreign country, we were regarded and treated as the great American company we were trying to become.

Upon our return midsummer of 1985, we mounted a new production of Lanford Wilson's third play in the Talley series. Originally produced in 1981 as a *A Tale Told,* Lanford had subsequently received good guidance from the *Los Angeles Herald Examiner* critic, Jack Viertel. Lanford took the advice to heart, and the resulting script was so new it demanded a new name, and so *A Tale Told* became *Talley & Son.* We mounted the production at the Saratoga Performing Arts Center (SPAC), where we were in residence each summer, and then we opened the seventeenth season with this production (thereby saving costs by using SPAC's money to pay the production expenses). Many of the original cast repeated their roles, like Helen Stenborg, who won an Obie for her performance; others grew into new roles, like Laura Hughes, who had played Avalaine in the original and was now old enough to play Olive; still others were new to the company, like Farley Granger, who took over the title role. Here was the essence of the advantages of a repertory company: bringing back a play that literally took years in development, with all the subsequent artistic growth in performance as well as in text. However, since we had presented the play only five years earlier, I wanted the subscribers to have an alternative, so we decided to play Paul Osborn's *Tomorrow's Monday* in rotating repertory with *Talley & Son* and let the subscribers choose which to see on their subscription (with the second play available at half-price, a device I had picked up from the Mark Taper Forum). The subscription audience liked both productions, although critical reception was far from enthusiastic. Nancy Donahue's poignant comedy *The Beach House* followed, with company actor Swoosie Kurtz and guest artist George Grizzard. Again, we had a big audience pleaser that critics denigrated.

Once more we faced the problem of space limitations at Sheridan Square. We had succeeded in keeping the whole sixteenth season in our own space, but now that we were launching a season of repertory, it was clear that we had to find an alternative space to house the three-play rep that was scheduled to fill the second half of the seventeenth season. Suzanne's search turned up only one space we could afford, even with the help of the National Endowment's grant for the Resident Ensemble

Program: Manhattan Community College's Triplex Theater, downtown near the World Trade Center. I hated the theater upon sight, but it was true that the space allowed the production of three plays in rotating repertory, and so we took it.

The three plays were a contemporary adaptation of Camus's *Caligula,* a revival of Lanford Wilson's *The Mound Builders,* and a new play by Canadian award-winning playwright Anne Chislett called *Quiet in the Land.* I had chosen *Caligula* as a vehicle to explore the growing concerns for understanding terrorism, and because it provided an outstanding part for Bill Hurt. But Bill's film of *Children of a Lesser God* ran over schedule, preventing him from joining us in what was our most important project yet. And so from the beginning, the REP seemed cursed. We took a company of twenty actors to Dorset, Vermont, for the month of November to allow us time in the country to focus on this challenging new task. In order to ensure all actors of sufficient role opportunities, it was necessary to double-cast all the shows. This proved to be a huge mistake. The actors hated sharing roles, because of the resulting sacrifice in rehearsal time for each actor. None of the plays lived up to their potential, although there were good reviews. Audiences hated the Triplex as much as I did. The atmosphere was antiseptic and academic, and it was located far from traditional theater paths. For most theater-goers, it was an unfamiliar area of the city, and once there, the audience found the plays strangely uncommunicative in the hostile arena.

Because all six plays of the season were mounted by mid-season, I was free to accept an offer to direct an all-star revival of *Picnic* at the Ahmanson Theater in Los Angeles, and this was to be followed with the cameras rolling on my first film, *The Front Runner.* From a personal point of view, it seemed as though I was finally getting the opportunity to see two life-long goals in direct contrast: the reality of creating a genuine repertory company and the chance to make a movie. Fortunately, the two goals did not seem in conflict. Unfortunately, the schedule did not materialize as expected, and so production of the film was delayed. I learned an awful lot about the business of making movies during the three years I prepared *The Front Runner,* and I directed a Showtime television version of my stage hit, *Picnic.* But I didn't get the movie made.

In the summer of 1986, one of my closest friends and collaborators, Neil Flanagan, died in Los Angeles of AIDS. We had a memorial service for him at the Mark Taper and then another in New York at Circle Rep on the following Monday. On Wednesday of the same week, my oldest and dearest friend, Rob Thirkield, the cofounder of Circle Rep, succumbed to the private struggles within his soul and committed suicide. This double blow left me reeling. Life was not a gift without end. Time is limited on this earth, and it was brutally brought home to me that if I had goals that I wanted to achieve, I had better go after them with the same vigor and commitment we had employed in creating Circle Rep.

All my life, I had longed to do work in film. I had used my sabbatical to explore the possibilites available to me, but as long as I was "tied down" by my responsibilities at Circle Rep, I could not aggressively pursue this goal. When the National Endowment announced that they were not going to renew Circle Rep's grant for the Resident Ensemble Program, I knew that I could no longer stay. Without the support to create a new kind of theater for America, I wanted to be free to throw myself fully into the new world of film. Although I had failed in my dreams of a national repertory theater, maybe I could succeed in bringing a new sense of collaboration to the art of film. In August, a third old and treasured friend, Marilyn Sutter (who was our first board member), died of cancer. Filled with the recognition of the sorrowful necessity of change, I submitted my resignation. I scheduled my departure for one year later, to be effective on July 14, the eighteenth anniversary of the founding of Circle Rep.

Due to financial restraints, Saratoga Performing Arts Center decided they would mount no more full theater productions, and so we were restricted to reading three new plays for one public performance each. I directed Brian Williams's lovely two-character play *In This Fallen City* for Lucille Lortel's White Barn Theater in Connecticut, as well as the reading at SPAC. And then I assembled an outstanding cast for reading Lanford Wilson's new play *Burn This*. Circle Rep's Jonathan Hogan and Lou Liberatore (both so brilliant in *As Is*) were joined by Steppenwolf's John Malkovich and Joan Allen. The results were spectacular. Lanford felt (characteristically) it was is very best play. The third reading was Ben Siegler's *Wandering Jew*.

Much of the eighteenth season was guided on long-distance telephone from Los Angeles. I mounted *In This Fallen City* at the Circle Rep to play in rotating repertory with Caroline Kava's *The Early Girl*, which we had developed from a PIP. Critics adored the second play (Robin Bartlett received a much-deserved, overdue Obie), but the audience seemed to enjoy both. Comment cards reflected the sentiment that we were back to doing the kind of plays our audience wanted to see. We had made arrangements to co-produce *Burn This* with our old friends at the Mark Taper Forum, where the play was perhaps the biggest hit in twenty years. Because John Malkovich had a film commitment, we had to play *Burn This* for a very limited engagement in New York, which obliged us to take a larger theater (at 890 Broadway) so we could accommodate all our subscribers. In fact, John's standby — a splendid actor named Cotter Smith — played two of the three weeks in New York. Naturally, since we could not offer the public an extended run with the original cast, we prohibited the press from reviewing this production, especially since we had the full commitment of the entire cast to return to *Burn This* for an autumn engagement on Broadway. At this writing, we are preparing to go into rehearsal for this venture, which will open at the Plymouth Theater on October 14, 1987, after a month's engagement at the Steppenwolf Theater Ensemble in Chicago.

The fourth play of the eighteenth season was John Bishop's satiric *The Musical Comedy Murders of 1940,* another play we had developed in our PIP process. This was our big hit for the season, and it transferred to the Longacre Theater on Broadway for a run of several months. The final offering of the season was the revival of *As Is* in rotating repertory with a new play by Murray Schisgal called *Road Show*. If I was going out, I was going out in rep! I hoped my selection of the last two plays should say a great deal about what I thought Circle Rep should be: a revival of the best play we had produced in recent years, which retains an awesome relevance to current times, in rep with a new play in which a wonderful American playwright took great risks in seeking a new direction for his writing. *As Is* was splendidly produced in revival under the direction of Michael Warren Powell, but small audiences forced a premature closing. *Road Show* experienced the kind of production problems a new play doesn't need, as the cast and director struggled to find the right tone and style for this very original piece. The critics did not buy it, and so my final repertory fizzled.

As I write this, we are launching the rehearsals for the Broadway production of *Burn This*. My cofounder and dear collaborator Tanya Berezin has assumed the job of artistic director and has announced a very exciting new play season for Circle Rep's nineteenth year. My film is still unmade, and I have moved on to other cinematic projects. Lanford Wilson, Terrence McNally, Jim Leonard, and Milan Stitt have been commissioned to write new plays for next season with the last money from the NEA ensembles grant. I will be returning to direct Jim Leonard's new play *V&V Only* at Circle Rep in the spring, following the premiere in a co-production with South Coast Rep in Costa Mesa, California. John Bishop's bill of one-acts called *Borderline* and *Keeping an Eye on Louie* will make the jump from PIP development to the mainstage, as will David Rappaport's *Cave Life* and Rafael Lima's *El Salvador.* Resident playwright Tim Mason has written us a new comedy called *Only You.* Suzanne Sato is leaving us to join the Rockefeller Foundation staff, but in her three years as managing director, she reduced the deficit enough that the continuation of the theater is assured. We are still bursting at the seams of our tiny theater in Sheridan Square.

And Circle Rep goes on.

MARSHALL W. MASON

Los Angeles

Postscript—The nineteenth season survived criticisms from a press always eager to jump to conclusions about trends. Tanya Berezin has survived their initial expectations that quality would suffer, and by the time *Borderlines* opened, her choices were being hailed as a new direction for Circle Rep, although we have continued to offer a variety of styles as we have always done.

Burn This opened on Broadway at the Plymouth Theater on October 15, 1987, and played for 487 performances before closing on October 30, 1988. Joan Allen won the Tony Award for Best Actress, but it was one of the scandals of New York that John Malkovich, Lanford Wilson, and I were overlooked by the nominating committee.

The Twentieth Anniversary Season got off to a splendid start with Craig Lucas's *Reckless,* which delighted Frank Rich as it "blew away the rigid walls of realism." I served briefly as the guest artistic director of the Ahamanson Theater in Los Angeles, which has the largest subscription audience in the world, and helped Robert Fryer to choose a vibrant season. Both movie and Broadway projects have proliferated for me, as we enter the new year of 1989. And Conchata Ferrell has organized and headed the creation of Circle Rep West, which will soon celebrate its first anniversary in Los Angeles.

The Company Roster

The First Company Roster—1969

FOUNDERS
Marshall W. Mason
Rob Thirkield
Lanford Wilson
Tanya Berezin

ARTISTIC DIRECTOR
Marshall W. Mason

MANAGING DIRECTOR
Rob Thirkield

ADMINISTRATIVE DIRECTOR
Tanya Berezin

EXECUTIVE PRODUCER
Beverly Landau

COMPANY MEMBERS
Tanya Berezin
Beth Bowden

Patricia Carey
Mona Crawford
Linda Eskansas
Michael Feisenmeier
Robert Frink
Stephanie Gordon
Spalding Gray
Ellen Gurin
Carl David Jessup
Jane Lowry
Sharon Ann Madden
Marshall W. Mason
Henry Mellor
Roddy O'Connor
Bill Oxendine
Burke Pearson
Suzanne Pred
Bob Shields
Maria Stefann
David Stekol

Tony Tenuto
Rob Thirkield
Alice Tweedle

PLAYWRIGHTS
Robert Kesser
Helen Duberstein Lipton
Matthew Silverman
David Starkweather
Doric Wilson
Lanford Wilson

COMPANY ARTIST
John Dowling

COMPANY ARCHITECT
John Deans

COMPANY COMPOSER
Alonzo Levister

The Company Roster as of 1984, the Fifteenth Anniversary Year

ARTISTIC DIRECTOR
Marshall W. Mason

MANAGING DIRECTOR
Richard Frankel

ACTING ARTISTIC DIRECTOR
B. Rodney Marriott

ASSOCIATE ARTISTIC DIRECTOR
Tanya Berezin

COMPANY MEMBERS
Samantha Aitkins
Michael Ayr
Kathy Bates
Tanya Berezin
Jacqueline Brookes
Timothy Busfield
Roger Chapman
Jordan Charney
Katherine Cortez
Lindsay Crouse
Jeff Daniels
Jack Davidson
Jake Dengel
John Dossett
Conchatta Ferrell
Neil Flanagan

Lindsey Ginter
Stephanie Gordon
Mari Gorman
Bruce Gray
Charles T. Harper
Trish Hawkins
Jo Henderson
Michael Higgins
Judd Hirsch
Jonathan Hogan
Ruby Holbrook
Barnard Hughes
Laura Hughes
William Hurt
Nancy Killmer
Ken Kliban
Swoozie Kurtz
Zane Lasky
Bobo Lewis
Robert Lu Pone
Sharon Madden
Debra Mooney
Edward J. Moore
Burke Pearson
Lisa Pelikan
Joyce Reehling
Christopher Reeve
Tony Roberts
Edward Seamon

Richard Seff
Timothy Shelton
Ben Siegler
Nancy Snyder
June Stein
Helen Stenborg
Danton Stone
Beatrice Straight
Elizabeth Sturges
Brian Tarantino
Rob Thirkield
Richard Thomas
Douglas Watson
Fritz Weaver
Jimmie Ray Weeks
Peter Weller
Patricia Wettig
Amy Wright

PLAYWRIGHTS
John Bishop
Jonathan Bolt
Julie Bovasso
Shelby Buford, Jr.
James Farrell
John Heuer
Corinne Jacker
Berillas Kerr
Jim Leonard, Jr.
Roy London
Terrence McNally
Patrick Meyers
Edward J. Moore

Claris Nelson
Marsha Norman
John Olive
Joseph Pintauro
Sam Shepard
Michael Skelly
Milan Stitt
Lanford Wilson

DIRECTORS
Neil Flanagan
Tony Giordano
Daniel Irvine
B. Rodney Marriott
Marshall W. Mason
Marshall Ogelsby
Elinor Renfield
Terry Schreiber
Rob Thirkield
Porter Van Zandt
R. Stuart White

DESIGN AND PRODUCTION
John Lee Beatty — *Set Designer*
Norman L. Berman — *Composer*
Jody Boese — *Stage Manager*
Laura Crow — *Costume Designer*
Chuck London — *Sound Designer*
Jennifer von Mayrhauser — *Costume Designer*
Dennis Parichy — *Lighting Designer*
David Potts — *Set Designer*
Fred Reinglas — *Stage Manager*

APPENDIX B

Chronology of Seasons

1969–1970

A Practical Ritual to Exorcise Frustration after Five Days of Rain by David
   Starkweather — Major Production
The Three Sisters by Anton Chekhov — Major Production
The Three Sisters by Anton Chekhov — Experimental Major Production

1970–1971

The Doctor and the Devils by Dylan Thomas — Major Production
Princess Ivovna by Witold Gombrowicz — Major Production
Sextet (Yes) by Lanford Wilson — Workshop
Waiting for Godot by Samuel Beckett — Major Production
The Ghost Sonata by August Strindberg — Workshop
Paderewski and the Garbage Thieves by Ronald Mele — Major Production
Death of a Salesman by Arthur Miller — Adaptation, Workshop
The Future Is in the Eggs by Eugene Ionesco — Major Production
The Doctor in Spite of Himself by Molière — Major Production
Time Shadows by Helen Duberstein — Workshop
Sextet (Yes) by Lanford Wilson — Film
Kit's Play by Berilla Kerr — Videotape

1971–1972

The Three Sisters by Anton Chekhov—Major Production
The Ghost Sonata by August Strindberg—Major Production
The Elephant in the House by Berilla Kerr—Major Production
Howie's by Richard Steele—Workshop
Denim and Rose by Richard Steele—Workshop
Time Shadows by Helen Duberstein—Major Production
The Empire Builders by Boris Vian—Workshop
Danny 405 by Conchatta Ferrell—Workshop
Ludlow Fair by Lanford Wilson—Workshop

1972–1973

Three New Plays by Lanford Wilson—Major Production
A Road Where the Wolves Run by Claris Nelson—Major Production
Canvas by David Roszkowski—Workshop
The Hot l Baltimore by Lanford Wilson—Major Production
Icarus Nine by Bruce Serlen—Workshop
Peace at Hand by Richard Wolf—Workshop
Great Jones Street by Richard Serlen—Workshop
When We Dead Awaken by Henrik Ibsen—Major Production
Offending the Audience by Peter Handke—Workshop
The Tragedy of Thomas Andros by Ron Wilcox—Major Production
Mrs. Tydings Mason-Dixon Medicine Man by John Heuer—Workshop
Smith Here by Ed Greenburg—Workshop
Snow Angel by Lewis John Carlino—Workshop
When You Comin' Back, Red Ryder? by Mark Medoff—Workshop

1973–1974

When You Comin' Back, Red Ryder? by Mark Medoff—Major Production
Straights of Massina by David Starkweather—Workshop
Prodigal by Richard Lortz—Major Production
*The Amazing Activity of Charlie Contrare and the Ninety-
    Eighth Street Gang* by Roy London—Major Production
Hothouse by Megan Terry—Major Production
him by e. e. cummings—Major Production
The Persians by Aeschylus—Major Production
One Person by Robert Patrick—Workshop
When Everything Becomes the City's Music by Lance S. Belville—Workshop
Not Enough Rope by Elaine May—Workshop
The Summer Solstice by Doug Dyer—Workshop
Busy Dyin' by Sheila Quillen—Workshop

1974–1975

Battle of Angels by Tennessee Williams—Major Production
Innocent Thoughts, Harmless Intentions by John Heuer—Workshop
Fire in the Mindhouse by Lance Mulcahy, Arnold Borget, and Dion McGregor—
    Workshop
St. Freud by David Roszkowski—Workshop
The Mound Builders by Lanford Wilson—Major Production
Down by the River Where the Waterlilies Are Disfigured Every Day by Julie
    Bovasso—Major Production
Scandalous Memories by Harvey Perr—Workshop
Afternoon Tea by Harvey Perr—Workshop
Harry Outside by Corinne Jacker—Major Production
Spring's Awakening by Frank Wedekind—Workshop
Not to Worry by A. E. Santaniello—Major Production
The Mound Builders by Lanford Wilson—Video Production

1975–1976

The Elephant in the House by Berilla Kerr—Revival—Major Production
The Loveliest Afternoon of the Year by John Guare—Special Event
Overruled by George Bernard Shaw—Special Event
Dancing for the Kaiser by Andrew Colmar—Major Production
Knock, Knock by Jules Feiffer—Major Production
Who Killed Richard Cory? by A. R. Guerney, Jr.—Major Production
Cavern of the Jewels by John Heuer—Major Production—Children's Show
Serenading Louie by Lanford Wilson—Major Production
The Lesson of the Master by Richard Howard—After Piece
When I Dyed My Hair in Venice by Helen Duberstein—Workshop
Solo for Two by Juliette Bowles—Workshop
The Magic Formula by Sidney Morris—Workshop
Terminal by Corinne Jacker—Workshop
Night Thoughts by Corinne Jacker—Workshop
The Confirmation by Howard Ashman—Workshop
Prague Spring by Lee Kalcheim—Special Event
Fog and Mismanagement by Jeff Wanchel—Workshop
Home Free! by Lanford Wilson—Workshop
Winners by Brian Friel—Workshop
Wildflowers by Richard Howard—After Piece
Dark Room by David Epstein—Workshop
Mrs. Murray's Farm by Roy London—Major Production
Listen, Please by Robert Abrami—After Piece

1976–1977

The Farm by David Storey—Major Production
A Tribute to Lili Lamont by Arthur White—Major Production
My Life by Corinne Jacker—Major Production
The Passing of Corky Brewster by Jerry L. Crawford—After Piece
Gemini by Albert Innaurato—Major Production
For Love or Money by Jay Jeffries and Jason McAuliffe—After Piece
Suicide in Bᵇ by Sam Shepard—Play-in-Progress
Allegra by Allan Bates—Play-in-Progress
To the Land by Claris Nelson—Play-in-Progress
Exiles by James Joyce—Major Production
Fat Chances by Charlie Peters—Play-in-Progress
Cabaret/New York Times: A Review by James Tobin—After Piece
What the Babe Said by Martin Halpern—After Piece
Mrs. Tydings Mason-Dixon Medicine Man by John Heuer—Play-in-Progress
Celebration off River Street by James Tobin—Play-in-Progress
The Brixton Recovery by Jack Gilhooley—Play-in-Progress
Unsung Cole by Cole Porter and Norman Berman—Major Production

1977–1978

Feedlot by Patrick Meyers—Major Production
Brontosaurus by Lanford Wilson—Late Show
Ulysses in Traction by Albert Innaurato—Major Production
Cabin 12 by John Bishop—Late Show
Lulu by Frank Wedekind—Major Production
Two from the Late Show by Lanford Wilson and John Bishop—Major Production
The 5th of July by Lanford Wilson—Major Production
This Living Hand by Mark Stevenson—Special Event
My Cup Runneth Over by Robert Patrick—Late Show
Pushing 30 by Jonathan Hadary—Late Show

1978–1979

Glorious Morning by Patrick Meyers—Major Production
Stargazing by Tom Cone—Late Show
In the Recovery Lounge by James Farrell—Major Production
In Three Easy Lessons by John Calene—Project-in-Progress
Total Recall by Martin Halpern—Late Show
The Runner Stumbles by Milan Stitt—Major Production
The Human Voice by Jean Cocteau—Late Show
Minnesota Moon by John Olive—Late Show

Winter Signs by John Bishop — Project-in-Progress
Winter Signs by John Bishop — Major Production
The Deserter by Norman Beim — Late Show
Perched on a Gabardine Cloud by Steven Braunstein — Project-in-Progress
Talley's Folley by Lanford Wilson — Major Production
The Poet and the Rent by David Mamet — Major Production — Children's Show
Life and/or Death by Herb Gardner — Late Show
Van Zandt Ellis Piano Recital — Special Event
A Woman's Life in the Theatre by Rita Gardner
Gertrude Stein, Gertrude Stein, Gertrude Stein by Marty Martin — Special Event
Buried Child by Sam Shepard — Summer Major Production
Gertrude Stein, Gertrude Stein, Gertrude Stein by Marty Martin — Summer
　　Major Production

1979–1980

Reunion (three plays) by David Mamet — Major Production
Mass Appeal by Bill Davis — Project-in-Progress
Some Sweet Time by Michael Cassale — Project-in-Progress
Hamlet by William Shakespeare — Major Production
Mary Stuart by Friedrich von Schiller — Major Production
Threads by Jonathan Bolt — Project-in-Progress
Innocent Thoughts, Harmless Intentions by John Heuer — Major Production
Child of the Clay Country by Marshall Ogelsby — Project-in-Progress
Back in the Race by Milan Stitt — Major Production
Spooky Lady by Barbara Baxley — Special Event
In Vienna by Roy London — Project-in-Progress
Box Office by Elinor Jones — One-Act Festival
On the Side of the Road by Gordon Dryland — One-Act Festival
Diary of a Shadow Walker by Shelby Buford, Jr. — One-Act Festival

1980–1981

The Diviners by Jim Leonard, Jr. — Major Production
Diary of a Shadow Walker by Shelby Buford, Jr. — Project-in-Progress
On Wayward Wings by Barbara Baxley and Michael Liebman — Special Event
Twelfth Night by William Shakespeare — Major Production
The Beaver Coat by Gerhard Hauptmann — Major Production
Gas Station by Shelby Buford, Jr. — Extended Reading
Snow Orchid by Joseph Pintauro — Project-in-Progress
The Bone Garden by Peter Maeck — Extended Reading
Childe Byron by Romulus Linney — Major Production
Say It with Music by Rita Gardner — Special Event

The Great Grandson of Jedediah Kohler by John Bishop — Project-in-Progress
In Connecticut by Roy London — Major Production
Charlie McCarthy's Monocle by Maxine Fleischmann — Project-in-Progress
A Tale Told by Lanford Wilson — Major Production
It's Only a Play by Terrence McNally — Project-in-Progress
The Diviners by Jim Leonard, Jr. — Summer Major Production

1981–1982

Threads by Jim Leonard, Jr. — Major Production
'night, Mother by Marsha Norman — Project-in-Progress
Bing and Walker by James Farrell — Project-in-Progress
What I Did Last Summer by A. R. Gurney, Jr. — Project-in-Progress
Confluence — Three One-Act Plays — Major Production
    Thymus Vulgaris by Lanford Wilson
    Confluence by John Bishop
    Am I Blue by Beth Henley
Presque Isle by Joyce Carol Oates — Project-in-Progress
Cat and Mouse by Claris Nelson — Project-in-Progress
How Women Break Bad News by John Bishop — Project-in-Progress
Snow Orchid by Joseph Pintauro — Major Production
Richard II by William Shakespeare — Major Production
The Great Grandson of Jedediah Kohler by John Bishop — Major Production
Spookhouse by Harvey Fierstein — Project-in-Progress
Young Playwrights Festival — Dramatists Guild Special Event
Screaming Eagle by Shelby Buford, Jr. — Project-in-Progress
A Think Piece by Jules Feiffer — Major Production
Double Album by Claris Nelson — Project-in-Progress
Foxtrot by the Bay by A. M. Appleman — Major Production
Johnny Got His Gun by Bradley Rand Smith — Summer Major Production
The Holdup by Marsha Norman — At Saratoga Performing Arts Center, Saratoga, N.Y. — Major Production
Angels Fall by Lanford Wilson — At Players State Theatre, Miami, Florida
The Great Grandson of Jedediah Kohler by John Bishop — Extended Reading
The 5th of July by Lanford Wilson — Video Production

1982–1983

Angels Fall by Lanford Wilson — Major Production
Rock County by Bill Elverman — Project-in-Progress
The Paper Boy by Jonathan Feldman — Project-in-Progress
Home Base by Jim Leonard, Jr. — Project-in-Progress
Black Angel by Michael Cristofer — Major Production

In Place by Corinne Jacker — Project-in-Progress
What I Did Last Summer by A. R. Gurney, Jr. — Major Production
Levitation by Timothy Mason — Project-in-Progress
Domestic Issues by Corrine Jacker — Major Production
I Won't Be Here Forever by Milan Stitt — Project-in-Progress
Young Playwrights Festival — Special Event
The Cherry Orchard, Part II by William Hoffman and Anthony Holland —
    Project-in-Progress
Faded Glory by Timothy Burns — Project-in-Progress
Fool for Love by Sam Shepard — Major Production
The Sea Gull by Anton Chekhov — Saratoga Performing Arts Center, Saratoga,
    N.Y. — Summer Major Production

1983–1984

Dysan by Patrick Meyers — Project-in-Progress
The Harvesting by John Bishop — Major Production
Listen to the Lions by John Ford Noonan — Project-in-Progress
Danny and the Deep Blue Sea by John Patrick Shanley — Project-in-Progress
Full Hookup by Conrad Bishop and Elizabeth Fuller — Major Production
The Sea Gull by Anton Chekhov — Major Production
Save the World by Berilla Kerr — Project-in-Progress
Levitation by Timothy Mason — Major Production
Hubbard, Ohio by Steve Nelson — Project-in-Progress
Danny and the Deep Blue Sea by John Patrick Shanley — Major Production, Co-
    produced with Circle-In-The Square Theatre of New York City
The Early Girl by Caraline Kava — Project-in-Progress
Balm in Gilead by Lanford Wilson — Major Production, Co-produced with Step-
    penwolf Theatre of Chicago
A Little Going Away Party by Sybille Pearson — Project-in-Progress
Circle Repertory Theatre's 15th Anniversary Benefit — Special Event

Chronology of Growth

The late seventies was the time of the Circle's greatest growth. It was also the greatest period of growth for the Literary Department. Milan Stitt's programs were continued, nourished, and grew almost organically once the processes had been established. Every year something new seemed to have been added to the entire Circle Rep process; these new things should be itemized in order to get the full scope of activity:

In 1977, the Friday Morning Readings were formalized in an ongoing process. Script readers were hired to help with the growing volume of unsolicited manuscripts. On September 27, 1977, Daniel Irvine presented the first Late Show.

In 1978, the Projects-in-Progress (PIPS) program was begun in conference with the playwright members—again, to formalize an existing program. The Playwrights Workshop was formed with Joe Mathewson, Mick Casale, Jim Farrell, Ralph Pape, Joe Pintauro, and Rod Marriott. By winter, Jim Farrell was hired as Assistant Dramaturg.

In 1979, with the revival of Stitt's *The Runner Stumbles,* the idea of creating a season of four new plays, one revival, and one classic was instituted. Stitt also worked out a plan to have a true revolving repertory system. By summer, the literary staff was swelling: James Farrell had succeeded Stitt as Acting Dramaturg even though Stitt officially remained as Dramaturg. B. Rodney Marriott was hired as Literary Manager; Mary Robinson, a former reader, was hired as Assistant Literary Manager; and by fall, Robert Meiksins was hired as a Literary Intern. A new Playwrights Workshop was begun under Marriott's leadership, with Joe Mathewson, Mick Casale, Jonathan Bolt, Joe Pintauro, Ellie Jones, Ben Siegler, Bill C. Davis, and Bill Elverman. Now Friday afternoons were reserved for Readings.

During the 1979–1980 season, there were 32 Readings of 40 plays. Of these, nine received major productions elsewhere, while five received full Circle productions. In addition, five PIPS were presented: *Mass Appeal, Threads, Some Sweet Time* (later *Elm Circle*), *The Diviners,* and *The Woolgatherer.*

In 1980, the First Annual Circle Rep Festival of One Acts began in May. By the fall, Robert Meiksins was hired as a full-time Literary Assistant. Extended Readings were begun as a step between a Reading and a PIP. The first two were *Bone Garden,* by Peter Maeck, and *Gas Station,* by Shelby Buford, Jr. Now all reading of unsolicited manuscripts was done by outside readers. For the first time, accurate archives were begun. Karen Gellman and Peter Oberlink were hired as Literary Interns. Jim Farrell was commissioned to write *Bing and Walker* with funds from the Drama League. It was determined that if an actor was auditioned for a PIP role, the role had to be offered to the actor if CRC produced the play on the mainstage. (This rule was changed in 1982 when Tanya Berezin took over as Casting Director.)

During the 1980–1981 season, there were 34 Readings of 38 plays. Of these, 11 received Major Production outside CRC, while eight were produced by CRC. Five PIPS were presented.

In 1981, by spring, the Extended Reading program was changed to be a step between a PIP and a mainstage. In the fall, Charles Kiselyak was hired as a Literary Intern. Daniel Irvine became the Director of Labs. The Playwrights Workshop was now called Playwrights Lab. The membership was up to 20. Outside regulars were permitted to attend. The Friday Readings were cut off from the Lab members. John Bishop was taken on as official company Dramaturg. Second readers were now being paid. It was determined that Dramaturgs should be assigned to PIPS on a regular basis selected from the Literary Department's personnel. The planned December Festival of One Acts fell through.

During the 1981–1982 season, there were 31 Readings of 33 plays. Of these, four received production outside, while six were produced by CRC. There were seven PIPS and two Extended Readings, after which the ER Program was terminated.

In 1982, movement within the department continued with unslackened pace. Jonathan Kalb was hired as a Literary Intern. Tanya Berezin was hired as Associate Artistic Director to cast the PIPS. B. Rodney Marriott became Acting Artistic Director to replace Marshall Mason, as he departed for a two-year sabbatical. Rob Meiksins became the Literary Manager. Janet Grillo, a former reader, became Assistant Literary Manager. Ari Roth was hired as a Literary Intern. Now the Extended Reading Series was reinstated, but was to be held only when needed (up to seven). Dramaturgs were assigned to every PIP and every ER for the first time. A Directors Lab was formed. Patrick Meyers was awarded the largest commission ever, $2,500, to write *Dysan*. The Playwrights Lab, which now had a membership of 25, was run by Rob Meiksins.

During the 1982–1983 season, there were 34 Readings of 39 plays. Of these, seven received outside production while four were produced by CRC. In addition, there were eight PIPS and six ERs.

1983 was the last year of growth for the Literary Department. In the winter, Robert Meiksins acted as Dramaturg, for mainstage production of Corinne Jacker's *Domestic Issues*. The Playwrights Lab was closed to outsiders. In the spring, the One-Act Festival was held out of the Directors Lab. There was also a Playwright Support Fund Benefit at Lortel Theatre on May 9, which included world premieres of 11 new plays. The process of reevaluation of Playwrights Lab membership was begun. In the fall, Ari Roth was hired as Assistant Literary Manager. Jackie Kanner was hired as Literary Intern. Now 3,000 unsolicited manuscripts were received. Tanya Berezin took on Casting for Friday Readings while she and Ari Roth acted as Dramaturgs for the mainstage production of *The Sea Gull*. At the same time, Berilla Kerr was nominated as Playwrights representative. Nancy Donahue was commissioned to write *Beachhouse* with Drama League funds. Plans were made for a Lab Workshop Production Series to be held in the summer of 1984, while John Heuer was commissioned to write *Rameau Labesque*. Lab membership changed; new members were brought in. It was determined that Dramaturgs should work on all mainstage productions.

The beginning of the 1983 season showed a full commission program of $6,000. One commission was to be awarded to an outside writer for $2,000. Three $1,000 commissions or six $500 commissions were to go to in-house writers to create new work.

In 1984 the budget cuts significantly curtailed all activities.

—————Notes————

1 The Climate

1. Lanford Wilson interview, New York City, April 11, 1984. His statement serves as an introduction not only to Wilson's unique shorthand style of speech, which for the listener can build into a highly emotional experience, but also expresses the shock that must have been experienced by provincials who came to New York City in the sixties. Much of the sixties counter-culture ambience is reflected in *Balm in Gilead,* which captures not only the drug scene and criminal elements to which Wilson refers, but also the individual despair and loneliness of those who lived and died through it.

2. "The first use of that term (Off-Off-Broadway) is generally attributed to *The Village Voice* critic Jerry Talmer, who was trying to call attention to a wide range of theatrical activity in New York City in 1960, theatres and productions with little in common beyond obscurity, poverty, and inexperience." Gerald Berkowitz, *New Broadways, Theatre across America 1950–1980* (Totowa, New Jersey: Rowman and Littlefield, 1982), p. 96.

3. Carlo Silvestro, ed., *The Living Book of the Living Theatre* (Greenwich, Conn.: New York Graphic Society, Ltd., 1971), ca. p. 40 (unpaginated).

4. Robert Brustein, *Seasons of Discontent: Dramatic Opinions 1959–65* (New York: Simon & Schuster, 1965), p. 80.

5. Ibid., p. 81.

6. Silvestro, ca. pp. 49–50.

7. Brustein, p. 81.

8. Marshall W. Mason interview, New York City, November 11, 1983.
9. Ibid.
10. Wilson interview.
11. Ibid.

2   The Four Founders—Plus Joe

1. Rob Thirkield interview, New York City, November 18, 1983.
2. William J. Sibley, "Lanford Wilson—Off Broadway: A Founder and Number One Playwright Honors the Circle Repertory Theatre on Its Fifteenth Anniversary," *Ladies' Home Journal* (Spring, 1984), p. 82.
3. Mel Gussow, "Lanford Wilson on Broadway," *Horizon* (May, 1980), p. 30.
4. Ibid., p. 32.
5. Emory Lewis, "Lanford Wilson," *Long Island Record,* February 28, 1973.
6. Alan Wallach, "The Long Island Review," *Newsday,* April 29, 1973.
7. Gerald Berkowitz, *New Broadways: Theatre across America* (Totowa, New Jersey: Rowman and Littlefield, 1982), p. 95.
8. Tanya Berezin interview, New York City, December 7, 1983.
9. Berkowitz, p. 98.
10. Wilson interview.
11. In order to capture the boundless activity and energy fundamental to the creation of off-off-Broadway by a young man who had played a very active part, this section of the April 11 1984 Wilson interview has been transcribed almost verbatim.
12. Lewis, "Lanford Wilson."
13. Mel Gussow, "When the Playwright's Life Is Visible in His Work," *New York Times,* August 26, 1984.
14. Brustein, pp. 307–11.
15. Jerzy Grotowski, *Toward a Poor Theatre* (New York: Simon & Schuster, 1968), p. 15.
16. John Simon, *Singularities: Essays on the Theater 1964–1974* (New York: Random House, 1975), p. 150.

3   The Core of a Company—1965–1969

1. According to Brockett, Stewart had been taking the La Mama troupe abroad since 1964, but this is not so. In 1964, La Mama had not even located on Second Avenue; it was still in a basement on 9th Street and completely unknown.
2. The revival of *The Clown* occurred at the Caffé Cino approximately one month after Joe Cino died. In it were Lanford Wilson, David Starkweather, Michael Warren, Robert Patrick, Claris Nelson, and Marshall Mason.

4 A Company Is Born—July 1969

1. Repertory stock theatre companies were standard theatrical organizations which flourished between 1850 and 1870 and virtually disappeared by 1900, undermined mostly by the advent of combination companies and the long-running play. Combination companies were acting companies that travelled with a star and a full troupe of supporting actors. Dion Boucicault claims to have originated combination companies around 1860 in England, although there is evidence to indicate that they were already in existence in America as early as 1852 with the Howard-Aikens company production of Harriet Beecher Stowe's *Uncle Tom's Cabin*. The expansion of the railway system made the transportation of full combination companies easier and more feasible, so that by 1886 there were as many as 282 combination companies on the road.

2. Harold Clurman, *On Directing* (New York: The Macmillan Co., 1972), p. 22.

3. Harold Clurman, *The Naked Image* (New York: The Macmillan Co., 1966), pp. 152, 296. It is not true, as stated in Foster Hirsh's book on the Actors Studio, that "In the vast panorama of the American Theatre, [Clifford] Odets is the only true company playwright, a writer with a theatre of his own" (pp. 98–99). Lanford Wilson has been working with "his own" company for almost fifteen years, while Odets's major contributions came pretty much within a one-year period; in addition, every other resident playwright at Circle Rep has the same luxury of working within their own company setting.

4. Ibid., p. 148.

5. Marshall W. Mason, "On Eleven Seasons," *Circle Repertory News* (Spring, 1980), p. 5.

6. Cited in Gerry Stern, "Good Enough to Be True," article in program for the Spring, 1984, Circle Rep production of Timothy Mason's *Levitation*.

7. Cited in Paul Gardner, "The Man Who Keeps Circle Rep Rolling," *New York Times,* October 3, 1976.

8. Brustein, p. 211.

9. Foster Hirsh, *A Method to Their Madness: The History of the Actors Studio* (New York: W. W. Norton, 1984), p. 73.

10. Clurman, *Naked Image,* p. 149.

11. Ibid., pp. 151–53.

12. Ibid., p. 148.

13. Ibid., p. 164.

14. Ibid., p. 150.

15. Brustein, p. 274.

5 The Early Days

1. Hirsh, pp. 76–77.

2. Mel Gussow, "The Quicksilver World of Off Off Broadway," *New York Times,* November 30, 1975.

3. John Willis, *The Theatre World — 1970–1971 Season,* Vol. 27 (New York: Crown Publishers, Inc., 1971), p. 6. Only Joseph Papp and the New York Shakespeare Festival seemed to have come out ahead. Papp's problems over permanent theatre space were resolved when he worked out a deal with the city of New York to rent the Astor Library, a historic village landmark on Lafayette Street, for the token sum of $1.00 a year in 1971. The Public Theatre reflected the alleviation of financial pressures by creating the greatest amount of activity during the 1971–1972 season. Two of its plays, *Sticks and Bones* by David Rabe and Shakespeare's *Two Gentlemen of Verona,* made the transition to Broadway.

4. *Danny 405* was deemed important mostly to give Ferrell the opportunity to work on it. This workshop is notable in that it gives yet another example of how much the Circle Rep was committed to the growth of its member artists, the process being, once again, more important than the product.

6   The Turning Point — 1973

1. Lanford Wilson, "Dammit Lady," *Performing Arts* (Vol. 7, No. 8, August, 1973), p. 48.

2. Gussow, "Lanford Wilson on Broadway," p. 34.

3. Actually, the original set of *Hot l* on West 83rd Street was designed by Mason and Wilson. Ron Radice, a scene painter, came in to paint it. When the play was moved to Broadway, Bloomgarten hired Radice to design the set. Many who had seen the original did not feel the Broadway set was as effective.

4. Clive Barnes, "The Theatre: Lanford Wilson's 'Hot l Baltimore,' Herald of a New Pattern," *New York Times,* March 23, 1973.

5. Emory Lewis, "Lanford Wilson," *Long Island Record,* March 9, 1973.

6. Alan Wallach, "Switched Off," *Newsday,* February 8, 1973.

7. Willis, Vol. 29, p. 7.

8. Willis, Vol. 30, p. 7.

9. Edwin Wilson, "A Dockside Romance," *Wall Street Journal,* April 19, 1974.

10. Mel Gussow, "Suddenly Real Plays About Real People," *New York Times,* May 12, 1974.

7   Changing Times, a Changing Rep, and Unlimited Growth

1. Mel Gussow, "Whither, Off Broadway?" *New York Times,* January 27, 1975.

2. Gussow, "Quicksilver World."

3. David Vidal, "Equity to Meet in New Code Today," *New York Times,* August 25, 1975.

4. Tom Buckley, "About New York," *New York Times,* May 16, 1975.

5. Vidal, "Equity."

6. Louis Calta, "Equity Is Accused on Theatre Code," *New York Times,* February 23, 1976.

7. Mel Gussow, "Showcase Code Is a Standoff," *New York Times,* October 2, 1975.

8. According to Robert Berkvist, "Notes: Wooing Big Money for Off Off Broadway," *New York Times,* February 22, 1976.

9. Cited in Paul Rawlings, "Mason Directs Sheridan Circle," *The Villager,* November 14, 1974.

10. Having worked with Lanford Wilson on *The Migrants* and *Summer and Smoke,* Williams became very fond of Wilson and wanted to remain on close terms. Circle Rep had been working on a new play of his, *Something Cloudy, Something Clear.* The developmental project was abandoned at the time of his death in 1983.

11. Daniel Irvine interview, New York City, November 18, 1983.

12. Mel Gussow, *"Battle of Angels," New York Times,* November 4, 1974.

13. Circle Rep occasionally still departs from the proscenium design. e.g., *Childe Byron* in 1981 and *Bing and Walker* in 1985, in which the audience entered through the meticulously detailed interior of a barn.

14. Louis Calta, "News of the Stage," *New York Times,* December 1, 1974.

15. Willis, Vol. 31, p.8.

16. The After Piece was a new late-night event, initiated by director Daniel Irvine, that would become The Late Show.

17. Michael Feingold, "Not All Great, but Great," *Village Voice,* July 7, 1975.

18. Alan Wallach, "Newsday Stage—New, Yes; Important, No," *Newsday,* December 16, 1975.

19. Emory Lewis, "Onstage," *Long Island Record,* March 11, 1976.

20. Howard Kissel, *Women's Wear Daily,* March 12, 1976.

21. Robert Brustein, "Art versus Arts Advocacy in the Non-Commercial Theatre," *New York Times,* July 4, 1976.

22. "Briefs on the Arts," *New York Times,* January 15, 1975. (Unattributed.)

23. Mel Gussow, *"Harry Outside* Enjoys Naturalism at Circle," *New York Times,* May 13, 1975.

24. T. E. Kalem, "Kooky Miracle," *Time* (February 2, 1976), p. 79.

25. Gardner, "Man Who Keeps."

26. Cited in ibid.

27. Mel Gussow, "Three New York Theatre Companies Get Ford Grants," *New York Times,* October 6, 1977.

28. Mel Gussow, "Stage: Bishop One-Acter at Circle Rep," *New York Times,* January 6, 1977.

29. John Simon, "Theatre," *New York Magazine* (November 13, 1978), p. 152.

30. Tish Dace, "Glorious Acting in Morning," *Other Stages* (November 2, 1978), p. 7.

31. Howard Kissel, "Glorious Morning," *Women's Wear Daily,* November 2, 1978.

32. Simon, "Theatre."

33. Clive Barnes, " 'The Recovery Room' Dispenses Many a Laugh," *New York Post,* December 8, 1978.

34. B. Rodney Marriott interview, New York City, December 3, 1983.

35. John Simon, "Folie à Deux," *New York Magazine* (May 21, 1979), p. 78.

36. Martin Duberman, "The Great Gray Way," *Harper's* (May, 1978), p. 81.

8   The Literary Department and Institutionalization

1. Lessing (1729–1781) is the author of *Miss Sara Sampson* (1755), *Minna von Barnhelm* (1767), *Emilia Galotte* (1772), and *Nathan the Wise* (1779). Lessing represents the high point of the German Enlightenment, and his work can safely be categorized as the beginning of the modern era in German drama.

2. One series of statistical notes regarding the readings is of interest. There were forty Friday Readings per year during the five-year period between 1979 and 1984. In the 1979–1980 season, with Marriott in his first year as literary manager, thirty-two readings were held of forty plays (some readings were of more than one one-act play). Of these, five have gone on to mainstage production by the Circle Rep — *Threads,* by Jonathan Bolt; *The Woolgatherer,* by William Mastrosimone; *Snow Orchid,* by Joe Pintauro; *The Diviners,* by Jim Leonard, Jr.; and *Am I Blue,* by Beth Henley. Another nine plays read that season have gone on to first-class production at other theatres. So at least fourteen of the forty plays that were read that season have been produced. So far, the most successful reading series has been during the 1980–1981 season, in which there were thirty-eight plays read, nineteen of which have had major productions either at Circle Rep or elsewhere.

3. John Bishop interview, New York City, April 18, 1984.

4. Ari Roth interview, New York City, November 29, 1983.

5. A separate $6,000 Full Commission Program, which had been set up by the Literary Department in 1983–1984, was also cancelled during the huge cutbacks.

6. See Appendix C, Chronology of Growth.

9   Transitions and the Changing Climate of the Eighties

1. See Appendix A for complete company roster.

2. Richard Frankel interview, New York City, February 10, 1984.

3. Marshall W. Mason, "#5. Changes in Current Operations," in Grant

Proposal, p. 5. (This is Mason's artistic statement which was submitted to the National Endowment for the Arts in support of the Circle Repertory Company's application for its Ensemble Grant.)

4. Mason, "#3. The Artistic Director's Statement," Grant Proposal, p. 4.

5. Within the confines of this funding, an interesting combination of experimental and traditional groups received Ensemble grants from the National Endowment for the Arts in 1985: the Arena Stage in Washington, which has the core of a company but wants to create a full company; the Circle Repertory Company; the Wooster Group, which has been a highly experimental company in New York City; the Spanish Repertory Company, which is a genuine repertory company operating within a Spanish area; the Trinity Square Repertory Company in Providence, Rhode Island, under Adrian Hall; the San Francisco Mime Company; and the Milwaukee Repertory Company.

6. Tom Thompson interview, New York City, February 9, 1984.

10 Strengths and Faults

1. Peter Buckley, letter to author, January 23, 1984.

2. In my opinion, for example, *Man of La Mancha, Hello Dolly, Mame,* and *A Funny Thing Happened on the Way to the Forum* lost a great deal in their translations to the screen. Even *Fiddler on the Roof* lost much of the impact of its opening sequence in the film version. Others, like *West Side Story, Oliver,* and *My Fair Lady* worked just as well on the screen as they did on the stage.

3. Mari Gorman, letter to author, November 14, 1983.

4. Ken Kliban, letter to author, November 7, 1983.

5. Richard Seff, letter to author, November 3, 1983.

6. Bruce Gray, letter to author, November 8, 1983.

7. Seff, letter to author.

8. Gary Stern, "Good Enough to Be True," in *Levitation* program, 1983.

9. Clurman made the point to the author during a personal discussion at Hunter College in the fall of 1978.

10. Buckley, letter to author.

11 The Circle Idea

1. Peter Buckley, "Circle Repertory Theatre—A Regional Troupe That's Generating Excitement," *Horizon* (May, 1980), p. 66.

2. Berkowitz, p. 262.

3. Jordan Charney, letter to author, December 20, 1983.

4. Marshall W. Mason, "Observations from the Sabbatical," Circle Repertory Company, Digest of Company Meeting, September 10, 1984, p. 1.

5. Typical of Thirkield, it was not he who revealed the extent of his support during the hours spent with the author. In fact, he barely mentioned it.

Mason, Wilson, and several others established the importance of Thirkield's support.

6. River Arts Repertory Theatre is at Byrdcliffe Theatre in Woodstock, New York, former home of the American Lab Theatre.

7. The Circle Rep is not a gay theatre and should not be thought of as such even though homosexuality is one important part of the theatre's lifestyle. However, since it does not seem to be any more important at Circle Rep than it is in the American theatre in general and does not seem either to contribute to or detract from the quality of Circle Rep's work, it is not dealt with as an issue in this work. Nevertheless, it is thought-provoking to note that Milan Stitt, a homosexual, feels that his lifestyle allows him the freedom to pursue his career as a writer without the financial responsibilities of raising a family. In college, he says he knew several writers whom he feels were more talented than he but who were forced to accept teaching positions in the Midwest in order to support wives and growing families.

8. Source prefers to remain anonymous.

9. In fact, Thirkield would commit suicide in 1986.

10. Clurman, *Naked Image,* p. 164.

11. Ibid., p. 149.

12. Stanley Kauffmann, *Persons of the Drama: Theatre Criticism and Comment* (New York: Harper & Row, 1976), p. 358.

13. Clurman, *Naked Image,* p. 149.

14. Oscar G. Brockett, *History of the Theatre,* 3d ed. (Boston, Allyn and Bacon, Inc., 1977), pp. 583–84.

15. Buckley, letter to author.

◉———Bibliography———

Books Cited

Berkowitz, Gerald. *New Broadways: Theatre across America 1950–1980*. Totowa, New Jersey: Rowman and Littlefield, 1982.

Blum, Daniel, ed. *Daniel Blum's Theatre World*. Vols. 17–20. New York: Crown Publishers, Inc., 1960–1964.

Brockett, Oscar G. *History of the Theatre*. 3d ed. Boston: Allyn and Bacon, Inc., 1977.

Brustein, Robert. *Season of Discontent: Dramatic Opinions 1959–65*. New York: Simon & Schuster, 1965.

Chekhov, Anton. *Four Great Plays by Chekhov*. New York: Bantam Books, 1971.

Clurman, Harold. *On Directing*. New York: Macmillan Co., 1972.

_____. *The Fervent Years: The Story of the Group Theatre*. New York: Alfred A. Knopf, 1945.

_____. *The Naked Image: Observations on the Modern Theatre*. New York: Macmillan Co., 1966.

Croyden, Margaret. *Lunatics, Lovers and Poets: The Contemporary Experimental Theatre*. New York: McGraw-Hill Book Co., 1974.

Ellis, John, ed. *Theatre World*. Vols. 21–40. New York: Crown Publishers, Inc., 1965–1984.

Evans, Rowland, and Robert Novak. *The Reagan Revolution*. New York: E. P. Dutton, 1981.

Gassner, John. *Theatre at the Crossroads*. New York: Holt, Rinehart and Winston, 1960.

Goldman, William. *The Season: A Candid Look at Broadway.* New York: Harcourt, Brace & World, Inc., 1969.

Gottfried, Martin. *Opening Nights: Theatre Criticism of the Sixties.* New York: G. P. Putnam's Sons, 1969.

Grotowski, Jerzy. *Toward a Poor Theatre.* New York: Simon & Schuster, 1968.

Guernsey, Otis, L., Jr., ed. *The Best Plays of 1975–76.* New York: Dodd, Mead, & Co., 1976.

Hirsch, Foster. *A Method to Their Madness: A History of the Actors Studio.* New York: W. W. Norton & Co., 1984.

Howard, Gerald, ed. *The Sixties.* New York: E. P. Dutton, 1981.

Kauffmann, Stanley. *Persons of the Drama: Theatre Criticism and Comment.* New York: Harper & Row, Publishers, 1984.

Lawlins, Chuck. *New York Theatre Guide.* New York: The Rutledge Press, 1981.

Little, Stuart W. *Off-Broadway: A Documentary History from 1952 to the Present.* New York: Coward, McCann & Geoghegan, Inc., 1972.

Neff, Renfreu. *The Living Theatre USA.* New York: The Bobbs-Merrill Co., 1970.

Obst, Lynda Rosen, ed. *The Sixties.* New York: Random House/Rolling Stone Press, 1977.

Silvestro, Carlo, ed. *The Living Book of the Living Theatre.* Greenwich, Conn.: New York Graphic Society, Ltd., 1971.

Rhodes, Richard, ed. *The Ozarks: The American Wilderness.* New York: Time/Life Books, Inc., 1980.

Rubin, Jerry. *Do It! Scenarios of the Revolution.* New York: Ballantine Books, 1970.

Simon, John. *Singularities: Essays on the Theater 1964–1974.* New York: Random House, 1975.

Taylor, L. B. *The New Right.* New York: Franklin Watts, 1981.

Writers' Project. *Texas: American Guide Series.* New York: Hastings House, 1940.

Books Consulted

Blum, Daniel, ed. *A Pictorial History of the American Theatre: 100 Years 1860–1960.* Philadelphia: Chilton Company, 1969.

Crowley, Alice Lewisohn. *The Neighborhood Playhouse.* New York: Theatre Art Books, 1959.

Deutsch, Helen, and Stella Hanau. *The Provincetown: A Story of the Theatre.* New York: Russell and Russell, 1972.

Kerr, Walter. *God on the Gymnasium Floor and Other Theatrical Adventures.* New York: Simon & Schuster, 1971.

Little, Stuart W. *Enter Joseph Papp: In Search of New American Theatre.* New York: Coward, McCann & Geoghegan, Inc., 1974.

Marcus, Robert D., and David Burner, eds. *America Since 1945.* 2d ed., 1977.

Price, Julia S. *The Off-Broadway Theatre.* New York: The Scarecrow Press, 1962.

Richard, Stanley. *Best Plays of the Sixties.* New York: Doubleday & Co., Inc., 1970.

Vaughan, Stuart. *A Possible Theatre.* New York: McGraw Hill Book Co., 1969.

Wetzteon, Ross, ed. *The Obie Winners: The Best of Off-Broadway.* New York: Doubleday & Co., Inc., 1980.

Journals, Magazines, and Newspapers Cited

Barnes, Clive. "Lemon Sky," *New York Times,* May 18, 1970.

_____. "The Theatre: Lanford Wilson's 'Hot l Baltimore,' Herald of a New Pattern," *New York Times,* March 23, 1973.

_____. " 'The Recovery Room' Dispenses Many a Laugh," *New York Post,* December 8, 1978.

Berkvist, Robert. "Notes: Wooing Big Money for Off Off Broadway." *New York Times,* February 22, 1976.

Brustein, Robert. "Art Versus Arts Advocacy in the Non-Commercial Theatre," *New York Times,* February 4, 1976.

Buckley, Peter. "Circle Repertory Theatre—A Regional Troupe That's Generating National Excitement," *Horizon,* May 1980.

Buckley, Tom. "About New York," *New York Times,* May 16, 1975.

Calta, Louis. "Equity Is Accused on Theatre Code," *New York Times,* February 23, 1976.

_____. "News of The Stage." *New York Times,* December 1, 1976.

Dace, Tish. "Glorious Acting in Morning," *Other Stages,* November 2, 1978.

Duberman, Martin. "The Great Gray Way," *Harpers,* May 1978.

Feingold, Michael. "Not All Great, but Great," *Village Voice,* July 7, 1975.

Gardner, Paul. "The Man Who Keeps Circle Rep Rolling," *New York Times,* October 2, 1976.

Gerard, Jeremy. "Will Success Spoil Circle Rep?" *New York Times,* March 14, 1982.

Glover, William. "Hot l Baltimore," *New York Times,* February 2, 1973.

Gottfried, Martin. "Hot l Baltimore," *Women's Wear Daily,* February 5, 1973.

Grover, Steven. "Little White Way," *Wall Street Journal,* August 21, 1979.

Gussow, Mel. "Suddenly Real Plays about Real People," *New York Times,* May 12, 1974.

_____. "Battle of Angels," *New York Times,* November 4, 1974.

_____. "Whither, Off Broadway?" *New York Times,* January 27, 1975.

_____. "Stage: 'The Sea Horse,' " *New York Times,* April 16, 1975.

_____. "*Harry Outside* Enjoys Naturalism at Circle," *New York Times,* May 13, 1975.

_____. "Showcase Code Is an Off Off Standoff," *New York Times,* October 17, 1975.

_____. "The Quicksilver World of Off Off Broadway." *New York Times,* November 30, 1975.

_____. "Stage: Bishop One-Acter at Circle Rep," *New York Times,* January 6, 1977.

_____. "Lanford Wilson on Broadway," *Horizon,* May 1980.

_____. "When the Playwright's Life Is Visible in His Work," *New York Times,* August 26, 1984.

Kalem, T. E. "Kooky Miracle," *Time Magazine,* February 2, 1976.

Kerr, Walter. "The Crazies Are Good to Listen To," *New York Times,* March 4, 1973.

Kissel, Howard. "Who Killed Richard Cory," *Women's Wear Daily,* March 12, 1976.

_____. "Glorious Morning," *Women's Wear Daily,* November 2, 1978.

Leo, John, as reported by J. Madeline Nash/Chicago and Elizabeth Taylor/New York. "The Revolution Is Over," *Time Magazine,* April 9, 1984.

Lewis, Emory. "Lanford Wilson," *Long Island Record,* February 28, 1973.

_____. "Lanford Wilson," *Long Island Record,* March 9, 1973.

_____. "Onstage," *Long Island Record,* March 11, 1976.

Raidy, William, A. "The Hot l Baltimore," *Long Island Press,* February 5, 1973.

Rawlings, Paul. "Mason Directs Sheridan Circle," *The Villager,* November 14, 1974.

Sharp, Christopher. "Mason Encircles City," *Women's Wear Daily,* April 12, 1974.

Sibley, William J. "Lanford Wilson—Off Broadway: A Founder and Number One Playwright Honors the Circle Repertory Theatre on its Fifteenth Anniversary," *Ladies' Home Journal,* Spring 1984.

Simon, John. "Theatre," *New York Magazine,* November 13, 1978.

_____. "Folie à deux," *New York Magazine,* May 18, 1979.

Smith, Michael. "Theatre Journal," *Village Voice,* February 8, 1973.

Stitt, Milan. "Pages from a Dramaturg's Notebook," *New York Times,* January 5, 1978.

Vidal, David. "Equity to Meet in New Code Today," *New York Times,* August 25, 1975.

Wallach, Allan. "The Long Island Review," *Newsday,* April 29, 1973.

_____. "Switched Off," *Newsday,* February 8, 1973.

_____. "Newsday Stage—New, Yes; Important, No," *Newsday,* December 16, 1975.

Wilson, Edwin. "The Sea Horse," *Wall Street Journal,* April 19, 1974.

_____. "A Dockside Romance," *Wall Street Journal,* April 19, 1974.

Wilson, Lanford. "Dammit Lady," *Performing Arts,* August 1973.

Journals, Magazines, and Newspapers Consulted

Albrecht, Ernest. "Skeleton in Closet Makes Bone-chilling Play," *Home News,* December 6, 1978.

Barnes, Clive. "The Theatre: 'Prodigal,'" *New York Times,* December 18, 1973.

———. "Stage: 'Runner Stumbles,'" *New York Times,* May 25, 1976.

———. "'Cabin' on Solid Ground," *New York Post,* January 7, 1978.

———. "A Lulu by the Circle Rep." *New York Post,* February 18, 1978.

———. "'Talley' Is No Folly," *New York Post, May 4, 1979.*

Beaufort, John. "Lanford Wilson's Latest—Offbeat and Appealing," *Christian Science Monitor,* May 9, 1979.

———. "Snow White and Black Vaudeville," *Christian Science Monitor,* October, 24, 1979.

———. "A Song-and-Dance 'Christmas Carol,'" *Christian Science Monitor,* December 26, 1979.

———. "One of the Off Broadway's Season's Funniest," *Christian Science Monitor,* March 12, 1980.

———. "Romantic Comedy from a Sensitive New Playwright," *Christian Science Monitor,* June 12, 1980.

———. "The American Heartland as Two Indiana Playmakers See It," *Christian Science Monitor,* October 24, 1980.

———. "Exceptional Acting Brings Byron's Ghost to Life," *Christian Science Monitor,* March 5, 1981.

———. "Lanford Wilson's New Drama: A Return to the Familiar," *Christian Science Monitor,* June 16, 1981.

———. "A North Carolina Homecoming Does N.Y.'s Circle Rep Proud," *Christian Science Monitor,* October 30, 1981.

———. "Circle Rep's Wildly Funny Broadside," *Christian Science Monitor,* March 25, 1982.

———. "Feiffer's Latest Play: Another Dour One, yet Sometimes Vivid," *Christian Science Monitor,* July 1, 1982.

———. "'Johnny Got His Gun' Transcends Its Grim Theme," *Christian Science Monitor,* August 19, 1982.

———. "An Engaging and 'Thoughtfully Serious' Comedy from Lanford Wilson," *Christian Science Monitor,* October 27, 1982.

———. "Morality and History Mingle in Drama of an ex-Nazi War Criminal," *Christian Science Monitor,* December 28, 1982.

———. Sensitive One-act Plays at Circle Rep," *Christian Science Monitor,* January 19, 1982.

Bondy, Filip. "'Buried Child' Is Another Feather for Sam Shepard," *Paterson News,* December 7, 1978.

Brukenfeld, Dick. "Block That Symbolism!" *New York Times,* December 20, 1973.

———. "Theatrical Nembutal—'The Mound Builders,'" *New York Times,* February 10, 1975.

Buckley, Tom. "Feiffer Fills Play with Food and Thought," *New York Times,* February 10, 1976.

Calta, Louis. " 'Changing Room' Is Critics' Choice," *New York Times,* May 24, 1973.

_____. "Circle Repertory Sets Three Works," *New York Times,* December 1, 1974.

Clurman, Harold. *"The 5th of July," The Nation,* May 13, 1978.

_____. Review of *Buried Child, The Nation,* December 2, 1978.

_____. Review of *Talley's Folley, The Nation,* June 28, 1979.

_____. Review of *Hamlet* and *Mary Stuart, The Nation,* January 19, 1980.

_____. Review of *The Woolgatherer, The Nation,* November 8, 1980.

Corry, John. "Broadway," *New York Times,* February 10, 1978.

Cyclops, C. "The World of the Joads Is Still with Us," *New York Times,* February 3, 1974.

Daniels, Robert L. Review of *In the Recovery Lounge, North Jersey Suburbanite,* December 13, 1978.

Davis, Curt. "Trips through Time," *Variety,* January 27, 1982.

Eder, Richard. "Stage: 'Runner' Strides toward Major Success," *New York Times,* June 15, 1976.

_____. "Stage: 'Winter Signs,' Drama by John Bishop," *New York Times,* March 12, 1979.

_____. "Theatre: Pat Carroll Plays Gertrude Stein," *New York Times,* June 28, 1979.

Eichelbaum, Stanley. "ACT's 'Hot l' Guests Weak Structure," *San Francisco Examiner,* October 24, 1973.

Flatley, Guy. "Lanford Is One 'L' of a Playwright," *New York Times,* April 22, 1973.

Feingold, Michael. "Theatre—One Night He Went Home and Shot Himself," *The Village Voice,* March 12, 1976.

_____. "Death Rap," *Variety,* April 7, 1982.

Flynn, Betty. "Lanford Wilson Has Checked in and out of 'Hot l Baltimore,' " *New York Times,* April 7, 1975.

Frank, Leah D. "My Cup Ranneth Over," *New York Theatre Review,* August/September 1978.

Freedman, Samuel G. "Will Success Spoil Nonprofit Theatre?" *New York Times,* July 22, 1984.

Gill, Brendan. "The Theatre," *New Yorker,* May 25, 1976.

Gluck, Victor. *"A Tale Told," Back Stage,* June 24, 1981.

Gottfried, Martin. "Playwrights; The Inner Four," *Vogue,* July, 1973.

Gottlieb, Richard. "A Dance That Can't Quite Fly," *New York Times,* December 18, 1975.

Gunner, Marjorie. "On and Off Broadway," *Rockaway Record,* April 18, 1976.

Gussow, Mel. "Three Lanford Wilson Plays Given Uptown," *New York Times,* May 22, 1973.

_____. "The Unwanted People of 'Hot l Baltimore,' " *New York Times,* February 8, 1973.

_____. "Stage: 2 Poignant Characters in Irwin's 'Sea Horse,'" *New York Times,* March 5, 1974.

_____. "Stage: 'The Sea Horse,'—Circle Repertory Gives Tender, Wistful Play," *New York Times,* April 16, 1974.

_____. "Stage: cummings's 'him'—The Circle Repertory Offers Revival," *New York Times,* April 20, 1974.

_____. " 'The Sea Horse' Star (and Its Author) Sheds Alias," *New York Times,* April 22, 1974.

_____. "Theatre: Wilson's 'Mound Builders,'" *New York Times,* February 3, 1975.

_____. "Stage: Clumsy 'Elephant,'" *New York Times,* November 4, 1975.

_____. "Stage: 'Knock, Knock,' Feiffer's There," *New York Times,* January 19, 1976.

_____. "Theatre: 'Lemon Sky,'" *New York Times,* March 3, 1976.

_____. "Theatre: 'Who Killed Richard Cory?'" *New York Times,* March 12, 1976.

_____. "Stage: Lanford Wilson's Early 'Rimers of Eldritch,'" *New York Times,* April 6, 1976.

_____. "Stage: Tale for Children," *New York Times,* April 11, 1976.

_____. "Stage: 'Serenading Louie' Harks Back," *New York Times,* May 6, 1976.

_____. " 'The Runner Stumbles' Marked by Fine Acting," *New York Times,* May 19, 1976.

_____. "David Storey's 'The Farm' Is Family Play about Forces That Hold People Together," *New York Times,* October 12, 1976.

_____. "New Drama Goes Off Off Broadway," *New York Times,* November 12, 1976.

_____. "Theatre: A Faded 'Lily Lamont,'" *New York Times,* November 29, 1976.

_____. "Stage: Fiery 'Brontosaurus,'" *New York Times,* October 27, 1977.

_____. "Theatre: A Nightcap without a Kick," *New York Times,* November 10, 1978.

_____. "Stage: 'The Deserter' Based on Eddie Slovik," *New York Times,* March 20, 1979.

_____. "Stage: Wilson's 'Talley's Folley,'" *New York Times,* May 4, 1979.

_____. "Stage: 'Reunion,' 3 Mamet Plays," *New York Times,* October 19, 1979.

_____. "Intimate Monologues That Speak to the Mind and Heart," *New York Times,* December 9, 1979.

_____. "Stage: Royal Dramas at the Circle Rep," *New York Times,* December 14, 1979.

_____. "Stage View: A Life-Size Approach to a Pair of Classics," *New York Times,* December 23, 1979.

_____. "Stage: Circle Rep Offers a Drama about a Loner," *New York Times,* March 8, 1980.

_____. "Theatre: 'The Diviners' Carries Audience Back to the Early 30s," *New York Times,* October 17, 1980.

_____. "New York's Stages Brush up Their Classics," *New York Times,* January 9, 1981.

_____. "Theatre: Tanya Berezin as Frau Wolf in Hauptmann's 'The Beaver Coat,'" *New York Times,* January 13, 1981.

_____. "Stage View—A Bold 'Lear' and 'Peer Gynt,'" *New York Times,* August 8, 1982.

_____. "Theatre: World War I, 'Johnny Got His Gun,'" *New York Times,* August 11, 1982.

Hughes, Catherine. "From Taylor to Talley," *America,* July 25, 1981.

_____. "Desert Days," *America,* December 11, 1982.

Humm. Review of *The Great Grandson of Jedediah Kohler, Variety,* April 7, 1982.

_____. Review of *A Think Piece, Variety,* June 30, 1982.

Isaac, Dan. "From the Editor's Notebook," *Other Stages,* March 25, 1982.

Jenner, Lee C. "On Theatre—'Stargazing,'" *Courier/Life Publications,* November 20, 1978.

Kakutani, Michiko. "I Write the World as I See It around Me," *New York Times,* August 6, 1984.

_____. "Stage: Out of the 19th Century, 'Macready!'" *New York Times,* July 30, 1980.

Kalem, T. E. "Crazy Farm—*Buried Child*," *Time Magazine,* December 6, 1978.

_____. "Blood Lust—*Fool For Love*," *Time Magazine,* June 6, 1983.

Kerr, Walter. "Hot l Baltimore," *New York Times,* March 4, 1973.

_____. "The Human Heart, Imprisoned," *New York Times,* April 21, 1974.

_____. "Stage View—Too Many Questions, Too Few Answers," *New York Times,* October 24, 1976.

_____. "Three New Plays, One 'A Treasure,'" *New York Times,* May 13, 1979.

_____. "Theatergoers Were Asked to Help Make Magic," *New York Times,* December 30, 1979.

_____. "Stage: 'Talley's Folly,'" *New York Times,* February 21, 1980.

_____. "This May Be 'A Tale Told' Once too Often," *New York Times,* June 21, 1981.

_____. "Stage View—When the Stage Is Just a Prize-Ring," *New York Times,* March 21, 1982.

_____. "Stage View—Jules Feiffer's 'A Think Piece'—Calculated Dreariness," *New York Times,* July 4, 1982.

_____. "Playwrights Are Growing Articulate Again," *New York Times,* October 31, 1982.

_____. "Stage View—How Can We Admire a Less Than Human Hero?" *New York Times,* March 6, 1983.

_____. "Stage View—A Parody That Fizzles, a Drama That Baffles," *New York Times,* January 9, 1983.

_____. "Stage View—Where Has Sam Shepard Led His Audience?" *New York Times,* June 5, 1983.

Kissel, Howard. "'Who Killed Richard Cory?'" *Women's Wear Daily,* March 3, 1976.

_____. " 'Glorious Morning,' " *Women's Wear Daily,* November 12, 1978.

Kroll, Jack. "Hope Against Hope," *Newsweek,* November 24, 1980.

_____. "Look Homeward, Playwright," *Newsweek,* June 22, 1981.

_____. Review of *Confluence, Newsweek,* January 25, 1982.

_____. "Toward the Apocalypse," *Newsweek,* November 1, 1982.

Kyd, Joanna. "This Runner Is a Triumph," *Our Town,* June 28, 1976.

Lahr, John. "On-stage," *Village Voice,* March 22, 1973.

Lardner, Ring, Jr. "Will 'Johnny' Finally Have His Day?" *New York Times,* August 6, 1982.

Lawson, Carol. "Blackstone Bringing 'Magic' to the Majestic," *New York Times,* April 16, 1980.

_____. "Broadway—'Fifth of July,' More on the Talley Family, Is Due in Early Fall," *New York Times,* May 2, 1980.

_____. "Erma Bombeck's 'Copebook' Coming to Broadway as a Comedy," *New York Times,* August 28, 1980.

_____. "3d Play in Talley Cycle Opens June 11," *New York Times,* April 15, 1981.

_____. "Circle Rep's Director, Citing Exhaustion, to Take a Sabbatical," *New York Times,* April 19, 1982.

le Sourd, Jacques. " 'In the Recovery Room' Is Terminal," *Gannett-Westchester,* December 8, 1978.

Lewis, Emory. " 'Kaiser'—the Dance Is Out of Step," *New York Times,* December 15, 1975.

_____. " 'Cory' Is Better as Poem," *New York Times,* March 11, 1976.

Mason, Marshall. "Artistic Excellence Is the Goal, *Sunday News,"* September 22, 1974.

McManus, Otile. " 'Sea Horse' Couple Don't Have to Act Their Play," *Boston Evening Globe,* December 3, 1974.

Moynihan, D. S. "Marshall Mason: The Inner River of Experience," *Drama Review,* Fall 1981.

Neff, Renfreu. "Speaking in Balloons," *Other Stages,* July 1, 1982.

Nightingale, Benedict. "Stage View—Early Lanford Wilson with a Touch of Today," *New York Times,* June 10, 1984.

O'Connor, Colleen. "Marshall Mason: Why Success Hasn't Spoiled Circle Rep," *Manhattan Catalogue,* December 1979.

O'Connor, John J. "TV: 'Migrants,' a Drama That Portrays Poverty," *New York Times,* February 1, 1974.

_____. "TV Review—'Hot l Baltimore' Signs ABC Register at 9," *New York Times,* January 24, 1975.

_____. "TV: Lanford Wilson's 'Mound Builders' Is an Ambitious and Puzzling Play," *New York Times,* February 11, 1976.

Oliver, Edith. "Back in Your Own Back Yard, *New Yorker,* March 28, 1977.

_____. "Off Broadway," *New Yorker,* May 8, 1978.

_____. Review of *Buried Child, New Yorker,* November 6, 1978.

_____. Review of *In the Recovery Lounge, New Yorker,* December 18, 1978.

_____. Review of *Reunion, New Yorker,* January 29, 1979.

_____. Review of *Minnesota Moon, New Yorker,* January 12, 1979.

_____. Review of *Winter Signs, New Yorker,* March 26, 1979.

_____. "At the Boathouse," *New Yorker,* May 14, 1979.

_____. "Present Conditional and Past Perfect," *New Yorker,* September 8, 1980.

_____. Review of *The Woolgatherer, New Yorker,* October 27, 1980.

_____. Review of *Twelfth Night, New Yorker,* December 29, 1980.

_____. Review of *Childe Byron, New Yorker,* March 9, 1981.

_____. "The Day Before the Fifth of July," *New Yorker,* June 22, 1981.

_____. Review of *Threads, New Yorker,* November 9, 1981.

_____. Review of *The Great Grandson of Jedediah Kohler, New Yorker,* April 5, 1982.

_____. Review of *Angels Fall, New Yorker,* November 1, 1982.

Quintero, Jose. "Where Are the New Directors?" *New York Times,* November 28, 1982.

Rabkin, Gerald. "Theater—The Bones Underneath," *Soho Weekly News,* October 26, 1978.

Raidy, William A. " 'Buried Child' Stimulating at Best," *Staten Island Advance,* December 6, 1978.

_____. " 'Richard Cory' Has No Central Theme," *Long Island Press,* March 11, 1976.

_____. " 'Buried Child' Unearths America Gone to Seed," *Star-Ledger,* December 6, 1978.

_____. "Lifeless Script Afflicts the 'Recovery Lounge' " *Star-Ledger,* December 9, 1978.

_____. "Chekhov's 'The Sea Gull' Hampered by Poor Players," *Star-Ledger,* November 25, 1983.

Reed, Rex. "Goody, It's Gershwin!" *Daily News,* May 3, 1978.

Rich, Frank. "Stage: 'Woolgatherer' at Circle Rep," *New York Times,* June 6, 1980.

_____. "Stage: William Hurt in 'Childe Byron,' " *New York Times,* February 27, 1981.

_____. "Stage: Richard Thomas Sparks 'Fifth of July,' " *New York Times,* April 9, 1981.

_____. "Stage: 'A Tale Told,' Part 3 of Talley Family Story," *New York Times,* June 12, 1981.

_____. "Stage: 'Threads' by Jonathan Bolt at Circle Rep," *New York Times,* October 26, 1981.

_____. "Stage: 'Confluence,' 3 One-Acters, at Circle Rep," *New York Times,* January 11, 1982.

_____. "Drama: Joe Pintauro's 'Snow Orchid,' " *New York Times,* March 11, 1982.

_____. "Theatre: Bishop's 'Jedediah Kohler,' " *New York Times,* March 23, 1982.

_____. "Stage: Jules Feiffer's 'A Think Piece,' " *New York Times,* June 29, 1982.

_____. "Theatre: 'Black Angel,' a View of the Holocaust," *New York Times,* December, 20, 1982.

_____. "Stage: Circle Rep Offers 'Sea Gull,'" *New York Times,* November 25, 1983.

_____. "Theatre: 'Full Hookup' at Circle Rep," *New York Times,* December 30, 1983.

_____. "Theatre: Revival of 'Balm in Gilead,'" *New York Times,* June 1, 1984.

_____. "Theatre: 'Bing,' by Farrell," *New York Times,* December 3, 1984.

_____. "Stage: 'As Is,' About AIDS, Opens," *New York Times,* March 11, 1985.

Shepard, Richard F. "Play with Liv Ullmann Will Help Off Broadway," *New York Times,* January 7, 1979.

Shewey, Don. "Near Myth," *Village Voice,* March 7, 1982.

_____. "A Playwright Asks Thorny Questions," *New York Times,* December 12, 1982.

_____. "Has the Regional Theatre Fulfilled Its Promise?" *New York Times,* August 7, 1983.

Simon, John. "Ascetic Realism," *New York Magazine,* April 9, 1973.

_____. "Theatre," *New York Magazine,* November 13, 1978.

_____. "Theatre," *New York Magazine,* November 20, 1978.

_____. "Blurred by Triple Exposure," *New York Magazine,* March 24, 1980.

_____. "A Different Drummer," *New York Magazine,* June 23, 1980.

_____. "All in the Family," *New York Magazine,* June 22, 1981.

_____. "Einstein in the Woods," *New York Magazine,* November 9, 1981.

_____. "Slow Flow," *New York Magazine,* January 25, 1982.

_____. "Ideals Lost and Found," *New York Magazine,* February 7, 1983.

_____. "Summer of 45," *New York Magazine,* February 14, 1983.

_____. "Childish Adults, Grown-Up Kids," *New York Magazine,* May 2, 1983.

_____. "Farcical Worlds," *New York Magazine,* December 5, 1983.

_____. "In Sickness and in Health," *New York Magazine,* March 25, 1985.

Smith, Michael. "Theatre Journal," *Village Voice,* February 2, 1973.

Stasio, Marilyn. "A Good Race—'The Runner Stumbles,'" *Cue,* May 29, 1976.

_____. "'Stargazing' Is up in the Air," *New York Post,* November 8, 1978.

Stern, Gary. "What's the Lure of Rep," *Backstage,* December 2, 1983.

Sterritt, David. "Do Playwrights Make Good Directors? Only Sometimes," *Christian Science Monitor,* January 21, 1981.

Sullivan, Gwyn. "Broadway Meets the Hinterlands," *News World,* March 16, 1979.

Syna, Sy. "Shepard's *Buried Child,*" *New York Guide,* December 25, 1978.

Thompson, Howard. "Theatre: 'Sheba' Is Back," *New York Times,* August 23, 1974.

Tretick, Joyce and Gordon. "Going Places," *News-Beacon,* April 26, 1974.

Watt, Douglas. "'Cabin 12' Looks at Grief," *Daily News,* January 10, 1978.

_____. "Shucks, Lulu's Back in Town," *Daily News,* February 18, 1978.

_____. "Take This One to Emergency!" *Daily News,* December 8, 1978.

Weales, Gerald. "The Diviners," *Commonweal Magazine,* September 11, 1981.

Wetzsteon, Ross. "The Most Populist Playwright," *New York Magazine,* November 8, 1982.

Wilson, Edwin. "A Moral Dilemma in a Parish House," *Wall Street Journal,* May 25, 1976.

_____. "The Play's Not Always the Thing," *Wall Street Journal,* March 13, 1981.

_____. "Scrawny Twirler's Fallen Angels," *Wall Street Journal,* October 29, 1982.

Interviews and Correspondence

PERSONAL INTERVIEWS (NEW YORK CITY)

Tanya Berezin, *7 December 1983*
John Bishop, *18 April 1984*
Richard Frankel, *10 February 1984*
Daniel Irvine, *18 November 1983*
B. Rodney Marriott, *3 December 1983*
Marshall W. Mason, *11 November 1983, 10 December 1983, 4 February 1984*
Ari Roth, *29 November 1983*
Rob Thirkield, *18 November 1983*
Tom Thompson, *9 February 1984*
Lanford Wilson, *11 April 1984*

TELEPHONE INTERVIEWS

Alan Feinstein, *4 December 1983*
Robert Lu Pone, *10 January 1984*

CORRESPONDENCE

Kathy Bates, *28 November 1983*
Peter Buckley, *23 January 1984*
Jordan Charney, *20 December 1983*
Jeff Daniels, *December 1983*
Mari Gorman, *14 November 1983*
Bruce Gray, *8 November 1983*
Michael Higgins, *18 December 1983*
Ruby Holbrook, *9 January 1984*
Ken Kliban, *7 November 1983*
Tony Roberts, *22 November 1983*
Richard Seff, *3 November 1983*
Michael Skelly, *5 January 1984*
Ted Sod, *18 November 1983*
Peter Weller, *January 1984*

Index

MARY S. RYZUK has worked as a singer, actress, and director. A member of the Authors' League of America and the Dramatists Guild, as well as the author of numerous produced plays and teleplays, she is also the author of *Stuffed Dolls,* an original screenplay published in 1980 by Unicorn Press. She received her Ph.D. in dramatic theory and criticism from City University of New York in 1986, and currently teaches at William Paterson College in Wayne, New Jersey.